The
Philosophy
of Love

Rebecca Ryan lives in Bradford with her three young children. Although she always loved writing, it hadn't really occurred to her that she could do it professionally. She recently left her job as a teacher to pursue writing full-time. She enjoys walking in the countryside and takeaways (if that counts as a hobby).

Also by Rebecca Ryan

My (extra)Ordinary Life

The *Philosophy* of Love

rebecca ryan

**SIMON &
SCHUSTER**

London · New York · Sydney · Toronto · New Delhi

First published in Great Britain by Simon & Schuster UK Ltd, 2024

3 5 7 9 10 8 6 4 2

Simon & Schuster UK Ltd
1st Floor
222 Gray's Inn Road
London WC1X 8HB

Simon & Schuster: Celebrating 100 Years of Publishing in 2024

Simon & Schuster Australia, Sydney
Simon & Schuster India, New Delhi

www.simonandschuster.co.uk
www.simonandschuster.com.au
www.simonandschuster.co.in

A CIP catalogue record for this book
is available from the British Library

Paperback ISBN: 978-1-3985-0928-3
eBook ISBN: 978-1-3985-0927-6
Audio ISBN: 978-1-3985-2969-4

Typeset in Bembo by M Rules
Printed and Bound in the UK using 100% Renewable
Electricity at CPI Group (UK) Ltd

For Mum and Dad

2010

Victory is nigh.

I can feel it, taste it. In the next ten minutes, that trophy is mine.

We're in the hall for the Year 11 awards assembly at Easington Roman Catholic High School. The blinds are drawn, and the air is thick with dust.

'I Gotta Feeling' by the Black Eyed Peas blasts from massive speakers whenever there's a lull in proceedings. There's even a photographer from the *Easington Gazette*.

Mr Hall, the headteacher, is on stage behind a little wooden podium, talking really, really loudly even though the mic is working. He's already announced some of the lesser awards – the ones voted for by the other pupils. Like the one for the person most likely to become famous. (Rachel Stone, which is fair enough because she almost got through to judge's houses on *The X Factor*.)

But now we're onto the biggest award of the night.

Mr Hall holds up the trophy for the academic excellence award.

I squirm in my seat, a bag of nerves. It's between me and Luke Priestly, I just know it is. Luke's been the best at maths and science since Year 7. But I'm the best in the arts. I like *all* the arts. English, history, actual art. But it's philosophy that I really love. If anything is going to win me that award, it's how well I've done in philosophy.

I sit up straighter, like I used to do when I was little, and I'd balance a book on my head to practise being a princess for the day.

'And the winner of the Easington High's academic excellence award goes to . . .' Mr Hall drums his hands on the little podium as his secretary passes him an envelope. He opens it as if we're at the Oscars. I can't take the tension anymore.

'Well,' he says. 'This is an unprecedented situation. Completely unprecedented.' I'm holding my breath. 'It's been awarded *jointly*. Alice King and Luke Priestly, come on up and collect your award!'

Hang on a second. What's happening here? He definitely said Alice King. That's me. *I'm* Alice King. But then he'd said Luke's name too.

'Come on, Alice! Luke!' Mr Hall calls.

My breath catches. The sound of people clapping feels far away. I'm so full of everything that I think for one horrible second I'm going to have one of my funny turns.

Please.

Not now.

But then the packed hall comes back into focus, people are smiling at me and reminding me that I've done well. What a relief.

I stand on shaky legs and start shuffling my way along the row filled with my friends, heading in the direction the stage.

'Well done, Alice!' Ms Small, my philosophy and ethics teacher calls from the front row where she's sat with the other teachers. I smile back, trying not to let the success go to my head.

So, I won it jointly with Luke. I still won. I won't have to tell people that I won it jointly. I'll just be able to say, 'yes, I won the award for academic excellence', there's no need to qualify it.

These thoughts make me feel a lot better. I smile and wave some more.

I make my way up the steps to the stage. Luke is already there. He's very scowly for a boy who has just won a trophy *and* some WHSmith book vouchers.

I try not to think about Luke and his scowls. Instead, as soon as my hands are on the trophy, I lift it up like it's the World Cup, only stopping when I hear Luke snort out a mocking laugh behind me. I give him a dirty look.

'Let's get a picture of all the winners, shall we?' The photographer from the *Easington Gazette* says.

'Great idea.' Mr Hall beams.

There's a few minutes of chaos while the other winners make their way back onto the stage with their trophies. I'm about to ask Luke how we should go about drawing up our trophy rota but there's no time. The photographer gestures for us to move to the front of the group, asks us to hold onto one side of the massive trophy each.

We're front and centre. Luckily, I straightened my hair extra carefully this morning. Aunty Moira let me use her ghds and everything.

Luke looks like he hasn't so much as looked at a hair brush this year. It's so far forward at the front I'm amazed he can even see to walk. But still, there's nothing to be done.

'Say cheese!' The photographer starts snapping away.

'Come on, act like you like each other,' he says, waving a hand over to me and Luke. We're stood really far apart. And my arm is starting to ache from holding the trophy up.

I shuffle an inch closer. Luke doesn't move. I notice that his school jumper is pulled over his hand so that you can only see the tips of his fingers where they're curled around his half of the trophy. His black nail varnish is chipped.

'That'll do,' the photographer sighs. He doesn't look especially pleased with us and I assume that's because of Luke scowling the whole time we were there. I was doing my biggest smile.

It's important to be nice though, even when people aren't nice to you. That's what I was always taught at church. So, while everyone moves around us, I say 'congratulations' and stick out my hand for Luke to shake. I don't exactly know what possesses me to do it, I don't normally go around shaking people's hands. But I'm almost an adult now and this seems like a sort of grown-up thing I'll be expected to do.

Luke looks at my hand and frowns an even deeper frown, which I didn't think was possible. I keep talking, my hand just hanging out in the space between us. 'You can take the trophy first if you like,' I say.

I pull away my hand because he obviously isn't going to shake it, which is kind of rude.

'The trophy's shit,' he says, brushing past me, heading for the stage steps.

The assembly is over and most of the teachers are dismissing their classes row by row.

The trophy's shit? It doesn't even make sense!

Luke is halfway down the steps but I need to say something back. To defend my trophy against this unprovoked attack.

'Well, I think you're shit!' I call, irritated that I can't think of a better comeback.

'Language, Ms King!' one of the teachers says and I wrinkle my nose, annoyed at the fact that I'm the one who got called out for swearing.

I huff out a breath, relax my shoulders like I've practised. I can't let Luke ruin today for me.

Hopefully, once we leave school for good, I'll never see or hear from Luke Priestly again.

Present Day

PART ONE

CHARLES

'Love shouldn't make you feel small.'

Chapter One

If there's one thing I've learned in the past two hours, it's this. It really doesn't matter how crappy your life is. Bad hair will always make you feel . . . well . . . bad.

'Sorry, but do you by any chance have any purple shampoo that I could buy, please?' I look hopefully at Stephanie, apparent hairdresser extraordinaire, currently wielding some heavy-duty tongs around the back of my head.

I'm thinking that I can just wash it as soon as I get home. Get rid of the ringlets. And the funny colour. Purple shampoo isn't a want, it's a need at this stage.

'You're out of luck, Alice, pet. It's V05 Smoothly Does It. Can't beat it.' She finishes another tight ringlet. Her final one.

'Okay, well thank you anyway, it's . . . really nice.' This is a lie. But still, there's no point in both of us feeling bad.

It had been Mum's suggestion to get my hair done. According to her, a new do is guaranteed to make you forget about the fact that six weeks ago you caught your boyfriend getting frisky with someone who isn't you.

Ex-boyfriend.

Charles had maintained that he didn't regularly get down and dirty on the living room rug. The shag rug I should add. Shaggy by name, shaggy by nature. But seriously, can any relationship survive the sight of someone else's finger up your boyfriend's bum? Ours certainly hadn't.

And so fresh out of the mother of all breakups, I find myself back in the former mining village I'd grown up in – Easington Colliery. I'm basically heartbroken and living in my childhood bedroom. The ghost of Vidal Sassoon himself couldn't make me forget that.

Mum had forewarned me that Heavenly Head Hairdressers still didn't take cards, so I pass Stephanie £30 cash, panicking about the fact that I really don't have £30 spare. The only faint silver lining of this morning is that with Easington prices being decidedly on the cheaper side of things, the new do only costs me £28. Still, it's possibly my first cash-based transaction of the last half decade. 'No, honestly, keep it,' I tell Stephanie as she tries to hand me my change. 'You did such a good job,' I finish, because I'm British and so I will take these ringlets to my grave before I admit my true feelings on the matter.

And really, brassy (read orange) curls should be the least of my worries. It's just that in the part of the stories where everything finally starts to go right, the heroine never, ever has bad hair. Even if she's been stuck in an unexpected downpour or some other freak weather phenomenon, it's always plastered to her face in an artful sort of a way. Stephanie has applied so much hairspray to my curls, I doubt that even an actual monsoon would cause them to budge.

Keen to escape a building with quite so many mirrors, I set off back home, walking slowly down the red-brick terraced streets towards Mum and Dad's house. I skirt around a worn sofa by the kerb, doing my best to blink away the tears that always seem to come when I'm alone.

It's when I'm on my own that I feel this overwhelming sense of hopelessness. Like the swell of a wave pushing upwards inside me.

Six weeks ago, I had a boyfriend, a job, a whole future in London.

And now I have none of those things.

I have to stop for a second to rest my head against a crumbling brick wall, the perimeter of someone's yard. Close my eyes tight against the world. Maybe it *would* just be easier if I expired round the back of a row of Victorian terraces.

What would my obituary read?

Alice King, found dead in the Easington gutter.

Am I even important enough for an obituary? Unlikely.

At this point, it's doubtful that I'd even be able to afford a funeral plan. Mum and Dad seem to get a daily flyer pushed through the letter box about them. They're crazy expensive. Do we still have pauper's graves anymore? Maybe I'd end up in one of them.

I push away from the wall, deciding against a gutter-based death, sternly reminding myself that aside from those old couples who die within days of each other, no one actually goes from a broken heart. And I would know. I've googled it.

Mum and Dad's house is one of those two-bed terraces that you sometimes see getting done up on *Homes Under the Hammer*. They've lived here the whole of their married lives. It's two doors down from where Nana and Grandad used to live, and my Aunty Moira is across the road. Basically, we Kings haven't so much as conquered a country, but we do rule over a small section of this here terraced street.

And if the thought of my ruling anything isn't farcical enough, I can't even claim a bit of the street. I left for university when I was eighteen and had never come back for more than a quick visit. Not until six weeks ago.

'I'm home!' I call, slamming the front door.

'Hi, pet,' Dad says as I come through into the front room. He's watching *Bargain Hunt*, from his designated armchair. It's one of those American-type ones where you pull a lever, and a footrest pops out. Like the one Joey had. It's older than me.

I'm braced for him to say something about my hair as I perch on the chair's arm and watch as the red team makes a tidy profit of £3. This past month and a half I've watched enough daytime TV

to make my eyeballs bleed. Approximately no one is made to feel
better about their prospects hearing the *Loose Women* complain about
the decline of the fish knife.

He pulls me in for a sideways hug without even breaking his
glance from the screen.

'Is that you, Alice?' Mum calls.

I reluctantly follow her voice through the dining room and into
the kitchen. If we were rich, you'd call the layout of downstairs
'open plan'. But we're not rich, so 'mostly one room' just about
covers it instead. The kitchen's a sort of wonky extension at the back
of the house, eating up fifty percent of our yard.

Nothing about it has changed since I was a little girl. The decor
is like a dysfunctional game of *Jumanji* – if the only things to emerge
from the vortex were pine cupboards.

The smoke alarm makes a half-hearted *beep* as Mum wafts at the
air with a tea towel. It always gets like this when she has her frying
pan out. Which is at all times. She said once that she'd be buried
with that pan and I'm not exactly sure that she was joking. Now
she's shaking it on top of the old gas hob that's liable to kill us all
in our sleep one day. Spam fritters hiss and spit from the blackened
pan, shooting flecks of hot oil into the air. A scorching drop lands
on my arm, and I retreat.

'It's bad, isn't it?' I ask. 'The hair.'

Doubtfully, Mum looks at the top of my head. 'Is that ... what
you asked for?' she asks.

'I'm not sure. I think I said the word "ash", but I can't be certain.'

And I really can't. It'd be just like me to ask for the wrong thing.
She peers a bit more.

'Well, I don't suppose it matters. You'd look like a super model
in a bin bag. Naomi Campbell or what's her face,' she gesticulates
with the spatula, 'with the legs.'

Naomi Campbell seems an unlikely comparison. I'm pasty, only two inches taller than mum and my natural hair colour is dark blonde. Or at least I think it is. I haven't seen it since some point in the late 2000s. Charles once said that my face was 'unusual'. Which I think is code for 'your eyes are too far apart'.

'At this rate, I'll be resorting to bin bags,' I sniff.

'Still no luck on the job front?'

'Nope.' I peer down at the floor miserably. Easington isn't exactly a hive of economic activity. The last success story we churned out was Billy Elliot. And he isn't even real.

'I'm sure if you just told people you'd been to university in London—'

I shake my head miserably. Barely completing exactly one year of a philosophy degree a decade ago really doesn't open many doors. Especially in Easington where there are so few doors to start with.

If I think about it too much, I start to get a stress rash.

I just don't exactly know what I want to do. Years ago, I had a plan. Go to university, get a job in philosophy, meet the love of my life. Wham, bam, thank you ma'am.

Except, university in London was hard. Way harder than I'd expected. I was a little fish in a capital city-sized pond.

At least in Easington I'd made the front page of the *Gazette* once. Mum and Dad still have the picture; it's framed on the mantelpiece taunting me about how much potential I used to have.

I wonder what Luke Priestly is up to these days.

Probably not dodging spam fritter fat in his mum's kitchen.

After I'd just scraped through my first year at university, I'd taken a summer temp job as an admin assistant at the head offices of Beck Health Cafés Incorporated. A chain of meat-free, dairy-free, gluten-free, wholefood cafés across London.

It was maybe half an hour after I met him that I realized I was in love with Charles, my new boss. He'd smiled at me and put his hand on the back of my office chair, and . . . I was gone.

I never went back to university after that summer. Instead, I just stayed working for Charles's company for most of the last decade, thinking that achieving fifty per cent of your life goals isn't too shabby. But here's the thing, breaking up with your boss leaves you sad *and* poor.

I've been wallowing in these less than happy memories for a fair few minutes. When I look up, Mum is staring at me, the fritters abandoned. 'It's just that I'm not exactly an appealing prospect,' I tell her. 'I don't have much experience beyond working for Charles. And, well . . .' I trail off.

Mum's lips press into a thin line. Same as they always do whenever Charles is mentioned. She makes a noise somewhere between a hum and a growl and returns to the fritters, flipping them like they've personally wronged her.

'That man really is a . . . a . . . pillock.'

Obviously, I'd spared Mum and Dad the more sordid details of our separation. Because no one wants to be responsible for explaining about the male G-spot to their parents. Being cheated on is humiliating enough.

'Agreed. Pillock.' Another sniff. 'Can we talk about something else?'

'I know!' Mum declares in her best I-will-cheer-you-up-if-it-kills-me voice, 'Why don't you go to Durham tomorrow? You could get something new to wear for your birthday.'

I get that odd sense of déjà vu. I'm almost certain that Mum said the exact same thing to sixteen-year-old me. It makes me wince.

And even if I am ridiculously grateful to them for taking me back, letting me live here rent-free, I really, with every fibre of my being, wish we weren't acknowledging me turning thirty in two days' time.

Thank God I put my foot down about a party.

And I absolutely cannot afford a dress.

Mum carries on. 'And are you sure you don't want to invite a friend? It doesn't seem right, spending your birthday with just us lot. They could stay in your room now that it has a double bed.'

Mum is ignoring the fact that the room itself remains frozen in time. There are statement fairy lights. There's a Barack Obama campaign poster pinned to the wall, and the complete box set of *Hannah Montana* on the small window ledge. There's my cork board, every inch covered with faded quotes from my favourite philosophers.

Plus the new bed's hostile land grab has left approximately one square inch of available floor space. Adding a whole other human into the mix would be tantamount to anarchy.

'So, what do you reckon?' Mum asks.

'About Durham?'

'No! About inviting a friend?'

A self-conscious shuffle ensues. From me, not Mum.

'I'd rather it just be a family thing, if that's okay?'

There's also the small matter of the fact that it turns out that most of my friends were actually Charles's friends, aside from Gabby who now lives several thousand miles and a fair few time zones away.

'All right ...' Mum speaks slowly as she gives the frying pan a good shake. 'Well, how about Durham tomorrow?'

The desire to do something, *anything* to erase the heavy feeling that settles over me makes me agree.

Sure. Why not? I can't afford a dress, but maybe I could get some purple shampoo at least.

I tell Mum I'll go.

She's beside herself with happiness.

'I just know you'll have a brilliant day.'

Mum serves up Dad's food. All carbs and variants of fat. She carries it through to him, so that he can eat in front of the telly. Dad last used the dining table at some point in the 1980s.

And to think that I ended up in the world of wholefoods. I half consider taking a picture and sending it to Charles. Imagining screaming *Hasta la vista, baby!* as the picture lands and he goes down clutching his chest at the dearth of micronutrients on Dad's plate.

The gradual unravelling of my mind must be on full display. I can't be certain I didn't mouth the whole *Terminator* line.

Mum reaches out to squeeze my arm and it's all just a little bit sadder than it was a few seconds ago. 'You know, Alice ... everything will be all right in the end.' I look at her face, searching for any sign that she really believes this. Her eyes don't even flicker.

I pass back through the dining room and the front room on my way to the stairs, suddenly heavy and desperate to be alone again.

'I'll be upstairs if you need me,' I tell my parents from the doorway to the front room.

Dad's words follow me up the stairs.

'Bloody hell, Alice. What have you gone and done to your hair?'

Chapter Two

The next morning, I wake up feeling mildly brighter. Heartbreak really does produce a maelstrom of feeling from the arse-end of the emotional spectrum. Charles would say I was 'big on emotions'. I didn't always agree but right now I see his point: amplified misery is no fun at all.

At least I have an actual semblance of a plan today that does not involve wearing my dressing gown until 4 p.m. and weeping snottily on Mum's shoulder.

Still, I don't move. Reluctant to acknowledge just how nervous I am at the prospect of going somewhere on my own.

I feel for my phone, swiping open Instagram. Like those people who leap from mountains in little webbed suits, I'm on Charles's profile before my brain can say, 'bad idea'.

As usual, my stomach squeezes at the sight of him. Ice blonde hair, not a strand out of place. It's hard to marry up the images with the man who ate cashew nuts out of my belly button on our third date. There's Charles completing a triathlon. Charles in his suit under the entrance of the new office headquarters. Charles at the latest Michelin-starred restaurant. The latest hip nightclub.

Charles has always been a commanding presence. Like how Ragnar Lothbrok might have looked had he been alive at the same time as Armani suits. But then running your own company at twenty-two would give anyone a fair old wedge of ego. Still, it's like

Charles took the Charlie I started dating when I was nineteen and buried him deep in the yard. It's impossible not to question whether Charlie ever really existed. Like Big Foot. Or Jesus.

My philosopher quote cork board is pinned on the wall adjacent to the bed. I'm sure it's mocking me. A post-it-note with Aristotle's 'We are what we repeatedly do' catches my eye. Teenage me had underlined it three times as a reminder to always be nice. Adult me thinks that if we are what we do, I should be one giant tear-drop by now.

Actually, staying locked in my room begins to hold little appeal.

I drag myself out of bed. That is, I stuff myself into the tiny slither of space between bed and wall and shimmy on down to pull some clothes out of my wardrobe. I haven't bothered to unpack properly and so am rotating the same few outfits on a daily basis. Most of my earthly belongings are still in suitcases, stuffed under the bed where they compete in a war of attrition with random teenage junk for floor space.

I blindly pull out some jeans, an old jumper and a handbag the size of a small country, before pulling my now erratic ringlets into a messy knot on the top of my head.

Standing still in front of the mirrored wardrobe at the end of the bed, I hardly even recognize myself. Which is ridiculous, because this is very me. Instead of wearing my heartbreak on my sleeve, I'm wearing it head to toe. I'm dripping in it. My skin is grey and my eyes are being propped up by dark purple bags. I'm heroin chic without the chic (or the heroin for that matter).

And my hair is still awful.

'That's a big handbag!' Mum smiles as I enter the kitchen. She not so subtly flings a tea towel over a bowl, but there's cake batter dripping from the whisk in her hand, which kind of gives the game away. A kernel of warmth worms its way into my cold dead heart.

'Happy birthday eve,' she says. Which I didn't think was a thing. But still, I smile and say thank you.

'What are you up to today?' I ask as I start pulling out blueberries, bananas, oat milk, basically everything I need for my breakfast smoothie.

'Taking your nan to the Welcome Centre,' Mum shouts over the whizz of the blender. 'They have a special on Friday — prawn sandwiches.' I stop blending just in time for her to yell the 'prawn sandwiches' bit while I'm decanting my purple goo into a glass.

'Part of their OAP meal deal,' she finishes off as I drink my smoothie. Pretending not to see Mum sliding the whisk under the tea towel.

The Welcome Centre is Easington's community centre slash charity venue. It's a sort of one-stop shop for any and all village activity.

I take another sip.

'I wish you'd eat more than those soup things, pet. You're too skinny. Some proper food would see you right. Shall I make you a bacon sandwich? I did your dad one earlier.'

It was confusing growing up with Mum metaphorically and physically chained to the kitchen, responding to Dad's every culinary whim. Not that Dad particularly had many whims, but he was very much the man of the house. It had bothered me as a teenager. But now, at almost thirty (even if I don't want to think about it), it doesn't bother me quite so much. Honestly, she seems really happy. I wonder these days what that must feel like.

'Thanks, but I'm fine. I like smoothies.'

And I do, mostly. But also old habits die hard. Charles was a mega fan of the smoothie.

I sip some more at my breakfast, playing for time. Staring off into the middle distance.

'Your dad and me could lend you some money, if that's the problem.' Mum is frowning at me as she speaks, worry etched into the lines of her face. Though it's equally possible that she just wants to finish her clandestine cake in peace.

'I'm not taking your money.' I feel every inch the almost thirty-year-old who's moved back in with her parents. Mum is a part-time dinner lady and Dad is Easington's third highest-rated plumber according to ratemytrade.com. Growing up, we never had much money. I remember the year the roof needed doing, how stressful it was. How precarious our situation felt. I hated it then. And I hate that I'm back in that position now, with only some meagre savings left in my bank account. I might not be penniless, but I'm definitely poor.

It doesn't feel like quite the distinction I'd like it to be.

'I really do think it'll do you good to get out, Alice.'

I guess this is it, then. Poor or not, I'm going.

Nowhere is particularly far in Easington Colliery. There's the main road through the village, optimistically named Sunshine Road and comprising of a butcher's, a pizza takeaway, a café and the hairdressers. There's row upon row of terraced streets branching off from it. As a general rule, there's about as many pubs as there are houses.

I'm waiting at the bus stop trying to burrow as far into my big coat as humanly possible. You can see the North Sea from here, its proximity ensuring that there's always at least a cool breeze. Heatwaves simply do not reach Easington, even in the summer. Now that it's November, it's positively arctic. My skin pebbles underneath many a layer. At least the hat I've pulled on hides the Great Hair Disaster of yesterday.

From behind my coat collar I stare off at the horizon. At the vast expanse of the murky sky and even murkier sea thinking that actually, it does all seem a bit pointless. And what do you know? I'm a nihilist now.

Really, there's only so long a person can stand silently crying at the sea, so I'm all but ready to abandon Mum's quest when hope arrives in the form of an old man with a Zimmer frame. I watch as he makes his way slowly towards the bus stop. This is good news. Old people are of one mind when it comes to bus timetables aren't they? Like the Borg. One must be imminent.

'Hi, pet,' he wheezes white knuckling his Zimmer frame.

'Hi,' I say, making it sound like more of a question.

'Alice, isn't it?'

I take a step back, startled.

'Yep, that's me. Sorry.'

'What you sorry for?'

I don't actually know.

'You might remember me as Mr Hall.' He gasps the words out.

'No way! Mr Hall from Easington High?'

Mr Hall does a soft chuckle. 'That's me. You can call me Peter, or Pete.'

I think of my last vivid memory of Pete . . . no, it's too weird. He's Mr Hall. At the school awards ceremony. He'd been so full of life, dad dancing to the music and being all over the top about the awards. He'd been old then. Maybe I hadn't quite realized just how old.

This version hardly looks like the same person. He pauses to cough, a full-body hacking cough that has so much force behind it, I'm amazed he doesn't dislodge a lung.

'I never forget one of my own. Especially not one as bright as you,' he continues, once the panting and wheezing has stopped. I'm seconds away from declaring a medical emergency.

I choose to ignore the reminder that I'd once had so much promise, instead asking, 'Are you okay?' as the hiss of a bus approaches.

'Lungs are giving out,' he says, patting his chest.

The doors of the bus clunk open and I step on backwards, still not entirely sure that Mr Hall isn't about to keel over and die on the pavement. Once he follows behind me, breathing relatively normally, I relax.

I'd really rather not have to get the bus. Not that I have anything against buses, it's just that they take ten times as long to get anywhere. It's almost an hour to Durham.

Part of me wishes that Mum and Dad hadn't instilled quite such a fear of credit when I was younger. It still haunts me to this day and it means that I'll be able to afford to a car round about never.

I plonk down in the first spare seat. Despite the smoothie I'm already hungry. Maybe I'll go to a café once my shampoo-based quest is over. I'm sure that Durham will have somewhere that sells wholefoods.

I'm startled to find my old head teacher making himself comfortable in the seat next to me when there's a whole half a bus of seats free. No one voluntarily sat next to anyone in London.

Honestly, he's a little closer than I'd like. Personal boundaries are something of a foreign concept in Easington. A bit like wild swimming.

For obvious reasons, I keep my hat on.

'Did I hear someone say you had some right posh fella down in London and it went a bit badly?' Mr Hall says.

The news that I'm being gossiped about isn't as surprising as it should be. Everyone knows everyone's business in Easington. 'Sorry, yes.'

Mr Hall looks at me. 'Doesn't do to dwell on these things.'

Clearly I do not look like a woman who's particularly coping with her new lot in life.

And instead of setting any sort of a personal boundary, I find myself giving Mr Hall a very PG-rated version of the end of my relationship with Charles. The version where I'd caught him cheating and then he'd finished with me and chucked me out of his flat.

'Well, he sounds like a right numpty,' is Mr Hall's summation of the sorry tale. 'You were always going to do great things, Alice. A teacher can tell.' He taps the side of his nose.

I manage a faint shrug, sitting back against my seat and letting Mr Hall do most of the conversational heavy lifting. No short ask for a man with significant oxygen requirements.

'Next stop Durham Central!' shouts the driver and I practically leap out of my seat to ring the little buzzer.

'Once will do!' chastises the driver as my thumb pauses its rather forceful press.

'Aren't you getting off?' I ask Mr Hall. There's something odd about chatting to your old head teacher as if you're equals. Even when you're both adults, it's still weird.

I now know that Mr Hall is a Newcastle United supporter, a widower and a dumpling lover. His daughter is his carer and he feels guilty about holding her back in life. I could have a good bash at ghostwriting his autobiography.

'I just come along for the ride,' he replies even though the B1283 isn't exactly what you'd call scenic.

'Okay, well enjoy the return trip.'

'Will do, it's my favourite direction. You have a good day now, Alice.'

The doors clunk open and I climb off the bus. Mr Hall waves to me as it pulls away and I hold up my hand back, feeling suddenly disorientated at the loss of his company.

Durham is everything I remember it to be. Quaint. Old. There's even bunting across the streets. The roads are cobbled because it's too fancy here for tarmac.

I Google Maps the Boots and hurry on. There are people everywhere and maybe I'm paranoid but I get an odd sense that they're all looking at me. I feel around the edges of my hat. Nope, it's not my hair. That's still firmly hidden.

Wow, there really are a lot of people here.

A bead of sweat works its way down my spine and my legs feel tingly. I will them forward. I've pinned all my hopes on feeling better once I get something to rectify the damage to my hair. I mean, my life might be atrocious but maybe my highlights can be saved.

Pushing through the chemist's doors, I try not to compare them to heavenly gates because that would make me insane. Heading to the hair section, there's a whole section for toners. I'm Frodo and the bottles promising ash hues are my Ring. We're drawn to one another.

If anyone clocks me having an out-of-body experience in the middle of Boots they don't let on. Though I notice that I'm being given a rather wide berth. Then again, my personal hygiene hasn't been what it ought to have these last few weeks.

My loose plan to buy toner and then find a café starts to seem vaguely aspirational based on the difficulty I have deciding which purple bottle to buy. After spending way longer than anyone should in the shampoo aisle, I grab the cheapest one and make a quick getaway.

In the queue, I try to make eye contact with precisely no one. I rummage around in my bag searching for my phone and then my hands are acting on autopilot, swiping open Instagram for my hourly Charles stalk. Honestly, I don't know why I do it. If I was watching me on a TV programme, I'd be screeching, 'Don't do it you tool!' at the telly.

And yet here I am.

Tool.

I watch as the screen fills with little Charles-based squares.

There's a new one.

My chest lurches.

You're mine #whenyouknowyouknow

There's Charles and the other woman, their heads pushed together for a selfie. Their smiles so white, I'm half dazzled.

You're mine.

Charles said the same thing to me. Over and over again.

You're mine you know?

It's like you were made for me.

No one else knows me like you do.

I feel sick.

It had always felt so good when he'd said it. But it was obviously an empty promise. Or else a threat. Because six and a bit weeks after we split up, Charles is using the very same line to social media announce that he's with someone else.

Ophelia. I recognize her from the shaggy rug. I try not to think where her fingers have been. She's bright-eyed and glossy-haired. Like those dogs with excellent fur that always seem to think they're better than the other dogs. An Afghan hound. That's it. She's like a sexy Afghan hound.

I click on her profile. There are several pictures of them together. Hashtag couple goals.

Charles is meant to hate couple photos, and yet Ophelia's profile is overflowing with them. At the top of the Shard, eating sushi at Nobu. There's a stabby feeling in my stomach.

#datenight #treatyoself

Ophelia poses seductively with an edamame bean between her lips.

I check the original photo. They've uploaded them at the same time. An hour ago. I'm still standing in the queue but everything seems to get darker, as though the world might be ending. My world. It's there in the sicky feeling you get at the back of your throat before you puke. The way my hands are shaking. Something terrible is about to happen. I don't know how I know, but I definitely do.

I look about. No one else seems to have noticed the imminent apocalypse.

'Next please!' I hear over the ringing in my ears.

But I don't move.

'I said, next please!'

'Are you going to pay?' the man in the queue behind me asks.

I feel my feet moving.

And then my hands, passing over the lone bottle of purple toner.

'You'll need to put in your PIN, pet. Contactless has been hit and miss all morning.' The cashier's voice is far away.

'Okay.' I put my card into the reader and enter what I think is my new PIN number. Except I don't feel good. And right now, who the fuck cares about shampoo when the world is spinning?

'Declined.'

I look up. See the cashier frowning at me. Her badge says, 'Hello, I'm Barbara'.

'Okay. Let me think.'

I have another go.

'Same again. Do you have another card?'

'No. I'm forgetful. It's new.' My voice doesn't sound right.

'I'm sorry, pet.' And Barbara does look sorry. Perhaps she too has fallen foul of the love of her life and had to live out her days with orange hair.

'What do I do now?' I whimper, mortified at the fact that I'm apparently mere moments away from weeping.

Time ceases to have any meaning as I stare at the card reader. Millennia pass, an epoch. I expect to look up and see that humans are extinct and fungi have taken over the world.

'Alice? Alice King?' Someone calls my name from the queue behind me.

I glance back wondering who has caught me now, at a time like this.

'Alice?' A figure I vaguely recognize is pushing his way to the front of the queue.

'Would you mind stepping aside?' Barbara suggests, ever so gently. 'I'll keep your shampoo here, shall I?' She shifts the box across the counter. 'In case you remember the PIN?' Barbara looks doubtful.

'Yes. Thank you.' I nod through the haze of humiliation.

The man that I clearly should know, but don't recognize, stares down at me.

'I almost didn't recognize you,' he says. I assume he means that I look significantly worse now than whenever he last saw me. Which would not be a surprise.

I manage to gather myself, feeling slightly less dazed. 'I'm sorry, but ... do we know each other?'

He's tall with dark hair swept to the side, features marred by a slightly angry expression. I want to run away and live out my days in the Alaskan wilderness.

'It's Luke. Luke Priestly.' His frown deepens.

No! Surely not. 'Emo Luke?' I blurt.

'Apparently so.' His jaw twitches. I'm being rude.

'Sorry, it's just that I was literally thinking about you yesterday. And Mr Hall ...' I'm shaking, and I'm not making a lot of sense. Luke frowns and I realize how odd this whole thing sounds, seeing as I haven't seen in him over a decade. I hurry on, 'I just didn't recognize you without the eyeliner. And you've grown, like ... a lot.'

'That tends to happen when ... people grow up.' His lip twitches.

This is the Luke who was on the front page of the *Easington Gazette* with me. Right here, in Boots. I haven't seen him in (I quickly do the maths in my head) fourteen years. Not since he went to a different sixth form.

School Luke was not exactly known for his sunny disposition. Not just because he wore black nail varnish. He had long hair and his nickname was Professor Snape. Teenagerhood is a cruel beast.

I massage my temples. Today is an onslaught from the past. Honestly, it's a lot.

'I didn't realize you lived around here,' he says. I wonder briefly why Luke is talking to me when everything about his body language, tone and – actually his entire demeanour – suggests he would really rather not.

'I don't. I mean, I didn't. I do now.' Six weeks holed up in my teenage bedroom and, clearly, I've forgot how to interact with people.

'Excuse me, Miss, would you like this or not?' A spotty teenager has replaced Barbara at the till and is waving my lone bottle of toner at me.

'I don't think I can remember my PIN. I'll get it next time.' There's no way I'm having another go in front of Luke.

'I can help you out?' Luke fixes me with the stare of a parent sick of telling an errant toddler to put their shoes on. I will defend these orange highlights with my life rather than take money from this man.

The teenager looks between us. 'Look, is one of you paying this £3.74 or what?'

Seriously, where is a nuclear holocaust when you need one? What I wouldn't give to be a silhouette on the floor right about now.

But before I can implore God for an end to humanity, Luke has handed over the bottle of moisturizer he was here to buy, inserted his card *and* PIN and now the teenager is shouting, 'Next please.' Luke hands me the bottle of toner.

We exit the queue. I feel irrationally annoyed at being cast into the damsel in distress role. Even though I am a damsel and distress is basically my personality type.

I fight down the annoyance. Luke was just trying to be nice. It'd be just like me to make him feel bad for it.

'I couldn't remember my PIN. It's not that I don't have £3.74. I forget stuff all the time.' I twist round to whisper to Luke.

'You're welcome,' he replies stiffly, pushing the door open with his shoulder and gesturing me through before him. The man must have taken some sort of a growth hormone. He's much taller than I remember.

I frown. 'Well, I didn't ask you to pay.' See, horrible.

Luke looks a bit alarmed and I can see that, objectively, it does suck to be him. Imagine popping to Boots, trying to do a good deed for someone you knew at school, only to find that she's unhinged and crying at you for paying for her shampoo.

I'm now full-on sweating, despite the November wind whipping through the streets. The band of my woolly hat is stuck to my forehead.

'I'm sorry. I . . . I . . . really have to go.' My voice breaks as I turn and run. Wishing I'd had the presence of mind to give Luke the toner back before I took off. Alas I did not and now I can feel it rolling around in my giant handbag.

I keep moving, rushing towards the bus stop, all thoughts of sustenance abandoned quicker than you can say 'panic attack'. At least there's a bus right ahead.

'Alice, wait!' I hear a voice call from behind me.

Luke.

'Sorry,' I cry, fishing around my chasm of a bag for the toner and waving the bottle above my head. 'Thanks for the shampoo.' I have basically just robbed the man of £3.74. I'll find a way to pay him back . . . I can't be indebted to him.

I dive into the bus's open doors, slamming my stupid card on the stupid card reader.

'Single to Easington, please,' I pant.

The machine beeps and I stagger forward.

'Same please, mate,' Luke says behind me. Distinctly not sounding like he's just summited Everest.

'What are you doing?' I round on him in the tiny bit of space by the ticket machine.

He rubs the back of his neck with his hand, looking uncomfortable. 'I'm ... getting the bus.'

I frown at him.

'You live in Easington?' My hands are on my hips and my hat is low on my head. I'm the embodiment of unhinged.

'Mum and Dad do, I have a flat in Durham. But ...' He pauses, glancing into the bowels of the bus where every single person is watching us with rapt attention. Mr Hall is there, leaned so far forward in his seat, he's at risk of toppling off it. Honestly? Are my life's myriad small humiliations merely a spectacle for other people? 'Look, I wanted to check that you were okay,' he mutters.

I take a breath out slowly. Realising that yelling at Luke for essentially being a nice person is not going to make me feel good about myself. I drop my voice to an almost whisper.

'I'm sorry about all of that back there. But you really ... honestly ... you don't need to follow me home. I can transfer you the money. What's your PayPal?'

Luke returns my whisper. 'It's not just that. It's a Friday. I always stay at Mum and Dad's on a Friday ... but my car is in the garage.'

I attempt a dignified nod.

'Right. I see. Okay, well, great ...' I make a sharp turn away from him. 'Mr Hall!' I cry out, as though he's my long-lost love, finally returned from war. 'What are you doing here?'

'All right, Alice pet. Thought I'd do another round trip. By the by, is that Luke Priestly? It's quite the little reunion we're having here!' He smiles as I sit next to him, and I realize that I'm a terrible human. Luke does one firm nod and then sits a couple of rows back from us.

He's being rude, if you ask me.

'You feeling okay, pet?' Mr Hall asks.

There's absolutely no way that I'm about to give Mr Hall the rundown of what will henceforth live in my mind as the Great

Boots Debacle. There's just no way to spin the fact that I discovered that Charles has a new girlfriend, the woman from the shaggy rug, and that the whole thing made me feel like the world was ending, causing me to forget my new PIN and peg it through the streets of Durham, fleeing the man I once co-won an award with.

Not with Luke in earshot at any rate.

Instead, I say, 'Why, yes, Mr Hall, very good thank you,' which makes me feel like I might have clawed back a modicum of dignity. That is until Mr Hall says loudly, 'I was hoping you were having a nice day. It's awful hard getting over a bad break-up.'

I'm starting to think that the world having ended when I expected it to would have been a kindness. To me at least.

Chapter Three

There's something to be said about not caring what you look like while you're alone in your bedroom. But then there's also something to the fact that running into a handsome old acquaintance will make your questionable fashion choices all the more questionable.

I tug my hat further down on my head.

'What are you *doing*?' I ask eventually, in a huff of frustration. It's actually very challenging, storming away from someone as they continue to walk next to you.

'Going this way.' He nods towards the far end of the main street, less than half a mile away, and the meagre collection of shops there.

'*I'm* going that way,' I tell Luke. Because I actually cannot go home yet. Mum probably hasn't even iced the secret cake.

'Okay,' he replies. He's wearing a sort of lumberjack jacket with a fleecy collar and his cheeks are rosy from the cold.

Neither of us speaks as we continue to march. The awkwardness of our silence is deafening.

I cave first. 'Where are you going?' I ask, speeding up.

'For lunch.' Luke matches my pace.

'That's what I'm doing too.' I'm out of breath again. I think we're in a race but I can't be sure. I speed up again.

'Okay.' Luke matches my pace easily.

We continue to walk, potentially looking like those athletes who took up fast walking as a sport. I'm no longer sure I know what's going on. The toner rolls around in my giant bag. We can't go to a café together. That would be ridiculous.

'We don't have to eat together,' Luke says.

'No, honestly, I'd be totally fine eating together,' I lie. 'It's just that I'm not sure I'll be the best company. I'm probably going to cry at some point in the next hour so—'

Luke chooses to ignore my happy prediction. 'Okay, fine.'

'Fine.' I nod. Unsure, exactly how we've arrived at this situation.

We walk in strained silence, passing the butchers and Bambinos – the local pizza takeaway – before we reach Star Bucks café.

I'd wondered, as a teenager, when the owners of Star Bucks had slapped a load of green paint on the sign and given themselves the new name, whether they were worried about being sued by actual Starbucks. But it turns out that no one from the real deal either knows or cares that there's a rundown café in Easington ripping off their brand. And anyway, the now cracked green paint is the only thing linking the international conglomerate with this three-star hygiene rating, belly buster bap serving local café.

And yet, Luke and I both slow to a stop outside the entrance. Because there is a tacit agreement that we come to Star's. Not because it has a particularly good bean of coffee, but because there are no other options.

Luke pushes the door and gestures for me to head inside, meaning that I have to duck under his arm. Silly tall men with their silly height.

'You here for the special? Liver and onion,' a bored waitress says, chewing gum.

'Am I okay to look at the menu instead?' I ask, because a serving of grey liver is absolutely not going to make today a better day.

She passes us two laminated menus.

'What if I'd actually wanted some liver?' Luke asks from behind me.

'Then by all means, don't deprive yourself on my account.'

Luke raises one eyebrow but says nothing.

Inside, Star Bucks hasn't changed — possibly in living memory. There are copious amounts of pine. Pine panelling. Pine tables. The chairs are pine. The café is long and narrow, so if you're seated towards the back — where Luke and I end up — it's like hovering on the perimeter of a black hole.

'Good spot for vampires,' I mutter, settling down into a seat that feels distinctly . . . sticky.

'Pardon?' Luke asks.

'Nothing.' I attempt to arrange my face into something like a normal expression.

Think! Think of something to say.

We stare at each other, my traitorous brain zeroing in on the fact that older Luke looks significantly better than school Luke. Luke.2 looks like he was created in a lab in a petri dish marked 'handsome'. I'd question that this is even the same person as Prof Snape if it weren't for the fact that the updated version seems to have the same standoffish personality.

We've now been quiet for way longer than is appropriate.

SPEAK, BRAIN!

'So, um . . .'

'How are . . .'

We start at the same time.

'No, you first,' I splutter, waving a sweaty hand. In fact, all of me is sweaty and I've no choice but to pull off my hat.

Luke's eyes go wide at the mass of dishevelled orange curls which pour out of it. Tactfully, he doesn't say anything. Instead, he leans back in his chair. 'I was going to ask if . . . if you're enjoying being back in Easington.' He picks an invisible bit of lint from his navy blue jumper. 'But that might be too personal.'

As it happens, I was just about to fill the conversation void by divulging a case of persistent shower mould that Dad dealt with yesterday, so in this instance, personal wins out. I blow a curl back off my forehead.

'It's okay, I suppose. A big adjustment. I lived in London before. It's um, different there.'

'I bet.' Something like sympathy ghosts across his face. 'I'm sorry, about your break-up.'

'Thank you. It's okay. He was my boss too, hence the penury. He's shacked up with an influencer from Soho. Might well have been shacked up with her since we broke up,' God, how many times can I say the word 'shacked'?

I'm feeling imminent doom again.

Thank God the waitress arrives to take our order.

'Do you want any chocolate cake? It's on offer.' She's really pushing those offers.

'No thank you.' My eyes make a hasty scan of the menu. There's a lot of bread. Baps in abundance.

'Do you do any salads?' I ask the waitress.

She blows a bubblegum bubble and shakes her head.

'There's the filled Yorkshires,' she offers unhelpfully.

'Okay, thank you, I'll bear that in mind, but for now maybe I could just have a cheese sandwich? On brown bread if you have it? Or seeded would be good too. Thank you.'

I'm sweating even without the hat now.

'Do you want it as part of the deal? You get a drink and a slice of cake too,' the waitress asks and Jesus it's a lot of effort ordering lunch.

'Yes, why not? I'll have a green tea, or just a regular tea to go with it too, please. But no cake. Luke, do you want some cake?'

'No cake for me either. I'll have what she's having.' He's cool as a cucumber. Knob.

'Great choice,' I say as the waitress leaves. I'm not entirely sure what I've actually ordered. I'm almost certain that I've earned us a reputation as the oddball table.

Luke seems confused.

'Cake can be really dangerous,' I tell him. 'Charles ran a chain of health cafés in London. He didn't like us to eat cake. And to be fair, there were these illegal sprinkles that everyone used a while ago. From America.' I get that I'm babbling. 'Sorry, I talk too much.'

He coughs.

'I see.' Luke looks as uncomfortable as it's possible to be when forced into close quarters with a woman ranting about illegal sprinkles. I adopt a no blinking stance. Because this interaction will not be enhanced by me starting to cry.

'Sorry, sorry.' I blow my nose into a napkin. 'I just miss Charles. And my life in London. And obviously there are people way worse off than me so it doesn't seem right to be so . . .' I grasp around for the words, '. . . messed-up, over all this. Even though you know . . .'

I attempt to recover a sliver of decorum by not wailing about Charles and the shaggy rug.

'Well . . .' Luke reaches forward as if he's considering placing a hand over mine before clearly thinking better of it. He sits up, his back straight against his chair. 'In the wake of a break-up, your nucleus accumbens is likely to be overstimulated.'

He must clock the vacant expression on my face. 'It's the part of your brain responsible for addiction. People who have recently left relationships where they felt a deep attachment have high levels of brain activity there. Plus you'll be readapting to lower levels of oxytocin. You'll feel better soon.'

Feeling better seems about as likely as Putin joining the Peace Corps. Still, oxytocin. I've heard of that. Charles's cafés released a 'happy breakfast pot' that claimed to be full of the stuff. What Luke's saying . . . it sounds almost like . . . science.

'Oxytocin? Isn't that the happy hormone?'

Luke's head tilts to the side. Just a touch. Maybe he's a tiny bit impressed. 'Yes. But it also works in tandem with neurotransmitters in the brain, dopamine and norepinephrine to create feelings of love. Even if the match isn't a good one, the confluence of hormones tricks several brain systems into believing that it is.'

Well, I was not expecting that. 'You sound like an expert on the matter,' I say, genuinely shocked.

'I am an expert,' Luke says. I grudgingly admire his confidence. 'I'm an evolutionary biologist. Based at Durham University.'

There's a vague memory of Luke being the only person to volunteer to dissect a pig eyeball in GCSE biology. At the time, it didn't do much for his social standing.

'Like that Richard Dawkins guy?'

'Yes, he's also a biologist.'

'Do you hate God too?'

'No.' Luke releases a breath.

'So, is this a big part of your research then? Love?' I ask him, genuinely, if reluctantly, interested.

'It's not an insignificant part. I'm working with an interdepartmental team from Harvard on the theory of love.'

He must see the disbelief on my face because he says, 'It's a team of biological anthropologists, psychologists and the Department of Biosciences We're even considering bringing in the philosophy department.'

'Thank you for mansplaining what interdepartmental means,' I tell him. 'That isn't, incidentally, why I was so shocked.' I begin to laugh.

'I didn't think that's what you were.' Luke looks unnerved.

'Sorry. Sorry,' I say. 'It's just . . . oh, the irony! Here you are . . .' I indicate him, '. . . the anti-Christ of romantic love. And here I am, a failed philosopher who wrote my entire A-level coursework on the philosophy of love. And then today there's been you and me and Mr Hall.' I laugh, mildly hysterical. 'And people deny that fate is a thing,' I finish.

I realize that my voice has turned too loud and so stare at my hands. I feel my eyes brim and wipe away a stray tear. At this stage, it could be a tear of despair or laughter. Who knows?

Luke looks confused. 'I thought you worked in food health?'

'I do. I mean . . . I did. My ex did. But I didn't start out that way. I did a year of a philosophy degree in London.'

Luke looks confused by my haphazard retelling of the last decade.

'Don't you remember I was properly into philosophy?' I ask him.

'Vaguely,' he replies.

'Only vaguely?' I'm forced to stop gesticulating as the waitress brings everything over. Meal deal was obviously code for 'lots of food,' because we have chips and the cake we didn't want too. It's some sort of dessert drowning in custard. At least I got my cheese sandwich. It's mostly bread.

Luke casts a wary eye over our table.

'I'm not sure this all goes together,' he says.

'Not with that attitude it won't.' I test out a wink, regretting it immediately.

'Like I was saying, we won that award. And then my A level coursework was all about the philosophy of love. I got full marks for arguing that Bertrand Russell was right when he said that to fear love is to fear life.'

'I remember the award, Alice.' Luke says it so quietly that I hardly even hear him.

'At the end, you said that it was shit and stormed off.'

'You were being nauseatingly pleasant.'

'There's nothing wrong with pleasant, Luke. You should give it a try sometime.'

A shadow crosses Luke's face and he takes a bite out of his sandwich with the air of a lion ripping into a gazelle.

'So, this study,' I manage, picking up a chip and putting it down again with as much dignity as I can muster. 'It sounds incredibly romantic, spending your days surrounded by love. I've always been so drawn to the idea that we all have this soulmate, that really we're not alone, or not completely.'

Luke looks up from where he's drinking his tea.

'Please don't tell me that you believe that there's such a thing as soulmates. How arbitrary.'

Luke says arbitrary the way some people might say genocide.

But he's on a roll. 'Love is the hallmark of the human animal, born out of the evolution of pair bonding, nothing else.'

I shuffle in my seat. 'I respectfully disagree, love is primordial. Philosophers have been trying to explain emotion for as long as time. Imagination, senses, emotions, the things we feel when we're in love, they're not rational things.'

'Feelings generate ideas that you test for evidence. I'm not saying that love doesn't exist, only that it is more rational than human tradition dictates it to be. Once you're aware of *why* you might feel a certain way, it's much easier to control and manage those feelings.'

'Are you a robot?' I ask.

'Not last time I checked.' Luke takes another aggressive bite of his sandwich.

'Well AI or not, I've never heard anyone apply the concept of free will to actual emotions.' I slam my spoon down following some aggressive stirring. 'What about those old couples who die right at the same time as each other because they can't bear to be apart. Like that couple at the end of that film *The Notebook*. There's no rational explanation for that.'

'Trust me, Alice,' Luke replies gravely. 'There is always an underlying health condition.'

I huff. Because that is the case in *The Notebook*. Yet I'm unwilling to concede the point.

'What about beauty?'

'Natural selection.'

'Romance?'

'The vagus nerve.'

'Marriage?'

'Divorce.'

'Those penguins who mate for life?'

'They're penguins. Look . . .' Luke implores like someone who is trying his best to be reasonable. The man at the table next to us is openly watching, a fork speared with a chunk of liver hovering halfway between his mouth and the plate. ' . . . I just don't feel that humans should be slaves to their emotions. I would have thought that you of all people might buy into that. Especially after, you know . . .'

He trails off, but it doesn't take a genius to figure out that he means the whole cheating ex-boyfriend situation.

I make a show of pouring out some more tea from the metal teapot with one of those spouts that makes the hot water go fucking everywhere.

'But falling in love with Charlie was amazing. The butterflies, the breathlessness, the feeling that nothing else mattered. There is no greater human experience. I just went and messed it up.'

'I thought *he* cheated?'

A bit of tea goes down the wrong way and for a second, I think I'm going to die being waterboarded by a cup of tea. The man at the table next to us takes it upon himself to whack me on my back.

'What? Oh, yes. He did. But he was very stressed with work.' I take a bite of my sandwich, my eyes watering from the almost choking.

There's so much bread it takes me forever to chew. I'm overcome with sadness, because being in love *is* amazing. I really believe what I said to Luke. That love is the thing gives meaning to it all. Without it, we're so . . . alone. It's just that losing love, when it happens to you, it's not something you're prepared for at all.

I finally swallow.

'So, your study then, it's *Love Island* with an academic flare?' I ask as Luke raises an eyebrow.

'Not quite.'

Why is he so prickly? Annoying man.

'What *does* it involve?' I press, keen to keep the conversation away from me and my recent dumping.

'Why, do you want to take part?'

'No. I'm too hung up on Charles. You have to be in the right mindset to fall in love. I'd be like the hidden landmine in the study. People would turn up thinking they're going on a nice date and then bang,' I slam the table for emphasis as tea spills over the top of my cup. 'You're missing a limb.'

Luke's expression morphs from vaguely alarmed to very much alarmed. Maybe that was a bit over the top. 'I thought love wasn't rational?' he asks. 'Surely, if that's the case, Cupid could strike at any time.' He uses my own logic against me. He also seems to be making much better progress with his lunch. Maybe he has a steel-reinforced jaw.

'It's not. Hell, if this was a romance story, *we'd* fall in love.'

Okay, now he's at outright panic.

'I thought we'd established—'

'I know, I know ... Apparently you don't believe in love.' I roll my eyes.

I'm not sure why I've taken such a personal affront to Luke believing that love is nothing but a bit of evolutionary fall-out. If anything, I should be the team captain of love is death.

'I believe that love is simply heightened activity of several brain systems. There's a difference,' he replies, looking significantly more put together than me at this stage in the proceedings. 'Actually,' he carries on, 'that's what the study is focused on. The theory that we each have four brain systems which dictate which traits we might be most drawn to in a potential mate. The research is being done in Boston, but we're helping to analyse their findings.'

'But how do you know which brain systems people have?' I ask.

'There's a questionnaire. We all have a mixture of all four, but one likely dominates. We then consider whether people are drawn to a partner based on this or not. Fifteen million people have taken part so far. That's why we've been drafted in to help with the analysis.'

'And you're expecting what, that love is ultimately explainable based on our brains?'

'Obviously,' Luke replies importantly, 'I'll be led by the evidence.'

'Obviously.'

'But yes, I expect that our findings will marry up with the preliminary assessments made by Harvard that feelings of love have a practical and reasonable explanation. Essentially, love is rational.'

'Well, you're wrong.' I pick up my teaspoon and put it down again. 'I bet it'll show the exact opposite. Love cannot be quantified. Or explained. It isn't rational. I could totally fall in love right now, when I least expect it.'

'How much?' Luke asks.

'Excuse me?'

'How much are you willing to bet?'

'Er . . .'

This has escalated quickly.

'What are *you* willing to bet?' I throw it back at him.

'£500.'

£500? Who has £500 lying around waiting to throw away on a bet?

Now, the sensible course of action here would be to thank Luke for his time, rise from the table and make a graceful exit. Neither seeing nor hearing from Luke and his ruinous theories again.

But then, poor life choices are fast becoming my calling card. In my mind, I'm the last stalwart in the defence against romantic love. The love of Shakespeare, of Emily Brontë, of David Nicholls.

'Done.'

Argh.

I attempt to backtrack.

'But how would we know? I mean you're in charge of the study. You could manipulate the findings.'

'We'd have to keep it separate from the actual study. It wouldn't be ethical for me to be involved. You say love isn't rational, I say it is. Let's keep this simple. If you fall in love within six months, at a time when recently heartbroken, you least expect it, you win. If you don't, I win.'

He uses air commas around the word heartbroken. I want to punch his smug, superior face. But I think of something better.

I narrow my eyes at him.

'What about you?'

'What about me?'

'Well, surely you'd have to admit that love is real if *you* went and fell in love. Seeing as you don't believe in it.' I look down at my hands, realising that I'm twisting the paper napkin around them.

He gives me a look.

'That's not what I said. I said that it can be explained. It's rational.'

'Tomato, tomato.'

I get another look.

'If I'm doing this then so are you. In six months if either one of us falls in love, I win.'

He thinks for a moment.

'Fine. But if neither of us falls in love, then the money is mine.'

'Deal.'

'Deal.'

We shake hands and I start to hyperventilate. What the fuck have

I done? Have I really just bet £500 on the philosophical premise that love is something you just *feel* when a) I've literally just been dumped by the man I thought was the love of my life and b) I'm a failed philosopher?

Luke doesn't seem like a failed anything. In fact, he seems worryingly competent on all fronts. His cheese sandwich isn't torn to bits on his plate like mine. I start to spiral. Jesus, my hair. No one falls in love with orange hair.

We engage in a staring contest as we finish our drinks. Or, at least, I think that's what's happening. I'm panting and silently catastrophizing but with Luke, there's always a chance that the robot version didn't come with eyelids.

We haven't even touched our dessert. I'll have to worry about the food waste at a later date.

To quell the panic threatening to overwhelm me, I change the subject.

'You know, at those awards at school, I voted for you as most likely to destroy the world.'

Luke leans forward ever so slightly. 'How amusing, I put your name forward for the same thing.'

'You did not!' I'm outraged.

'I did. It's always the ones you least expect.'

My eyes water as I give in and blink.

'But why me? I mean you, yes. You looked like the sort of kid to fashion a pentagram with your own blood of a Tuesday morning. I was the metaphorical head of the cheerleading squad.'

'We didn't have a cheerleading squad.'

I roll my eyes. 'Hence, metaphorical. All my school reports said, a pleasure to have in class.'

He shrugs, pulling on his lumberjack coat. 'Of course they did. Well, we were both beaten to it by Leo Payne, anyway, weren't we?'

'That's right. Good memory,' I concede.

'I think he's a Lib Dem councillor now.'

'Accurate then. Anyway,' I stand up, 'this has been interesting.'

'I think I'll go home and look into minibreaks. Be nice to get away with *your* money. Eastern Europe maybe.' He zips up his jacket.

I'm mostly flailing with my own Puffa coat. The arm of one sleeve is inside out and it's defeating me.

The guy at the table next to us has actually turned in his seat to watch.

'Well, I hear Romania is lovely. It'd be so nice to return to the land of your ancestors. Pity you won't make the homecoming after all.'

Luke stands up too, peers down at me.

'Because you're a vampire,' I elaborate weakly. Why am I so short?

'When did you discover your thing for vampires?'

'What? I don't have a thing for vampires.'

'You've mentioned them twice already.'

'Must be because I see you and think, there is a man who looks like he'd feast on the blood of the innocent. Just the vibe you give off.'

Luke pauses before reaching into his jacket and pulling out a pen. Of course he carries a pen in his pocket. Of course. He's probably got a bunker full of tinned food somewhere.

'Write down your number and I'll text you,' he says. I think about writing down the wrong one, just because I can. But then that would be like admitting I was wrong, wouldn't it?

I write it on the back of the bill and hand it to Luke.

The waitress appears by our table with the card machine.

'I'll be in touch.' Luke taps his card. I follow suit, holding my breath until I see that it's been accepted without the need for a PIN. Boots round two is the absolute last thing I need.

'Not this weekend, please. It's my birthday and I'll be celebrating. You know, with alllll the people.'

I pull my hat back on, heading back through the café towards the street.

'And just to confirm, you're not planning on following me home now?' I ask Luke over my shoulder.

'I can assure you that I am not.'

'Good.'

'Good.'

'Goodbye, Luke.'

'Goodbye, Alice. I'll be in touch'

And in what is fast becoming my signature exit, I turn and run.

Chapter Four

Me: Hi Charles. How's things? I just thought I'd check,
    because I saw the picture on Instagram of you
    and Ophelia and I wondered if it meant that you're
    together. Obviously you're together in the picture. But
    are you together, together? Anyway, I hope you're
    well, Alice

I'm sweating by the time I hit send, elbows propped up on my
mattress. The message has taken me forty-five minutes to compose. But after the debacle of today, my brain won't quieten down.
It's like Luke set out to make me question everything I thought
I knew about love. Surely he has to be wrong. Because knowing
that my neurotransmitters are all out of whack doesn't seem to
make it any easier to deal with the fact. I feel more muddled
than ever. In dire need of some clarity. And for that, my brain
has latched onto the word, Charles. Running it through me like
tickertape.

Charles: Yes, Ophelia and I are together. C
Me: But we only broke up a few weeks ago?
Charles: If you continue to harass me, Alice, I will be forced
    to contact the family solicitor. And block you. That too. C

I might not know much, but there is one thing which I'm sure holds true. True love doesn't threaten to set the family solicitor on you. And it shouldn't make you feel quite so small.

I block Charles's number.

There's a sort of hollow emptiness once I do. The gnawing realisation that I'd pinned everything on what turned out to be the Trojan horse of love. I'd welcomed it, embraced it with open arms and then, just like the good people of Troy – boom! – the walls are on fire and your people are dead.

Was Charles always like this? He can't have been. I trawl through my memories of us. Charlie kissing me for the first time in the nightclub by the Millennium Dome. Him dancing up behind me and snaking his hands around my hips. The flowers. The jewellery.

I should feel calmer. Happy Charles-based memories have got me through the darkest moments of the last six weeks. But for some reason they don't work so well this time. In fact, they don't work at all. Something has changed. Even if I'm not exactly sure what.

I go to bed thinking that at least tomorrow can't be any worse.

A weak light creeps into my bedroom, pulling me to a state that's somewhere between asleep and awake. There's a sort of vague hope that maybe yesterday was one of those stories that ends with . . . *And then it was all a dream* . . .

Damn it. I'm properly awake now, and it was very much not a dream. Charles . . . toner . . . Luke . . . the bet. Oh God, the bet. What on earth was I thinking betting on the fact that love isn't rational? So irrational that I could go and fall in love again in within six months?

Clearly, I wasn't thinking straight.

It's just that something about Luke got under my skin. Not in a good way. More in the sense that impetigo might.

I do a long breath out.

'Happy birthday, pet!' Mum calls through my bedroom door.

I groan.

Mum starts hoovering the landing furiously on the landing. She gives me a one-armed hug on my way to the bathroom, refusing to fully let go of the Dyson knock-off.

For reasons that cannot possibly be good, Mum blocks my path downstairs.

'It's your birthday,' she shouts over the noise, 'I'll bring you a cup of tea in bed.'

'Honestly, I don't mind, it's not like we're doing anything.'

Mum does a nervous titter of a laugh and I narrow my eyes at her. She flicks the hoover off.

'Mum.'

'Now, now, Alice.' She begins manhandling me back into my bedroom. 'You just stay in there for a while. Don't worry about a thing.'

She closes the door in my face. My own mother.

'Maybe you could sort out that hair of yours?' she calls from the other side.

Defeated and feeling slightly nervous at the prospect of whatever Mum has planned, I reach inside my bag. I mean, since Luke bought this toner for me, I might as well put it to good use.

I'm obviously growing as a person because I don't even check Instagram while the toner sets. Instead, I'm deep into the Biological Sciences prospectus from the University of Durham, which isn't a particularly normal way to spend the first hour of your fourth decade either. I'd been hoping to gather a bit more intel on Luke, but he's listed as a course tutor and that's it. There's no info on this love study of his either.

Another hour later and it's becoming increasingly difficult to ignore the fact that something is afoot downstairs. My stomach rolls at the prospect. I want nothing more than to hide for the whole day.

I hear Mum greeting Nana. Followed shortly by a shriek and a loud shushing from Mum. Aunty Moira must be here then.

My hair, though now significantly less orange in tone, is still damp. The ends bleed little patches of water onto my jumper.

'Alice, love! Are you coming down?' Mum calls. There's more hushing and I steel myself. I am not so awful now that I'm going to ruin whatever Mum has planned for me. I will smile through this party if it kills me. I can cry later on.

'Just a second!' I call, quickly pulling my wet hair into a bobble.

I thump down the stairs loudly, giving them plenty of warning that I'm on my way, and hear a few muffled, 'She's coming, get ready's as I near the bottom step.

I fix my biggest, fakest smile on my face and round the doorway. There's a hotchpotch of 'Surprise!' and 'Happy Birthday' as I emerge into the front room.

'And ... now!' Mum cries. There's the pop of party streamers from everyone, apart from Nana and her arthritic hands. They explode in my face before tiny swirls of paper fill the air, slowly drifting over me.

I swallow, feeling strangely spaced-out. As if I'm watching the scene, but not in it. *Smile, damn it,* I command myself.

'I had no idea!' I tell them all as Mum pulls me in for a hug.

Mum drapes a birthday banner over me as I look around the room. I was right, there's Mum, Dad, Nana, Aunty Moira and Fred, Aunty M's latest beau. Basically, it's everyone that Mum could muster. No wonder she wanted me to bring a friend.

Goodness, being so bitter and twisted is hard work.

Beneath the window, I spot Dad's fold-out decorating table, always brought in from the shed for occasions like this. A table-cloth has been thrown over it, but I still recognize it. It's covered in beige party food and paper plates. There's a small mountain of mini sausage rolls and little cocktail sausages on sticks. Okay, it's a sausage-heavy party platter. There's also some pink wafers for Nana. Because she's low-key obsessed with them.

I'm still stood in the middle of the room, potentially with a rather vacant expression on my face. It's just a lot to take in.

'Thank you, everyone . . .' I cast a hand around uselessly, '. . . for all this.' And I really do mean it. This is the first birthday I've spent at home in a decade. I actually don't deserve any of it.

'Come here, pet.' Aunty Moira envelopes me in a bear hug.

Aunty Moira is two years younger than Mum and is widely known as the glamorous one in the family. She's been rocking blue eye shadow and pink lipstick since the Eighties. Today she's wearing a red satin blouse and black trousers. Those wet-look ones that always seem to go baggy at the knee and look good on basically no one. Still, you have to hand it to Aunty M, she really commits to a hug.

'Do you want to open your cards, Alice?' Mum asks, reaching for the small pile stacked on top of the fireplace.

'Yes, why not?' I head for the couch, almost sitting down on Fred.

'Fred, move out of the poor girl's way,' Aunty Moira barks at him. Fred gives me what I internally describe as his 'help me' look and shuffles along as I plop down next to him.

There's something a little bit awkward about having people watch you open birthday cards. I try to draw it out. Reading the poem on the front of Nana's card. A £5 note floats out of it. Nanas always have your back, don't they? I choose not to dwell on the fact that unless I find a job soon, that £5 could well be the entirety of my net worth.

There's another from Mum and Dad, and one from Aunty Moira and Fred. The last card though, I don't expect. The envelope reads:

To Alice King, Easington Colliery, England. I think she said North Street once. Her parents are Cheryl and Gary. Her Dad's a plumber. Thank you!

Mum looks over my shoulder.

'The postie said they had a hell of a job working out that one. It only arrived this morning.'

I recognize the handwriting on the dog-eared card though, and all of the Australian stamps. I'm actually nervous to open it in front of everyone.

They're all still looking at me though, so I've no choice.

To Alice, Happy 30th birthday you old cow! Sorry to hear about everything that went down with Charles, you were always way too good for him. I hope you're not fucking miserable over there. Don't be a stranger (again). Love Gabs xxx

I swallow the lump in my throat.

Gabby was my closest friend in London. Suffice to say, she'd never been Charles's biggest fan. Two years ago, she left to work in Australia and I let the distance affect our friendship more than it should have done.

'I don't make much of that card,' Mum says, taking it from me and putting it with the others on the mantelpiece, next to the picture of me winning my award.

I can't help but laugh. Gabby's card is a picture of a smiling woman and says 'The only things lower than your taste in men are your tits'. It's exactly what I'd expect Gabby to send. There's no time for me to dwell on exactly how I feel about her getting in touch. Early indicators are that it's gratitude served with a massive dose of guilt. So that's nice.

Mum has retreated to the kitchen and re-emerged with a small pile of presents. I swallow thickly as she shuffles about nervously, watching while I unwrap their gift.

It's a mug in the shape of Mrs Potts from *Beauty and the Beast*. Underneath it says 'You're my cup of tea'. I daren't look up. I don't want anyone to see how watery my eyes are.

'You always loved that film,' Mum reminds me.

She's not wrong, I went through a phase of watching it every day. Granted, this was when I was a child, but I get the feeling that Mum is determined to erase a good chunk of the last ten years and start afresh.

I hold up the mug, examining it from all angles and making some appreciative hums. I'd always been drawn to stories about love. Desperate to experience it for myself. The *Twilight* phase had been particularly intense. Maybe it's Edward Cullen's fault that I'm like this. And Disney's. All those princesses and their happily ever afters tied to finding 'the one'. We never really stood a chance.

The moderate high I'd been coasting off mere moments ago evaporates. I open my eyes wide, trying not to let tears fall. Because that's what we all want, isn't it? Someone to pick us. And yes, it'd be helpful if that person looked like the Beast after he gets turned back into a human. But just for someone to choose us. Luke was wrong yesterday. It's not about synapses or science. It's about someone saying 'You're it for me'.

'I thought you could have your smoothies in it on a morning,' Mum says, nervously glancing at the mug.

'Thank you so much. I love it. Honestly.' I hug the mug to my chest.

I realize that everyone is busy chatting. Only Mum is watching me.

'Could I open the rest of the presents later?' In reality, there's only two more and they'll both be statement jewellery from Aunty Moira; she always wraps the earrings and the necklace separately. But still, I'd rather not risk a DEFCON 1 emotional meltdown in the face of another undeserved present.

'Of course, love. Everyone, let's eat!' Mum declares.

Dad claps his hands together and heads to the buffet table with intent.

'Do you want me to get you something, Nana?' I ask. Her wheel-chair has been pushed next to the couch. She's busy playing sudoku on an iPad. Ever since Grandad died, Nana has got into puzzles in a big way.

'Go on then, pet. Nothing too chewy. Definitely some of those wafers.'

I approach the buffet table with no small amount of trepidation and stand next to Dad. I notice that his plate is 90 per cent sausage. I grab some Wotsits and some cheese and pineapple sticks before balancing a couple of pink wafers on top of everything.

I rest the plate on the arm of the sofa between me and Nana, eating my cheese and pineapple. It's coated in a thin layer of pink biscuit dust. Everyone chats while we eat and it feels good not to be at the centre of things anymore. Aunty Moira, who works at the council, is in the middle of a story about the Welcome Centre.

'Bloody Dave is thinking about selling it. Says it'll cost too much money to repair. But he went all the way to Turkey for,' she waves an arm about, 'that hair transplant. Waste of money if you ask me, he'd have been better off with a wig. Like the one Nelson got.'

I'm vaguely confused as to who Dave is (and Nelson for that matter), but judging by the scowl Aunty M is making, we are not Team Dave.

'Who's Dave?' I ask.

'He owns the Welcome Centre.' Aunty M is in the middle of the room, sat on one of the dining chairs Mum has brought through. 'Inherited it after Edna died.' They all make the sign of the cross.

'I knew all that brandy would get her in the end,' Mum says. 'But I always had a bad feeling about Dave.' She's perched on the arm of Dad's chair.

'Way too big for his boots if you ask me,' Aunty M agrees.

'But surely he can't sell it can he?' Dad has a mouth full of sausage roll.

Aunty M shrugs. 'Apparently he's thinking about it.'

We take a moment of quiet for the Welcome Centre's troubles.

I've been so wrapped up in Aunty M's Dave-bashing that I've finished my cheese and pineapple sticks, eaten half the Wotsits and I'm two bites into a beef paste sandwich. I drop it like it's running an electrical current.

'You heard from that fancy man of yours?' Aunty Moira asks, still holding court from the middle of the room.

'I told you not to mention him, Mo,' Mum interjects.

'Why not? Good riddance, I reckon.'

I assure Aunty Moira that I haven't heard from Charles since the split, which is a lie, and nor do I want to. Also a lie.

I'm trying to think of something to say when the front room light cuts out.

'Close the curtains,' Mum calls from the kitchen and I know what's coming.

I'm right. Mum emerges from the kitchen. Her face positively aflame with the thirty candles covering every millimetre of the cake she baked yesterday. It's more candle than cake.

'Feel the heat off that!' Dad gasps as Mum does a slow walk past him.

Mum starts up a slow rendition of 'Happy Birthday' that everyone else joins in with. She hovers the cake in front of my face and Dad was right, it is quite warm. I try not to think of how much of my spit I must cover the cake in blowing all the candles out.

'Who wants cake?' Mum asks.

Everyone does.

'I'm not sure,' I say.

'But you have to have cake on your birthday!' That's Dad. He looks genuinely aghast. If he were wearing pearls, he'd be clutching them.

'You can't miss out!' Aunty Moira is so concerned that she stands up to really emphasize her point.

'Um . . .' I'm paralysed by indecision.

'You used to love birthday cake when you were little,' Mum says. She's right, I *did* used to love cake.

'All right, maybe just a little slice.'

A Charles-shaped devil appears on my shoulder spouting off.

'What about the addictive properties of sugar, Alice?' he asks in my head. I've made his voice much whinier than it is in real life.

'Go away, Charles. You don't get to tell me what to do,' I tell him, also in my head. Apparently, this is the decade where I start talking to myself. 'I don't belong in your world anymore,' I finish.

Now that I'm not talking to my Charles-devil, I'm forced to consider the fact that I don't belong here either. I don't belong anywhere. I'm saved from dwelling on my lack of belonging by the slab of cake Mum passes me, its girth so substantial she's presented me with my very own *Man v. Food* challenge.

I take a tentative bite.

It's just cake. Why am I being weird?

I try a few more. I think I'm chewing too much.

I'm not sure if it's the cake or the bite of a beef paste sandwich, but suddenly I don't feel so well. Maybe I should have listened to devil-Charles. I try to have another conversation with him, but my tongue feels weirdly thick.

'I think she's gone a bit doolally,' Aunty Moira says as my stomach ache settles well and truly around my middle.

'You okay, pet?' Mum asks.

'I don't know. I don't feel great to be honest. I think I just ate too much.'

'Why don't you go and have a lie down?' Mum asks.

I nod. 'I think I will.'

I stumble upstairs, somewhere between relieved and sad that I'm escaping my own surprise birthday party.

If this is my thirties . . . I don't want it.

Chapter Five

On my first official day of being 'in' my thirties, I wake up with a desperate craving for Coco Pops, which feels like rock bottom. Maybe this is the point where things really start to turn around for me.

Except ... it's a Sunday. Day of rest. No one turns their life around on a Sunday.

I'd spent the rest of my actual birthday in my bedroom with Mum bustling in and out at half-hourly intervals, mostly bearing cups of tea and a sort of pinched expression of worry.

I check my phone (though, and this is an important point, not my Instagram). It's 9.05 a.m.. There is one thing I need to do, so I open WhatsApp.

Gabby's WhatsApp picture is of her in the middle of a road, riding a traffic cone like a cowgirl (or something a bit less PG, if you were feeling that way inclined) and swilling from a bottle of champagne. We'd met in our first-ever philosophy seminar but unlike me, Gabby had sailed through.

Still, we'd stayed friends after, and I hadn't even been bitter about it when she'd gone on to do her PhD. Or when she'd moved to Sydney to work at the university there.

Without thinking too much about what a crappy friend I'd been this past couple of year, I fire off a text.

Me: Hi Gabs, I got your card yesterday, isn't the Royal
Mail amazing? Anyway, I just wanted to say thanks for
sending it. And hope you're good. Bye xx

I hit send and then read it back, cringing. I don't expect a reply
any time soon, even if it is only early evening over there. Gabby's a
terrible replier. She once told me that she agrees with the philosophers who argue that as humans can't actually see time, it isn't real.
Essentially, she used reductionism as an excuse for being late 99 per
cent of the time.

My morning task done, I look around. For the first time in weeks,
it's like my bedroom walls are getting closer somehow. Trapping
me. 'Happiness is the key to success' one Post-it note declares. That
cork board is coming down.

Okay. Time to leave the bedroom. I pull on grey joggers and a
white T-shirt, a look best described as 'convict on day release'.

'Morning, pet,' Dad greets me from his favourite chair in the
front room. The birthday cards are lined up along the mantelpiece,
even the one from Gabby. 'Oof, are you all right? You look a bit
peaky,' he asks.

This is parent code for you look a state.

'Yeah, honestly, I'm fine.' Mum comes through from the kitchen
join us. 'Is there any of that cake left, Mum?' I take a breath.
'Actually,' I remember yesterday's stomach ache, '... ignore me, I
think I had enough.'

My parents side-eye each other. It's got to be hard, being lum-
bered with a problem child at their age.

'I'd best be off if I want to drop this stuff down the
Welcome,' Mum says.

'What stuff?' I ask, sitting on the couch.

'They have a golden oldies thing there on a Sunday now, for after
church like. Your nana goes some weeks. I'm taking the leftover

party food for them. I can't believe how much there is! But I've got to dash otherwise the pork won't be ready for dinner.'

'Doesn't matter to me if we eat a bit later,' Dad says smiling up at her. Apparently, he's unable to work the oven.

'I'll run it down for you, if you like?' I tell Mum.

She stops, one arm in the big coat she has for winter.

'Would you, Alice? That would be ever so helpful. We already dropped Nana there, but then I forgot the sausage rolls and so I had to come back home but they're all expecting them. And I need to check on the Yorkshire pudding batter and there's the pork too.'

I pull on my own big coat as Mum relays her morning at break-neck speed. I wait while she loads my arms up with silver trays full of food; apparently, she'd had emergency sausage reserves ready to roll. At the last minute, I make an executive decision to stuff a packet of pink wafers into my coat pocket. Nana had eaten like a million of them yesterday.

'You remember the way?' she asks, balancing a tub of twiglets on top of everything.

'Yeah, don't worry,' I tell her, my arms already aching.

The Welcome Centre is actually older than me so, I've never known Easington without it. According to Mum, however – who has lived here her whole life – it's new and it'll always be new. It's a red-brick building from the 1980s that's just off Sunshine Road.

'Right, well, thank you, Alice.' Mum drifts back to the kitchen.

'No problem, and thank you, you know, for the party.'

Dad waves from his chair, his eyes never veering from the TV and causing me to feel a pinprick of irritation. I shake it off quickly, because I really don't need to be adding irritation into the mix right now. Not when there's already a significant lack of any of the decent emotions as it is.

I feel like Scott of the Antarctic battling the elements as I set off to the Welcome Centre. The wind is biting, and my now ashy but still choppy hair whips me in the face. The ache in my arms grows and I wish I could shove my hands into my coat pockets. There's a genuine risk that I'll get frostbite and lose a couple of fingers in my quest to deliver day-old sausage rolls to the geriatric masses of Easington.

I stomp on, turning the corner from Sunshine Road and spotting the centre further up the road.

From what I can remember, the Welcome Centre is run mostly by a team of volunteers. There's a chef, I think, who I presume gets paid. Basically, if anything is happening in Easington, there's a good chance it's happening at the Welcome Centre. Food bank, mum and baby groups, golden oldies groups … Mum and Aunty M come to a fitness class here every week. When I was younger, they used to run a youth club for teenagers. We'd all pay 50p for ten tonnes of sugar from the tuck shop and then dance to Maroon 5 like we were being exorcized. I had my first kiss in the Welcome Centre. With Stephen Cole who'd tasted mostly of cheese and onion crisps. Luke had even come a couple of times. He'd hover around the edges of the dance floor, scowling at people.

The Welcome Centre of today looks to have aged as badly as the perm.

It's a sort of square building with a flat roof. I'm no trained builder but the cracks in the brickwork cannot be good. Nor can the fact that the felt roof is peeling off at the corners. The whole thing just looks sad and tired and structurally a bit dodgy.

I push the doors into the glass entrance; it's no discernibly warmer on the inside than it was outside. I sidestep a couple of strategically placed buckets and head into the main space, with its blue walls and bumpy lino floor.

If push came to shove, I'd deny this. But I'm starting to think that Dave with the hair from Turkey would be better off without this place.

All the old people are sat around tables nursing cups of tea with their coats and hats still on.

My hands are full of sausage roll, so I do a head jiggle at Nana who looks a bit surprised to see me and then take the boxed-up food to the little kitchen which hasn't changed in years. There's still a hatch into the main room. 'Hello,' I venture to two people moving around in there.

One, the chef I presume judging by his almost white outfit, comes and finally relieves me of the food. 'The sausage rolls are here!' he calls past me to the main hall.

A cheer goes up.

'Want to help me put these out?' the second person asks, picking up one of the boxes. She's about my age, and even though we can see our breath misting the air as she speaks, she looks incredibly chic. It takes a special sort of grace to pull off a roll-neck jumper and a crystal pendant, I feel.

'Course,' I reply. 'I'm Alice, by the way.'

'Hannah,' she smiles. Great teeth. Hannah comes to join me from the kitchen.

'Am I okay to stay a little while?' I ask her. 'My nana's here, so I thought I'd say hello.'

'No problem. My dad's over there somewhere.' She does a one-handed wave towards the far table. I fathom who she's waving at.

'Your dad is Mr Hall?' I ask, though I shouldn't be surprised. Everyone in Easington is linked to everyone else if you dig down deep enough on Ancestry.com.

Hannah tilts her head at me. 'I haven't seen you round here before.'

'I've been in London the last twelve years. I just moved back. We got chatting on the bus a couple of days ago. Course, I remember him from school too.'

Hannah smiles. 'His horoscope said he'd make a new friend this week!'

We move around depositing the sausage roll platters. Old hands snatch out to grab them, like it's one of those Hungry Hippo games. Arms finally free, Hannah and I stand by the table closest to Mr Hall.

'Alice, pet,' he wheezes, 'I didn't think I'd see you again so soon.'

Hannah fusses around him, handing him a handkerchief from his pocket when he starts to cough. Again, loath to agree with Turkey Dave, but it's so dilapidated in here that it's an actual health hazard. And Mr Hall does not look like he'd withstand a bout of pneumonia.

'I come bearing sausage rolls,' I declare grandly, and Hannah grins 'I'd better get on,' she tells me. 'I need to tidy the place up.' I do a quick scan of the room. The paint up by the ceiling has turned yellow. I can't help but wonder what Hannah could possibly do to tidy that up without access to some fairly extensive scaffolding.

'I won't keep you, I'll just go sit with Nana for a bit.'

Hannah smiles and walks towards the entrance, pushing her jumper up her arms, the universal sign for 'I mean business'.

Nana is on the middle table. I unstack a chair from the back corner of the room and pull it in next to her.

'Hi, Nana.'

'Hi, pet. Nice to see you here. Let me introduce you.'

I sit still while Nana tells the table who I am, following it up with a much-enhanced version of my life story since I left Easington, bigging me up the way that all good nanas are wont to do. Everyone nods along as she rounds it off with 'she gets her brains from me'.

'You done?' I ask.

'Leave me be. I hardly see you, I don't get chance to brag half as much as I want to.'

Ouch. Guilt makes me do a full body shiver. It's even worse because it's the truth. I haven't visited Nana anywhere near as much as I should have done these past twelve years. I don't even know what the inside of her care home looks like.

'I brought you wafers.' I hold out the packet of pink wafers I'd snaffled from the kitchen drawer, hoping that wafers are a reasonable apology for being an absolute shit show of a granddaughter.

'My favourite.' She looks at me from behind jam-jar glasses. Nana seems to be getting smaller every time I see her. Like Easington's answer to Benjamin Button. Or Yoda. 'You look sad, pet.'

'I am sad.'

'Do you want to tell your nana about it?'

I actually think it's the guilt making me feel sad this particular time. But still, I stick to the script. 'It's just the usual, really. No job. No Charles.'

I wonder at the virtue of throwing myself a pity party with a woman who lived through a world war, rationing and the threat of nuclear annihilation. She makes a sort of a pfft noise. 'That idiot. I never liked him at all. Good riddance I say.'

Why does everyone keep saying that? Nana must see the despair on my face because she pats my hand.

'There, there, pet. It'll be all right.' I catch her eye as mine become filled with water. She gives my hand a squeeze.

'I just wish I knew that things *would* be okay. Like, I could get through the next few weeks or months or whatever if I knew that I'd come good in the end.'

'You will, pet. You're a force of nature. Always were, even as a little un. Remember when you ran that campaign, so that girls could wear trousers to school? Me and your mum were ever so proud.'

'It's not really a lifetime achievement.' I sigh.

It was literal decades ago.

It's like instead of growing into a better version of myself, I'm regressing. Getting less good with age.

I heave a dramatic sigh.

'Tell me about how you and Grandad met again.' I need a

distraction desperately. I know the story like the back of my hand, but it never fails to cheer me up.

Nana closes her eyes and her face settles into a familiar smile. 'It was down by the beach. I was with me mam and dad. And your grandad was there, with his friends, like. Course, my dad knew him. They'd worked down the pit together, and from church, like. And he knew your grandad was a decent sort. So, no one minded at all when he came over bold as brass and asked if I wanted to go for a walk along the beach. And, well ... you know the rest.'

There you have it. Straight out of the pages of Shakespeare. Or at least *Brassed Off*.

In the end, Grandad had got to be a hero fighting the Nazis and they'd married the day he came home.

'I'm so happy that you had that.'

'Me too, pet.' She taps my hand.

'Especially when I'm worried that I've missed the boat.'

'Which boat?'

'The boat which sails you off to happily ever after. Like twelve years ago I knew what I wanted. Now I just feel so lost. Is it possible to get less wise with age?'

She thinks for a second. Chews on a wafer. 'I don't know. Randolph over there thinks that a potted plant is his dead dog. So maybe.'

Nana clearly realizes that this was not the answer I was hoping for.

'He's gone funny though. In the head. What exactly did you want all those years ago that you can't have now?'

I go to speak but she cuts me off, 'And I don't mean that muppet.'

I laugh, even though it's depressing as hell. 'I wanted to get my degree.'

Nana finishes her wafer.

'Do that then.'

I laugh, because it's ridiculous.

'Nana, I managed one single year at uni. Everyone knew way more than me. It was terrifying.'

I look at her. She's like a hamster, her cheeks are full of pink dust.

I hadn't planned to drop out of uni forever. I thought I'd take a year, get back into it. I'd felt intimidated, like I didn't deserve to be there. But I *had* planned to go back, after I'd maybe regrouped a little.

Except . . . I just hadn't. I was good at working for Charles and I enjoyed being the best admin assistant I could be. And anyway, eventually Charles said philosophy wasn't a secure way to make a living.

Nana has a drink of her tea.

'Yes, that's it. There's only one thing for it, go back to university.'

I throw my head back and laugh.

'You make it sound so easy.'

'It is easy.'

'Nana, people from Easington don't get to be philosophers.'

'People from Easington are yet to embrace double glazing, Alice.' We both look to the Welcome Centre's glass porch as it's rattled by a particularly blustery bit of wind. 'Which is why you need to break the mould,' she finishes off.

'Pardon?'

'Do what you've always wanted to do. Prove them wrong. Get any old job for now and then go to uni. Simple.' She thinks for a second. 'Durham is a good university isn't it?'

I laugh again. 'Nana, it takes three years to get a degree. Three!'

She fixes me with a stare from behind her glasses. 'No need to go stating the bleeding obvious, Alice. I'm well aware of how long a degree takes, thank you very much.'

I shake my head.

'Honestly, Nana. There's no chance. You know I applied to be a chef at the Wacky Warehouse? Didn't even get an interview and they microwave their food.'

Nana takes hold of both of my hands. Hers are so wrinkly, it's like her skin is made of tissue paper. 'Alice, I will say this once and once only. Don't have any regrets. Please.'

It's really bad form to argue with people in their nineties.

'Okay, I'll look into it.' She looks sceptical. 'I promise I will.' I rub my hands together. 'God it's freezing in here!'

'I know, the heating has a mind of its own.'

Hannah does the rounds with a giant teapot, topping up cups. She smiles at me. 'Do you really think I could do it?' I ask Nana.

'Not a doubt in my mind, pet. Not a doubt.'

Chapter Six

When I get home, Dad is busy watching the football and Mum is deep in the kitchen trenches, making the Sunday dinner. I head to my room, my cold hands working at my phone just enough to see that I have two messages. It's been quite some time since I had two messages. One is a reply from Gabby.

> **Gabby:** Alice! So glad the card found you. I wanted it
> to be a surprise! It's the middle of the night, darling.
> I'll message properly soon, we need a catch-up,
> much love! X

I smile. It's impossible not to around Gabby. I like her reply and then click on the other message. From an unknown number.

> **Unknown:** Alice, Luke Priestly here. I hope your birthday
> was pleasant. I've been thinking about our bet and I
> believe we might need to clarify the exact parameters.
> Would you like to meet again?

I am not enamoured with a text from Luke. Not enamoured at all. I decide not to share with him that regarding my birthday, five people, mostly blood relatives, threw me a surprise party.

Me: You know what, I'm not sure I'll have time. Now that I've
thought about it some more, I'm going to be very busy
with important things
Luke: Aren't you unemployed?

Knobhead.

Me: Between jobs. And actually, I'm thinking of going back
to uni as a mature student. I've been planning it out
all morning

Obviously, this is a total lie. But it turns out that getting one up on
Luke has done what Nana's motivational 'regrets' speech only partly
managed. It's given me some drive.

Luke: Very admirable. And would you like to make payment
by cash or bank transfer?

I file away the fact that Luke thinks me going back to uni is admirable, not ridiculous, to consider at a later date. Unless, of course,
he's being sarcastic. Actually, it's probably that.

Me: Come on, it's not like we signed our names in blood
or anything
Luke: Is that how you normally make bets? Dark

I let out a big huff. Why is this man so frigging annoying?

Me: Right! Fine! What do you want to sort out?
Luke: If you're free, let's meet next Sunday
Me: Okay, Star Bucks at 2?
Luke: Yes. See you then. Luke

Me: I know who you are

Luke: Pardon?

Me: I know who you are, you don't need to sign off
with your name

Luke: Okay

I don't reply. It feels like a win.

My phone pings again and it'll really be a win if Luke has mes-saged to ask why I didn't reply. No such luck, however. Instead, the Indeed jobs app tells me that there's a role available at the local Chinese restaurant. It's new-ish. Set up in what used to be one of Easington's many pubs. I think back to what Nana said about work-ing while I study. I mean, I *could* do that. Maybe. I vaguely worked in the restaurant sector, that could work in my favour.

If nothing else, there's the fact that beggars can't be choosers. And unless I find a job soon, begging is fast becoming a distinct possibility.

It's therefore because I have absolutely no other option that two days later, I find myself across the street from the Lotus Flower, ready, in some vague sense of the term, for my interview.

At least the whole *making up a whole extra life in which I have an abundance of waitressing experience* has served as a distraction from Charles. And with a bit of luck, if I get the job, I'll be far too busy carrying plates of Chinese food to wallow in misery quite so much.

Just go in. I will myself forward.

'A job's a job.' Dad said. 'You can always look for another after.' I hadn't mentioned that maybe, potentially, I'm half considering going back to uni to Mum and Dad. Not when I'm ping-ponging between thinking it's a good idea and thinking it's the worst possible idea so often I'm one rapid U-turn away from whiplash.

Impending poverty at the forefront of my mind, I head inside for my interview. The lions that had once stood either side of the entrance have been beheaded. Replaced with giant plastic flowers in a sort of half plant, half beast type situation.

Inside there's an array of different-sized tables all squished together in a slightly hotchpotch fashion. I wonder how you're even meant to waitress between them.

A singer a few years older than me is busy murdering 'Lady in Red' from a little stage along the back wall, even though the restaurant is empty. He's wearing a bandana. A brave choice for anyone who isn't an Australian surfer. His T-shirt reads 'Karl Marx: Sharing is Caring'.

I hover awkwardly in the doorway as the manager – at least, I'm guessing that's who he is – approaches. 'We provide entertainment Wednesday through Saturday. He's warming up,' he says, just as the singer tries and fails to make the high note.

'Here for the interview?' he asks.

I nod.

'Then you must be Alice.'

'Yes, that's me.' I attempt my brightest please-hire-me smile and I'm sure my lip splits.

'I'm Paul.' The manager has blonde hair and slightly yellow teeth. He offers me a hand. It's a grubby handshake that makes me want to wipe my palm down my trouser leg. I resist, but I'll be hitting up some antibacterial gel once I'm done here.

'Come, sit.' Paul directs me round an expansive bar to some battered leather sofas directly in front of the stage. I wince as the singer starts up with the Pogues' 'Fairytale of New York'. In November.

'It's the only song he's even half decent at,' Paul says apologetically.

I almost lose my footing on my way to the sofas.

'Careful, floor's a bit slippery.' He gestures towards a yellow and black sign hidden behind a plant. 'There are warnings up, though, so you can't sue us.'

'I see. Can I just say what a beautiful restaurant you have here?'

It's very obviously a line. However, now that I'm here, I am committed to employment.

'Eh, it's all right like. There's eight waiting staff. You all get your own area. Tips are put in the shared pot at the end of the night. If I catch you sticking them in your waistcoat, you're out.'

'Waistcoat?' I ask faintly. Paul is not wearing a waistcoat.

'Aye. That's the uniform. Black trousers, white shirt and we provide the waistcoat. Pink for the girls, blue for the boys.' By way of an explanation, he rummages around in a black bin bag by his feet and holds up a cheap satin waistcoat. It's dark pink with gold dragons embroidered across it. Quite frankly, it's hideous.

'Why do the girls have to wear pink?'

'Pink's for girls, innit?'

'*You maggot . . .*' The singer gives it some welly.

Give me strength.

'How much does it pay?' I ask weakly.

'£50 a shift. Three shifts a week. Five till close. Free meal when you're finished. Six-month probation period.'

£50. God, that wouldn't have even paid for Charles's Bloom & Wild subscription.

'It's only carrying plates from the kitchen and back.' Paul finishes his little spiel. 'Not exactly rocket science. We have an induction and everything.'

I remember what Nana said. How this could be a way to partly fund a philosophy degree and cling to that very faint, if not invisible to the naked eye, possibility.

I nod, swallowing the last morsels of my pride. 'I'd really appreciate the opportunity.'

Paul smirks and I feel slightly nauseous. 'You start tomorrow.'

If there were to be one cardinal rule in the post break-up world, it should be this. Do not check your ex's social media unless you have it on good authority that they are a) recently maimed or b) living in a bin. Checking your ex's social media to find them advertising his and hers flavoured lube with their new girlfriend is guaranteed to make you feel bloody angry at the world. In fact, you might even have to bury your head in a pillow and scream.

It is, therefore, with the misguided sense of optimism that I am now a woman for whom things simply cannot get any worse, that I shove my arms into my new pink and gold waistcoat, ready for my shift at the Lotus Flower. I've teamed it with a Calvin Klein white shirt that Charles bought me one Christmas, and some black trousers that belong to Mum.

I squeeze myself into the tiny gap between the bottom of the bed and the mirrored wardrobe, only to discover that it doesn't matter how on point your eyeliner is, absolutely no one can pull off embroidered gold dragons.

Mum and Dad are waiting in the hallway as I come downstairs, ready to wave me off for my first shift. I try to focus on the niceness of their gesture, rather than the fact that it's the sort of thing you'd do for your twelve-year-old off on their first paper round. Because that would be completely tragic.

'All right.' Paul appears from behind the bar the second I step through the doors.

'Yes, excited to get started really.' I think it's fair to assume at this stage that almost everything I say to Paul will be a lie.

It doesn't matter because he ignores me anyway.

'You're on tables one through twelve.' He points towards a crowded bundle of tables on the right-hand side of the restaurant as I try to pull my coat off while looking keen and raring to go all at the same time. I end up just removing my coat with unnecessary vigour, almost whacking myself in the face with my own arm. Paul is still rattling off instructions. I have an awful feeling that this might be the induction he mentioned. 'You take the order, you give the sheets to the kitchen, you serve the food, you clear the table.'

'Okay.' I try to remember. Order, kitchen, food, serve, clear, I chant.

'The set menus are the most popular. They'll all ask for banana fritter *and* ice-cream for dessert. But it's one or the other. Like it says on the menu. We're not a charity. I can't afford to be doling out both. They want extra they need to pay for it.'

'Banana fritter or ice-cream. Got it,' I say, refusing to dwell on the fact that I apparently need to have strong opinions on desserts.

'You get your wages last shift of the week. You're only on tonight and Friday, so you'll get paid—'

'Friday.'

'All right, smart arse.'

Paul is touchy. I'm not smart and my arse is nothing to write home about. I cling to the reminder that I'll at least be earning money. I'm already planning to save as much as I can. I think I'll feel less like I'm forever walking on cracked ice if I can just get some savings behind me.

'That's it. You're set. Joanie will show you how to carve the duck. Joanie!' he calls.

I presume Paul becomes less snappy when paying customers arrive.

Joanie (who is stood by a table approximately three metres away) leaves the stack of napkins she'd been turning vaguely into swans. She's probably in her late teens, with thick eyeliner and a nose ring. Her hair is dark at the roots but turns bright blue halfway down. It clashes even worse than mine with the waistcoat.

'Joanie's in charge tonight,' Paul adds before walking off and disappearing into the kitchen. I think his part of the induction process might well be done.

'Hi,' I say to Joanie. She's miniscule. Paul has left a child in charge.

'What do you want to know?' she asks with a slightly antagonistic tone.

'Um, Paul said something about duck?'

'Oh, right. It's part of the experience. You carve the crispy duck at the table. Two forks, basically rip the fucker to shreds.'

'Part of the experience?' I ask.

'That's what people come for. It's all about the crispy duck. I swear, the slobs around here all have a hoisin sauce fetish. Other than that, all you need to know is that Paul's a prick.'

'Duly noted.'

'And Andy's enthusiastic but shit.'

'Andy?'

'The singer. He's meant to be on Wednesday through Saturday, but he basically turns up when he wants. Like tonight, he isn't here. Consider it a blessing. You need to train your ears to buzz when he sings. He'll one hundred per cent try to get you to join the Communist Party. He's like a wasp, ignore him and eventually he'll go away.'

I nod, trying to remember it all.

'Okay.'

'Oh, and if they ask for a banana fritter and ice cream, just give it to them. It's not worth the aggro.'

I actually think I quite like Joanie.

'Got you.'

We're blasted by a freezing wind as the restaurant door opens.

'First customers are here.' She looks towards the door where a family of four are waiting. 'You're up.'

I hurry onward, wanting to look keen. I mean, how hard can this be? Joanie is obviously smashing it to be in charge like she is. In fact, none of the other waiting staff seem to be much older than teenagers.

Unfortunately, as the evening wears on, it becomes increasingly, glaringly obvious that I've done basically nothing in my life that might have prepared me in any way for a night as a waitress in Easington's foremost Chinese restaurant.

Foremost only in the sense that there are no others.

Even walking around the place proves to be a challenge. Joanie tells me that the floor isn't real marble, it just looks like marble. Either way, it's like an ice rink. All night customers slip and slide to their tables, grabbing at the edge of the bar as they move.

'Our John broke his wrist in here last year,' one of the more seasoned veterans informs me. 'Couldn't sue cause of those bastard signs.'

'I see,' I reply, trying to write down everyone's orders.

Time seems to do funny things in the Lotus Flower, my shift passing in the blink of an eye but also feeling like the longest six hours of my whole entire life. I get orders and table numbers wrong. I bash into other waiters like we're in a game of dodgems.

Joanie seems to be running the place, barking out orders at people and intercepting my mistakes when she can.

According to Paul, who mostly sat behind the bar all night, I don't look cheerful enough. I mean, not that I think anyone would care, but I don't feel particularly cheerful. And clearly, I underestimated how achy I'd be. My feet are killing me.

I also hadn't anticipated that the smuggling of frozen goods would feature so heavily in my evening.

But despite risking Paul's banana fritter-based wrath, I have no tips to pour into the communal pot by the end of the night.

Joanie has plenty. She unloads them all into the empty ice cream tub marked 'tips' while glaring at Paul.

'We wait on the couch now while they cook our tea,' she informs me.

Even though 11 p.m. is not a recognisable mealtime by any

stretch, my stomach grumbles. The devil-Charles who made an appearance at my birthday party is back. I shrug him off before he can even say the words MSG. Because quite frankly, I haven't got the energy for him right now. I'm exhausted.

I sit back on the couch, relieved to just not be stood up anymore.

'So, where you from?' Joanie sits next to me. I likely smell, but she doesn't seem to care.

'I grew up in Easington.'

'Really?' The corners of Joanie's mouth turn down, like she doesn't believe me.

'Yeah, like ten minutes away from here. Why?'

'You don't sound like it, that's all.' Joanie's accent is thick like Mum and Dad's. On the few occasions they'd met Charles, he'd hardly been able to understand them.

Nope, not going there right now.

'Well, I lived in London for the last twelve years, I only moved back six weeks ago. I guess I changed my accent a bit.'

'Got ya. But you're here to stay now?' she asks.

I can't help but let out a slightly hysterical laugh. Because I am here to stay.

'Yep.'

Joanie eyes me like I might be an unexploded bomb.

'You know anyone round here then?'

'Nope, reluctant lone wolf right here.' This statement is perhaps something that might have been better kept in my head. And not just the fact that I described myself as a wolf. I *had* friends. I hung out with loads of people when I was at school. And I'd thought about trying to get in touch with some of them on and off over the past six weeks. Something had stopped me though. Something that felt suspiciously like embarrassment sprinkled with a dusting of shame.

One of the chefs comes out from the kitchen, carrying takeaway boxes full of chicken curry and rice.

'Thank you,' I say, taking one of the forks that's been dumped in a pile on the middle of the coffee table in front of the sofa.

For the first time since I came back to Easington, I'm actually starving. Still, I stop eating after I've had half of my box. Joanie does the same. Her box is still mostly full of rice when she puts the lid back on it.

'Bit heavy on the five spice,' she says.

'Do you not like it?' I ask, gesturing down to her box on the table.

'Nah, it's all right. I always save half for Tyler.'

'Is Tyler your partner?'

'Nope, son.'

'Son?' I obviously do a very poor job of hiding the shock on my face because Joanie laughs.

'He's two. Had him when I was nineteen. Me mam's looking after him now. Tyler's a good lad.'

'Cute name.'

'Thanks.'

I change the subject. 'Does it get easier? Here, I mean. I was useless tonight.'

'You weren't that bad. You want my advice? Better shoes.'

We both look down at the patent leather ballet pumps I'm wearing. In contrast, Joanie has on a Velcro pair with a thick rubber sole. And this is what it's come to. I'm coveting shoes based on the depth of their tread.

'Anyway, I have to go. I catch a lift with one of the chefs.' We look over. One of the kitchen staff is waiting by the door, car keys in hand. 'When's your next shift?' Joanie asks.

'Friday.' Two days away.

'I'm in Saturday.'

She stands and shrugs on her leather jacket, flicking her blue-tipped ponytail over the collar. Then she turns back to me.

'If you want to meet for coffee on Saturday, I'll be down Little Daisies about one.'

'Little Daisies? I don't know it.'

'Out towards Peterlee way.'

'Er,' I hesitate, not quite believing that Joanie is actually asking me to meet up with her.

'There's no pressure like, I just thought with you not having any mates.'

'No! Honestly, I'd love to come. I'll see you there.'

As Joanie leaves, I manage my first small, yet genuine, smile in quite some time.

Paul comes out from behind the bar.

'Well, you're a bit crap. I thought you had a shit ton of experience?' he asks me, heading past the couches on his way to the toilets.

And failure, my old pal, is back in the room.

Chapter Seven

I found Mum waiting up for me when I got home from my shift. This despite the fact that she likes to keep a regular 10 p.m. bedtime. It's almost like she knew that I'd be feeling a bit flat about the whole thing, sad in a way that feels different to before. Less of a panicking sadness, and more a fear that I'll be trapped in this life now. I decide to definitely look up philosophy courses in Durham. But tomorrow, when my eyelids aren't quite so heavy.

Obviously, I avoided talking about any sort of sadness to Mum. Instead, I mainly ranted about Paul and then spent a good ten minutes talking with wonder and awe about Joanie's shoes.

It's possibly not a massive surprise then, when I venture downstairs the next morning that my eyes snag on a similar pair on top of the sideboard in the front room. Mum has pinned a note underneath them.

ALICE I POPPED TO THE BIG TESCO EARLY
AND GOT YOU THESE. I HOPE THE SOLE IS BIG
ENOUGH. LOVE MUM X
    PS ME AND AUNTY M ARE GOING TO OUR
DISCO EXERCISE CLASS DOWN THE WELCOME
LATER IF YOU WANT TO COME.

The shoes are approximately 50 per cent sole, and potentially the ugliest things I've ever seen. Still, I grin at them like a kid who has just unwrapped the one thing they asked for on Christmas morning.

I dig my phone out from deep in my dressing gown pocket to text mum.

> **Me:** Thanks for the shoes, they're brilliant. Will come to
> disco thing xx

My biceps are actually aching from all the plate carrying last night, so today is perhaps not the day to embarking upon a new fitness regime. But I really want to go.

My tragic yet heart-warming moment is interrupted by my phone vibrating in my hand. I expect it'll be a reply from Mum, so my heart sinks when I see Luke's name.

> **Luke:** Hello Alice, Luke here. I just thought you'd like
> to know that our preliminary findings are due to be
> published today. 'Love' has more to do with our brains
> than our hearts. In precis, it is rational after all

Seriously, I must have been awful in a previous life. Why is he contacting me now? And why is he so annoying?

> **Me:** Have you really messaged me to gloat? Also, you
> don't need to say, 'Luke here' when you text. Like I said
> before, know it's you, your number is saved in my phone
> **Luke:** I thought you'd be interested, that's all
> **Me:** Well, our bet has nothing to do with your little study.
> It's simple. One of us falls in love, we pay up. Actually,
> I've been thinking myself, on Sunday, we should sign up
> for a dating app. That way you won't just be able to hide
> from women (or men) for the next six months.

> **Luke:** I've no intention of hiding

Stupid stomach, stop swooping. I remind my stomach that it's Luke we're dealing with here. Still, all the swooping messes with my mental faculties. My fingers are flying over my phone, not giving due consideration to what they're typing.

> **Me:** I still think we should sign up. Not that I'll need it personally.
> I think I'll be in love well before these six months are up
> **Luke:** Have you met someone already? You don't mess
> about King

I think of all the men I've encountered in Easington. Paul, the singer, Mr Hall. None of them exactly scream 'love of life'.

> **Me:** Not exactly. But I can just feel it coming I smirk,
> thinking about how much my next words will
> annoy Luke. In my waters I type.
> **Luke:** I'm not even going to dignify that with a response
> **Me:** It's actually a school of philosophical thought, fatalism.
> That whatever's going to happen is going to happen and
> there's nothing we can do about it
> **Luke:** Is that what you think?
> **Me:** Not fully . . .

I admit that reluctantly because while I might have done in the past, now it's impossible to ignore the fact that my actions have at least played a part in my current, less than joyous, predicament.

> **Luke:** Thank God
> **Me:** Anyway, it's been a delight as always. But I've got
> places to go, people to see

Luke: Good
Me: Bye

Luke doesn't reply. Damn him!

I'm actually a little bit out of breath by the time I've finished doubling down on the bet that I should never have made in the first place because 1. My annoying traitor of a brain is still hung up on Charles, despite the whole Ophelia lube situation. And 2. If I lose, I'll have to sell a kidney to be able to pay.

It's just that something about Luke, well it just makes me want to win.

My competitive spirit has somewhat abated by the time I join Mum and Aunty M en route to the Welcome Centre for some disco exercise. After tea (more pig) Mum asked me to call for Aunty M from over the road. Fred sent me upstairs, where Aunty M was changing, and if I'm ever rich enough to afford therapy, watching Aunty M pull on a thong will be point one to discuss.

'Stops too much chaffing,' she told me from where I stood frozen in horror in the doorway.

Now the three of us are rushing towards the Welcome Centre in the dark, the cold robbing even Aunty M of her ability to talk. Inside, the Welcome is lit up. There's a group of middle-aged woman, all wearing their coats still, huddled in the middle of the room. Mum goes to chat to them while Aunty M nudges me with her elbow.

'Psst,' she says. I don't think people normally say psst, but still, I look her way. 'Dwaine, two o'clock.' She tilts her head to the far corner of the room, where a man is knelt down fiddling with a speaker.

He stands up and . . . Dwaine is quite something.

Aunty M smiles. 'Why'd you think I come here every week.' She strips off her coat, revealing the leopard print leotard and leggings that will be point two on my therapy agenda.

I also pull off my own coat. I'm wearing some of the expensive workout gear that Charles bought me one Christmas. Maybe the fact that I didn't wear it all that much was a factor in him picking Ophelia. I've seen her Instagram, she's a Sweaty Betty ambassador for Christ's sake. Maybe she finds sticking to Charles's diet easier than I did.

At least I get a little kick out the gear Charles bought getting its first run-out at Easington's damp and draughty community hub. Petty, thy name is Alice.

Aunty M drags me to the front row of women just as Dwaine seems to notice my presence. He's tall and he's wearing a skin-tight sliver workout top. I can see *at least* a six-pack underneath it. Like a modern-day bionic man.

There's an annoying little titter in my brain reminding me that Dwaine isn't Charles. Not that I want him to be Charles. Charles cheated on me and lied to me. But my brain does not seem to be getting fully with the programme. Instead, it's wasting energy coming up with all sorts of fantastical scenarios. Nothing too specific, just Charles finding out that I'm being checked out by other men (and I think Dwaine *is* checking me out) and galloping into Easington on horseback to win back my hand.

Like I said, nothing too specific. I'm in the middle of my daydream when the music starts to boom.

And I mean boom.

Dwaine has a little mic that curls around his face to his mouth. Everyone gives him their rapt attention. Possibly because he's about to lead us in a disco-based workout, but also because he looks like that Duke from *Bridgerton* that everyone went batshit crazy for.

'And stretch,' he calls, as 'Dancing Queen' rings out around the place. It's impossible not to get swept up in a bit of Abba. We all dutifully stretch.

Warm-up done and having discovered that Aunty M is surprisingly flexible, we move on to the main part of the session.

'We'll run through the dance routines, just for the newbies,' Dwaine says, definitely looking at me. I feel my cheeks go red, and not just because I'm worryingly warm after just the warm-up.

Without the music, Dwaine leads us through a dance routine. 'Gives you an arse of steel, this,' Aunty M tells me, executing a move that's somewhere between a squat and a hip thrust.

I do my best to follow suit, thinking that an arse of steel might make shifts at the Lotus Flower a bit more manageable.

'Then two box steps to round it off, and strike a pose,' Dwaine says, going to fiddle with the phone he has plugged into the speakers.

'Papa Don't Preach' starts to play and immediately everyone launches into a side lunge, touching arms to toes. I try to copy, but the wrong arm goes to the wrong toe and I almost take Mum's eye out.

'Now spin!' Dwaine calls and everyone starts waving their arms above their heads as they turn. Except I'm somehow going the opposite way to everyone else.

It carries on like this. The rest of the class moving with the coordination of a synchronized swim team, me just trying my best.

Part way through the third 'routine', a floor-based number, Dwaine starts to laugh. I know it's at me, because I'm sat with my head between my knees while everyone else carries on with the jazz hands sit-ups they're doing, but I can't even feel offended. I laugh too. And before I know it, I have a laughing stich. Or a partly laughing stitch at any rate.

We do a cool-down to 'Two Become One' and I genuinely think there's a good chance I've entered the twilight zone.

Still, there's no getting away from the fact that despite being god-awful, I've had fun.

'Alice,' Aunty M says, swiping at her head with the neon green towel she'd brought. 'Go ask Dwaine when the next class is.'

On hearing his name, Dwaine looks up and smiles.

'Mo, you know the timetable well enough by now,' Mum says, frowning.

'I just thought our Alice might want to get to know Dwaine a bit more, that's all. She's always on her own, it's not good for her.'

Aunty M talks as if I'm not stood literally half a foot away.

'Yes, I agree but Alice has had quite enough to do with you-know-what, don't you think?'

I presume in this instance 'you-know-what' refers to the entirety of the male species.

My gaze flits between the two of them as they bicker about whether or not I should go and speak to Dwaine.

Except, it very much looks like Dwaine is coming to speak to me. Walking slowly across the room towards where the three of us are stood, his eye contact so intense there's a chance I'm being hypnotized. I half expect him to crook a finger at me, like when Patrick Swayze rescued Baby from that corner ... and I *really* need to stop imagining my life as a romance movie.

'You're new,' Dwaine says, coming to a stop in front of us.

We all go quiet, Aunty M gazing up at him in a way that probably puts women's rights back a couple of decades.

I nod, my chat desperately lacking.

'Come on Cheryl,' Aunty M says louder than necessary, 'let's leave the young uns to it. The food bank's on tomorrow, better get the tables out.'

Mum is (reluctantly) dragged away by the top of her arm, disappearing into a giant storeroom at the back of the Welcome.

And now it's just me and Dwaine. A fact I'm not quite sure how to feel about.

'Good session,' Dwaine says, and I laugh.

'I'm pretty sure I was rubbish.'

'Nah, this lot have been coming for months, that's all.' We look around at all the middle-aged women, now working together to unfold tables all round the edge of the circular room.

'I wonder why,' I say without thinking and then immediately go red. Because that properly sounded like a flirt. Can I tell Dwaine that it was an unintentional flirt? Is that a thing that people do?

'Why is that then?' I look up at Dwaine; he's smiling. And it might be the all the exercise releasing some much-needed endorphins, but I don't think I mind Dwaine smiling at me like that.

I laugh to cover the fact that I don't have a good comeback. It sounds louder than I planned.

'So, do you want to get together or something?' Dwaine has a hand on the back of his neck. And I'd never have expected it from a man who can do the splits (the grand finale of routine two) but he actually seems a bit nervous.

I don't have an awful lot of thinking time. Long pauses are never good after a question like that, are they? But a montage of emotions flashes through me. Terror, because what if the first date landscape has changed completely in the last ten years? Sadness, because I never thought I'd be here again. Excitement, because Dwaine seems nice and like I said, six to eight pack. Plus glee. At the prospect that I'll be able to gloat to Luke.

'I'd love to,' I rush out.

Dwaine smiles and chats away as I put my number in his phone. I start to feel vaguely nauseous, but I ignore it.

'I'll be in touch,' he says.

'Got ya.' I point my two index fingers at him. Wondering why I decided that now would be a good time to test out that move.

We say our goodbyes and I walk to join Mum and Aunty M where they're waiting by the doors.

'What did Dwaine want?' Mum asks as we rush home, bracing ourselves against the cold.

I tell them that he asked me out, eliciting a frown from Mum and a squeal of delight from Aunty M.

I'm still not sure how to feel. I'd agreed, at least in part, to go out with Dwaine because of Luke. I need to work harder at not thinking about him. Or Charles for that matter.

At least the prospect of a date might encourage me to shave my legs.

PART TWO:

DWAINE

'Love shouldn't put you down.'

Chapter Eight

My phone vibrates deep in my waistcoat pocket and I make a quick dash to the toilets to check it, almost crashing into one of the other waitresses. It's not that I'm particularly desperate to see who's messaging me. It'll be Dwaine. He texted this morning to ask me out to brunch tomorrow and we've been messaging on and off all day.

No, the reason for my quick escape is that Andy had turned up for his shift tonight and he is midway through, 'I Will Always Love You'. It's wrong, isn't it, to wish illness on someone? But it wouldn't be the worst thing in the world if Andy was struck down with a bout of laryngitis. An extensive and long bout.

The only place he's muffled is in the furthest corner of the disabled loo.

When a fellow waiter emerges, I see him wince as the door opens. I rush inside, leaning against the back of the door and closing my eyes for a second.

My second shift is going as badly as my first did. Only this time I don't have Joanie to entertain me through it. I check my phone. It is Dwaine, letting me know where to meet tomorrow. I send a thumbs up and a smiley face emoji before taking a few deep breaths and bracing myself to face the music, in the loosest sense of the term, again.

Paul is waiting for me on the other side of the door. 'You're spending too much time in the toilet.'

Paul, I've quickly realized, is a waiting manager in name only. I don't think I've seen him lift so much as a chopstick yet. He mainly just sits behind the bar, playing on his phone and yelling at us all.

'You can't stop people going to the toilet,' I tell him, not exactly sure of the law, but sure that going for a wee is some sort of a basic human right. Let's just ignore the fact that I was actually in there checking my phone.

'Just don't make a habit of it, especially since you're on probation.' He stalks off and I clench my fists down by my side.

Two hours later, I'm aching again. The only, and I mean only, upside of Andy having a stab at 'Figaro' was to clear the place.

At least I've banked a hard-earned £100.

Come Saturday morning I fear that from now on I will never not smell of hoi sin sauce. I've been in the shower so long that Mum bangs on the door asking if I've drowned.

In honour of my brunch with Dwaine I do my best with Stephanie's choppy layers, dedicating many a hair grip to the cause. I put on jeans and a nice top that's crinkly but passable and I'm ready.

Not, I should add, ready in the sense that I'm physically or mentally prepared in any way, but I'm dressed at least.

It's Saturday, and Mum is therefore busy putting the net curtains through a hot wash, so I've been able to borrow the van. And if recent events weren't enough to bring me down a peg or two, driving around in a clapped-out old banger with, 'Gary's Golden Showers and Other Plumbing Services' emblazoned down the side ought to do it. In fact, there's now a very good chance that I am a woman for whom there are no more peg rungs.

I stop at a cashpoint and withdraw £50 in cash. My budget for the week. I spend a bit of the drive wondering if there's anything I can do as a side hustle for extra money.

Wrestling with the clutch while attempting a reverse park at least distracts me from all the hustling I'm not doing. And from the panic of being on a date with a man who isn't Charles. I mean, it's not like I haven't been on my own with a man since Charles. I've been to Star Bucks with Luke. But we have so little spark, a burning rag and cannister of petrol couldn't get us going.

The gear stick on the van screeches as I aim for fourth and end up in second. I lurch forward, ramming my foot down onto the clutch. I didn't exactly drive a lot in London. Never, in fact. So, by the time I finish parking the van in the café car park, the back of my neck is wet with sweat.

I hadn't accounted for the ten minutes it would take me to manipulate the van into a spot. So I'm also late.

On unsteady legs, I head inside. The café Dwaine has picked has a sort of Australian theme. There are surf boards stuck to the wall and the staff are all wearing Hawaiian shirts. There's a giant blow-up kangaroo in the corner.

Dwaine waves to me from where he's sat on a high stool, looking out of the window. I'm so queasy it'll be a miracle if I manage to keep anything down. I walk over, trying to ignore the fact that Dwaine is blatantly checking me out. 'Hi,' he says, leaning down to peck my cheek. 'You look nice.' I feel my cheeks go red, nice is good.

I attempt a less than graceful manoeuvre to haul myself onto the stool.

'Find it okay?'

'Yeah, fine thanks. Did you?' He laughs as I bury my now luminous face behind the menu. 'Course you did. Sorry. What's good here?'

'I get the egg whites and tomatoes. With a side of spinach and avo, you know to make sure I hit those macros.'

I nod along like I'm also deeply concerned about macros. I'd sort of hoped that jazz hands Dwaine wasn't too much of a fitness fanatic. But actually, I'd watched Charles bemoan how hard it was to get abs over the years. So, getting a ton of them, like Dwaine has, must take some serious dedication and effort.

'Dwaine, man! Good to see you!' A waiter in a Hawaiian shirt with blonde dreadlocks appears. He and Dwaine high five. I imagine Charles high-fiving a waiter and snort with laughter. Dwaine and the waiter both stare at me. Must stop thinking about Charles.

'Sorry,' I say.

'What can I get you then, folks?'

'The usual for me,' Dwaine answers. 'No butter on the spinach though, mate. And I'll get a green goblin smoothie.'

I'm not even close to deciding what I want. So rather than put us all through the agony of my indecision, I just ask for the same as Dwaine. Hopefully he'll be impressed. Charles would have approved.

Argh. Get lost Charles!

I start to consider that thinking about your ex at regular three-minute intervals might not be a good sign when it comes to my readiness to date again.

I put the menu back on the narrow table in front of us and then wonder what I'm meant to do with my hands. I cross them like the Queen. Then uncross them again. I'm sure they're bigger than they used to be. I'm so focused on my giant hands that it takes me a second to gather that Dwaine is talking.

'How're you finding Easington so far?' he asks as our green goblins arrive. It's very spinach-y.

'Yeah, it's good.' Obviously, I'm grossly exaggerating the success of my return. But even if the dating landscape has changed a lot in the last ten years, it's sort of a timeless thing, isn't it? Not voicing to the man I'm on a date with that I spent a solid six weeks crying and wondering if I'd be alone for all of time. I ignore my brain's dark turn, instead putting all my energy into trying to suck up more of the thick smoothie through the straw. The straw's circumference isn't quite wide enough to let a right lot through. I give in. 'I grew up here actually.'

'I thought you must have done when you came to class with your mum and Mo.'

'I don't recognize you though, from school I mean,' I tell him.

Dwaine drinks some of his smoothie. Clearly his lung capacity is far superior to mine, because I see the green whizz up his straw.

'I'm from Sunderland. But I do classes all over the place.'

'You seem really good at them. I don't think Mum has missed a session since I came home.'

He smiles at the compliment. And aside from not knowing what to do with my hands, I think this is going well. Imagine what Luke will say when he hears that I already have one successful date under my belt. I sit up a little straighter at the thought of being able to needle him. Dwaine is talking. 'It's all right, like. A lot of people *say* they're into fitness but then when it comes down to it, they don't have the drive. It's a way of life.'

'It sounds like you're really clued up about it all. Has it always been something you were interested in?'

Dwaine doesn't get to reply, because the waiter is back.

'Food's up, folks!' He slides plates in front of us and I appreciate a good protein heavy breakfast as much as the next sane person, but . . . I don't know. It looks a bit sad. Imagine that. It's the first nutritionally complete meal I've had since I got here and I think it looks sad.

Dwaine snaps a picture before tucking in, answering my question with a fork full of eggy spinach hovering just in front of his mouth.

'Yep. Had my black belt by the time I was eleven.'

'Karate?'

He nods, taking a bite. I wonder what Mum would make of the knowledge that Dwaine can probably chop through a piece of concrete with his bare hands.

As we eat, he tells me about some horror stories from the world of fitness. Honestly, I could have probably done without knowing that some steroids cause erectile dysfunction. I presume the personal trainer–client relationship doesn't require the same vow of confidentiality as, say, the medical profession. Or the priesthood.

'Everything okay with the food?' The waiter is back.

'Yes, thank you, delicious.' It's actually all a bit watery. But no one likes a complainy date.

As we finish our meal, Dwaine goes back to talking about the importance of fitness and I zone out a bit.

'So, do you want to go out again?' He puts down his knife and fork.

I'm taken aback. I mean, I think I've had a nice enough time with Dwaine. And the bits that weren't so good, like the watery meal and me not knowing where to put my hands weren't exactly his fault.

But ... imagine what Luke will say when he hears I'm already onto a second date.

'That would be great, thank you.'

We have another go at some small talk, and this time, I try to be a bit more involved. I go into quite a lot of detail about the kimchee rice pot I'd helped develop for Charles's café chain.

'You know, fermented cabbage is good for gut health,' I tell Dwaine as we head to the tills to pay.

'I do know that.' His reply is enthusiastic and look at us, we have things in common.

We split the bill and coat up, ready to go back outside.

'Meet me by the beach on Tuesday for a workout?' Dwaine asks as we emerge back into the car park.

'You really want to see me again?' I ask.

'Course,' he smiles. I get that he's just being nice, but my cheeks go red anyway.

Dwaine waggles his eyebrows. 'Things can get pretty intense when I work out, you might want to bring a shake.'

'A shake?' I ask.

'Whey. Or something that'll aid muscle recovery.'

This whole chat is taking some of the shine off the prospect of a second date with Dwaine. He must mistake whatever expression my face is making for confusion. Or shake-based reluctance at least.

'I can make it for you if you need me to. I tend to go for two scoops of chocolate.'

I can't have that. It's dating 101 that you don't start out needy. You can get needy later on. But you don't start out that way.

'No, honestly. I can make my own. I love shakes. Whey. Chocolate. Got it.' Charles had never liked protein shakes, too synthetic.

'Great. I guess I'll see you Tuesday at 11 then.'

Dwaine moves imperceptibly closer and I don't think, I just act, diving towards the van. Opening the door so hard that it bashes into the parking post next to it. Pretending not to notice, Dwaine smiles, raises an arm and heads in the opposite direction.

I watch him disappear from view, realising that I'm breathing really fast again. And the back of my neck is clammy.

What the hell is wrong with me?

Dwaine was going to kiss me. And okay, I didn't expect us to get to that point after one date, but I don't particularly object to the thought of kissing him. I quite like kissing, actually.

But I'm nervous. It'll just be nerves. I haven't kissed anyone but Charles in years and he was very particular. He'd never have kissed me after I'd eaten egg. Not in a million years.

That'll be it.

I steady my breathing. Relax my hands on the wheel. And hope that the panicky feeling I had just now doesn't come back. Even though deep down, in the part of me that I'd rather not visit, I know that it probably will.

Chapter Nine

Once I'm feeling a little more 'with it' I set off to meet Joanie.

Dad had told me where I might find Little Daisies in Peterlee. Except this can't be right because I've ended up outside a massive unit on an industrial estate. An enormous green hippo holding a daisy is stuck to the front. 'Welcome to Little Daisies Soft Play Area' the dragon announces.

I drum my fingers on the wheel, having avoided the trauma of another car park and just pulling to a stop across the road.

Surely Joanie would have said if she'd wanted me to come to a soft play. People need to give you the option of declining, don't they? Soft plays are not the sort of place anyone goes by choice. Especially childless people.

But then Joanie had been really nice, asking me to meet her like she did. And on that note . . . I'm out of the van and wrestling with the non-central lock before I can think too much about it.

'One adult, please.'

'You're on your own?' The young girl at the entrance eyes me suspiciously. She's dressed as one of the 101 Dalmatians.

'Yes, but my friend should already be here.' My mini meltdown has rendered me ten minutes late. I try to peer behind her into the expanse of soft play, looking for Joanie. I hope that I'm in the right place.

'What's your friend's name? I'll see if she's already signed in.'

'Sorry. Sorry.' I start randomly apologising. 'It's Joanie and, er, Tyler I think she said.'

Dalmatian girl raises a single eyebrow at me, causing the splodge of black face paint she has around one eye to stretch out.

'There's no Joanie that I can see.'

I'm moments away from having to explain myself out of a very awkward situation when Joanie comes barrelling through the entrance from the car park. She's wearing ripped jeans and Doc Martens with a baggy hoody.

'Alice! You're here. I wasn't sure you'd come. Tyler, say hello to Aunty Alice.'

I'm not sure how I've been bumped up to Aunty quite so quickly. But still, Tyler holds out his hand. 'Hello, Aunty Alice,' he offers. It's pretty cute actually. Tyler has pale skin, grey eyes and a rather solemn expression. Like a scaled-down Forrest Gump.

'Hello, Tyler. Nice to meet you.'

We shake hands. His is warm and firm but ridiculously small. It's so weird that they make hands that small.

After our handshake, Tyler and I stare at each other. Because I've no idea what to do now.

'Two adults and one child,' Joanie tells the Dalmatian. 'Hang on, I've my loyalty card here somewhere.' She rifles through her handbag, extracting nappies, snacks, baby wipes, the head of Hulk. 'Here it is!' She hands over her card to be stamped.

Finally, we're buzzed through the entrance gate.

Now Charles always said I had a tendency to overreact. And perhaps the man had a point. Because entering Little Daisies is like stepping into the seventh circle of hell.

The floor is sticky. The air smells greasy. 'Let It Go' blasts from speakers. Hordes of children swing from various brightly coloured contraptions, or else emerge screaming from ball pits.

Joanie and Tyler stop at a table with three chairs, a laminated menu propped up against the ketchup.

'Shoes off!' Joanie commands.

Tyler obliges, neatly lining up a pair of Spider-Man trainers under Joanie's chair before running, screaming, into the abyss of the main play area.

'It's good for them to burn off some energy,' Joanie explains, watching as he belly flops into a pit of multi-coloured balls.

I nod in agreement when honestly, there's not one child in here who looks even close to burn-out.

'You want coffee? They do a muffin deal.'

'Er ...' I do want a muffin. I haven't eaten since brunch, which granted was only half an hour ago. But ... I don't know. God, I can't even make up my mind about a muffin. No wonder my life is appalling.

'How about I get you one, then if you fancy it, you can eat it?' Joanie asks.

'Okay, sounds good. Thank you.'

Joanie goes to order from a young man who appears to be dressed as a Christmas elf, while I perch on the edge of my lime-green chair.

Occasionally a child stumbles past our table, red-faced and sweaty, as if returning from battle, guzzling Fruit Shoots. Gangs of them run laps of the place in pack-like formation and then, for no discernible reason, rugby tackle each other to the ground.

Joanie swerves a situation where one child has another in a head-lock to make it back to our table, her tray laden with an orange Fruit Shoot, two coffees and chocolate muffins.

'Thank you.' I slide Joanie £5 and take the coffee. 'So, do you come here a lot?' I have to shout over what looks like the beginnings of a flash mob. Olaf is leading a gang of children in a hokey cokey.

'Most Saturdays,' Joanie shouts back. 'It's my weekend day. I used to meet some other mums here. He goes to his dad on Sunday.' She takes a big bite of her muffin and considers. 'Hmm, not enough baking powder.'

'Used to?'

'Pardon?'

'You said you used to meet some other mums here.'

'Oh. Yeah, when I was pregnant with Tyler I did these courses at the hospital. How to keep a baby alive, that sort of thing. Met some other women there. They were all right, for a bit.'

'What happened? I mean, you don't have to tell me. If you don't want to.'

I pull my own muffin towards me having resisted for longer than I expected to.

'I don't mind. Honestly, I don't know if it's a hormone thing, but having babies turns women bat-shit crazy. It was like they were friends, but they hated each other too. Like I said . . . hormones.'

'Wow, I'd no idea.'

I've never really spent a lot of time around kids. I think when I was younger I always imagined that I'd have a family. But that reality seems further away than ever. Especially now.

'Yep.' Joanie, doesn't seem to notice my internal conflict, instead crossing her eyes to denote the level of crazy she was dealing with. 'And none of my school friends wanted to hang out with a baby. Which is fair enough. Just been me and Tyler really.'

Joanie, who has been tracking Tyler's movements the whole time, smiles. I look over to where he's scaling the netting up the side of the play area.

'He seems really cute.'

'He is.' She has a drink. 'But what about you? Why don't you have any mates?'

It's a direct question, for sure.

'It's a bit of a story but . . . basically, I lived in London for years, after uni. And it's a long way, on the train. Then I broke up with my ex. You might have heard of him actually – Charles van der Beck, Beck Health Cafés?'

Joanie looks blankly at me in a way that suggests she hasn't, in fact, heard of Charles.

'And so, I found him in a ... um ... compromising position in the living room. With another woman.'

Joanie has a mouth full of muffin. For some reason, I keep talking.

'And he was my boss, so when he dumped me, I got the sack too.'

'Hold on, he dumped you?'

I half shrug.

'He sounds like a twat.'

Joanie's voice drips with I Hate Men vibes. A sentiment I absolutely should get behind.

At that moment, Tyler rejoins us. He appears to have lost his T-shirt and is now in only a vest. He squeezes orange Fruit Shoot down his throat before running back off without a single word.

I peel a lone chocolate chip off the top of my muffin. It melts on my tongue, making the inside of my mouth silky. I push my plate away a fraction.

'I'm trying to move on. I had a good date this morning with a guy called Dwaine. Very muscly.' I pull my plate closer again as a means to avoid Joanie's inscrutable gaze. 'How about you? Anyone special?'

'God no. I've got enough on with Tyler and work.'

'I bet. Charles always said working parents have it so hard.'

'Do you always talk about this Charles guy so much?'

'Er. No.' I make a mental note not to, at least when I'm around Joanie.

'Good, then we can be friends.'

I laugh. There is something refreshing about never wondering what Joanie is thinking. 'How long have you worked at the restaurant?'

'Ever since I had Tyler. I need to work evenings so that me mam can watch him. Once he gets all his free hours at pre-school, I'm out of there. He starts next September. I'm on a countdown. I swear, I can't fucking wait to tell Paul I'm quitting.' She makes a stabby movement with her muffin knife which I presume is aimed at Paul.

'Does . . .'

I pause, wondering how personal to go on a first friend–date. Gabby has no filter, like zero. The first time we met she talked me through getting her coil inserted. Still, I decide to go for it.

'Does Tyler's dad help?' I ask.

'Yeah, as much as he can, like. He didn't run off or anything, but he's young.'

'So are you,' I add without thinking. Joanie looks like it's the first time she's been presented this fact.

We pass the rest of the session pleasantly enough, discounting the moment when the ball pool needs to be evacuated after a rogue kid pukes in it. Joanie regales me with the minutiae of Tyler's birth ('and then I said "if someone doesn't get me an epidural, I'm going to start smashing shit"'). She assures me that it was worth it ('kid's the boss').

My suspicions that I might quite like Joanie were well-founded. She's like an angry garden gnome. She scowls at the clown worker who tries to clear Tyler's Fruit Shoot before he's finished with it. And her face takes on an air of pure venom if the conversation veers anywhere near the Lotus Flower. She tells me about a time a customer got their hand stuck in the hinge of the toilet door and ripped the top of their finger off. 'Paul asked the ambulance drivers if they wanted to order takeaway.'

'Is Paul the owner?' I ask.

'No, manager. The actual owner is some sort of drugs lord.'

'No way! Seriously?'

'Yep.'

I don't ask any more questions just in case I'm ever forced to rely on the concept of plausible deniability to avoid jail time. 'I'm thinking of going back to uni next September, if they'll have me.'

'Don't blame you. TYLER,' she shouts as I file away the fact that yet another person doesn't seem at all shocked by this. 'Our time is up!'

Tyler is not happy about this fact. And for such a small person, he makes his displeasure well known, wavering between going rigid or else fully floppy. A table is dragged. At one point, he latches onto my arm and Joanie has to peel him off, finger by finger. She instructs me to sing to distract him and so I give the most enthusiastic rendition of 'Humpty Dumpty' that I can manage, given the circumstances.

'Bye, Aunty Alice,' an upside-down Tyler calls from over Joanie's shoulder as we all stand in the car park, finally.

'Bye, Tyler! Thank you so much for inviting me. I had a really nice time.'

It's true, I did. I climb back into Dad's van looking forward to another trip to the soft play place far more than the idea of smoothies and sweat on the beach with Dwaine.

Chapter Ten

'Alice.'

Luke arrives at our table in Star Bucks, greeting me with the formality of a dusty old business type about to address some sort of board meeting. Well, aside from the small leaf in his windswept hair, right at the front. He hasn't noticed it.

'Luke.'

'Do you want to eat again?' he asks me, sitting down as our waitress hovers at the edge of the table.

'No thank you, no budget for cheese sandwiches. Just a tea for me,' I tell the waitress.

'I see.' Luke seems exasperated and we're only two minutes into our meeting. Or maybe he's the sort who sees poverty as a personality flaw. 'I'll just have a coffee,' he says to our waitress.

'You can eat,' I tell Luke. He's a university lecturer, they can surely afford the odd cheese bap every now and then.

'I know.'

'I just meant don't not eat on my account.'

'I'm not.' I feel like my hackles are up already. But then, to be honest, I'm not exactly sure what a hackle is or how I might feel if it's up. I do think that Luke is unnecessarily prickly, though.

I just can't help but needle him.

I sit back in my chair, stretch my fingers out. Luke eyes me warily.

'So, guess who's already been on a date?' I smirk.

'You,' Luke says. Missing the point of this little game entirely.

'You're meant to play along and say you don't know.' I frown.

'What a complete waste of time and effort.'

I huff. 'This bet might be over before it's even got started. Though of course, I'll miss our chats.'

Our drinks arrive. Luke stirs sugar into his coffee, swirling the spoon in what I consider to be a very menacing fashion.

'In love already, huh? Must have been a pretty spectacular date.' It sounds friendly, but as he's full-on scowling like a Disney villain, it doesn't *feel* friendly.

I think about the watery spinach as Luke takes a sip of his coffee. Arsehole.

I sit up a little straighter, desperate to put us on a more level footing. 'Well, I've been thinking about the bet. I don't think its premise is sound,' I say. I have a drink, giving him a sort of touché look with my eyebrows.

'I mean,' I carry on, 'how will we even know that the other one is in love. We could just lie. You might be in love but not say and I could just pretend.' I'll be honest, I'm a little bit smug at this.

'I've been thinking the exact same thing,' Luke says.

'You have?'

He nods. Once. 'And the solution seems entirely obvious.'

'It does?' Jesus, brain, please try and muster something, *anything* that doesn't make me seem like a completely useless person.

'Yes.' I feel like if Luke had a stack of papers, he'd straighten them. 'The person we're claiming to be in love with will need to love us too. Or not, if my theory is correct.'

I slam my cup down harder than I need to, making tea splosh all over and forcing me to borrow napkins from the surrounding tables to clear it up. By the time I look at Luke again, the table is covered in rapidly disintegrating soggy brown tissue.

'Think about it, it makes perfect sense,' Luke says. 'In order for romantic attachment to fulfil its basic evolutionary principle ... babies ... feelings of attachment need to be mutual.'

'It's actually the same in philosophy,' I reluctantly acknowledge. Doubly annoyed that Luke has just suggested that we make our bet even harder, but also that he might be right. 'Aristotle said that true love amounted to two bodies and one soul.'

That at least riles Luke a bit. He starts drumming his fingers on the table, *drum, drum, drum*. I'm sure he's doing it to try and break me, but I cannot be broken. I mean I can. Obviously. But not today, Satan.

I start my own tap back. We're a symphony of table noise.

'So, you agree that for you to win the bet, both parties would need to declare their love?' he asks.

I throw my hands in the air. 'Yes, fine, if you say so. This still doesn't solve our other problem, the fact that you could just hide from women for six months.'

'Five months and three weeks remain of the bet. And I told you, I've no intention of hiding.' His gaze is so intense that I start to fan myself with the plastic menu. Why has God wasted eyelashes like that on a man like Luke? It's quite frankly a travesty.

'Yeah, but you're never going to fall in love over a quick ... you know, one-night thing,' I say.

'Who said anything about quick?'

I stop fanning. Luke, seemingly realising what he's said, actually goes a bit red. 'Sorry, that was inappropriate.'

And I can't help it, I start laughing as Luke watches on horrified. There are tears rolling down my cheeks and I have to reassure the man at the table next to us that I'm laughing, not dying. It's the same liver keeno who was here last week.

The thing is, I'd bet my life that Luke *is* a hit with the opposite sex. Because if there's one thing that womankind is good at, it's picking a man with the emotional range of a paper clip.

'Anyway,' I say, wiping tears from the back of my hand and having well and truly lost the plot. Luke's expression is stony. In that he looks like he's been carved from stone. 'Don't worry about it.' Another titter escapes me. 'Plus, like I said, I've thought of a solution for this one.'

'The dating app?' He still looks a bit ashen.

'Yep. You should sign up for one, actually go on dates.'

Luke leans back in his chair.

'I'm on a dating app.'

'Fuck off.' Clearly, I've not yet regained my equilibrium.

'It's true. I'm on Tinder.'

'Well, that's where you're going wrong. You want to get on Bumble or something like that. That's where my Aunty Moira met her Fred. Everyone on there is serious. Tinder's just for hook-ups.'

Another pointed stare.

'Let me see your profile then,' I say, making a grabbing motion with my hand.

'Why would you want to see that?'

'We can make it a bit more romance friendly.'

Luke rolls his eyes but reaches into his jeans pocket and pulls out his phone, unlocking it and passing it to me.

I eye it warily.

'You don't have a dick pic as your profile picture, do you?'

Another Medusa-like stare. 'No.'

'No dick pics of any description?'

'Jesus, Alice.'

I hold the hand not grabbing his phone up like I'm in a shoot-out. 'Sorry just making sure, your bits are the last thing I want to see today.'

The man at the table next to us leans over to say, 'I think his bits would be pretty lovely, myself.'

'Thank you.' Luke tilts his head in the man's general direction and I go red for the second time. Getting a cup of tea with Luke is like one long stress test.

We order another round of drinks as I settle down to look at Luke's Tinder profile. The signal in Easington is patchy, so it takes a while to load. But finally, I'm on Luke's profile and ...

'That's the picture you use?' It looks like a mug shot. He's much more handsome in real life.

'Yes. Why?'

'No reason.' Poor guy must just not be very photogenic.

'There must be a reason, otherwise you wouldn't have mentioned it.' Luke is back to drumming his fingers on the table.

'It's just ... are you sure you want something so ... severe?'

In the picture, he's glaring face-on at the camera. A plain white wall behind him. Like I said, mug shot.

'What would you suggest?' His tone is the one he does so well. Neutral with undertones of scathing.

'I don't know, maybe one where you're laughing or something more relaxed? Laugh now and I'll take a candid shot.' I open his camera, noticing the vein pulsing in his forehead. 'Okay ... three, two, one – now, laugh!'

Luke clenches his jaw. He's gone from mug shot to predator. 'Maybe you should just stick with the original,' I say as our second round of drinks arrives. A muscle in the side of his jaw twitches again.

I recommence scrolling. 'Okay, so under interests, you've put the word biologist.'

'Have I?' He stirs more sugar into his coffee. 'Damn it, I thought I'd changed that. It was supposed to say "biologist, former Satanist."'

Tea sprays out of my mouth. This meeting is wetter than I thought it would be.

'No one is going to go out with a Satanist.'

'I was joking.'

'Oh, right . . . I didn't know you did that.'

He glares at me.

'So just biologist then?' I ask, earning another glare over his coffee cup. 'Concise, to the point, I like it.'

I scroll down the rest of Luke's profile.

'And under occupation . . . again, the word biologist. You can't put that twice.'

'Why not?' he asks.

'Because one hundred per cent of your answers are the word biologist. It makes it look like you're married to your job.'

'What if I am married to my job?'

'Then lie. What sort of music do you like?'

He looks like he's thinking for a minute. 'I listen to Radio X in the lab.'

'Right, so go for something like this . . . *my work is my passion*,' I think off the top of my head. '*But I'm also interested in indie rock music. I enjoy exercising and I'm close to my parents, but I'd love to meet someone to share it all with.* Do you want me to write it down for you?'

Luke's angry vein is back. Actually, I think it's found a friend. 'I would never say that.'

'Which part don't you like?'

He shakes his head. 'The whole lot. I'll add music to my interests if you're so bothered about it.'

I have a drink of tea.

'So, you really don't date?' I ask. He shakes his head. 'Not even the odd sexy séance?' I ask.

'No, Alice, I don't date. I don't do well with . . . people.' He shifts in his seat and starts to look a bit uncomfortable. I'm transported back to Easington High. Luke had maybe one friend at school, and a whole bunch of people who picked on him. He kept to himself as much as possible. I remember one time in maths, I asked if I could borrow his pencil sharpener. He looked so shocked at being spoken to that he just slid it across the table to me and mumbled 'thanks' when I passed it back. In fact, whenever I spoke to him in school, he barely answered.

Maybe Luke really isn't good with people.

I don't want to make him feel bad about that, so I just start talking.

'I used to love dating. For our first date, Charles took me on the London Eye. And we went to the zoo this one time too. It was so much fun.'

I try to inject a healthy dose of cheer into my voice, but it falls a bit flat. I'd always thought that the time I spent with Charles was exciting. But now the word doesn't feel quite right. Intense, yeah that's it. It was intense with Charles. I close my eyes for a second, just for a mini regroup. When I open them, Luke looks to be mid eye twitch.

'At most, a walk is perfectly adequate to ascertain how compatible you are as a couple.'

I give him a long stare. 'And they say romance is dead.'

'*They* say that romance is a societal construct.'

I hand back his phone.

'Aren't you setting up a dating profile?' he asks, draining the last of his coffee.

I shake my head. 'I've got Dwaine remember. If it all goes tits up, I'll think about it.' I pause a second. 'Obviously, you'll be my go-to person if I do need to set up a profile.'

'Fine,' Luke says.

'Fine.'

'So, what are you and Dwaine doing for your second date?'

I had seriously been considering calling off my exercise date with Dwaine. He's a nice enough person but ... there's just something missing. Plus I don't actually want to exercise. Things are bad enough around here without adding exercise into the mix. But now maybe I'll have to go, just because I've gone on about it so much to Luke.

'Exercising on the beach. It's no bubble pod but you have to compromise in relationships. And anyway, a beach is a beach. I can't wait.'

'A bubble pod?'

'All the influencers are going in for them. Like a pod that you put in the garden full of fairy lights and flowers and stuff.'

A dark shadow passes over Luke's face. So, he's mortally offended by the concept of a bubble pod. Big surprise.

It's so obvious that I'm annoying him. I'm loving it.

I offer up a whimsical sigh. 'Are you okay, Luke?'

He pulls a hand over his face. 'I just don't understand how you believe in all this, after everything that's happened? I knew you were a philosopher, but still.'

'I don't know what you could possibly mean.' I stick my little finger out as I take a sip of tea. Just to really bother him.

'And anyway, one year of a philosophy degree does not a philosopher make,' I say.

'I thought you were going back to uni?'

'I'm still weighing up my options,' I declare grandly. Because now is not the time to be disclosing to Luke that whenever I looked at Durham's philosophy course, I was hit by the memory of what it was like in London the first time round. How I'd been expecting it to be, if not easy, manageable. Only to feel like I was way out of my depth the whole entire time. I am terrified at the thought of putting myself through that again.

Luke's phone vibrates on the table between us and he reaches for it. Whatever is on there makes him do this small smile, where the corners of his mouth turn up just a smidge.

Luke is distracted by his phone as I keep talking. 'You're right though. Philosophers aren't exactly known to be lucky in love. Sartre had a ton of affairs and Nietzsche proposed to the same woman three times and got turned down.' Maybe it's the same for me and I'm doomed to be unlucky in love.

No, get it together, King. That attitude will not help me to win this bet.

Luke finishes up on his phone.

'We done here?' I'm slightly snappier than I planned to be.

'Yep. Enjoy exercising with Dane.'

'Dwaine.'

Luke's phone vibrates again.

'Dwaine,' he says, 'that's the one. I presume you'll let me know if he makes you swoon.'

'Did you just say the word swoon?' I pause mid putting my coat on.

'Apparently.' He looks positively murderous.

I laugh.

'Right, well I'm going to go work out right now. And buy some whey.' I stand up. 'As always Luke, it's been real.' I've literally no idea why I'm talking like an American.

He's distracted by his phone again.

'Sorry,' he says, 'I'm just messaging Lucy on Tinder. Clearly my profile is just fine. She has such kind eyes.' His voice drips with sarcasm.

I lean over his shoulder. He smells irritatingly nice. 'Let me see her, then.'

Luke flashes his phone. There's something prominent about Lucy, and it isn't her eyes.

'Oh yeah, sure it's the eyes.'

I scoff in a way that I hope says *Men*.

'Well, enjoy Lucy.' I pause. 'That sounds weird. Let me know if you have any tummy flutters.' Another pause, 'Okay, I'm going.'

Luke doesn't even look up from his phone.

Insufferable man.

Chapter Eleven

'Now, squat!'

I want to yell at the woman in matching workout gear to fuck off, but screaming at the TV is not going to make me feel any better about my life. Instead, I snatch my phone off the mantelpiece, clicking off the YouTube fitness clip because it's not exactly brilliant is it? Discovering that you're weak of both mind *and* body.

I go to make up a couple of shakes. Having discovered that whey protein powder costs a small fortune, relative to my wages at least, I'm now committed to upping my protein intake whether I'd like to or not. Though the less said about the keto pancakes I attempted the better. They'd turned into a sort of cheesy scrambled egg and attached themselves to the bottom of the pan.

Shake in hand, I hurry onward for my second date with Dwaine.

Obviously we'll be exercising so I've had to factor that into my outfit choice. As I have the fact that it's as balmy as the North Pole outside. I've gone for my workout leggings and then a couple of T-shirts and a hoodie. The bobble hat that had hidden my hair through its orange ringlet era is back in the game too.

Dwaine texted me last night, telling me to meet him at the steps to Hartlepool beach. And I have to say, so far, points for being an unproblematic date. In a rare moment of good fortune, Dad said that he didn't need the van this morning, meaning I can avoid getting the bus. Though as the van shudders along the A19, the windscreen alternating between fogging up and dripping with condensation, I wonder how much of a good turn this really is.

We used to come to Hartlepool beach some weekends when I was little. Admittedly, it's seen better days. My favourite former arcade is a pile of rubble with a barbed wire fence around it.

I feel a stab of annoyance at the politicians who have so obviously abandoned this corner of England.

I mean, *I'd* abandoned the area, but that's different.

There's a long winding promenade with quite a few sets of steps down to the beach. But aside from a couple of brave (or foolhardy, depending on your perspective) dogwalkers chasing their dogs along the wet sand, the place is abandoned. So it's easy to spot Dwaine off in the distance.

I rush over, careful not to spill my shake.

'Morning!' I smile, waving my drink at him.

'I tried chocolate like you suggested,' I say.

'Great!' He looks pleased. And I aim to please. Unless it's Luke, then I aim to irritate.

I give my head a little shake. Not literally, that would be weird. Internally. Because Charles had invaded my first date with Dwaine, I'm not having thoughts of Luke bother me on this one.

I try to have a drink but it's sort of a congealed mass at the bottom of the cup I'd also had to buy. Blowing a tub of whey-sized hole in this week's budget.

'It's so cool that you were psyched for this. I love working out with a partner.'

I get a flicker of a warm glow at the word partner, it nestles itself somewhere in my chest. It's a good job too, seeing as it's freezing. 'It's so important to share hobbies and interests, you know?' I say, thinking that 'psyched' is pushing it.

'I do. You ready to get started?'

I nod. Even though I'd been hoping for a little more small talk to avoid the actual workout part of our date. Still, probably best not to start complaining just yet.

'We should warm up.' Dwaine promptly begins jogging on the spot. I follow his lead, trying to hide how hard I'm breathing.

'You look good.' Dwaine nods towards me. It's reassuring, because I don't feel good. I seem to be out of breath already, and sweat is pooling in strange places – like behind my knees.

We're only on the warm-up and this already seems a bit more hardcore than the jazz hands and high kicks routine he'd led us in down the Welcome.

'Thanks, I need this. My diet hasn't been great lately and my ex used to say I'd put on weight looking at a chocolate bar.' I try a sort of self-deprecating laugh that doesn't quite ring true. And even though I've made that half joke hundreds of times, I feel flat. Like I'm realising that was actually a crappy thing for Charles to say.

'Shall we head along the beach?' Dwaine doesn't seem to notice that I'm in the middle of a revelation.

'Okay.' I smile, shaking out my fingertips to dispel the noise in my brain. And to get a bit of blood into them.

We descend some partly eroded and therefore mildly perilous steps to the beach. The sky is a jumble of grey clouds, and sea fog hovers in the air, so it's not exactly the romantic beach setting, but beggars can't be choosers. Like I said to Luke, a beach is a beach.

And anyway, no date is enhanced by running.

Despite what *Baywatch* implied, sand is actually a very unforgiving surface to run on. Every step I take seems to slide backwards, meaning that it takes more effort than it should to propel myself forwards.

Dwaine doesn't seem to be at war with the sand.

'Did you enjoy the rest of the weekend?' I pant, attempting to claw back the date element of the . . . date.

The sentence takes me so long to get out we make it to the other side of the beach before I finish it. I find to my dismay that Dwaine has dropped to a plank, right there on the sand. I try to copy, pretty certain that my forehead shouldn't be on the floor right now.

Honestly, I can hardly breathe. It feels like someone has an elastic band around my chest. I do that thing where people put their hands on their knees and breathe. It makes me cough. Hard.

'Yeah,' Dwaine says, barely catching breath, 'got a new PB on a half marathon on Sunday.'

Marathon sounds so much like muffin. I could really go for half a muffin. A full muffin even.

Dwain looks down at me with pity. 'Do you want to go get a drink or something? You look, kind of . . . in need of it.'

'Sure, why not?' I attempt to sound breezy but come off as asthmatic.

He waves a hand towards the steps up from the beach, indicating towards a cafe. We ascend, me clinging to the rail for dear life, my limbs trembling.

'That place does a good protein shake.' He points towards the aptly named Shake Hut and I'm genuinely amazed that he is good to go for yet another shake.

He pulls my hand into his as we walk towards it, lacing our fingers together and I really don't like it. But I don't know how to get my hand free without being rude.

Dwaine chats away as I stare down at our interlinked hands. 'You might want to up your protein some more.' It's delivered in a friendly enough tone, but it's still a bit judgy, isn't it?

'Might I?' I sound high.

He nods.

In contrast to the general ambiance of the morning, the sign to Shake Hut is bright pink, surrounded by giant plastic sweets and chocolate. Finally, Dwaine lets go of my hand to order.

Still dazed by the exercise and the hand-holding, I take an inordinately long time to decide, plumping in the end for mixed berry shake and a chocolate muffin. I probably won't eat the whole thing. But surely I deserve at least some amount of muffin after that.

'Sorry.' I join him in a little booth. He's already drunk half of his. 'I'm terrible at making decisions.'

'Duly noted.' He smiles but it's not exactly convincing and I get the impression that my lacklustre planking has signalled the beginning of the end for Dwaine and me. Plus the way he's glaring at my muffin like it insulted his mum, well . . . final nail, meet coffin.

'And sugar has all sorts of dangerous properties, it's pretty addictive if you're not careful.'

The room spins. 'What did you say?'

'About sugar? It's just best avoided, especially if you're bottom-heavy.' He looks down at my legs.

The room tilts.

I think I'm going to die.

Something is so, so wrong.

I hear Dwaine ask if I'm okay but his voice is so distant, and I've had to shut my eyes tight to get away from the visions spreading out in my brain.

'I'm just thinking about your health.'

'You'd lose the last bit if you put your mind to it.'

'I can't believe you're eating chocolate in bed, gross, Alice.'

Memories slam into me. Each of them sounding exactly like Charles. I'm pushing my back up against the booth, trying to get away but trapped.

Why has no one else noticed that the world is ending?

Dwaine touches my arm and I practically leap out of the booth.

'I need to go.' White-hot panic fires through me, lighting me up from the inside out.

'Are you okay to drive?' Dwaine asks.

We're back at Dad's van. How did we get here?

'Yeah. I think I am.'

'I could take you? If you like?'

'No.' I flash horror across my face as Dwaine steps towards the van. He stops.

'I'll be fine. I just need to, to get away.' I'm more breathless than ever.

'Please, leave me alone.'

I hope that Dwaine knows that I mean that in every sense of the word.

'Don't sweat it, honestly. If you're sure that you're okay?'

I nod.

'Okay, I'll see you around, Alice. Take care of yourself.' His voice comes through faint and blurry.

What the fuck was that?

Chapter Twelve

I crawl into the van in a whole heap of confusion.

And not just about Dwaine.

I don't know how to make sense of what happened.

I make it home, feeling unsteady and disorientated as I lay down on my bed, I look at my phone, feeling like my phone should be able to give me some answers here. After all, it's never let me down before. I'm just not exactly sure what questions I need to ask.

In the end, I call the only person who I think might be able to help.

'Alice! I'm I dreaming this call? It's almost midnight here.'

'Shit, Gabby, sorry, I didn't even think.'

'It's fine, I'm out anyway. One second,' I hear her tell whoever she's with and then she seems to move outside. 'Sorry, I can hear you properly now. What's up, lovely?'

Suddenly, the thing I actually called about doesn't seem like the most important thing. Because while I want to ask about Charles and me, and Charles and me together, what I really need to say before I do any of that is this.

'I . . . I just wanted to say I'm sorry for being a really shitty friend.'

And now I'm crying again. Credit to my eyeballs for dredging up some more tears.

'Hey, hey none of that. Talking about being a bad friend,' her voice has taken on a faint Australian twang, 'I did move halfway around the world.'

'Yeah, actually that was a dick move on your part.'

Wherever Gabby is, it sounds busy, but I can still hear her laughing really loud over the noise. It's all so different to the quiet of my room.

'We're okay now, aren't we?' she asks.

I hope we are.

'I won't keep you, you're obviously out, I'm so pleased it's going well there. I just wanted to ask, because you're the only person who really knew me with Charles. But do you think that he, like, put me down sometimes?'

'Shit, Alice, I didn't expect this tonight.'

'I know, God I'm so selfish. I'm literally ruining your night.'

'Hey, I didn't say that. Hang on, let me go somewhere quieter, that's all.'

I wait, biting the skin at the side of my nails while Gabby moves down the road, away from the entrance to wherever she was.

'There, that's better,' she says. 'You know, I'm always here if you want to talk about Charles stuff.'

'Thanks, you were the only person I thought to call. It's just I was remembering some stuff today about what he used to say to me about like what I ate and what I looked like and do you think it's right if the person you're with puts you down sometimes?'

The other end of the phone is quiet for a few moments. I can hear my own heartbeat. And then Gabby's voice, more serious than I've maybe ever heard her. 'I think if you're asking it Alice, deep down, you already know the answer.'

'Alice, wake the fuck up, will you? Table seven need their prawn crackers.'

'I don't think managers are meant to speak to their staff like that, Paul.'

Joanie isn't working tonight which is a shame because she would make the whole shift more bearable. To my utter amazement, I'm even missing Andy murdering 'Uptown Girl' and handing out the *Socialist Worker* newspaper in the toilets. At least he sometimes tells Paul to leave us alone.

'Just get the prawn crackers.'

I want to tell Paul to go stuff himself and his vat of prawn crackers. But with some serious willpower, I manage to keep my peace. My self-esteem will bottom out entirely if I end up failing my probation and getting the sack.

I'm so shaken up by this afternoon. I had some panic attacks when I was a teenager, mainly around exam time. The pressure just got too much sometimes. It was scary working out what was going on but eventually, I'd learnt a few breathing exercises to manage them. And I hadn't had one since I left uni. Well, not until that day in Boots with Luke. I don't think I can ignore the fact that they're obviously back. And these feel much worse. It's hours later and I still feel all spacey.

Unfortunately, there's no time for spacey because Easington's appetite for crispy duck doesn't wane on a Tuesday night.

'Table for three please. We've not booked. Is that okay?'

I'm loading a tray with drinks at the bar, so I don't immediately look up.

'No problem, sir,' Paul says. 'Alice will show you to your table in just a moment.' His 'customer voice' makes my skin crawl.

'Thanks.'

I look up to see who my next happy customers are.

Oh God, no.

It's Luke. And two other people who aren't Luke. But Luke is here. There. In the doorway of the restaurant.

If there is a God, please let's have another extinction event. One that includes me.

I still for a moment.

Nothing.

I'm frozen. My hand hovers uselessly in mid-air, ready to pick up the pint of Carling I'd been set to deliver.

'Alice.' Luke nods.

I feel a red stress rash start to climb its way up my throat.

'Alice. Take the drinks and then come back and show these people to their table,' Paul snaps. 'Sorry. She's new.'

I scurry off with the drinks tray.

'Watch it!' a customer warns as I drip Carling on the black and white stripes of his football top. I hurry back to the bar.

'Just this way,' I mumble to Luke and his parents. Luke's face is a mishmash of them both. His cheekbones are high like his mum's, but he has his dad's eyebrows. It's obvious that his parents got more cheerful DNA than Luke; his dad positively beams whilst I dodge eye contact.

'How did it go with Dwaine?' Luke asks as we swerve round tables.

'Badly.' I think of the morning, of what I'd remembered about Charles and frown. It was hard to care so much about fleeing Dwaine with that clouding out my every thought. I need to pull myself together. 'How about Lucy?' I ask, gesturing with the menus to their table.

Luke does his small smile. 'Very well thank you.'

I'm about to ask if he thinks he might be in love, but his dad interrupts me.

'Do you two know each other then?' he asks, sitting down.

'We went to school together,' Luke mutters.

I remain mute.

'I thought I recognized you!' His mum smiles. 'You won that award, with Luke didn't you? In Year 11?'

'Yeah, sort of,' I reply faintly.

His dad's hair is grey and a bit thin on top. His mum has a neat, dark bob. Plus she's coordinated her purple top with dangly earrings. Considering the rumour that Luke used to spend his spare time offering up sacrificial mice at a hand-crafted altar in his bedroom, his parents seem suspiciously average.

I realize that the three of them are staring at me.

'What can I get you to drink?

'White wine for me please,' his mum says.

'Kronenbourg,' Luke snaps. His mum glares at him and some more of my brain fog clears. 'Please.'

I hide my smirk behind my notepad.

'I'll have the same as Luke please, love,' his dad says as I scribble away.

I take their food order, feeling more stress evaporating off into the ether when they only order two courses. At least I won't have to lead them through a five-course banquet extravaganza.

Luke's mum seems to be on some sort of health kick. She orders soup and then steamed fish and plain rice. I'm not entirely sure that the kitchen staff will know what to do with a steamer.

'Slimming World,' she offers by way of explanation, as I under-line the word 'steamed' three times on my notepad.

I look up. 'You don't need to, at all,' I tell her.

'Ooh, she's nice. Isn't she, Luke?'

Luke doesn't answer.

Arsehole.

'I used to be a waitress!' his mum continues, oblivious to her son's scowl. What is Luke's problem? 'My first job when I was fifteen. Loved it.'

I manage a smile and then leave them to it, handing in the order sheet to the kitchen and seeing to my other tables, all of which are in the same crowded corner as Luke's. It's like I can feel his eyes on me, judging my waitressing abilities. Or lack of them.

Unfortunately, football shirt man, a mere table away from Luke, is getting a bit handsy. I manage to dodge his wandering paws while I clear his table. He then enquires loudly why I have a face like a slapped arse.

I try to catch Luke's eye, but he's staring murderously upwards. I wonder what his parents have said to him. Everything about him is so intense, it's a miracle is he isn't blowing out blood vessels on the regular.

The intensity unsettles me, making me a worse than usual waitress.

I knock over a bottle of wine on the bar. According to Paul it's coming out of my wages.

I mess up Luke's mum's order. Presenting her with fried as opposed to boiled rice. She assures me that it's no problem at all. But then she doesn't eat any of it, so I feel doubly bad. By the time they ask for the bill I'm feeling pretty miserable. I tot up what they owe and hand it over with three little sweets.

'Er, I think there might be a problem with the bill,' Luke says.

I close my eyes.

'It says we owe £610. I think it should be £61.'

It's obviously a mistake. You could probably buy the place for £600. I, however, look like the sort of person who doesn't know basic maths.

'Oi, love!' Football shirt man with the wandering hands chooses this moment to start heckling me. 'Are you getting our mint chocolate bombs or what?' He slurs his words, well on his way to pissed.

'Sorry, just a second,' I call over. For some inexplicable reason, my eyes start to well up.

'You said that five minutes ago.'

'One second.'

I look down Luke's bill, wondering where I've gone wrong. Except the items are all blurry.

'Hey, hey, don't worry about it. It's no harm done.' Luke's Dad reaches up and takes the bill from my shaking hands. 'Here, let me take a look.' Him being nice to me makes things a million times worse.

'That's it. I'm going to speak to the manager,' football shirt calls over from his table.

This is all so like me, making stupid mistakes. Not thinking straight.

I try to gulp in air, something to clear the fog in my head but it's like the walls of the restaurant are closing in on me.

'I'm sorry,' I say to Luke's family. 'I need to go actually.'

I drop the bill on the table and run for it.

I push past Paul by the door, only half hearing as he shouts, 'What the fuck is going on?'

I'm outside, taking big gulps of fresh air and letting the tears come freely.

Chapter Thirteen

Without thinking, I set off home, the sub-zero air meaning that there's a chance I'll arrive looking like one of those arctic explorers with icicles for eyelashes.

It's really something isn't it? Failing at a job that literal sixteen-year-olds excel at. I just want to be good at something.

I hug myself to keep warm.

'Alice!' It's Luke. He catches me up further down the road, his stricken face illuminated by the streetlight.

'Sorry,' I sniff. 'You must think I'm insane.'

Luke tilts his head like he might be considering the fact.

'I can add up,' I continue. 'I must have just forgotten to carry the one. Or maybe I carried an extra one. I'm not sure. Anyway, like I said, I'm sorry,' I finish miserably.

'Stop saying that,' Luke growls.

'Stop saying what?'

'Stop saying sorry.'

I go to say sorry again but catch myself, settling on opening and closing my mouth a few times.

I sniff, making the cardinal error of underestimating the amount of snot I'd produced in the last five minutes.

Luke, tactfully, says nothing.

'I didn't realize that I . . . say that a lot?'

'All the time. It's unnecessary.'

See, this is why Luke is so confusing. He's actually being *nice*. Ish. He's being nice ish. But he has this tone of voice that makes him sound like the lead detective in a murder enquiry. You know, the sort who broods a lot and has deep personal trauma in their past.

It's cold. Emotionless.

I manage another slightly more demure sniff. 'Yeh, so I, er, apologize. I've had a weird day. I think I'll just head home.'

'I'll walk you.'

I'm still shaking from the cold.

Luke side-eyes me.

'Here, you can take my jacket,' he offers.

'But you'll freeze.'

'I'm fine. The oestrogen in your body makes you more sensitive to the cold.'

Alrighty, then. Who am I to argue with the science?

I shrug his jacket over my shoulders, enjoying the fleecy lining.

Luke doesn't seem to notice the cold. He's probably trained his body to regulate its temperature on a cellular level. I'm so pleased with my joke that I share it, only for Luke to say . . . 'That's biologically impossible, Alice. It's simply the case that taking into account body fat percentages versus oestrogen levels, on balance, you are more likely to feel the cold.'

'So you are cold?'

'Yes.'

'Then you should take your coat back.'

'No.'

He breathes out slowly through his nose.

I really ought to stop poking the Luke-bear. But after a few moments, I lose all sense of self-preservation. 'What do you mean, body fat percentages?'

Luke looks to the sky before saying, 'Merely that I weighed up which of us was most likely to succumb to the cold given our relative percentage of body fat.'

'But you're not fat, Luke.'

'I know. You have more body fat than me.'

I stop walking.

'Are you calling me fat? Because if one more man mentions my weight, I swear to God I'm going to get punchy.'

'I am not calling you fat, Alice. I'm simply stating that as a man, I am likely to have less body fat.'

'Right.' I try to calm down. At least having the good sense to recognize that most of my anger should not be directed at Luke.

'What do you mean, another man?'

'Pardon?'

'You said "if another man mentions my weight".'

'Oh, that yeah. Dwaine kind of said something today. He didn't mean anything by it but it ... er ... well, it just reminded me of some stuff Charles used to say about what I should eat and stuff.'

'I see.'

Strike me down now, render me mute O Lord. Anything to stop me speaking.

'I know I'm not like universally attractive or anything.' I wave my arms around. 'But don't you think that your partner should like you regardless? Or does even caring about this make me a bad feminist? I mean, I get that how we look is meant to be the least interesting thing about us. I just ... argh. I don't know.'

Luke isn't speaking. He isn't even looking at me. He's glaring straight ahead.

'And now I'm going to die of embarrassment for wailing about this to you. Nice knowing you.' My hands cover my face.

'Alice.'

I shake my head.

'Alice.' Luke has the lightest grip on my wrist.

I relent. Because walking in the pitch black over uneven paving slabs is challenging enough.

'Sor—' I begin but catch myself. 'Can we just pretend that the last ten minutes never happened? Actually, the last ten hours. It's for the best.'

Luke glances down at me. 'No, a partner should never make you feel like that. As you know my . . . practical application is limited, but I believe that you should be each other's biggest advocate, in all regards. That's what numerous participants of the study suggest at any rate.'

'You mean the proper Harvard study and not our knock-off one?'

Luke smirks. 'Exactly.'

'Okay. Right, thanks for that.'

Luke's words do settle something in me, but my embarrassment hasn't completely abated.

We walk in silence. Past the butcher's, Bambino's and Star Bucks, me leading the way down the streets of Easington on my way home.

'You don't have to walk me all the way back,' I say.

'It's no problem.' His voice is level. 'Mum and Dad would disown me if I didn't.'

'I see.'

We walk in silence some more. Almost home.

Luke clears his throat.

But doesn't speak.

He does it again.

Poor man, he must think I'm ridiculous. He's right, I *am* ridiculous.

'So, Dwaine is—'

'Out.' I finish the sentence for him, omitting the part where I'd had the mother of all meltdowns.

'Good.'

'Can I transfer you your winnings in instalments? Like a payment plan,' I ask.

'No.'

'But whatever happens, I'll lose. I *always* lose. I'm on my own and I'm a loser!' At some point I've started to almost shout.

'Keep it down, will you?' I leap into the air as there's a call from a window in the darkness. 'I'm on earlies tomorrow!'

'No.'

I drop my voice to a whisper. 'Talk about kicking a woman while she's down. All right, how about I clean your flat?'

'No.'

'Polish your shoes?'

'No.'

'Well, I'm not being your sex slave. That's my line in the sand.'

'Your line in the sand is being a sex slave. Jesus, Alice.' Luke looks exasperated. 'You're not backing out of this now.'

'Why not? I've said you can win. I thought you were going to head off on a minibreak?'

'You're not backing out because you *think* you'll lose. You'll pay me my winnings fair and square when you *actually* lose.'

'But why?'

Luke looks like he's wondering that very same thing himself. After some time and careful deliberation, he replies, 'I don't think quitting will make you feel good.'

'I suppose it won't,' I say carefully. 'But I still don't get why you'd want to help me. You don't even seem to like me.'

He tilts his head. 'I'm wondering the same thing myself.' He looks across at me. 'I don't dislike you, Alice. I'm just not like you ... all friendly.'

'Luke, I have, at a push, two friends.' I think about Joanie and Gabby. 'Maybe two and a half if you include Tyler. He's two by the way. Is it bad form to be third-best friends with a small child you've met once?'

'Not as bad as saying the phrase "third-best friend".'

'Jesus, are you smirking?'

'No.'

'Oh.'

'You used to have lots of friends. At school. I found you suspiciously jovial.'

'How ironic. I just found you suspicious. You made me super nervous the whole time.'

I'm sure his lips twitch in an upward direction.

We arrive outside my house. 'I'm here,' I say before we stand awkwardly staring at each other in the dark. Luke's face all sharp angles in the streetlight.

'Fine, it's still on. I'll regroup,' I add, wondering if humans get a finite number of fresh starts in life.

'Tell me though,' I carry on, 'do you never worry that you'll end up alone and unloved? Because I think about that *a lot*. I think I might have always been a bit ... lonely.'

Luke shrugs. 'There's no point worrying about it.'

'Interesting.' What sort of person thinks, *Hmm, there's no point in worrying about that* – and then actually stops worrying? Psychopaths, that's who.

I've probably already said too much. 'Right, well I'd better get in.' I go to punch his shoulder and then think better of it, pulling my hand back and letting it hang by my side. Luke looks at it like I might have leprosy. 'See you, fourth-best friend.'

'Goodbye, Alice.' He starts to walk away as I reach for my key. 'And for what it's worth, you are.'

I look up and realize that Luke is facing me again.

'I'm what?'

His face is scrunched up like he might be in actual, physical pain. 'Universally attractive. You'd have to be an idiot not to think so.'

I'm too stunned to speak for a moment.

'Right. Right. Okay, thank you, Luke. That's very kind.'

'No problem. Just stating a fact. My favourite. Goodnight.'

'Yeah, night.'

Luke watches on as I fiddle with the keys, finally unlocking the door.

It's weird but I can feel his eyes on me long after I go inside.

Chapter Fourteen

Joanie's anger rings out around Little Daisies, the soft play where we've met for the second week running.

'I'm sorry, but what a dick.' Her face is puce, but then she has just come back from yelling at the parents of a kid who pushed Tyler over. To be fair, Tyler had chicken-legged the little girl with pigtails mere moments before. They're all playing together in the ball pool now.

So Joanie was already irate before I even mentioned Dwaine. She slices her muffin in half in an overly aggressive manner. 'What is wrong with men? Here you are, fit as fuck, and he's saying you should lose weight.'

She balls up her fists and I worry that she's about to start punching random members of the opposite sex by proxy. A worker in a cow onesie busy wiping down the next table edges away from us, dishcloth abandoned.

'He didn't say I needed to lose weight. Just implied that I was a bit bottom-heavy. And I'm not fit as fuck.' I, at least, lower my voice to a whisper, keen to avoid a lifelong Little Daisies ban. Tyler shrieks with delight as the other kids bury him in the ball pit. No, we can't get banned, not when Tyler enjoys it here so much.

'You are fit. You remind me of that Elle Fanning, you know who plays the princess in *Maleficent*. Loved that film when I was younger.'

Brilliant, a reminder that Joanie's celebrity points of reference are years younger than mine. But I do know who she's talking about.

'Please, I'm like the bargain bucket version.'

Joanie rolls her eyes at me.

'At least I didn't get the sack.' I attempt to inject some positivity into proceedings.

Joanie nods. 'Paul said that Luke had a go about that guy trying to feel you up.'

The thought of Luke defending my honour me makes me shift in my seat and take a tentative bite of my own muffin. Because every time I think about not eating something, Charles's voice comes back to me. The whiney one I imagine in my head. And I realize I don't want him to have that power.

'Paul was proper annoyed.' Joanie is still talking. 'Spent all of Thursday night ranting about the *snowflake generation*.' She smiles. Anything that annoys Paul is cause for celebration in her book.

'We really need to unionize or something. The conditions are actually appalling.'

Joanie shrugs. 'We won't be there much longer. I'm out next year and I thought you were going back to uni.'

'I'm still thinking about it,' I say, forcing myself to take another bite. It should not be this hard to eat a muffin. It's a bloody muffin.

'Seriously though, you all right? About the Dwaine thing?'

I nod, chewing through my ambitious mouthful.

'I mean, we'd been on two dates,' I say after swallowing, 'so it's hardly a massive deal. I think I'll probably avoid going to his disco exercise class from now on, but so long as I don't dwell too much on the fact that I might be alone and unlovable my whole life, I feel fine.'

Joanie's kohled eyes narrow.

'You,' she picks up her muffin knife to point at me, 'need to be a bit fucking kinder to yourself.'

I reach over to gently take the knife out of Joanie's hands, careful to make no sudden movements. Even if it is so blunt that it'd struggle to saw through butter.

'You know, man or not, I find myself pretty fucking amazing,' she says.

'Do you?' I ask in genuine wonder.

'Yep.'

'I don't think I'm amazing.'

She leans back in her chair. 'You don't say.'

'I guess I just always thought that love conquered everything. Like it didn't matter how I felt about me, so long as someone loved me.'

'That's bullshit, Alice. Sorry but it is. Love doesn't conquer everything. I love Tyler like mad, but if I can't afford to feed him, we're still fucking screwed.'

Tyler runs towards us, his little arms powering him forwards, his face smeared in ambiguous dirt. Joanie attacks it with a packet of wet wipes.

I watch them, all the while wondering when, exactly, Joanie had become so wise. It has been a long time since I thought I was amazing. Or even that I was perfectly satisfactory.

'Have you lost the bet, then, now that you're single again?' I've already filled Joanie in on the bet with Luke.

'No. Luke wouldn't let me quit. And anyway, I'm not sure I want to give up on love entirely.'

She shrugs. 'Your funeral.'

'Do you want to come to church, Alice?' Mum calls through the bedroom door. She'll have been up early this morning, preparing the Yorkshire pudding batter.

My ears are still ringing from Andy's vocal majesty last night. He spent a good deal of time stomping around the little stage 'singing' 'I'm Gonna Be (500 miles)'. He interspersed it with a couple of quotes from *The Communist Manifesto* which was actually pretty funny. Especially when he pointed at Paul and shouted, 'Let the ruling classes tremble!' Paul had looked white-faced and terrified. I suspect that he might be more than a little afraid of Andy. Which is great.

'No, thank you. I'm going to sort some stuff here.'

We always went to church together when I was younger, and I felt all sorts of confused when I started thinking that maybe I didn't agree with a lot of the stuff being said up there by Father Hogarth, my childhood priest. I have a vivid memory of my first confession . . . of feeling really muddled about the fact that I *thought* I'd been good, but Father Hogarth saying that I *must* have something to confess.

I just made some stuff up in the end, and then didn't sleep for worrying that lying your way through your first confession was probably the sort of thing that got you sent straight to hell.

I've long since made my peace with being a poor excuse for a Catholic, but that guilt still lingers around the edges of my thoughts sometimes.

Like right now, I'm worrying that Mum is annoyed at me. Even though she doesn't say anything except 'no problem'.

I lie in bed listening to the sound of her footsteps retreating and then swing my legs out. I'm not sure when I finally made the decision to unpack properly, but I think it might have something to do with realising all that rubbish Charles used to say about the way I look. And Luke's 'biggest advocate' speech, or semi-speech, at least.

I haul the cases out from under my bed. No mean feat in a room this size. I throw the lids open and gaze at the contents. I don't even recall owning half these clothes; they look like they belong to another life, all smooth fabrics and block colours. As I go about transferring them to my wardrobe, I realize that none of these things look like they should belong to me.

Adulthood would be much easier if it came with a manual telling us what we're meant to be.

Anyway, as I simply do not have the means to overhaul my entire wardrobe I plough on with the unpacking.

'Is everything all right up there?' Mum calls from downstairs.

'Yeah, great, I'm just unpacking,' I call back.

This is met with a few seconds of silence.

'Okay, we're off to church.'

I sense them waiting for a response. 'Have fun!' I call cheerily, even though ... do people have fun at church? I'm not sure I ever did.

The front door slams as I wade back into the battle of the suitcases, sure that at any moment someone is going to appear and drag me onto one of those secret hoarder TV programmes.

I look around. My room was already 90 per cent bed and now that I've emptied the entire contents of my suitcases, it'll take the team that rescued those Chilean miners to prise me out. I can't help but wonder why I have so much stuff in the first place.

I don't take my cork board down, but I do rearrange the faded Post-it notes so that the more in-your-face inspirational ones are slightly hidden. Now there's one from Shakespeare informing me that 'expectation is the root of all heartbreak', which seems much more in keeping with my vibe these days.

I stand back (i.e. flatten myself against the back of my bedroom door) to survey the finished room. It looks awful. Like, truly awful. But then, at least it's *my* awful.

It's been so long since I felt a sense of achievement, I hardly even recognize it.

I shower and get changed into some of my newly unearthed clothes. The whole thing has taken me so long that by the time I head downstairs, Mum, Dad, Nana and Aunty M are already back from church.

'Alice!' Aunty M opens her arms wide, almost smacking Dad in the face. 'Come here!' I'm squished against her boobs and I don't even care. I'm smiling about it. Not especially about the boob thing, but the hug at least.

'I'll get lunch going, shall I?' We all follow Mum through into the front room.

'Do you want any help?' I ask.

'No, pet, I'll manage fine on my own.' This is code for keep out of my kitchen or else. 'Anyway,' she carries on, 'that programme you used to like is on now I think, the debate one?'

Dad, a man who can wield a TV remote like no other, has found a politics debate programme in mere seconds. It's not the same as the one I watched when I was younger, *The Big Questions* that was called, it was more philosophy than politics. I think they ended it now. But this still looks interesting.

I sit cross-legged on the floor while Dad, Aunty M and Nana settle on the chairs and sofa.

Charles hated politics. He said that they were all corrupt anyway so what was the point in engaging.

He isn't here to comment today though so I get to watch as two politicians debate how much the NHS should pay for expensive treatments that prolong rather than save a life.

It all gets a bit heated and whether they mean to or not, the politicians are arguing along the lines of Kantianism and utilitarianism, causing some dark crevice of my brain to wake up and stretch.

'You applied to university yet, pet?' Nana asks.

There's a nanosecond of silence before . . .

'What's this, Alice?' 'Come again?' 'I thought you'd already been to uni?'

Mum, who apparently has the hearing of a bat, is out of the kitchen in an instant, tea towel in hand.

Nana gives me a look from behind her glasses that can only be described as 'over to you.' I narrow my eyes at her. We'll see who has the last laugh when all the pink wafers mysteriously disappear.

'I've been thinking about it,' I say delicately, talking to no one in particular. 'I can't exactly work at the Lotus Flower forever. And anyway, I don't want to.'

'But what would you study?' Mum asks. Her mouth is hanging open, just a touch.

'Philosophy,' I tell her.

'Again?' Dad sounds so incredulous that I start to wonder that going back to uni is the absurd notion that I suspected it might be.

'Leave her alone,' Nana says. 'There's nothing wrong with wanting a bit more for yourself.'

There's another second of quiet before Aunty M smacks me on the back and declares, 'Good for you, Alice. I say go for it.'

'Aye, if that's what you want to do.' Dad shrugs.

Mum looks unconvinced; she's twisting her tea towel around her hands. 'I just worry,' she says gently. She's sat next to me and is almost whispering. 'I don't want what happened last time . . .' She doesn't finish the sentence.

'I get it.' I tell her, twisting round fully to speak to her. 'I won't lie, the thought makes me feel a bit . . . ill. But I think I have to do it, to prove that I can. Even if it's hard.'

Mum nods slowly. 'Then you have our full support, of course.'

I breathe out a sigh of relief. Today is going very well. Heck, maybe you *can* turn your life around on a Sunday.

'What's the latest with the Welcome Centre, Aunty M?' I ask, keen to move the conversation on and avoid any more drama. For the rest of my life, if that's at all possible.

Aunty M draws herself up gravely, her voice drops low, and she says darkly, 'Not good, pet, not good at all.'

Mum goes back to the kitchen. I take it she's already heard all there is to hear about the Welcome Centre's woes.

'He's wanting to put it up for sale. Dave.' Dave is public enemy number one. He doesn't live in Easington anymore. But if he did, I get the feeling he'd be run out of town. 'He said there's too much that needs repairing.'

'What's wrong with the place?' Dad asks, flicking the TV over to a football match.

I think Dad probably hasn't been down the Welcome for quite some time; we'd have a quicker go talking about what's right with it.

'The roof mainly,' Aunty M says. 'Needed completely replacing last year. The walls are already plenty damp. Boiler's on the brink too.'

'Where will we go without it?' Nana asks.

We all make concerned noises.

'I know,' Aunty M sighs. 'There's so much going on there. Not just for the oldies, there's the fitness class and the food bank of course. They were hoping to put it on an extra day.'

It still feels crazy, at a time where rich people are going into space for fun, that some people can't afford food. I make a mental note to speak to Paul about donating some of the extra food from the restaurant. From what I can tell, there's always a ton of waste.

'Plus there's the Women's Aid group that meets on a Monday night,' she continues.

'Women's Aid?' I ask, my voice faint.

Aunty M nods. I can feel all their eyes on me.

I swallow thickly, not at all sure what I'm meant to do with this information. It feels significant though, massive even. Suddenly, me going back to uni feels small fry.

'What's going to happen next?' I ask when I can't take the silence anymore.

We wait while Aunty M has a drink. 'We've got a bit of time. The council have marked it as an asset of community value, so he can't sell it right away. We're going to try and raise the funds to buy it. They've got me liaising with all the charity groups. Every day they're calling, panicking about what's going on. All because bloody Dave wants his fifty grand.'

'Fifty grand?' I ask. 'It doesn't seem like a lot.' Not for a full-on building, albeit a crumbling one at that. But then house prices are way cheaper here in Easington.

'Aye, that's what he wants for it. Greedy bastard.'

I nod. The whole thing just seems ridiculously unfair. People from Easington already have so much to contend with, they deserve to keep their decrepit charity slash community venue.

The sense of injustice worms its way deeper under my skin.

It's just wrong.

I look around at my family, deciding there and then that if I'm here, if I'm getting another shot at this, I'm doing it right. I'm going to uni and getting a philosophy degree. And the Welcome Centre cannot be allowed to close.

Chapter Fifteen

Luke: Do not love Annie

That's it. The extent of his correspondence. Still, I deduce that Annie must be another Tinder match.

Me: Oh no! What happened?
Luke: Nothing. We went for a walk. No 'flutters'
Me: One walk? That's not enough time
Luke: Trust me, I realized quickly
Me: How quick is quick?
Luke: Pardon?
Me: You said you realized quickly
Luke: The whole thing lasted half an hour
Me: 30 minutes! No way is that long enough! Sometimes you don't think someone is going to be your soulmate and then you kiss and realize that they are. Friends to lovers. It's a whole trope. You need to put more effort in

I hope Luke really is all right.

Luke: Who says we didn't kiss?

I'm now distinctly flustered.

Me: You said it lasted half an hour

Luke: More than enough time for a kiss. It's over,
King, move on

Is it weird that I quite like being called King? Maybe.

Me: Well, we're a hopeless pair

Luke: The situation is unfolding exactly as per my
expectations

Me: Wow, so helpful. Honestly, has anyone ever told you
your personality is SO warm

Luke: I'm wounded. I thought we were friends now

Me: I think we're still hovering between friends
and frenemies

Me: Do you know what a frenemy is?

Luke: I can work it out

Me: Always a delight, Luke. Have a good day

Luke: Thank you

Me: You're supposed to say 'you too'

Luke: You too

Me: I give up

Luke doesn't reply. Frenemies indeed.

The motivation which had seen me pledge to protect the Welcome
Centre propels me through a university application.

In the end, I apply to Durham, Newcastle and Northumberland
universities because I want to stay local. Durham would be easiest
because I could live at home and keep working at the Lotus (cue full
body shudder). But I'm casting a wide loop. I'll have to resit my first
year and the thought of all that debt only occasionally sends shivers of
panic down my spine. It'll be worth it, I tell myself, deep in a Reddit

article about the earning power of graduates. Me and my student loans can live a long and happy life together.

Driven less by motivation and more by impending mountains of debt, I make the seminal decision to stop highlighting my hair, thinking that I should make cutbacks where I can. In what's possibly a brave, possibly a foolish move I ventured back to Stephanie to have it stripped back to its natural colour, emerging once more with ringlets. Stephanie favours a tong, and that's all there is to it. At least I declined to have it cut again because I think, no, I hope, that some of my choppy layers are looking a bit less choppy. My actual hair is approximately two shades darker than the colour I've been dyeing it for the last couple of decades.

Me and my new do are at work in the Lotus Flower tonight. My last of the week. As ever, Paul is on hand at the end of the shift to dole out some motivational cheer.

'You've been about as much use as a chocolate fireguard tonight,' he declares.

'I just objected to that old man telling me to smile. If I want to smile, I'll smile,' I reply.

'Preach,' Andy and Joanie call at the same time as Paul stalks off.

I check my phone. Luke has sent me that gif of Leonardo DiCaprio chucking money off the side of a boat in *The Wolf of Wall Street*.

'Urgh. He's so infuriating.'

Joanie peers over at my phone and snorts. 'You need to get on another date. It's been two weeks since the exercise freak.'

'I know. I do,' I say with absolutely no enthusiasm.

'At least you eat a bit more like a normal person now,' she tells me. I'd say I'm still struggling a little with that one, but I'll take a compliment wherever I can find it.

'How about this Luke dude? What's he look like?' Joanie asks.

'He's okay, I suppose.' An image of Luke looking severe floats into my head. 'It's hard not to see him like he was back at school. He had this long leather jacket.' I think about Luke's fitted jeans and lumber-jack jacket. 'I suppose, objectively, he's handsome.'

'He's fit? Go out with him, then!'

I wrinkle my nose. 'It's not like that. Luke's attractive in the way that you might appreciate the architecture of a good building. Like the Shard. Beautiful, but soulless.'

Joanie rolls her eyes.

'He's far too serious for me. The exact opposite of what I go for. No, I need someone romantic, like Charles was at the start. Yes, that's it. Like Charles, just *not* Charles.'

'Charles without the twat.'

'Yes,' I reply weakly.

'I reckon you're writing off this Luke dude too quickly. It's always the ones you don't expect it to be.'

'Yes, in romance novels. Do we look like we're living in a romance novel?' Together, we gaze around at the peeling walls of the restaurant, listen to the rain outside battering against the windows.

'No, we don't,' Joanie agrees.

'Exactly. Anyway, Luke and me aren't suited at all. He's successful.' I hold my hands up as Joanie starts to speak. 'I'm not being down on myself. I'm just saying I need someone a bit more towards the train wreck end of things.'

Speaking of train wrecks . . .

'I'll go out with you if you like?' Andy, the singer, leans around Joanie.

'Pardon?' I ask.

'This is a private conversation, Andy.' That's Joanie.

'You want to go out with me?' I ask.

'Course. There's no life without love.' He puts a hand over his heart.

'Yes. My thoughts exactly.'

I look afresh at Andy. He's not what I would describe as classically attractive. Not in the same way as Dwaine or Charles anyway. He has a bit of a beer belly and a mildly waxy pallor. Like one of those imitation Elvises that have gone slightly to seed.

But then maybe that's where I've been going wrong. Paying too much attention to looks. Looks fade, don't they?

I look past Joanie.

'Just to be clear, what is your take on cellulite?'

'Couldn't give two hoots! All about the mind, me.' He taps the side of his head, presumably to demonstrate where his brain is stored.

'Alice,' Joanie snaps. 'There has to be some other way.'

'Hey!' Andy protests, standing up and doing a little bow. I'm not entirely sure why. Possibly so we can get a good look at him. Maybe if you were being generous you could describe him as rugged. But then he must be about ten years older than me. He's ageing well, really. 'I know how to show a girl a good time.' He takes a big swig of his pint of Stella. 'Scout's honour.' He holds up three fingers.

'He might be a better fit than Dwaine,' I tell Joanie. 'Andy and I have more shared interests.' I talk almost to myself. 'I'm interested in philosophy. It's not far off politics. They're in the same faculty at some places. I mean, what have I got to lose?'

'All semblance of self-respect?' Joanie doesn't miss a beat.

'You know I'm right here,' Andy says, straightening the Karl Marx T-shirt which he is rarely without. It might be nice, going out with someone who actually cares about the rights and wrongs of the world.

'What do you say then, lass? Shall we give it a go?'

I think for a second. It's looking increasingly likely that it's going to be up to me to fall in love. Luke couldn't even fall for Lucy with the impressive ... eyes. Really, he's left me no choice.

'Yes. Why not? It's a date.'

I spend some time social media stalking Andy ahead of our date, which is set for the coming Thursday. It's the first week of December now and Easington is colder than ever, but becoming more

Christmassy with each passing day. The Lotus Flower is decked out with a bright pink tree — an assault on all the senses, while Mum and Dad have resurrected their twenty-year-old fake tree. It has, at best, two thirds of the branches it's meant to have.

By the flickering lights of the tree, I check out Andy's socials. His Instagram is a mishmash of flattering selfies, clips of him singing and angry quotes about the ruling classes. Surely I've got something of a shot with someone who posts 'All history is the history of class struggles'?

I can't see Andy not speaking to me like Charles did just because I tried to chew an oyster at his twenty-fifth birthday meal and then apparently ruined the whole thing.

Perhaps class is a bigger issue than I'd ever considered. Like in *Lady and the Tramp*. Because if Tramp had fallen in love with someone from his own social circle, then maybe he wouldn't have had to share that bit of spaghetti like he did when he was clearly the malnourished one. And everyone knows there was room on that chunk of wood for Leonardo DiCaprio. No working-class girl would have shoved him off into the Atlantic Ocean.

Maybe there's a power imbalance when you're with someone so much better off than you. I was drawn to the security Charles offered. Financially, I mean. He bought me all sorts, let me live in his flat, kept me in a job. He even told me what I could and couldn't afford. I think that because he was doing so much for me, I felt like I had to make myself fit into his life. I'd told Joanie that my accent faded, but that was my doing, wasn't it? I didn't want to sound like I was from the Deep North.

At least Andy has his finger on the socialist political pulse. And if he is all about the brain, I decide that it's time to get mine back in working order.

I get dressed in my ever more compact bedroom. As a minimum I need a T-shirt, jumper, hoodie and coat before I even consider leaving the house. Layered up, I set off towards Easington library.

Just across the road from the Welcome Centre, the 1970s building has an ugly pebble-dashed facade and narrow prison-like windows. It's small. I wonder how sizeable their collection of left-wing literature might be.

Obviously, I could research on my phone. But it seems wrong somehow to use an iPhone to brush up on socialism. Aren't Apple one of those companies that dodge their tax?

'Hello,' I greet the motherly looking librarian. 'I'm looking for some information on the working classes.'

She smiles and starts tapping away on the old desktop computer behind her desk, hitting each key with quite a bit of force. We watch as the screen slowly fills.

'Maybe some history or politics-type books?' she asks.

'Yes please, exactly that sort of thing.'

'Right you are, well history is down there. Politics at the end of the row.' She points down a corridor of books.

I thank her and wander down, breathing in the library smell. Granted there's a fair amount of damp too, but books always smell good, don't they?

The general history section seems to follow a loose chronological order. There's a couple of rows of books on the Romans and then we skip several hundred years to the Tudors. And then it's straight to the world wars. All generic tomes.

I try the local section, which is filled with books and pamphlets about the history of mining. The pit disaster of 1951 dominates. I learnt about it in school, how eighty-one miners died after an explosion. I remember Nana telling me once that almost everyone knew someone who'd been killed. I gather up some of the pamphlets on that, feeling a bit despondent at the fact that the people of Easington have had more than their fair share of troubles.

The politics section is a bit more promising. I pull out a handful of angry red books, all with titles like, *A History of the Socialist*

Movement in England, The Luddites and Workers' Rights and *The Revolution Cometh* and sit down at one of the few desks, grappling with an introduction which begins, 'When the workers rise up'. I take note of the 'when', not 'if'.

Do I agree that 'the prospect of a utopian socialist ideal is fundamentally flawed' and that 'violence is the only way through which the means of production can be controlled by the worker'? I'm not sure, but I have to say I'm enjoying doing some proper reading and there's a massive crossover between this and philosophy. Karl Marx literally wrote about the philosophy of poverty, and lots of philosophers argue that global poverty is an ethical issue. Maybe Andy and I really are going to get along. I'm deep into the story of the Tolpuddle Martyrs when my stomach growls (it does that now) and I realize how much time has passed.

I take the books to the counter, filling out a form so that I can get a library card and check them out.

'Alice, pet,' someone wheezes from behind me.

I swivel round. 'Mr Hall.' I smile, 'How are you?'

Mr Hall is linking arms with his daughter Hannah, who also smiles.

'Not bad, thanks to this one.' He taps Hannah's arm. 'Just checking out another jigsaw. We like to do them on a night, don't we, Hans?'

'Absolutely.' Hannah shuffles her and Mr Hall to the counter, checking out their 5,000 piece jigsaw.

'I haven't seen you on the bus in weeks,' Mr Hall gasps and I feel a bit guilty. My ex-headteacher is likely my fifth-best friend now. I make a mental note to text that to Luke later, just to wind him up.

'No, I haven't been back to Durham for a while Maybe I'll go soon.'

'All done, Dad,' Hannah says.

My books too, are all checked out. The bright red cover for *The Revolution Cometh* tops a small pile.

If Hannah and Mr Hall think it's a bit weird that I'm clearing the place of its Marxist literature, they don't say anything.

We all head to the doors. 'Are you doing anything nice this afternoon?' I ask.

'We're just popping to the Welcome, aren't we, Dad?' Hannah says. Mr Hall nods, wiping his mouth with a tissue. Over the road, there are people milling around outside the centre. 'I need to clear away the food bank tables.'

'Do you work there?' I ask.

Hannah shakes her head. 'No, I just volunteer. Dad goes so often it makes sense that I help out. Vinnie, the chef, is the only paid member of staff. And even he works part-time.' She turns to Mr Hall who she's back to linking arms with. 'We'll get you a nice cup of tea when we're there,' she tells him.

It could be the vow I've made to be more helpful, or the fact that I've just spent the morning getting increasingly deep into the history of class strife, but I offer to help Hannah.

'That would be lovely, thanks.'

We make our way across the road, slowly, because Mr Hall can't move particularly fast, arriving at the Welcome to see a handful of people boxing up bits and bobs from the fold-out tables which are all around the edge of the room.

Hannah leads Mr Hall to a chair. He sits and takes a few deep breaths through his nose.

'All right Hannah, love,' a middle-aged man calls from one of the tables. 'We'll be out of your way in a sec. Not much packing up to do, the place was cleared again this morning.'

Hannah rubs her hands together against the cold.

'I'll go make us a tea, shall I?' I ask her.

'There'll be a hidden packet of biscuits in the top cupboard too.' She smiles. Hannah, I feel, is one good deed away from being canonized.

There's no chef Vinnie in the kitchen today, and I can only find the big teapot, so I hunt down the teabags in a cupboard and chuck a handful in before using the hot water dispenser to fill it up. I find the biscuits too and stand at the little hatch looking out to the main area. Tables are being folded away and Hannah is peering in a strategically placed bucket, looking between it and the ceiling where water is dripping through. Mr Hall appears to have fallen asleep.

I stir the teapot with a long spoon, looking around the place. There's a noticeboard, on the wall opposite, directly in my line of vision. I've never noticed it before, and it's too far away to make everything out clearly. But one poster catches my eye.

There's a red fist, shaped into a heart, and underneath the words 'love shouldn't hurt' look like they've been spray painted on. I don't know why, but I can't take my eyes off the poster. I just stir the tea and stare at it.

I shake my head.

Look away.

Except the poster draws my gaze again. I'm a compass and the poster is due North.

Hannah comes over to pour herself some tea and realizes what I'm looking at.

'There's a support group on Monday evenings,' she says. 'Women's Aid run it.'

I nod, still a little dazed even though Aunty M had told me all of this a couple of Sundays ago. 'We need to make sure that they don't shut this place down,' I say, my voice surprisingly steady.

Hannah nods. 'I agree. It's too important to the community.' She moves away, cradling a cup of hot tea.

I'm still looking at the poster. I mean, it's obvious isn't it, of course love shouldn't hurt. Not the break-up bit, that's always going to be hard. But being *in* love, that shouldn't hurt, should it?

And if it does hurt, is it really love at all?

PART THREE

ANDY

'Love shouldn't tell you what to believe.'

Chapter Sixteen

It turns out that when you're already feeling a bit off, immersing yourself in all the shitty things that have happened to the working classes is not a particularly bright idea. I slam a book on the Luddites closed, stamping down an urge to take a hammer to my iPhone.

There's one thing that is guaranteed to cheer me up a bit though.

> **Me:** Guess who has a date tonight?
>
> **Luke:** You I presume
>
> **Me:** Again? Couldn't you have played along even for a second?
>
> **Luke:** OK. Ooh, who could it possibly be?
>
> **Me:** Too late. Hey, did you know the Tolpuddle Martyrs were transported just for setting up a trade union? And don't even get me started on what happened to the Luddites
>
> **Luke:** You're anti progress. What a shocker. Are you going out with a Luddite?
>
> **Me:** You're much wittier over text

I dodge the question. In reality, it's very feasible that Andy would identify as someone who smashes up rich people's machines.

> **Luke:** Thank you

Me: Wasn't a compliment

Luke: Thank you. So, who's the working-class hero?

Me: Andy, we work together. We're off to The Buccaneer

Luke: The Buccaneer?

Me: Yeah, why?

Luke: No reason. Enjoy. I have a date now, too

Me: You do? Another Tinder hook-up?

I'm suddenly very interested in Luke's date.

Luke: Nope

Annoying man.

Me: Well, let's hope this one lasts longer than half an hour.
     Both of us on dates, I am so winning that bet

Luke: It's coffee, not a marriage proposal

Me: Yet. It's not a marriage proposal yet

Luke: OK. Bye

Me: You don't say bye over text. At most, you send that
     waving emoji

Luke: *A single waving emoji*

I spend the rest of the day feeling irritated at Luke and pissed off on behalf of the proletariat.

I get ready for my date with Andy, not entirely sure if it's that I'm genuinely interested in working-class history, or if I'm trying to prove a point to Luke about the randomness of love, but I dedicate more time and effort than a sane person would to this. In a nod to the Russian peasantry who simply did not have access to lip gloss, I lay off mine. I still take time to brush my teeth with Colgate, not baking soda, because in some instances capitalism really did come through for us.

The Buccaneer is a working men's club. So I need an outfit suitable for that. Something which looks nice and yet also conveys my commitment to class warfare all rolled into one.

In the end, I plump for skinny jeans, ankle boots and the floaty rainbow halterneck top that Aunty Moira got me for last Christmas. It's so synthetic that I'll go up like Guy Fawkes if I'm even in the vicinity of a naked flame, but all in all I don't think I look too bad. Not quite the self-love that Joanie has been encouraging me towards, but I actually manage to look in the mirror and think I look . . . not bad. Which is a start. I add a little black beret-type hat that I think I wore for fancy dress once, hoping to channel French Revolution vibes.

On a whim, I order myself a Che Guevara flag for my bedroom. I don't use Amazon because big business is scum of the earth and instead find a little ethical company that allows me to pay cash but charges twice as much as everyone else. Hopefully, I'll notice the difference in the quality of flag.

By 7 p.m. I am raring to go.

'You look fancy, pet,' Dad says from his chair as I pull my big coat on in the front room.

'Thanks, Dad,' I smile at him.

Mum is sat perched as far on the edge of the sofa as possible without actually falling off.

'And you'll be okay?' she asks.

I zip up my coat and try to reassure her. 'We're going somewhere really busy and I have the van. I'll leave if I want to.'

'Okay, if you're sure.'

I smile, straightening my beret.

'I'm sure. I'll see you both later.'

'Bye, pet,' they call as I head out to the van, making a mental note to speak to Dad about the headlights which don't seem to particularly illuminate my path as I navigate towards the edge of the village and The Buccaneer.

I pull the van up on the street opposite, using both hands to haul the handbrake into place.

I look across the road.

It's not what you'd call romantic, The Buccaneer. Flat-roofed, with a faded picture of a pirate and concrete steps. I see that there's been a great deal of pebble dashing, Easington's foremost design choice. And the small windows have bars across them, never a particularly welcoming sign.

Reminding myself not to be a judgemental cow, I set back my shoulders and push through the blue double doors.

Inside, it seems unnecessarily bright. I'm not sure where I'm meant to be meeting Andy. There are several rooms off a main foyer, and I start to peer into each one.

In the one labelled 'Smoking Lounge', there's a pool table. Several pints rest on the edge. But no Andy. In the 'Lounge' there's a lively game of darts. I immediately duck back out, not wanting to hang about drunk men with sharp pointy things.

Finally, I spot him in the 'Saloon'. He's not alone. He's sat at a table with five other men, each one slightly more gone to seed than the last. It's like looking at a montage of Andy's future.

There's a faded carpet and the walls are covered in textured wallpaper. Christmas streamers are Blu Tacked across the walls and there's an LED light-up tree in the corner. The pine bar takes pride of place in the middle of the room, an assortment of tables gathered around it. Andy is sat at the one closest to the fire exit. Beer mats and copper plates decorate the wall above the bar.

I'm considering whether to stay or go home when Andy spots me hovering in the doorway.

'Alice!' he calls. 'Come in!'

I rush over before I can chicken out.

'Everyone, say hello to Alice.'

There's a grumble of hellos.

'I'll just go get a drink.' I look towards the bar behind me.

'Sit down,' Andy smiles. 'I'll go for you.'

The others shuffle along the bench, making room for me.

I'd hoped that they might leave me and Andy in peace, but one of them slaps me on the back and loudly declares, 'Our Andy always gets the lookers. Handsome twat!'

'What can I get you to drink?' Andy asks standing up, an oddly formal note to his voice.

'Er . . .' I peer over at the bar, remembering a time when Charles had made us leave somewhere because they didn't have samphire gin, and laugh. 'I don't mind, surprise me. I'm driving though.'

Andy goes to the bar, leaving me with his friends.

'What are you reading?' I bravely embark upon conversation with a man whose face is so deeply wrinkled that it appears to be melting right off his skull.

'Sartre,' he replies.

I think he's joking until I see that he is, in fact, reading Jean-Paul Sartre's *The Age of Reason*.

My eyebrows shoot up of their own accord. Good on melty-face man.

'So, um, how do you find it?' I ask tentatively.

He licks his finger and turns down the corner of the page.

'Freedom,' he intones, 'is everything. Freedom from the state, from the market, from the past. It's all about freedom. Sartre got that.'

I think for a moment. 'But it's a lot of responsibility, isn't it? The fact that we're all free to make these decisions about our life? What if we mess it all up?'

Melty-face man looks at me from over the top of his battered copy. It's hard to tell through the deep lines, but I think his features have arranged into mild appreciation.

'Then Sartre would say you can't blame anyone else, lass. That's what.'

'Here you go!' Andy returns, carrying two pints. 'You can have one. And I got you these, too.' He drops a bag of pork scratchings next to the drink. I open the packet and peer inside. My stomach rolls, not sure that my efforts to be less controlled around food extend to pig hair.

'Have you seen the news?' melty-face man asks, putting down his book.

'Aye. The bastards!'

Everyone murmurs their assent.

'What news?' I ask, taking my first and only sip of my pint of Carling. Because I don't want to be rude, but I struggle to drive the van stone cold sober. I'd never make it home alive if I had a pint too.

'Unemployment at a record high. The bastards.'

I think it's the government that are the bastards.

'Privatising the NHS too,' someone else calls.

'I know what you mean,' I add enthusiastically. 'I needed my tonsils out when I was twenty-two. The NHS didn't have capacity, so they outsourced me to some private place. It was very nice, but it shouldn't be like that, should it?'

My tonsils story prompts a thirty-minute discussion as to the pitfalls of privatisation. Things get a bit heated, despite the fact that we all essentially agree.

'And that is why the Tories are bastards,' melty-face man concludes.

'And Labour,' someone else adds.

'Aye, and Labour.'

I'd ask which political party they do all support, seeing as they've just slated all of the major ones, but I'm actually enjoying myself. Okay, there are more people involved in my first date with Andy than is ideal, but still, watching a load of middle-aged socialists shout about the inherent weaknesses of liberal democracy really is quite good fun.

Andy returns once more from the bar. He's been at least twice during the debate. I realize that if I want the two of us to have a real conversation, I need to get in there before he starts to slur his words.

'So, Andy.' I turn to him. 'How did you start out as a singer?'

It dawns on me that Andy should be at the Lotus Flower tonight. This must be one of the days where he has opted to simply not attend.

'Well, course Dad was a miner, and four generations before him.'

'Course,' I agree. Totally caught up in the socialist fervour.

'But . . .' He points his finger at me. 'I said to myself, you're a good singer,' I aim for what I hope to be a very neutral facial expression, 'so I thought I'd give that a go. And here I am! Do a bit of painting and decorating through the days, like.'

'How exciting. And useful. People always need things painting.'

'Aye, that they do, lass. My heart is in the singing, though.' He sighs and closes his eyes, his lips curving up at the corners.

Right on cue someone taps a mic, making it screech.

Before I can confirm that Andy has, in fact, brought me on a date to watch him sing, he's stumbled past me and is grabbing the mic from the barman.

He taps the foam cover, sending out another ear-piercing screech. 'Testing, testing!'

'Go on, Andy, lad!' a punter calls.

I assume that Andy sounds somewhat better when you're halfway to pissed already. I sip the Coke I'd asked him to get me on one of his trips to the bar.

Andy takes to the little stage, testing the mic. There's a foil garland sellotaped to the wall behind him, sagging down in the middle. It's a solidly ridiculous visual but I can't help laughing along at all the catcalls.

He opens with a roaring edition of 'Uptown Girl'. Which he directs at me. It's quite the feat to attempt to sing, drink a pint and roll a cigarette at the same time.

We then move on to some Billy Bragg. Which is much more palatable as most of the words are spoken. It causes all the old miners to link arms and sway, which I appreciate.

Finally, Andy finishes with the bold choice of Taylor Swift's 'Trouble', which he just sort of shouts at us, pointing his index finger at me as he shakes his hips.

It dawns on me that Andy's vocals are perhaps better appreciated in this sort of setting. Here it has a – potentially unintentional – comedic air. It's only when you're trying to waitress that you start to think about self-perforating your eardrums.

By the end, I'm clapping along with everyone else, genuinely enjoying myself. The man is hilarious! How did I never notice this before?

Having downed several more pints during the course of his act, Andy is now distinctly swaying as he makes his way back to the table. I gather my things.

'You're leaving already?' he slurs.

'Past my bedtime.' I try out a mild flirt. 'I need my beauty sleep.'

'Nah, you're all right as you are, lass.'

We walk through the foyer to the exit.

'Thank you, Andy, I had a nice time.' And it's true. I did. The whole evening was really good fun.

'Me, too. You know, we're going on a rally up Newcastle on Monday. Tag along if you want.'

'What are you protesting?' I ask from under the doorway.

'The council.' He slurs a bit. 'They've upped the parking charges down the hospital. Fifteen quid a day to park there now. It's shocking.'

That does seem really unfair. I pause to consider the offer.

'Okay maybe I'll come along, thank you.' Hopefully, there won't be as much alcohol involved if we meet in the day. Plus, just imagine how annoyed Luke will be.

Andy leans forward an inch and taking no chances I duck out from under him and dart through the car park.

'Bye, Andy,' I call, not waiting for a reply.

Apparently, I don't ever consider kissing on a first date.

Chapter Sixteen

Me: Had such a good date last night. Second date in the
   bag too. Get counting that money, loser
Luke: In the unlikely event that you win, I will simply go to
   the bank and withdraw £500. Or are we paying each
   other in gold coins?
Me: Ha ha. I told you, I'll be paying you in toil
Luke: I never agreed to that
Me: Why not? You look exactly like the sort of person who
   gets off on a master-slave relationship

I realize a nanosecond after I send the text how inappropriate
that sounds.

Me: Not in a sexy way
Also me: Just like platonic bondage
Also me: NOT bondage. Slavery. Platonic slavery
Also me, now seriously regretting waking up this
   morning: Can we forget I said anything?
Luke: I'm enjoying this immensely
Me: I hate you
Luke: I'll live
Me: How was your date?
Luke: Amenable

Me: Do you think you'll see her again?
Luke: Doubtful
Me: Brutal

Luke ignores me.

Me: Soo, any exciting weekend plans?
Luke: I have tea at Mum and Dad's every Friday night.
Apparently, we're having curry tonight. There's some
work to finish up in the lab tomorrow

The thought of Luke in a lab coat sends the tiniest of thrills through
me. Clearly, I've completely lost my faculties.

Me: God, I'd kill for a curry. Dad can't handle any spice. I
made paella this week. The paprika gave him such bad
heartburn Mum had to go to the 24-hour pharmacy at
Tesco for Gaviscon
Luke: Come over if you want
Me: Ha, sorry I wasn't trying to wrangle an invite.
Luke: I know you weren't. But you can still come

I blow a rogue bit of hair off my face, wondering how I end up so
flustered every time I speak to Luke.

Me: It doesn't sound like you want me to come
Luke: I wouldn't have invited you if that were the case, would I?

Okay then, it looks like I'm going to Luke's.

Later that evening, I'm oddly nervous as I stand outside Luke's
parents' house. I've bought wine. Because my job pays nowhere

near a living wage, it's only one step up from the bottle which had declared, 'This is a bottle of red wine'. But at least I haven't turned up empty-handed.

I pick at the cheap price label, watching as it curls under my fingernail.

Luke's parents live in one of the more modern areas a couple of miles outside Easington. It's quite astonishing how quickly you adjust to new surroundings. Charles's Chelsea flat had been straight out of the pages *of Modern Homes* magazine. All shiny surfaces and sharp angles. Only a couple of months later and I'm now mildly in awe of what looks like a three-bed semi with its own garage. Compared to my parents' terrace, it's practically palatial.

I walked here, the arctic evening breeze preferable to dicing with death in Dad's van. The beginnings of hypothermia have begun to set in by the time I ring the bell and hear Luke shout, 'I'll get it!'

He opens the door and a blast of warmth hits me. Luke looks ... softer somehow. He's wearing a cream jumper that looks so warm and snuggly I could bury my face in it.

'You look cosy,' I say

Clearly the part of my brain responsible for rational thought has just frozen right off.

'Hello,' he answers. I shuffle about, partly because I'm self-conscious about the turn of my thoughts just a second ago, partly to restore some feeling to my frostbitten toes.

'Don't leave her standing out there, she'll catch her death!' his dad calls.

I follow Luke inside, pulling off my coat and feeling oddly embarrassed at my own jumper which is decidedly bobbly.

Thankfully, Luke doesn't notice how weird I'm being and just leads me through to the kitchen. It's a few decades more advanced than Mum and Dad's, with cream cabinets and wooden work surfaces. Brightly coloured tiles go all around the wall. Beyond a little breakfast bar is a dining table set for four.

'I brought wine.' I hold out the bottle, the label turned towards me.

'Excellent.' Luke's dad appears, taking the bottle from me and searching for a corkscrew. He may as well not bother; it's screw-top.

'Hope a curry's okay?' His mum is wearing another matching top and necklace combo, this one turquoise. 'It's been so long since Luke brought a girl home.'

'It's not like that, Mum,' Luke says, almost at the same time that I laugh, 'Not at ALL.' She looks between me and Luke as I rush out, 'Curry is great thanks. Fantastic, even.'

I take a few steadying breaths.

'We're so glad you could come,' his mum says. 'I love your jumper.'

It's blatantly obvious that she's just being nice. My jumper is dark blue, and it has big snowflakes stretched out over it. But it's something that I bought myself, quite possibly, a decade ago.

'Thanks, I just thought Christmas jumper, what with it being nearly Christmas.'

Luke's mum nods along gamely.

'Thank you for inviting me, by the way,' I carry on. 'Oh, and thank you so much for smoothing things over with Paul when you came in the restaurant. I'd just started there ... as you could probably tell. I'm not quite as rubbish now.'

'It was mostly Luke who spoke to Paul,' his mum says. 'I don't normally take against people, but that man set my nerves on edge.'

'Yeah, he's awful.' I look around for Luke, surprised that he was the one who stuck up for me to Paul, and realize he's retreated into the furthest corner beyond the dining table. Almost like ... is he embarrassed? I didn't realize he had that in him.

We move through to join him. There's a sideboard filled with DVDs, the surface topped with myriad different candles, all of them giving off a waxy scent.

There are placemats. I've missed placemats.

My stomach rumbles at the aroma coming from the kitchen and Luke's mum brings out platters of food as we take our seats. I'm ping-ponging between excited and overwhelmed in the face of so much food.

We are surrounded by dishes of curry and rice. There's naan bread and poppadoms too. It's almost too much and I've never been great at sharing food. I tend to worry that people will think that I've taken too much.

But then I think about the people at the Welcome Centre, relying on a food bank. Really, it's a privilege not to have to go hungry. I reach past Luke for a poppadom, thinking that I'm going to give this my best shot

Luke spends most of the meal looking as though he's eaten a bee, rather than a curry, but once I get past the weird food thing, I have a great time.

It turns out that Luke's parents are relaxed and, most importantly, fun. Nothing like their son. I ask how they met. (Friend of a friend. Classic.) Oblige them to go into the minutiae of their wedding. (Registry office because she was knocked-up with Luke. Another classic.)

Things seem to have worked out fine though. Luke's dad turns sixty next week and his mum is throwing him a party.

I make some non-committal sounds at their demands that I have to come. Because Luke has got particularly stabby with a bit of chicken.

The curry is great. I'm high on spice (the non-prison variety) and possibly a fair bit of red wine. Luke is teased in a good-natured sort of way, which makes him look like he's constipated, and makes me howl with laughter.

'And then there was the time he tried to dye his hair dark blue, and it came out sort of green!' His dad laughs as he shovels another forkful of rogan josh into his mouth.

'Yes, and the less said about the gel phase the better,' his mum adds, wiping her face with a paper napkin. 'We thought he'd been electrocuted!'

'Ooh,' I add, 'I remember that.' I point a fork at Luke. 'It looked like he was wearing a dead hedgehog as a hat.'

'At least he could use both of his eyes then. The number of times he walked into a doorframe during the fringe era, honestly.' We all laugh. Well, all apart from Luke.

'We couldn't all be Little Miss Popular at school,' he says.

'Luke,' his mum remonstrates gently and I feel a bit bad for getting so caught up in all the Luke-bashing when I'm in his childhood home, eating his parents' food.

'At least you're successful now though,' I add quickly. 'I swear that being popular in school just means you're going to be a crappy adult. What's the point in being a success at sixteen, only to fuck it all up later?' A moment after I've spoken, I realize that my thoughts may not be exactly suitable for a wholesome family meal.

Everyone is looking at me. They all go to say, 'You haven't!' at the same time, which is all sorts of embarrassing.

Luke narrows his eyes.

In a bid to fill the awkward silence, his mum bravely embarks on a three-minute monologue as to the merits of squeezy mango chutney.

'Those jars just get awfully sticky around the rim,' she finishes up.

'Alice and I have something to discuss,' Luke suddenly says. 'We're going to my room.'

'Remember to use a condom. I'm too handsome to be a grandad,' his dad jokes, earning him a punch in the arm from his mum and a scathing look from Luke.

I burst out laughing. Even *I* appreciate that falling for someone who doesn't properly believe in love has bad idea written all over it.

Luke leads me into his bedroom. Like mine, it's still a shrine to his teenage years.

I peer round. Luke has three posters along his wall, each one depicting the human body in various states. Poster one is naked humans and the third is a skeleton. Poster two, the muscle one, really gives me the creeps. It's the hollow eyes.

Other than that, the bedroom is remarkably normal. 'No tank I see,' I say. 'People at school said you were a snake owner. But honestly, this is way nicer than my room. I'm not sure you'd want to be my friend anymore if you saw my place.'

I think about my crowded bedroom that is mostly bed.

'Are you quite done?'

'Yes.'

He goes over to an old-fashioned stereo on a shelving unit in the corner and hits play. Arctic Monkeys fill the room quietly, and I can almost see the stress leave Luke's body. His shoulders relax and he stops scowling quite so much as he sits on the bed.

'The eyes on the skeleton poster are following me.' I walk up and down past the edge of Luke's bed.

His eyes closed as he says, 'You're not the first person to say that.'

'Luke, are you bringing girls back to your room? How scandalous.'

He shrugs, leaning back against the headboard and stretching his legs out along the bed. His legs are freakishly long. 'It was a long time ago. But they freaked out Sarah Smithins, if you must know.'

'Nooo, not Sarah. She was really mean to you, Luke.'

I have a very vivid memory of Sarah trying to glue a nasty sign to the back of Luke's long leather coat, even though the school's glue sticks were in no way sticky enough to hold up a piece of A4 paper that said 'loser'. I'd told her she was being horrible. Weirdly, Luke had sat at the same table as me for lunch that day. He hadn't said anything, he'd just sat there silently.

'Yes . . . in public she was. We never told anyone.'

My stomach squirms. Not one bit of me likes the thought of Luke being some dirty little secret of a teenage mean-girl.

I finally stop pacing and sit on the edge of the bed. I turn to face where he's still leaning.

'I can't believe you were snogging her. You wouldn't even shake my hand at the awards ceremony.'

Luke doesn't say anything and we just sit for a few minutes while the music plays quietly. I have this gnawing sense that there might be something more to Luke not believing in love than he's willing to admit.

'So, what did you want to discuss?' I ask finally.

'Pardon?'

'You said downstairs that we had something to discuss. To your parents.'

A deep sigh.

'I did, didn't I? I just wanted to make it stop.'

'Make what stop?'

'The whole thing.'

Another hand.

I mentally run through the evening. His mum and dad poking fun like that. Everyone laughing about teenage Luke. Everyone except Luke.

I'm feel like a magpie, picking up titbits of information about Luke as if they're nuggets of gold. Except nothing I learn makes me feel good. It's not like Luke and I were particularly friends at school. But we knew each other as well as two people who go to the same school and grew up in the same small town could. We were both always top of the class. Him in maths and the science subjects, me in the arts.

'I'm, um, sorry if school was ... was all a bit rubbish.'

I'm not sure where my apology comes from.

He waves it away. 'You were never unkind to me.'

'No, but I could have done more. Called them out more than I did. You know, first they came for the goths and I did not speak out—'

Luke tilts his head.

'Are you comparing my teenage experience to genocide?'

'Of course not. That would be ridiculous.' I pause to gather my thoughts, weirdly determined to make Luke feel better. 'Like I said downstairs, at least you're a success now.'

I shuffle back to sit next to Luke against the headboard. We only just fit. I can feel his warm legs inches away from mine.

'Why did you leave university?' he asks.

And 'tis the season for sharing apparently, because I answer as honestly as I ever have. 'I never felt clever enough to be there. I'd thought it was going to be this big amazing adventure but it just wasn't. God, some people could hardly understand my accent. And then I nearly failed and thought I'd have to come home. That's ... why I ended up working for Charles for so long. It felt like being an admin assistant was something I could do. I was so grateful to him for making me feel useful. Like I was good at something, you know? Even now that I've actually applied to uni, I'm just so scared that I'll get there and discover that my brain is all shrivelled up.'

Luke looks at me dead-on.

'You're far too young to be losing cognitive function. It's much more likely that you're suffering from the Pygmalion effect.'

'Pardon?'

'The Pygmalion effect. Whereby high, or in your case low, expectations impact upon one's level of performance. It could be that you think this for yourself or that someone has made you feel unintelligent. But in layman's terms, you don't believe yourself to be clever, therefore you aren't. Plus, from what you've described, you have imposter syndrome too. It's very common in people from low-income backgrounds.'

I frown, not at all sure if Luke has just paid me a massive compliment or thoroughly insulted me.

'No, I don't think I have that.'

The music plays for a little while.

'So, your date was only passable?' I want to cover up the weird atmosphere.

Luke twists round to look at me, brushing against the side of my arm and giving me goosebumps through my snowflake jumper.

'Pardon?'

'You said over text that the date was only okay.'

He rests his head back again.

'She was nice enough, but can I see myself in irrational levels of love with her? Or her me? I don't think so.'

I nod, understanding a bit more than I did before. 'Any kissing?'

'Yes.'

'What? Again?'

'Kissing is an important biological indicator of attraction.'

'No. You cannot ruin kissing for me. I love kissing.' I laugh nervously at the fact that I'd fled at the first indication that Andy wanted to snog.

'Okay then.'

There's a few more moments before I cave.

'Fine. Tell me what happens when we kiss.'

My cheeks blaze red.

'Not *we* as in me and you.' I flap about. 'We as in humanity, the adult species, people with lips.' I trail off.

Luke gives me a pointed look.

'During a kiss, lip sensitivity causes a chemical reaction in our brain resulting in a natural high. Dopamine and oxytocin in particular. With tongues, testosterone is released for men, increasing one's sex drive . . . would you like me to go on?'

'What, why?'

'You're looking a little flushed.'

'Am I?'

'Yes.'

'I think it's just warm in here.'

Luke frowns. It isn't hot at all. It's just that hearing Luke talk about kissing has made me feel tight. Like my skin is too small for my body.

And I'm really, honestly, not sure what to do about that fact.

Chapter Eighteen

I think I might have a little crush on Luke.

Just a small one though. Insignificant really. And honestly, it's just like me to go for someone like that. Someone who has told me on several occasions that he doesn't believe in love. Someone who has bet literal cash on the fact that love isn't a real thing.

I'm determined to ignore it.

I'm on my phone, scrolling through Luke's incredibly sparse Instagram, when a message from Joanie appears.

> **Joanie:** Can you come over? I need someone to watch
> Tyler. Mum's sciatica is playing up

I am in no way in possession of the skills required to spend an evening in charge of Tyler. I've seen Tyler run up the front of a slide in the soft play, his little arms pumping while he let out a war cry – he's way stronger and more determined than me.

> **Me:** Can't I just do your shift for you? You can
> have the money

It's always dead on a Sunday and working for free seems preferable, though neither is particularly appetising. However, Joanie makes up fifty per cent of my friends now so I can't really let her down.

Joanie: Already checked. I get paid more than you and
Paul says he's not paying you the extra because you're
a bit rubbish

Fucking Paul.

Me: I'm on my way. Text your address

Joanie lives in a social housing flat. A small two-bed affair in a low-rise block built out of red brick. It's the sort of place that would go for half a million quid in London. Here, it just looks run-down and a bit sad. There's an empty bike rack outside and the adjacent wall has been sprayed with some graffiti. I'm not sure who Mikey Knaves is, but apparently, he's riddled with STDs.

'Thank God, come in.' She opens the door and I follow her through the narrow corridor towards the lounge. We pass a small kitchen on one side, and on the other there's three doors which I guess must be bedrooms and a bathroom. I follow Joanie to the final room at the end of the corridor. The lounge has a dark red carpet and red-and-cream stripy wallpaper.

'Bath is at six-thirty, then a snack,' Joanie starts to rattle off. 'He can have a glass of milk with his snack, but he has to brush his teeth *after* he has them. Then it's story at seven and lights out at seven thirty sharp. All okay?'

'Bath, snack, teeth, story, bed. But Joanie, why are there so many cakes?'

Every available surface is covered in cakes, biscuits and brownies all in various stages of decoration. There's a white unicorn cake, propped on a shelf with *Ella is 2!* on it. And hundreds of cupcakes all with swirling coloured icing.

'Oh, them. I'm the Cake Fairy, aren't I?' She's shrugging on her coat.

'The Cake Fairy?'

'On Facebook. For extra money. I make cakes and shit. Here.'

She hands me a business card from out of her pocket. *The Cake Fairy* it declares. *Make all your sweet dreams come true!* Then there's a sort of pink Tinkerbell waving a magic wand.

Joanie fiddles with her nose ring. Her look definitely does not tend towards the pink and fluffy.

'I wanted to be a chef, see, before I got knocked up. Here.' She hands me a cupcake. 'This one's a spare. Help yourself. Anyway, got to dash. Good luck. Bye, Tyler. Love you. Be good.'

'But—'

And she's gone.

I'm still hovering awkwardly in the lounge, cupcake in hand. There's a mini Christmas tree on the windowsill, Tyler's Advent calendar propped next to it. Tyler, lying on his stomach in front of the TV, turns to give me an appraising look.

'Hello Tyler.' I venture.

'Hello.'

He turns back to the TV, resting his hands on his chin.

'Er, what are you watching?'

'Bing.'

'Can I watch too?'

He nods, without breaking eye contact with the screen.

I sit down cross-legged next to him.

Ten minutes in and I've developed a strong dislike towards Bing, the moany oversized rabbit. In the episode we've just watched, he killed a butterfly with his big giant paws.

Tyler has barely moved a muscle. Kid seems riveted.

Another episode starts up.

'Does your mum normally let you watch cartoons for this long? Only I thought she said bath at six, or was that the snack?'

'Cartoons with snack.'

'Okay, snack time then.' I haul myself up from the floor, one leg dead. 'What can I get you?' I do a little bow that goes unacknowledged.

'Hollandaise eggs, please.'

'Excuse me?'

'Hollandaise eggs.'

He says it like Holland days.

'Er, I don't think I know how to make that. Anything else?'

'Frittata?'

'Or that. Something less egg-y?'

Tyler, clearly realising that he is dealing with an imbecile, asks for a toast house.

'One toast house coming right up.'

'With milk.'

'No problem.'

I retreat down the hallway to the kitchen, passing the prolific bakes of Joanie en route. She probably makes amazing toast houses.

Finding myself a fraction of workspace in the kitchen, I set to work. Twenty minutes later I emerge flustered but carrying a 3-D structurally sound toast house. Complete with chimney, garage and garden shed. I present it with a flourish to Tyler, who takes the plate without looking up, 'Thanks.' He proceeds to make a gallant effort at eating the eight slices I've used in the construction process.

Come 8 p.m., I don't think, I *know* we're behind schedule. Except, I'm not sure exactly how to get Tyler to bed.

After the toast house I'd suggested we head to his bedroom for stories, to which he'd replied, 'No, thank you,' while passing back his plate. Now we're stuck. It's wrong to manhandle three-year-olds, isn't it?

Tyler sways where he's sat three inches from the TV.

We've been watching YouTube videos of kids unboxing toys for the past hour.

He sways again and I shuffle to the edge of the couch, tracking his movements like a lion watching a pack of gazelles.

His eyes shut, before snapping open again.

But then he lays down.

I can taste victory.

I turn down the TV, watching his breathing turn deep and slow.

Scooping him up, I carry him to bed, still in his jeans. The whole affair is as far from Joanie's instructions as it's possible to be.

Tyler's bedroom, I note, is the only room in the flat that Joanie appears to have decorated herself. With dinosaur wall stickers and a diplodocus nightlight.

My charge finally in bed, I collapse on Joanie's couch and flick through the TV channels, wondering how she does this every day, looking after Tyler while working two jobs. This evening, I've struggled to do just one of those things.

I pick at the cupcake Joanie left me. It's delicious. Like sweet, but not too sweet, air.

I've just finished it as the front door bangs shut.

I sit up on the edge of the couch, giving the impression that I've been as alert as a guard dog all night. 'Was everything okay here? Did Tyler go down all right?'

'Yeah, totally fine, just like you said,' I lie.

'Great. Routine is everything at his age.'

I gulp as she flops down next to me on the couch. She looks exhausted.

'Cupcake was amazing by the way. You should go on *Bake Off.*'

'I thought about applying once. But there's this animalistic connection between me and Paul Hollywood. It's those eyes. Not sure it'd be fair on the other contestants. Plus how do you concentrate on your kneading when you're horny as fuck?'

'Right.' I draw the word out, wishing I hadn't heard any of this.

'I want to work in a café.'

'Well, if you cook as well as you bake, you'd be amazing.'

'Thanks. I was doing a course when I got pregnant with Tyler.'

'What's stopping you now?'

'Money.' She pauses for a minute. 'Any chance you're one of those secret millionaires and now you're about to make all my dreams come true? Because I'll sign whatever you want me to. In fact, lead me to thy dotted line, maestro.'

'Joanie, I have Velcro shoes. Velcro.'

'Oh yeah, right,' she sighs.

'Work okay?' I ask.

A shadow passes over Joanie's face. 'Fucking Paul.'

'You shouldn't let him make you do everything all the time.'

'It wasn't that.' She sighs again.

'What happened?'

'Someone vomited all over the toilets.'

'Wait, what?'

'Paul offered extra money if one of us would clean it up.'

'Go back a second.'

'You know how much he offered? Five pounds. Five actual pounds. To clean up human vomit.' She starts to massage her temples.

'I still don't understand why there was sick in the toilets.' I'm more than a little confused.

'Please. It's not the first time. Normally someone off their fucking face.'

'It's a Sunday night.'

'Doesn't matter.' She sighs the deep sigh of someone who is bone-tired. 'I just worry,' she carries on, 'that I'll never manage to leave.'

I squeeze her hand. 'You will. I'd buy your cakes. Your cupcake was the bomb.'

'Did you just say "the bomb"?'

'I did say that. I wish I had some money for you. It could be like the Fleabag café, just without the guinea pigs.'

'So just a café then. I'm just stuck because I can only work short hours till Tyler is at school and even then ...' She shrugs. 'It feels impossible.'

Her words remind me of Friday night at Luke's, what he'd said about the importance of self-belief.

'You know, Luke said that thinking you can do something is half the battle. He was talking about me going to uni but the same applies to you,' I say.

Joanie raises one pencilled-on eyebrow at me. 'What like manifesting? Because that's bullshit, Alice. No one thinks, "I know, I'd like to become a millionaire" and then miraculously a million quid lands in their bank. Especially not round here.'

I laugh. 'I'm pretty sure Luke would rather volunteer for *Married at First Sight* than admit to the psychic power of manifestation. No, I mean, both of us could do with having a bit more faith in ourselves. I've already decided that I'm going to try and be more useful round here.'

Joanie sighs. 'I'm plenty useful, I have two jobs, Alice. Two.'

'I know, you're too busy to be of any more use. But you could start by thinking that it's not impossible, that one day you'll get to be a chef.'

She pulls her hair out of its ponytail, running her fingers through it. She looks so tired, crumpled. She deserves more than this.

'Maybe,' she says. 'And what about you, any news from uni?'

'Not yet, I think it'll be a little while. And that's if they even invite me for an interview.'

Joanie slaps my thigh harder than is really necessary.

'Proud of you, mate.'

'I might not get in. But I'm done with being a low-key fatalist.'

Joanie laughs. 'Come again?'

'It's basically this argument that philosophers have over whether we have free will over our futures. I always thought there was a degree of fate in it all. But now, I don't know, maybe there have to be elements of free will too. We have to have some agency over our futures otherwise what's the bloody point?' I ask. 'That's why I want to give Andy a fair shot too. Because if I want to have a loving relationship *and* win £500, I need to invest time in it.'

She looks at me, long and assessing. 'You'll be all right, you know? At uni, I mean.'

I grin, feeling a warmth settle over me. 'And you, you'll get there, Joannie. We'll make sure of it.'

Chapter Nineteen

It's with a sense of optimism that I wait by the kerb, ready for my second date with Andy.

In many ways, this date is ticking all the boxes for the newly motivated me. I'm taking ownership of my destiny. Spending time with Andy and doing some good at the same time.

Even Andy uploading a reel of him belting out 'All I Want for Christmas Is You' to Instagram ahead of our date hasn't put me off. I didn't have to work particularly hard to deduce that it was for my benefit. He tagged me in the post.

In an about-turn to end all about-turns, Joanie left a comment on the post saying that she could 'listen to him all day', while Paul had popped up to warn us against 'shagging in the toilets'. Andy had replied to Paul's comment with a row of laughing face emojis.

And yet, here I am, carrying a cardboard 'NO to hospital parking charges' sign that I spent a good chunk of yesterday, and precious funds, creating. And let me tell you, there is nothing like propping yourself on your teenage bed, colouring in some block capitals with a marker pen to make you feel alive.

Mum, clearly fearing that I'm about to be imminently arrested, reminded me not to glue myself to the road before she left for work. Apparently, she'd seen a load of climate protestors do it once.

Andy pulls up in a battered old Ford Fiesta. It's like one of those clown cars, there are so many people crammed inside, waving madly

at me. I wave back, feeling somewhat hyped up on adrenaline. They
have placards, too, balanced on their knees. Melty-face man with a
passion for Sartre has so many swear words on his, that I wonder if
it might serve to turn people against the cause. No one wants the
C bomb dropped on them before 10 a.m. on a Monday. At least I
get to sit in the front.

Andy leans over like he might be about to kiss me, so I duck
down, rummaging around for absolutely nothing in the rucksack
I've brought and plonked at my feet. We're moving again by the
time I right myself.

'I don't think we'll make it all the way up the A19.' Andy smacks
the dashboard of his Fiesta, prompting an ominous rattle. 'We'll
have to get the train from Seaham.' He's wearing his favourite Karl
Marx T-shirt and some heavy-duty boots. The sort favoured by the
Russian mob.

'No problem,' I tell him.

We settle into our carriage on the Seaham train which moves at
approximately 3 mph because the infrastructure round here really
is poor. One of Andy's comrades produces cans of Carling, forcing
the other passengers to get up and leave, throwing nervous glances
at our placards. Clearly I was wrong to imagine that we wouldn't
be drinking during the day.

Things progress further downhill when, perched under the massive Christmas tree by the Lord Nelson monument in Newcastle
centre, the rest of the group starts hurling abuse at unsuspecting
shoppers. No one seems to really mention the car parking charges,
preferring instead vague promises about the governing classes being
'bastards'.

In the cold light of day, militant socialism is rapidly losing
its appeal.

'What have you done for the cause?' Andy shouts at a mum and her young daughter. The mum huddles her daughter close to her and scurries away.

'Tory scum!' another one shouts.

I can't let them keep this up.

'Andy!' I tug at his arm. 'What about the hospital parking charges?'

'Good point, lass,' he says, before shouting out, 'Down with a money-based economy!'

I shuffle away again, disappointed. I'd imagined a sort of protest march. Like those inspirational ones you see in movies. With hundreds or even thousands of people all linking arms, holding candles and sporadically breaking into song before facing off against a line of shielded riot police. Instead, we've met up with two other people, making us a total of seven. One of them has brought a trestle table to display copies of *The Socialist Worker* which no one buys. And we're not marching anywhere.

'Government bastards!' one of them shouts and the others cheer.

'Yes!' a random passer-by calls faintly in solidarity. Theirs is the only voice of assent. Most people eye the group with indifference, or else downright hostility, yelling at us to 'get a job' or, better yet, 'get in the bin'. Basically, whatever the cause might actually be, this protest is damaging to it.

Enthusiasm for my do-gooder protest about the parking charges has all but evaporated by lunchtime. Now I'm mainly just embarrassed to be here.

The others take a breather as flasks are being opened and corned beef sandwiches passed round. Having seen quite enough corned beef at home and not particularly wanting to share a meal with people who heckle toddlers, I decline and slink off.

I plan a quick walk round the block. It's not like I can do any shopping. I've brought £12 with me today and I've already had to spend half of that on a train ticket for both Andy and me.

But there in the distance, I see it.

Pret.

Pret is home and I am a millennial homing pigeon. I feel myself dragged towards it. This is the sort of place I should be avoiding. It's the sort of place Charles loved. He kicked the wardrobe once when our local one temporarily closed for refurbishment.

'You *know* I can't function without my skinny turmeric latte,' he'd complained, hopping about rubbing his foot.

Looking back, it was a bit of a wanker move, but also . . . a rainbow slaw super bowl. What I wouldn't give for a rainbow slaw super bowl. Even if my want does make me a member of the emergent middle classes, I can't help myself; I buy one and eat it down the side of an alley, as though I'm shooting up crack.

I'm unfortunately forced to return to Andy for want of water. I couldn't afford any in Pret.

Disappointingly, our posse has finished their lunch and has begun a chant.

'What do we want?' Andy leads.

'An end to capitalism!'

'When do we want it?'

'Now!'

'Piss off!' someone calls.

It seems almost ridiculous now that I'd considered a second date with Andy. In fact, this isn't really recognisable as a date at all. When I think back, he hadn't actually helped me to have a good time on our first date – he'd been too enthralled with himself. So what am I even doing here?

Oh, yes. Trying to win a bet. Apparently, I will stoop very low for that. Like, low, low. And the hospital charges thing. I look over at Andy, watch a fleck of spit leave his mouth as he shouts, 'Death to the state!'

Somehow, I don't think Andy is the one who will win me the

bet. And he's about as unfortunate an ambassador for socialism as Andrew Tate would be.

'Alice! Come and join us!' he calls over.

'No, thank you! I think I'm going to head off actually,' I shout.

He moves to join me, carrying his placard over his shoulder.

'What's the matter, lass?' he asks, voice hoarse.

'I'm not sure I agree with all this.' I wave a hand around.

Andy blinks, seemingly astonished. Neither of us speak.

'Alice!' It's Luke and his mum. Because obviously I was an absolute dick in a previous life and now I'm being punished for it over and over and over again in this one.

'Are you with these guys?' Luke asks, looking towards the protesters who've now cornered a young man and are questioning him aggressively on his loyalty to the cause. This is the first time I've seen him since my little crush realisation. So of course, I'd be holding a homemade placard.

'They have that young man by the lapels,' Luke says, his face flushing with outrage. Police community support officers are already heading towards the scene. This doesn't look good.

'Knock it off!' Andy shouts, before looping an arm around my shoulders. As quickly as I can, I shrug him off.

Luke's mum rearranges her face into a neutral expression. 'Well, they seem . . . passionate.'

Luke scoffs and I throw him a dirty look.

We stand even further back as the PCSOs move in to reprimand the protestors. Protestors who I'm technically with. What was I thinking? Mum's fears that I might be arrested don't seem so ridiculous anymore. I drop the placard.

'Time to go, Alice.' Andy casts a nervy glance at the police. 'Looks like our right to protest is being violated. And I have a painting job this afternoon.'

'Thank God.'

'Is everything all right, Alice?' Luke's mum asks, gnawing her bottom lip.

'Are these your friends?' Andy asks, sounding surprised.

'I'm Luke.' Luke pulls his shoulders back. 'An old school friend of Alice's. And this is my mum.'

It's probably a stretch to describe me and Luke as friends from school. But I don't say anything as his mum is talking now.

'We're just off to Fenwick's to pick up some bits for the party on Sunday. Luke took the day off specially to come along. I'm making blinis!' she announces, waving a hand at Luke. 'I really hope you can make it, Alice. Remember, it's Mick's 60th. Did Luke text you all the details?' she asks me.

I notice a muscle twitch in Luke's jaw, almost as though he can't bear to talk about it. 'Not yet.'

His mum ploughs on, clearly oblivious. 'Well, no harm. I'll get him to message you later, shall I?'

Andy looks at the placard by my feet and sort of puffs out his chest. 'You didn't tell me about a party, Alice?' he asks in an accusatory tone which seems to put Luke's heckles up.

'Actually, I'd *love* Alice to come along,' Luke goads Andy.

This has gone far enough, we're mere seconds away from one of them weeing in a circle around me.

I snort in a way that hopefully suggests – *men!* – to Luke's mum. But she's busy glancing between the pair of them, a frown creasing her eyebrows.

Her eyes dart between Luke and Andy. 'You can bring your . . . um . . . friend if you like, Alice.'

I've absolutely no intention of bringing Andy, but now is not the time.

'Sounds great. Text me the details, Luke. But you two had better be off,' I say, practically shoving them towards Fenwick's.

'Nice to meet you, mate!' Andy calls after them with a more combative air than is necessary.

I breathe out slowly as he turns to me. I'm about to give him a piece of my mind when he says, 'I don't want you to see that guy.'

What the hell? That odd sensation, like my body is heating up from the inside and my skin is becoming too small, starts up again.

'Pardon?' I ask, gobsmacked.

'That tosser and his mum. Blinis!' Andy makes his voice high like Luke's mum and my irritation skyrockets.

'She's probably never eaten blinis in her life before. But even if she had, it wouldn't matter. She's lovely.'

'Alice . . .' Andy begins in a patronising tone that probably forces all women in a three-mile radius to prickle. 'They are obviously a middle-class enemy in our midst.'

'God, Andy you don't know anything about them! You have no idea what Luke has been through. He might come across like an arse, I'd be the first to admit that, but he's a good person. And his mum . . .'

In truth, my commitment to Andy's quasi-socialist stance was already on its last legs. But him being mean about Luke and his mum is the final straw.

I want to go home. Right now.

The other 'protestors', under the guidance of the PCSOs, busy themselves folding the trestle table and generally pretend not to hear our domestic.

'Nah, lass. You're wrong about them. Totally wrong.'

'I don't think I am.' Oh fuck, I'm struggling to breathe.

'You just don't understand.' Andy punctuates every word. 'I'm looking out for you.'

'Leave it off, lad,' melty-face man tells Andy, tilting his head towards me.

Andy grunts in assent. I, however, am engulfed in dread.

I'm cold again.

Paralysed.

It's like everything has tilted.

It's happening again. A surge of memories seems to be shoving to the front of my brain. Battering every other thought out of the way.

'You wouldn't understand, this band are better.'

'It's important that you learn to fit in with my friends.'

'I can teach you everything you need to know, don't worry.'

I jerk back as each one surfaces before black creeps into the corner of my eyes. I feel someone catch my back as I fall, then the cool pavement underneath me.

I'm not sure how much time passes. My head feels thick and I'm clammy all over. There's a hand under my head and I think for a second it must be Luke. He was here, wasn't he?

'Are you all right?' Andy asks. I open my eyes and see his face above me, the cloudy sky behind him. 'Sorry if things got a bit heated back there.'

Everything is muddled. I thought Luke was here, but I can't see him. Maybe he doesn't care about me at all and now I just have Andy.

He puts his other hand on my forehead and I jolt.

I nod but can't speak. My throat feels hoarse, like I'm the one who has been yelling about the benefits of Marxism all morning.

It takes an age for me to feel steady enough to stand up and then even longer to limp back to the station, flanked on either side by Andy and melty-face man who hover like I'm about to collapse at any second. Which maybe I am.

I feel sick on the train home, not saying anything as the others talk in hushed tones all around me. And when Andy finally drops me off at home, I limp upstairs to bed. The whole time I wonder when things might start to get easier.

Chapter Twenty

There's just no getting away from the fact that the panic attacks I thought were long gone are back with a vengeance. When I was younger, they were almost always linked to exams, tests, that sort of thing. But now they're forcing me to remember things about my time with Charles. Things I think I'd rather forget.

I'd always seen Charles as someone who saved me, gave me a job, somewhere to live ... and maybe he did. But I can't ignore the fact that things were obviously wrong too. Charles controlled everything. Not just my food. But what I watched, listened to, everything. He always made it seem like he was doing me a favour, making a ton of mini decisions for me every day but ultimately, he told me what to think. What to believe. And surely, *surely* love shouldn't do that.

I look at the stack of socialist books in the corner by my bed.

I've let the same thing happen with Andy.

I lose a whole hour on Charles's Instagram. Looking at a picture of him and Ophelia handing out food parcels to the homeless of London (though you've really got to wonder whether they have the means to cook quinoa). I stare hard at the image of them both, hoping that some sort of an answer might suddenly present itself.

Someone made you feel unintelligent.

Luke's words from that night in his room come back to me.

I look again at the picture of Charles and Ophelia, wondering if she still manages to think for herself.

I feel like an idiot.

I text Luke, something about his sureness of himself appealing to my inner turmoil.

> **Me:** Sorry about earlier. I don't know why Andy was being like that
>
> **Me:** And sorry about being sorry. I know I'm not meant to be . . .
>
> **Luke:** There's no need for you to apologize for Andy's actions
>
> **Me:** Okay, thank you. This really sounds like I'm fishing for compliments – I promise I'm not – but as a biologist, could I get your professional opinion on whether I am, in fact, a stupid person?
>
> *Some time, and I imagine a great deal of suffering later,*
>
> **Luke:** As a biologist I cannot give a definitive conclusion. However, as a frenemy, I'd say absolutely not. Also, why are you texting me at 1 a.m.?

Crap.

> **Me:** Sorry, didn't realize the time. I'm just lying in bed wondering about my brain. I thought, Luke is probably up for some brain chat
>
> **Luke:** And you would be right. I do enjoy brain chat
>
> **Me:** Distract me. Tell me a fun fact about brains
>
> **Luke:** ••••
>
> **Luke:** Brains can't feel pain. You can perform surgery on a brain without anaesthetic, because they don't need it
>
> **Me:** That cannot be true
>
> **Luke:** It is. No pain. Only pleasure

I look at the text. It causes my stomach to swoop a little. Something about the word 'pleasure'. Immediately I realize . . . I'm officially crazy.

> **Me:** You learn something new every day

Like the fact that Charles used your insecurities to completely change you as a person, my average yet unhelpful brain contributes.

> **Me:** I'm worn out. I should get to sleep. Thanks
>   though. Night x
> **Luke:** Goodnight, Alice

I look at my phone, feeling like something is not quite finished, though I can't put my finger on what.

> Luke again. **Luke:** You're smart Alice. You've always been
>   smart. Relax.

And there it is. I've sought out Luke, again, to help me deal with something. At least sleep comes easily, my phone clutched to my chest. Hanging on to Luke . . .

Another message wakes me up at 6.30 a.m., dammit.

> **Luke:** Dad's party is at two on Sunday. Just to warn you, it's
>   in the garden and it's December.

Apparently, pleasant Luke is like the luna moth. Only comes out at night.

> **Me:** Okay. Good morning to you too, by the way. Thanks for
>   the invite, but do you even want me to come?

> **Luke:** Yes
> **Me:** Only because your mum said that you should?
> **Me:** Because now I don't know if you're inviting me
> because your mum said so
> **Me:** Or if you're inviting me because as your frenemy, you
> actually want me there

I wait as the little scrolling dots tell me that Luke is composing a reply.

> **Luke:** Are you quite done?
> **Me:** Yes
> **Luke:** I have no objections to you coming
> **Me:** Seriously?
> **Luke:** Fine. I would like you to come
> **Me:** Then I'd love to. Cue string of emojis
> **Luke:** I can absolutely assure you there will be no
> flamingo dancing
> **Me:** Spoilsport
> **Luke:** I presume you've broken up with what's-his-face?

I assume he is referring to Andy.

> **Me:** Not exactly . . .

I haven't even thought about Andy actually.

> **Luke:** Okay, Alice. See you Sunday

Little Daisies, I've discovered, has several themed rooms hidden at the back, where they host birthday parties. Today, we're in the 'medieval' room, celebrating the third birthday of one of Tyler's preschool friends. Said theme is largely ignored. The birthday girl, wearing a pink tutu, is mid meltdown over something to do with her sock. Tyler, sat on her right, is pulling funny faces every time she looks at him, promoting a fresh bout of wailing. People dressed as a knight, Little Red Riding Hood and the Abominable Snowman are busy serving platters of beige food to already feral children.

'Cut it out, Tyler!' Joanie yells over to him. Tyler doesn't in fact, cut it out. But he gets much better at doing it when Joanie isn't watching.

To be completely honest, I've only tagged along because Joanie begged me to come for moral support. And now that I'm here, I kind of get it. None of the other parents have really spoken to her. Or sat with her. They're all about a decade older than her and while I'm trying to grow as a person, I immediately dislike them.

'They don't want to not invite Tyler,' she'd told me when I met her outside. 'Because then they'd feel bad. But they don't actually want me there either, in case teenage pregnancy is catching.'

'So, Andy . . .' I start. That's the price of my coming. That Joanie has to listen to me try to work through whatever happened with Andy. I don't think I'm ready to talk about the Luke thing. Not when it doesn't feel like we're frenemies anymore.

'Look, I know I've said in the past that he repulses me, but you know what, you do you. Maybe he's not that bad. Tyler!' she barks suddenly, catching him with his tongue out again.

'He isn't?' I raise an eyebrow. Suspicious.

'Nope, he's like one of those poisonous spiders. Unpleasant, but necessary for the biodiversity of the planet.' Unpleasant sounds about right, I think, remembering the 'protest' we'd been on. Even if he had been sweet when I fainted, I never quite imagined my soulmate to be quite so shouty.

I look at Joanie a second longer.

'Fine, I just want you to win the bet,' she admits.

'Yeah well, save your breath,' I tell her. 'Andy's not the one. I don't want someone to tell me how I need to be. I'm going to end it with him.'

'Thank God. It was giving me a hernia, pretending to like him.'

An impromptu conga line weaves around us, headed up by Humpty Dumpty. We're encouraged into joining and are forced to continue our conversation while bobbing along behind Tyler who, for the record, is a very enthusiastic conga-er.

We bob and kick and Tyler leaps three feet into the air.

'It does mean I'm further away from winning the bet though,' I call over Joanie's shoulder.

She looks back at me, grabbing tighter onto Tyler's T-shirt as he jumps about.

Another kick.

'So, what are you going to do next?' she asks. 'Another date?'

'Maybe . . .' I trail off. Not sure how keen on the idea I actually am. I still have four months to win the bet, maybe I could just take a bit of a break, regroup in the new year. The truth is, after I've realized all this stuff about Charles and me, I'm not sure I properly trust myself anymore.

'There's that thing people say, the only way to get over one man is to—'

'Stop right there!' I tell her and she smirks.

Tyler breaks away from the conga line, making a beeline for the luminous orange squash that's appeared on the buffet table.

'Slow down, Tyler!' she calls as Tyler chugs like he's necking a pint on a night out. One of the other mums gives Joanie a funny look. Which is rich. I saw her kid launching party rings like mini frisbee missiles less than five minutes ago. Joanie looks worn out again.

'You know,' I tell her, 'I was thinking, if ever you wanted me to watch Tyler so you can like catch up on baking, or just have a rest, I'd be happy to.'

Joanie turns to look at me. 'You'd do that, for me?'

'Course, I love hanging out with Tyler.'

Over Joanie's shoulder I see him stick two breadsticks up his nose and take off at a run.

'That would be amazing.' Joanie beams.

'It's nothing, honestly.'

She smacks me on the back with such force that I take a step forward. 'You're a good friend. I won't take the piss and ask all the time.'

I smile, that sense that I'm doing well at something is old and familiar. But then it's not just that. I want to help Joanie because I like her and I like Tyler, but I don't feel like she'll take more than I can give. She'll not make me feel daft because I can't do something, or push for more. It feels a bit like trust. Or maybe boundaries. Either way, it's a good thing.

There's a text waiting for me as I leave Little Daisies.

> **Andy:** Do you want a dick pic?

How is it possible that my taste in men is getting *worse?*

> **Me:** You know people don't usually ask that before they send them. But just to be clear – NO
> **Andy:** Are you sure?

I get more and more annoyed.

> **Me:** Yes
> **Andy:** All my other girlfriends wanted them

I don't even respond. I just block and delete his number. Because
if there's one thing that might ruin today for me, it's a close up of
Andy's penis.

By the time my shift rolls around that night, I'm all geared up to
dump Andy.

We don't get the chance to talk before customers arrive, mainly
because Andy is two hours late and he doesn't like to be disturbed
once he's 'in the zone', so I've had to wait until we're all sat in our
usual spot on the couches at the end of the night. Joanie is sand-
wiched between Andy and me, and one of the kitchen staff has
served us takeaway tubs of sweet and sour chicken. I really need to
speak to Paul about the plastic waste this place produces.

'You going to speak to Andy tonight?' Joanie whispers, putting
the lid on her half-eaten meal.

'Yeah,' I reply, standing up and stepping round Joanie's legs
towards him. 'Andy, could we . . .'

Andy gestures at me to stop talking, his mouth full of food, and
I wrinkle my nose.

'Actually, I don't think we should see each other anymore,' Andy
says, while I stand there like a tool.

He saws at a bit of sweet and sour chicken with the edge
of a spoon.

'Pardon?'

'You don't like my singing.'

I can't deny that. I'd run to the kitchen every time Andy had
started singing to me.

'Well, er—'

'Plus not one nude.' He gives me a very pointed look.

'Shocking.' Joanie's grip tightens on her fork.

'And then there's the fact that you're openly mingling with the
bourgeoisie,' he finishes, with another spoonful of chicken.

'So, just to be clear, you're breaking up with me?' I'm dumb-founded that what I think might be happening is actually happening.

'Fraid so, lass.'

'Don't lass me.' I'm starting to think that my appraisal of Andy's personality was ridiculously optimistic. Well, it wouldn't be the first time.

'You bloody idiot, Andy,' Joanie barks. 'She's so far out of your league it's ridiculous. She only went out with you because she has crazily low self-esteem.'

I am very grateful that Joanie doesn't announce to all the other staff that I'd partly agreed to go out with Andy to win a bet. They're all watching us like we're a live soap opera as it is. It's also nice too, the stuff she said about leagues.

Andy shrugs.

I feel mildly hysterical. Not at all about the breaking-up part; that's an enormous relief. Just about the fact that it's Andy who is doing the breaking up.

'But, but—'

'Come on now, lass, don't get desperate. We can still be mates.'

'No. No. Did he just use the "we can be friends" line with me?' I ask Joanie, so unbelievably over talking to Andy.

'Afraid so. Least you're rid of him. We'll find you someone else.' Joanie pats my knee.

'Right. Well. Right. I'm going home.'

'Night, Alice,' Andy offers.

Joanie gives me an unexpected hug. 'Don't let the bastards get you down.'

Chapter Twenty-One

Me: What do you think of this one?

I snap another picture of my outfit in the mirrored wardrobe at the end of the bed and send it to Gabby. Totally because it's hard to know what to wear to a BBQ in December and not because I'm bothered about what I should wear in front of Luke.

My phone pings with her reply.

Gabby: Whit-woo. I'd do you

Another message.

Gabby: But pin the front of your hair back. The butcher's layers are distracting

Gabby refers to Stephanie as 'the butcher'.

I look down at my outfit, still unsure. On Gabby's instructions, I've opted for cord trousers and a purple rollneck jumper, going potentially a bit overboard with an eyeliner flick. As far as I'm concerned, I look like I've got dressed in the dark in the Sixties.

Me: I don't know

Immediately, my phone starts ringing in my hand.

'Will you quit it. You look great.' Gabby has always had a loud phone voice. Deafening Charles used to say.

I flop down to sit on the edge of the bed, putting Gabby on speaker and going about pinning my unfortunate layers back off my face.

'And the trousers don't look too tight?' I ask, trying not to panic about the fact that my clothes have definitely got a little snugger.

There's a whirling down Gabby's end of the phone.

'No. If they're digging in, do the hair bobble thing that pregnant people do. You look great.' Her voice gets louder to shout over the whirling.

'What's going on down there?' I ask.

'We're having the floors done, a man with a machine is here. Can you stop that for a second?' she asks him. The noise cuts off. I picture Gabby in her amazing apartment in Sydney, getting the parquet floors sanded on a Sunday night.

'Sorry, darling. As I was saying, you look fantastic. Much healthier. But why do you care so much? It's only a barbecue in Eas-ing-ton isn't it?'

I snigger at Gabby pronouncing all of the letters in Easington.

'Yeah, it's no big deal really.'

She hmms and the line goes quiet for a second. Downstairs, I hear the muffled tones of Aunty Moira talking rapidly to Mum.

'There's a man,' Gabby declares. 'Alice King, you sly thing, is there a man over there?'

'No!' I shout out. 'I mean yes, there is a man, but he's not ... I mean, it isn't about him,' I finish weakly. Both sounding and being very confused about the whole thing.

'But he'll be there?' she asks.

'Yeah, it's his dad's birthday.'

'And he's good to you?' Serious Gabby freaks me right out.

I think of Luke. The stern set of his features when he's being serious. The way he doesn't let me get away with anything, like the bet. But then underneath, he does seem to care, in a way.

'I guess he is. I don't know how to know for sure though.'

I pick absentmindedly at a loose thread on my trousers.

'It makes sense,' Gabby says, 'Give it time.'

Suddenly, I really want to get off the phone. Not to get away from Gabby, just to be on my own for a moment.

'Yeah . . . you know, this must be costing a fortune from Australia. I'll let you get off.'

If Gabby cottons onto my evasive tactics, or the fact that it's a WhatsApp call, she doesn't let on.

'Don't be a stranger,' she singsongs down the phone.

'I won't. Speak soon.'

'And you.'

I cut the call off and then sit still on my bed, staring at the same worn beige patch of carpet.

I don't trust whatever it is I might or might not be feeling for Luke.

It's confusing. Everything swirling round in my head. I wish my brain would take a day off.

'If you want a lift, we're leaving in a minute!' Mum shouts up the stairs.

They're going to meet Nana down the Welcome.

I stand up, calling back, 'I'm coming.'

I try to shake the unsettled feeling as I jog downstairs. Aunty M is mid rant about her soon to be ex-partner Fred. 'The man pegs his teabags out, for God's sake,' she says to Mum as we all pull our coats on.

'You liked that at the start, Mo,' Mum replies in a measured tone. 'You said it showed that he was savvy with money.'

'There's being savvy and then there's being a tight-arse.' Aunty M zips up her coat.

'Are you going to the Welcome too?' I ask her.

She shakes her head. 'Nah, we won't all fit in the van.'

I hadn't thought about that. It's actually probably pretty illegal for three of us to be in there, to be honest.

'I can walk, if you want to go,' I say.

'Don't worry yourself, pet. I'm gonna go have it out with Fred. Once the spark has gone, it's gone,' she adds wisely.

I'm not exactly worried about Aunty M. My whole childhood, I'd never seen her be particularly cut-up about a break-up before. Chances are, she'll have reactivated her Bumble profile quicker than you can say Ben & Jerry's.

'Take care, Mo.' Mum and Dad make for the door as Aunty M gives me a wet kiss on my cheek.

'Have fun,' she says, 'Don't do anything I wouldn't do.'

I don't let on, but I'm not exactly sure that excludes an awful lot.

The van clunks to a stop in front of Luke's parents' house. It's midday, and the sky is looking decidedly murky.

'This is a nice place, don't you think, Mick?' Mum asks, peering through the windscreen from where she's squished between Dad and me in the front of the van.

'Very fancy,' Dad agrees.

I give the door to the van a shove. I almost go sprawling across the pavement a good distraction from the fact that now that I'm here, I feel a bit nervous.

I say a quick bye to Mum and Dad and then I've no option but to walk down the drive and knock on the door. I'm treated to the symphony of Dad maxing out the revs on the van as he does a three-point turn round the bottom of the cul-de-sac.

'Alice!' Luke's dad opens the door. He's wearing a bomber jacket and hat with those comedy sunglasses which declare 'birthday boy' above them.

'Happy birthday,' I smile, holding out the box of chocolates I'd bought for the occasion.

He takes them from me. 'You didn't have to do that, pet!' He pulls me in for a hug. 'Come in, come in, Luke's just outside with Hannah.'

I follow him through the hallway to the kitchen. It's a week from Christmas and their decorations are up. Very tasteful, lots of grey. But I'm not paying much attention to the tasteful grey decorations. I'm stuck on the word 'Hannah'.

Mick speaks over his shoulder, 'I have to say, I thought a barbecue in December would be a disaster . . .'

He's cut off by Luke, who steps round the patio doors from the garden at that very moment.

'Is that Alice?' he asks.

'How nice that you hear disaster and think of me,' I say, just as an offensively attractive woman steps into the dining room behind Luke. Holding his hand.

It's Hannah. As in Mr Hall's daughter Hannah. Carer of the sick and volunteer of the Welcome Centre. The shoe-in for an OBE. Hannah does not look like she's been catapulted through a worm hole from the 1960s to be here. No, Hannah looks effortlessly chic. She is wearing many a floaty layer. Long dress, long jumper, big scarf. All in pastel hues. I'd look like a two-man tent fit for the Sahara Desert, but Hannah has the willowy frame that lets her get away with it. And I've already met her and know that she's nice, so I can't even dislike her.

'Alice.' Luke nods, looking incredibly uncomfortable. 'This is Hannah.'

'We've met before actually,' I say, trying to smile but feeling like I might be coming off a bit like that emoji that's meant to convey shock, or fear, or something bad anyway. The one that's all teeth. Luke looks between us.

'At the Welcome,' I explain. 'Hannah is Mr Hall's daughter, our old headteacher. Remember, you met him on the bus back from Durham that day,' I add, the reminder of the day Luke had paid for my shampoo giving me just the boost I need right about now. Not.

Luke looks taken aback. 'I didn't realize,' he tells her.

'There's no reason you would, our first date was less than half an hour.' She laughs and smiles up at him and wow, they are both bringing some serious genetic material to the table. Maybe Luke is right, and you *do* just go for the person your DNA matches you to.

He turns back to me.

'Where's Andy?' he asks.

'He dumped me last night,' I say breezily.

Luke frowns, his little forehead vein making a reappearance as Hannah's eyes dart between us.

'It's fine, I'm not bothered. He was pretty awful,' I tell Hannah.

'Been there, done that.' She's still looking between me and Luke. He's glaring like he's either about to kiss me or kill me. I can't quite tell. It's very intense.

'Do you want a drink?' he finally snaps.

My yes is nothing if not enthusiastic.

'Mulled wine all right?' Luke is still looking at me.

'Ooh, I love mulled wine,' chimes Hannah in a sing-song voice.

'Perfect. Thanks.'

Luke nods and leaves in a manner that can only be described as stompy, meaning that Hannah and I are alone.

Hannah watches him leave then turns back to me. We're still stood by the open patio doors, so we sort of shuffle further into the dining room. Outside, I can see people huddled in groups. I don't have a massive desire to join them.

'I'm sorry again about your boyfriend,' she says.

'No problem. Honestly, he was an arse.'

She laughs.

'Can I ask though, and tell me if I'm crossing a line or something,' I get a sort of sicky feeling in the back of my throat as she carries on. 'But is there like, a thing, between you and Luke? I won't mind if there is, I just don't want to waste my time here either.'

'What, NO!' I say overly emphatically, giving her shoulder a nudge with my balled-up fist. I'm not entirely sure why. 'Why would you think that?' I force out a laugh.

She lets my weirdness pass. 'Just a feeling, that's all.'

We both look over at Luke in the kitchen and catch him with his head turned towards us. No, towards me, I think.

'He keeps looking at you,' Hannah says.

'Nooo he doesn't, does he? I don't think he does. And if he does do that, which I don't think he does, it's probably not a thing,' I babble. I shake my head side to side for emphasis. 'We go way back, that's all. At school we won this prize together, your dad gave it to us actually. So me and Luke have a bit of history,' Hannah looks very interested at this, 'but not much history.'

'Okay, if you're sure?' she asks.

'Completely.' I smile.

Luke returns, holding three little glasses of mulled wine between his hands. He doesn't even look shaky as he carries them and really, it's unfair that he's so unfailingly competent at everything he does.

He hands them out.

'Should we go outside?' I suggest, still reluctant to freeze but hoping that maybe there'll be another guest that I recognize so that I won't have to spend the entire day third-wheeling on Hannah and Luke's date.

'Are you okay?' Luke asks, following as I lead the way outside. A quick scan tells me that I know basically no one.

'Yeah, sorry. Just weirdly emotional.'

'Mercury is in retrograde. That'll do it,' Hannah says and I'm surprised that Luke doesn't comment. I'm pretty sure that if I suggested that our moods were dependent on the position of a planet millions of miles away, I'd get a lecture on the workings of the limbic system.

There's a marquee set up at the far end of the lawn that we gravitate towards. Inside, people cling to the heaters.

We take our seats at a white plastic patio set that isn't as close to a heater as I'd like it to be. But all the best spots have been taken, so it'll have to do. It's a bit of an awkward silence and Luke isn't looking at either of us.

If this is how all his dates go, no wonder they're short-lived affairs.

'So how did you two meet?' I ask.

'We ran into each other in Stars.' Hannah smiles, looking at Luke like he's hung the moon even though I think he's being a bit of a rubbish date. A strong jaw will get you far in life it would seem.

'It's only our second date but Luke invited me to his dad's party. Isn't that cool?'

I almost choke on my mulled wine at Luke being described as cool.

Luke, presumably realising that he's being a bit of a dick at this point, stops staring off into the middle distance and reaches over and gives Hannah's hand a squeeze.

I decide that maybe now would be a good time to get drunk.

'So, how're you finding being back in Easington?' Hannah asks, blowing on her mulled wine. She has these gloves with the fingers cut out, little pearls along the top, that I can't stop admiring.

'A bit better now, thanks.' I try to snap myself out of my weird mood. 'Have you always lived here?'

She nods. 'I think I was four years behind you at school.' Course she bloody was. 'Dad was already in his fifties when he had me.'

Despite her youth, I can't find it within myself to dislike Hannah. She's just really . . . nice. Saintly almost. She tells us about what it's like being a carer for her dad ('it has its ups and downs, but mainly I'm glad it's me'). And how hard it's been to meet people now that he needs so much of her time. She tells us that it's felt like all her school friends are moving on, but how she loves living round here.

I start to think that my chances of winning this bet are looking pretty good. Luke is bound to fall in love with Hannah. Heck, I think I could have a good go at falling in love with her at this point.

'I feel exactly the same,' I tell her, having another drink of mulled wine, though not feeling any drunker for it despite some very determined efforts. 'At eighteen, I was desperate to get away. Now I wonder why I ever thought it was so bad here in the first place.'

'I think it's a normal teenage thing,' Hannah says. 'I mean, I might have gone if Mum was alive and Dad wasn't sick. What do you think, Luke?' She tries to involve him in the conversation again.

He sits up a little straighter. 'The teenage brain is predetermined to strive for independence. It's a biological change. Mice and rats experience the same phenomenon.'

I drain the rest of my drink, realising two important things then and there.

1. It is impossible to get drunk on mulled wine. In fact, drink too much of the stuff and it leaves you with red lips and liquid sugar for blood.
2. It's pretty hot when Luke talks science.

I'm not sure how long passes as I stare at Luke. 'I'll be back in a moment,' Hannah says, heading for the toilet.

'You and Hannah seem to be getting along well?' I ask. 'I think maybe I won't have to worry about losing this bet after all. She's already in love with you and who wouldn't fall in love with her?'

Like bad bout of the Black Death, Luke swoops down to whisper in my ear, 'We need to talk later, King.'

The back of my neck goes all goosebumpy.

I ignore him. I feel unsettled and I don't like it.

'Have you told her, about our bet?' I ask instead.

He shakes his head. 'It hasn't come up.'

'Don't be a div and lie to her.' I cross my arms. 'You don't want to go messing it up with someone like her. Trust me.'

Luke looks at me long and hard, like he's trying to figure me out when I can't even figure myself out. I look about wildly, the human equivalent of a rabbit caught in the headlights.

'Is there any more booze around here? It's impossible to get pissed on mulled wine,' I declare.

'That's because the cooking burns off the alcohol.'

I did not know this.

'Really? Well then, they should take the wine bit out of the title. It's false advertising.'

Luke snorts. Then looks horrified at the fact that he's just snorted, which in turn makes me laugh.

I hear the sound of a fork clinking against a glass. Oh no. Speeches. I'm not sure how I feel about speeches. Luke stands up and moves to the edge of the marquee to watch. I follow, and peering over his shoulder I can just see his dad holding aloft a prosecco flute. Luke catches me and moves to block my view. I shove him out of the way.

'Knob,' I whisper.

'Brat.' He's smirking, though, and – oh God, where did all the air go?

'I'd just like to thank you all for coming,' Mick begins. 'I'm especially pleased to be here at my sixtieth birthday party because it means I'm not dead.'

Everyone laughs.

'I can never understand why people don't like these big birthdays.' I think back to my own birthday and look about guiltily. 'Not when it means you've made it into another decade. Always cause for cele-bration in my book. Anyway, I won't go on, I know you're all only here for the free food. But I just wanted to say a very public and very embarrassing thank you to my beautiful wife, Lilian.'

Lilian smiles and then says, 'I told him to say that.'

'She might be a woman who organizes a garden party in winter. But without her, I'd probably be dead already and without her I might not care so much either way. To Lilian, everyone.'

We all toast. 'To Lilian.'

My good feeling evaporates as the speech ends.

'Alice?' Luke asks.

I sniff. 'I'm going to go. Look, there's Hannah.' She's hovering round the patio doors positively radiating serenity.

Luke looks a bit pained. His mouth is set into a tight line.

'Sorry,' I say. 'Sorry, I know you don't like it when I say sorry.'

'Alice,' Luke calls after me as I rush past Hannah.

'I'm going to go find some real booze,' I tell her. 'It was really nice seeing you again.' I keep moving.

'I'll be one second,' I hear Luke tell her.

'I can occupy myself, look there's a nimbus cloud shaped like a broom up there.' I don't know what sky Hannah's looking at. All I can see are rain clouds.

'Alice!' Luke calls me back as I'm halfway down the hallway to the front door. I haven't even texted Dad to come get me, but I'm determined to set off. The confused tinkering of my brain this morning is now a deafening cacophony of sound and I need to get somewhere quiet to clear it.

I turn to face him.

'Are you okay?' he asks frowning.

I shake my head. 'I don't know, I don't know what's wrong with me. The party is lovely and Hannah is lovely, you're ... you.'

'Is it the Andy thing?' Luke takes a step towards me. 'Because, you know, you're better than them. Those other men, I mean. I didn't think, I mean, I don't want you to get hurt, just because of a bet.'

He's so close that I can see a tiny patch of hair along his jaw that's just a smidge longer than the rest. He must have missed it shaving. I have such an overwhelming urge to touch that patch of hair with my finger that I jolt back. Like I've been electrocuted. I look at Luke, terrified at what I think I might feel.

'It's not the bet. Or maybe it is the bet. It's everything. I ... I can't do this. It's wrong.'

And it *is* wrong. Luke is here with Hannah. Lovely Hannah who has been nothing but nice to me. Lovely, normal-not-broken Hannah. My bottom lip starts to tremble. I can't look him in the eye, too scared of what I'll see there.

'I'm sorry, Alice. You don't need to pay me anything. It was a stupid bet.'

'For fuck's sake Luke! It's not about the bet. I'm going.' He makes to come after me as I turn away. 'Just please, let me leave.'

And with that, I walk away.

Chapter Twenty-Two

Alice King,
   We request your presence at an interview at Durham
University on 9 March 2023 . . .

I stare at the message in my inbox. Blinking a couple of times, just to check it's really there. But it is, it really is.

I embark on a little solo celebration in my bedroom, bouncing up and down and clapping a lot. There's a good chance I sort of squeak, so it's a good job no one is here to see it.

Scanning to the bottom of the email, I see there's some information on an event-type thing specifically for mature students that's taking place this week. I figure I'll go to it. It'll be good to gather whatever intel I can ahead of my interview which is, I double-check the date, in three weeks. I'm going to need flash cards. Lots and lots of flashcards. I need to learn everything there is to know about philosophy and then wow them with my philosophical brilliance. Then they'll have to let me in.

I tap away on my phone, arranging next-day delivery for an emergency order of 500 blank flashcards.

Two months have passed since the garden party with Luke and Hannah. Seventy days since I spoke to Luke. Not that I've been counting or anything.

The restaurant was busier than ever over the Christmas holidays.

Apparently nothing screams 'birth of Our Lord' like beef in black bean sauce. But the day itself was nice. Quiet and spent just with my family, but nice for it. More and more I appreciate what I was missing out on, being so distant from them all those years.

I haven't even minded the time I've spent on my own quite so much. Occasionally, I've craved it (normally after a visit from Aunty M). And I'm mainly just reading or listening to music, we're not talking about anything ground-breaking here. But it's really been an awfully long time since I felt happy in my own company.

A week after Christmas, I saw Luke with Hannah. They were going into the Welcome Centre as I was coming out of the library, returning all of my socialism books. I'm trying my best to be happy for them. Luke and Hannah, I mean. Not the socialist books.

I head downstairs to tell Mum and Dad my good uni news, texting it to Joanie and Gabby on my way.

'That's excellent, Alice, I knew you could do it,' Mum says when I tell her. She's in the kitchen again, trusty frying pan in hand. 'Let me make you a cup of tea to celebrate.' She reaches over with one hand still on the pan to flick the kettle on.

I move round her.

'Don't worry, I can do it. You want one?'

'Go on then.' I pass her again, pulling out teabags and milk and the single sweetener she has in her tea.

'It's not in the bag yet,' I tell her, 'but I'm another step closer at least.'

'Have you heard from the other two? Newcastle and Northumberland, I mean?' Mum's voice gets louder as the kettle boils.

'Not yet.'

'Well, Durham would be easier. That way you can keep living at home.'

I smile and stir in the water, using it as a distraction to avoid revealing to Mum that while my initial plan was to stay home, I'm starting to think that maybe I should live in Durham next year. If I get in, that is. I've no desire to move away like I did when I was eighteen, but I maybe would like to live somewhere a little bit bigger. Somewhere people don't all know everything about each other. Over Christmas, Debbie from four doors down got done for fiddling her benefits. People are still talking about it. And I'm pretty sure that out of earshot, the villagers call me 'sad Alice'.

But there's no point in talking to Mum about it until I actually have a place, and I have an extra shift at the Lotus Flower tonight, so I need to go get ready.

'I'd better take this upstairs.' I hold up my Mrs Potts mug of tea, thinking that having a favourite cup goes a long way to making me happy. 'I'm at work tonight,' I remind her.

'I washed your waistcoat, love,' Mum tells me. 'It's on the radiator in the bathroom, that one always gets the hottest, so it should be dry by now. Will you be bringing some you-know-what back?' She's dropped her voice to barely a whisper, looking around as if at any moment she expects a SWAT team to come bursting through the front door.

'Yeah, that's why I agreed to go in. They bin loads of stuff on a Tuesday. I'll smuggle out what I can when Paul isn't around.'

Mum nods, her lips pressed together in a thin line.

Paul had not taken kindly to my request that we donate some of the food waste to the Welcome Centre. Even stuff that is literally about to go in the bin. So Joanie and I had taken matters into our own hands. We basically do our best to smuggle out all the out-of-date vegetables we can, and then Mum takes them down for the food bank.

Mum had only agreed to take part in our clandestine semi-criminal enterprise because Aunty M had told her that they struggled to get fresh food for the food bank and also because I assured her that the stuff we stole was only going to be thrown out anyway. And okay, smuggling out-of-date cabbages into a box in

Dad's van while Paul is on the toilet isn't exactly how I'd envisaged spending my working life, but here we are.

'Go, go, go!' Joanie holds the kitchen door open for me and I peg it through the restaurant to the van parked right outside, a carrot and a cucumber pilfered from the 'to throw away box' in each of my hands.

The kitchen staff had been more than happy to help us undermine Paul. They might hate him even more than us, and I didn't think that was possible. The other wait staff don't help, but they haven't grassed us up either. Though that could be because Joanie spent a fair bit of time saying, 'snitches get stitches'. She was joking, obviously. I think.

I chuck the stuff in the van and then head back inside. Paul's there, his visit to the loo must have been shorter than usual.

'What are you doing outside?' he snaps from where he's stood on the far side of the couches. Joanie is busy handing out our evening meal, she doesn't look up at me.

'I just . . .' I will not cave under interrogation. I urge my brain to come up with something sensible, a credible explanation. But instead of this sensible, credible explanation, it manages, 'I really like the dark. It reminds me of being asleep.'

Joanie rolls her eyes and shakes her head a bit, handing out the last meal and sitting down.

I do an exaggerated yawn, doubling down on my awful excuse. 'I love being asleep, don't you?' I ask Paul.

He pulls a face of disgust and walks towards the kitchen, not even bothering to answer me but muttering something about 'crazy millennials'. I go to sit next to Joanie.

'That was the best you could come up with?' she says around a massive yawn of her own.

'What would you have said?' I ask, starting on my rice.

'Wanted a bit of fresh air, needed to check I'd locked my car ...'

'Yeah, those are better. You're good at lying.'

Joanie yawns again. 'What can I say? It's a gift.'

'Are you okay?' I ask.

She nods. 'Just worn-out.'

'Do you want me to watch Tyler tomorrow night? You could go to your mum's for a bit again?'

She shakes her head. 'We always do a movie on a Wednesday night. It's our thing.' Joanie pauses for a second for her biggest yawn yet. 'You could come on Thursday night, though, if you don't mind.'

'Course not, I'd love to babysit.' I look down at her food; she's hardly touched it. 'Do you want to get back? Save that for tomorrow?'

Joanie nods and I have to half carry her to the van.

Durham the city might be beautiful but the Durham Students' Union is not. It looks like a high-security prison. Or else the sort of place we'll all move to when the planet gets too hot. It has walls of sheer concrete and these tiny little slits for windows. And, oh Jesus, they're playing Radio 1 in the atrium. If I didn't feel old before, I certainly do now.

Everyone is bustling about, a hive of activity. I rush over to the Information Point just because it seems like the thing to do and also because I'm more than a little nervous that I'll see Luke here. I think it's for the best if our paths never cross again.

'Excuse me,' I say to a man whose hair is pulled into a very neat man bun, 'could you tell me where the mature student event is?'

'I want the same thing actually.' A man behind me smiles.

The receptionist taps away at his computer and then points a finger towards the back corner of the atrium to where someone who is definitely a teenager is sat under a banner that reads, 'Durham University Welcomes Mature Students'.

I head over, looking about like I'm trying to lose a spy who is hot on my heels.

The teenager is on her phone, but when she sees me and the man approach, she sits up and smiles. And look at that, she has braces.

'Hi!' she says to us both. 'Welcome! Are you thinking of studying with us next year?' In front of her, several leaflets are fanned out.

If I had to guess, the guy next to me is a couple of years younger than me. He's pale and thin with black hair and greyish eyes.

'Yes,' I say to the teenager, 'I have an interview in a couple of weeks. Philosophy.'

She nods excitedly.

'I've been accepted onto a computing course,' the man says as we both reach for a leaflet that's called 'Mature Students, Funding and You'.

'You first,' he says.

'Thanks, I'm really going to be needing the funding.'

'Me too.'

We turn back to the teenager.

'How *old* would you say is too old?' I ask her. 'To be a mature student.'

'You're never too old to learn, that's what I say!' It's obviously a line from a girl who has her hair in actual bunches, but it's a nice sentiment nonetheless. Which she then ruins by saying, 'Once I think we had someone who was like *fifty*.' She says the word fifty as if referring to the prehistoric era. The man next to me laughs.

I think we're done here. I gather up a couple more leaflets, including one which talks about 'balancing your family life with your studies' which I absolutely don't need but which I take anyway because a freshly printed leaflet is hard to beat.

'Thanks for your help,' I tell the girl.

'Good luck with your interview,' she replies, already back to her phone.

'Was it me, or was it a bit of a stretch to call that an event?' the man asks as we head back towards the exit, walking in the same direction.

'Total stretch,' I agree. 'I'm Alice, by the way.'

He nods his head. 'Shaun.' He holds out his hand to shake. He's thin and his hand is cold but he's quite nice to look at. A sort of skinny Legolas, with short black hair.

'So, computing?' I ask.

'Yes, I'd like to work in online games design.'

'Sounds cool.' We're outside now. I'm babysitting Tyler tonight, so I decide to just get the bus straight home.

'You local?' he asks as I move towards the bus stop.

'Yeah, Easington Colliery if you've heard of it? I've got to get back now, actually, but maybe I'll see you around next year, if I get in that is.' I laugh.

'You're from Easington?' Shaun asks. I nod. 'I am too. My Dad runs Bambino's.'

Bambino's is the local (read only) pizza takeaway in Easington.

'No way! My Aunty Moira says you do the best kebabs.'

'Why thank you.' Shaun does a little bow. 'Dad wanted me to take over the business, but I've no passion for pizza or kebabs.'

We're still stood outside the atrium. 'No, I can imagine,' I tell him.

'Do you think . . .' Shaun starts and then stops. It takes me a second to recognise what is happening. 'I mean that is, would you like to come over one day? I could show you a bit of the online gaming world?'

Shaun seems nice. He's not intimidatingly attractive like Dwaine, or a bit gross like Andy. He's not Luke either, my ever–unhelpful brain chimes.

'It's okay if you'd rather not.' He looks down at the floor, shuffling his feet a little, and maybe this is what I need. Someone uncomplicated, just . . . nice.

'You know what, that would be great,' I tell him, feeling reassured about my decision when I see how happy it makes Shaun.

We swap numbers and say our goodbyes. Shaun is going to look around the uni more, so we don't have the pressure of a bus journey back together. All in all, I'm feeling pretty good about the whole thing. I take a selfie, making sure I capture the University of Durham sign in the background, and upload it to Instagram. Because it feels right, being here. Like maybe this ugly concrete building is where I should have been the whole time.

'So, Tyler,' I say, 'why do you think we're alive?'

Tyler eyes me warily. I think by now he knows that we're not going to stick to Joanie's five-step bedtime routine. Instead, we mostly just watch TV until he passes out in front of it while I make ever more elaborate toast houses. I brought my own loaf of bread today and really went to town. There was an orangery and everything.

Tyler twists round from where he's watching the TV and just says, 'Bing.'

I have my newly arrived flashcards around me and I'm writing out philosophical questions on them in preparation for my interview.

Gabby has emailed me some suggestions of things to focus on too.

'Yes, but does Bing really exist?' I ask an ever more confused-looking Tyler. 'Does his existence hold up against the naïve comprehension principle?'

Tyler frowns at me and then says, 'But he's right there,' and points at the TV to where Bing has captured a worm in his giant paws. For my mind, Bing really needs to keep away from the wildlife after what he did to that butterfly. But at least Tyler has the makings of a great philosopher.

He starts to sway, and I don't know if it's my top-notch philosophy chat or the fact that he's three hours deep into a Bing marathon, but he finally falls asleep and I carry him into bed. I'm clearing up the remnants of my toast mansion when my phone lights up with three notifications.

The first is a missed call from an unknown number which I ignore. Obviously.

The second is from Facebook, an invite to a school reunion in two weeks' time that I will absolutely not be going to. I hit the decline button, pleased that I don't have to tell people to their face, or even come up with an explanation as to why I don't want to go to their party. What a time to be alive.

The final notification is a comment on my photo from earlier. All my regular commenters (i.e. Gabby) have already said something nice about it, so I'm a bit surprised when I see that a random account with a flower for a profile picture has written 'disgusting' and posted a sick-faced emoji underneath it.

I scrunch up my face, not willing to let some internet troll ruin my good day. How I've got myself a troll when I have twenty-two followers is beyond me. I delete the comment and am just sitting down on the couch when Joanie comes home.

'Thanks again for tonight,' she tells me, sitting next to me and looking a bit more rested for once in her life.

'No problem, we had fun. Are you feeling any better?' I ask.

'Yeah. I just went to Mam's and had a bath in peace. How did the Durham thing go?'

I shrug. 'It was okay. I can get a student loan still, so that's good. And this guy asked me out. He's from Easington too, he wants to be a computer gamer or design games or something.'

'He sounds like a man-child,' Joanie says.

'They're all man-children,' I reply.

'I always thought you'd end up with that Luke dude, you know?' Joanie is already falling asleep.

'Let it go, Jo. He's already forgotten about me.'

PART FOUR

SHAUN

*'Love shouldn't control who
you're friends with.'*

Chapter Twenty-Three

I quickly discover that Shaun is completely suited to a degree in computing. The man is never not online.

He invites me round to his house the next Saturday, and before I agree, I ask some very pertinent questions.

> **Me:** Can I just check; do you hold any extreme political views?
>
> **Shaun:** No
>
> **Me:** And you're definitely not bothered how long I can hold a plank for?
>
> **Shaun:** Don't think so
>
> **Me:** Close enough
>
> **Me again:** And finally, do you have a narcissistic personality?
>
> **Shaun:** Are narcissists generally found working in kebab shops?
>
> **Me:** Probably not. Excellent then, it's a date
>
> **Me:** A friendly date
>
> **Me:** Two friends hanging out on what might, or might, not be described as a date
>
> **Shaun:** Got it. See you soon, Alice

'Alice! Alice, pet?' It's Aunty Moira. I'm deep in the middle of a text conversation with Joanie. We're batting around ideas for ways that she could make some hard cash that aren't illegal or involve us seriously relaxing our thoughts about organ harvesting.

'Here!' I call from my bedroom.

'The taxi's coming in fifteen minutes!' she says from the bottom of the stairs. I've agreed to go to the bingo with Mum and Aunty M. Aunty M has finally broken up with Fred, and had been heard declaring loudly at 8 a.m. when she called round to borrow some tea-bags, that she was ready to, in her words, get back in the man saddle.

Fifteen minutes? I look at the time on my mobile. Who goes for a Friday night out at 5.15 p.m.?

'Okay,' I call, dropping the phone to throw on a red shift dress and pulling my hair into a bun.

Mum and Aunty M are waiting in the front room when I come down.

'Howay then, you look nice, pet,' Aunty Moira says as I perch on the edge of the couch to pull on some ankle boots.

Aunty M is wearing her wet-look leggings and a fluffy pink jumper adorned with the odd fake pearl. Mum embraced the advent of the jegging years ago and has never looked back. She's in her trusty blue pair with an oversized roll-neck top.

'You both look nice too.'

'Thanks, pet,' Aunty M replies. 'You know I love a bit of pink. And I like to let me hair down when I'm single and ready to mingle.' She shakes her boobs at us.

'Come on, Mo!' Mum protests, zipping up her coat. 'None of that now.'

There's a beep from outside and the three of us shuffle towards the door.

'Ladies.' The taxi driver has rolled down the window and is resting his elbow on it as he gives us a nod like an ageing Danny Zuko.

'All right, our Glen.' Aunty M settles herself in the front. 'How's the pigeons.'

Apparently, Glen keeps homing pigeons. Or, from what he tells us about them as we weave through the streets of Easington, just pigeons, because they don't seem to return home all that often.

I'm not quite sure how she manages it, but Aunty M then segues into the details of a documentary she watched this week. I zone out as she declares with conviction that 9/11 was an inside job. Something about the melting point of steel beams.

'All those people and the government behind it all. So sad, isn't it? And you look better now, Alice.' I tune back in at the mention of my name. Aunty M twists round in her seat to look at me.

'Pardon?'

'I was just saying to your mam – wasn't I, Cheryl?' She doesn't give Mum chance to respond. 'I was just saying that our Alice looks a lot healthier these days. Bit more meat on your bones. Not like when you were with that posh twat. What's his name?'

Again, no response time is given.

'Charles. That's it. You always looked knackered when you were with him. When we saw you, that is.'

Aunty Moira continues to talk for the rest of the journey, and after dropping us at the entrance to the Mecca Bingo, our Glen leaves in a suspiciously speedy fashion.

'Three ladies for the Big Friday Night game,' Aunty M tells the woman behind the counter. 'Eeh, is that you Agnes? Cheryl, you didn't tell me Agnes was working here now!'

It's like a who's who of Easington.

I wait while the three of them catch up. Mum assures Aunty Moira that she did tell her that our Agnes was working here now. Agnes gives a quick precis of her life since they were all at secondary school together.

I like to think that I'm distinctly less of a snob now that I've moved back to Easington. Mainly because no one gets to be a snob with a weekly budget as miserable as mine. But still, this place seems a bit much.

For one, the lights are incredibly bright. If you're going to have such harsh lighting, you really need to make sure the decor is more tasteful – or, at the very least, clean. There are these nondescript black stains all over the carpet, like little globules of tar, and the walls are dirty. The colour scheme appears to be blue and orange. Colours that don't complement each other in any way.

By the time Mum, Aunty M and Agnes have finished bemoaning the surge in popularity of paper as opposed to plastic straws – *They just make my teeth feel funny!* – a queue has formed behind us. We're given our bingo sheet and ushered through.

The bingo hall reminds me of a cattle market. Except instead of penned-in cows, there are hordes of middle-aged women clustered around blue and orange tables.

A table of people shrieks at us as we enter, patting spare chairs.

'Cheryl, Moira! Over here!'

The women are all a similar age to Mum. Most have deep wrinkles. From what Mum said when she invited me, it's a mixture of her work colleagues and some of their old school friends.

'I'll go to the bar,' one of them declares, shifting out of her seat. 'What can I get you ladies?'

There are various calls for pints of cider, some with blackcurrant. Mum has a lager shandy. Aunty Moira asks for a double vodka and Coke. And then it's my turn.

'Er, rosé wine please. Here, I'll give you some money.'

'No need, Alice pet. These are on me.'

I don't ask how she knows who I am. No doubt Mum has been confiding in them about her problem child who moved back home at twenty-nine.

It's not an unfair appraisal of the situation.

'I'll go with her,' says Aunty Moira. 'Help carry the glasses, and I want to order a basket of chicken and chips. You want one, Cheryl?'

'Go on then, why not?'

'And you, Alice?'

'Maybe just some chips please.' I had a late lunch, busy adding to the three thousand flashcards I'd made of potential questions ahead of my interview next month. It's hard to remember to go and get yourself a jacket potato when you're compiling arguments for and against the premise that the universe is essentially meaningless.

But still, chips. I'm as likely to find meaning in fried potato as I am in anything.

'That's it, pet. Men like something they can grab on to.' Aunty Moira's hips thrust.

This hilarity prompts a fresh bout of laughter. I really should counter her statement with some sort of feminist soundbite suggesting that women don't owe men anything regarding their appearance. But, in light of recent events, I recognize that would make me a total hypocrite. I spent the past decade changing myself to make a man happy.

Food ordered and drinks delivered, we get down to our first game of the evening. The room is hot and damp by now, and we're surrounded by other cramped tables of bingo fans. I'm surprised to learn that the prizes are ... substantial. There's £10,000 up for grabs this evening. Suddenly, I clutch my giant bingo pen all the tighter.

Let's do this, Alice! Let's win the world!

Four hours in, and the numbers on my card are starting to blur. Someone else wins the jackpot and my enthusiasm for blotting out numbers on my card wanes somewhat. Replaced instead with enthusiasm for Mecca Bingo's rosé wine.

I decide to get pissed. Again. And this time, there's no mulled about it. No burning off the alcohol in these bad boys.

The first glass was disgusting – warm and cloying. But then, as if by magic, glass after glass appeared. And because it was hard to join in a conversation centred mostly around the politics of the school dinner lady rota – Mum's friends are all dinner ladies – I've drunk glass after self-filling glass. Now I love the wine so much. So very, very much.

'Look, everyone!' One of them suddenly points, leaning over the table. 'Alice looks sad.' Everyone stops what they're doing and stares at me. 'Why are you sad, Alice?' She pulls an unhappy face.

I glance around the gathered faces, hot and greasy beneath the too-bright lights. 'Because all I have is wine, even though I love wine.' As if to prove the point, I take another big swig.

Mum is looking at me funny and I wonder if she's a bit sad too. Maybe I was right all that time and making bacon sandwiches for Dad doesn't make her happy. I wish Mum was happy.

'No. That's not right.' It's Aunty Moira talking now. Or at least one of her is. I blink a couple of times. 'Your mum says you had a . . .' She looks coyly around the gathering, '. . . gentleman friend who walked you home.' What is this? An episode of *Downton Abbey*?

If I were more sober, I'd be astonished that Mum had even clocked Luke walking me home literal months ago.

I stare into the bottom of my glass, which surprises me by being empty. 'That's Luke. Luke is handsome. More handsome than I thought. But Luke isn't Shaun. Luke has a girlfriend and Shaun is easy, you know? I just want something to just be easy.'

'But Luke is handsome. So, Shaun smorm!' one of the group cries. Even drunk-me recognizes that isn't a word. This prompts a bout of enthusiastic, slurred chanting that makes me want to throw my hands over my ears. 'Luke is handsome, Luke is handsome!' Which isn't the most imaginative chant in the world. Still, they make a valiant effort.

'But what's wrong with Shaun?' I interrupt, raising my voice above the caterwaul, wondering what Shaun has done to the dinner ladies of Sacred Heart Primary.

'He was right up his own arse. You could tell when he came up for a visit with you that one time. Didn't eat any of Cheryl's dumplings. She makes brilliant dumplings, our Cheryl,' Aunty Moira tells the table.

'No, *Charles* was up his own arse and didn't like the dumplings. Not Shaun,' I explain. It's a nice feeling to admit in public that my primary boyfriend was actually an arse. Which he was. Is.

'Well, who's Shaun when he's at home, then?'

By this stage, I'm starting to get confused myself.

'Shaun runs a kebab shop. Or at least, his dad does. I met him at the uni thing for mature students.' I never realized how much of a tongue twister 'mature' is.

'We love kebabs, we love kebabs. Shall we get one?' Aunty M bashes the table in time with her chant.

'I think it's time to go home.' Mum seems significantly less drunk than the rest of us. Probably because half of her drinks have been lemonade.

'No, wait! I know!' It's one of Mum's dinner lady friends. She has short hair that appears to be growing upwards, like a cactus. Cactus head. I laugh at my own joke. 'Alice should message Charles. I mean . . . I mean, the other one. The one with the kebab shop. The one who walks her home.'

'Luke!' someone offers.

'Shaun!' another voice cries.

'No, no, no!' I'm surprised to hear that it's me shouting over the others, as though this is suddenly important. 'Luke and Charles, they make me sad. I shouldn't love either of them. I don't even know if I love Shaun yet.' I slam my glass down. 'I'm so confused!'

The others laugh, as though this should be no surprise for any woman in the world ever.

Aunty M slings her arm over my shoulder. 'You message this . . . Luke or Shaun or whatever . . . and tell him you want a shag. Get it out of your system! You're still young!'

'I think that's quite enough!' Mum announces.

'Want a shag! Want a shag!' they all chant, pointing at me. The other bingo players are starting to look round, and one woman holds a finger to her lips.

'Want a shag! Want a shag!' The voices get even louder. It's 8 p.m. and I'm considering hiding beneath the table at this point.

'You know what they say.' It's cactus-hair again. 'The only way to get over one man is to get under another.'

Remembering Joanie, I'm starting to think this saying might be the unofficial Easington motto.

'Pardon?' I ask, faintly aware that lots of people are talking to me.

'Which one do you really want to get under?' one of the group calls.

I scrunch up my eyebrows, thinking hard.

'Luke, I think. I'm scared to get under Luke. And what if Luke won't let me get under him?'

'Course he will. He has eyes in his head, doesn't he?'

'Yes. Yes, he does have eyes. They're the best shade of brown. But if you get really close, there's bits of gold too.' I find myself staring into the middle-distance, probably looking like a lovesick fool. It's a very blurred middle-distance, my bingo card long forgotten. My eyes fill with tears, because I shouldn't want to get under Luke. Luke has Hannah. Plus maybe it's not enough to want to get under someone, maybe there's all sorts of other stuff I should be thinking about. Like Shaun, Shaun is nice. 'Oh, God! What should I do?'

'Message him.' It's Aunty Moira again. 'Tell him . . .' She thinks for a moment, adjusting her boobs in the pink top before her face lights up with inspiration. 'Tell him that you want to tear his boxers off with your teeth!'

'Jesus, Mo.' That's Mum.

'It's one of my best moves!' my aunt protests. I am getting far too much insight into her sex life. Mum starts bickering with Aunty M, telling her to be quiet.

Still, and before I even know what I'm doing, I find myself clumsily reaching for my mobile.

> I eant ro

I delete and start again.

> I wsnt tit

I give my head a shake. Luke won't like a messy text.

> I want to tear your boxers with my teth Close enough.
> It's taken me an age to type the message. 'Who am I
> sending this to again?'

Everyone seems as confused as me.

'The post twat!' one of them shouts.

'Shaun!'

'Luke!'

I hit send.

Mum announces the taxi is here and we need to go. We take at least twenty group photos before we finally get out of the door. I do a mass upload to Instagram, even though they probably aren't even story material. I have a faint sense that I've done something I'll regret in the morning. But I drain my drink and the nasty thought disappears as the three of us scramble to leave.

'STOP! Stop here!' Aunty Moira screams. The taxi driver (who isn't Glen with the fly-away pigeons) does an emergency stop and as I lunge forwards, I nearly throw up.

'What, what's wrong?' Mum asks.

'I need a kebab.' Aunty M is already unbuckling her seatbelt.

'You only had chicken and chips a few hours ago.'

'But I *need* one. Alice, you want a kebab, don't you?'

I'm drunk, but I'm still not drunk enough to eat a kebab.

'Alice, more chips?'

I lift my head up. 'Er . . .' I don't think I do want more chips.

'That's my girl. Taxi man, will you wait for us? Come on, Alice.'

We stumble out of the car and into the takeaway, passing the local Easington massive hanging about outside.

I peer at a man behind the counter.

He pauses mid kebab shave.

'Hi, again, Alice.'

I feel all the colour drain from my face. It's quite a sobering experience coming face to face with the man you just semi-sexted.

'Aunty Moira, this is Shaun. You know, the one I was telling you about. The nice one,' I say through gritted teeth.

Aunty Moira appraises Shaun.

'Bit skinny for me. I like something I can grab on to.'

'She's said that already tonight,' I tell the whole shop – which would be Shaun and his dad, who looks miserable in a sort of 'I came here for a better life and have to put up with shit like this' type of way.

Aunty Moira orders a large kebab and a portion of chips for me.

'Have you had a good night?' Shaun asks, going back to shaving the kebab. He hasn't mentioned the sext, which is a bit confusing. Maybe he hasn't seen it yet.

'Yeah, it's been lots of fun. I'm sorry though, I think I accidentally texted you, could you maybe delete it before you open it?' I watch as Shaun uses one hand to pull his phone out of the back pocket of his jeans.

'There's nothing here,' he says. He turns his attention to me. 'Are you still on for tomorrow?' He seems nervous, but a drunk Aunty Moira is a terrifying thing.

That's really strange about the text though. I'm sure I decided that it was Shaun I should be texting.

'Absolutely.'

'I'm looking forward to it.'

There, see. Nice and safe and nice.

'Me too.'

Aunty Moira and I gather up our takeaway, steam rising from the lamb and chips. 'Bye, Shaun!' we call back over our shoulders.

'I wonder where your message went?' Aunty Moira asks, as we get back into the taxi.

Chapter Twenty-Four

I wake up with one side of my face planted in a plastic container of salty chips and mayonnaise. I retch, and not only because I have mayonnaise on my forehead.

I catch myself in the mirrored wardrobe. I look a state. This isn't me being down on myself. This is a cold hard fact.

Snapshots of the previous night flash through my mind.

Struggling to keep up with the bingo.

All the wine.

Seeing Shaun in the kebab shop.

At least I'd had the presence of mind to turn down a kebab. My stomach rolls again as more and more memories of the evening assail me.

The chanting.

The message. Oh my God, the message!

Who did I send it to?

From somewhere deep inside my bedding, the phone pings. My fingers shake as I fumble to unlock it to see who I texted.

> **Luke:** It's highly unlikely that your mandible (lower jaw) bone possesses the power required to rip the material of standard men's underwear

No. No. No.

Also, who uses brackets in a text?

I attempt some damage limitation.

> **Me:** LOL. Sorry, oldest excuse in the book but I didn't mean to send that to you. Obviously
> **Luke:** ☹
> **Me:** Did you just use an emoji voluntarily?
> **Luke:** Yes
> **Me:** I thought you'd be with Joanie on this one
> **Luke:** What does Joanie say?
> **Me:** That emojis are the beginning of the end for humanity
> **Luke:** She sounds sensible

There's a long pause. It's almost like the past months avoiding Luke haven't happened. But they have. I feel like I should apologize again.

> **Luke:** It's okay, Alice. It was only a message
> **Me:** Okay, thank you. Hope you're well

The entire mini exchange is mildly confusing. Though it's possible that my alcohol-addled brain simply isn't processing rational thought right now.

However, I've no time to dwell on my reaction to Luke's texts or that another random account has replied 'ugly' to my seven picture Instagram bonanza from last night. I mean, looking at the state of us, they're not wrong.

Mouth parched, I drag myself downstairs in desperate search of water. Mum has left paracetamol out on the kitchen counter for me, which I count as excellent mum behaviour.

Aunty Moira groans from the couch in the front room, so I take her some too.

After that, I attempt to sweat out the booze in a hot shower.

Once I'm perilously close to fainting, I drag myself out. Back in my bedroom, I pull out the clothes I've picked for the date. It's just jeans and a nice jumper, not the gamer chic T-shirt I'd considered ordering online. Because I'm not letting myself be moulded to the whims of a man anymore, remember?

If I didn't feel so deathly, it might feel like more of a victory.

You know what? Toddlers have the best social life. I've lost count of how many Little Daisies parties Tyler has been to at this stage.

I sip at my tap water, the only liquid within my meagre budget. 'Rough night down the Mecca,' I explain to Joanie.

'That *is* rough.' Joanie shoves half a muffin towards me as I gaze at her like she might be the Messiah.

As usual, we're sat away from the other parents in a little corner. I have my back to the chaos of the kids' party and I jolt as a wayward balloon smacks me in the back of the head.

'That's not even the worst of it.' I attempt a shouty whisper, doing my best to be heard over 'We Don't Talk About Bruno'. 'I accidentally sexted Luke while I was drunk.' I glance nervously at Joanie.

'I knew you liked him!' Joanie bobs up and down and I get nauseous just watching her. 'Hang on, I thought he had a girlfriend now?' she asks.

I put my head in my hands, 'I'm an awful person! And after what Charles did to me too!' I bash my head against the table. 'I'm a mess.'

'You're not,' Joanie intervenes. 'Okay, maybe a little. You have to tell me, though ... what did you say?'

'That I wanted to rip his boxers off with my teeth.'

'Excellent.' She laughs and rubs her hands together. 'Your life is like living in a soap opera. One of the sleazy ones. Like *Hollyoaks Later.*'

Another balloon pings off the back of my head. Joanie shouts 'Oi' but I don't even flinch.

'Do you think I'm an awful person? Should I tell Shaun? Maybe I should go find Hannah down the Welcome and confess.'

'All that depends on whether you're planning on actually shagging Luke?'

'Course not!'

'Then don't worry about it. What's a little sext between friends?'

I look round to where all the kids are gathered. They're sat in a circle playing pass the parcel. Two of them have said parcel in a vice-like grip, their faces turning slowly purple as they refuse to give it up to the other.

Dropping my voice to a whisper, I say, 'Will you stop saying sext, we're in the presence of children. And I told you – it was an accident. A slip of the fingers.'

'You know,' Joanie carries on as if I haven't spoken and I take the chance to stuff some muffin in my mouth, 'I called this months ago. You and him have always had a thing.'

'You've never even met him.'

'Just the way you used to talk about him. There's definitely some intense brooding there.'

My head is on the table again. Behind me, I can hear various parents shout out, 'You've got to pass the parcel ... pass it!'

'I don't think there is brooding.' My lie is weak, even to my own ears.

'You did sext him, Alice,' Joanie reminds me unhelpfully.

I groan. 'I'm literally going to Shaun's house in an hour. And whatever happens in the future, Luke is with Hannah now.'

She ignores me. 'Look, frankly, I don't care who you sext.'

I nod as she finishes with, 'Still think you'll wind up with Luke though. Or no one, no one is an option too.'

I glance up at her. 'Look,' I implore. 'Beautiful, saintly girlfriend aside, even I know that the chance of me falling in love with a man like Luke – who doesn't believe in love – is never, ever going to happen.'

I let my statement hang in the air, waiting for her to agree. It is highly irritating when she doesn't say a word.

Shaun's family live above their kebab shop. Still hungover, I ring the doorbell beneath the green and red Bambino's sign. At least he has a short commute.

I adopt what I fear might be a slightly nervy smile as Shaun opens the door, headset already in place, ready for our game. The computer game, that is.

He holds up a hand and speaks into the mic. 'N'Zoth has been spotted in Hearthstone. I repeat. N'Zoth spotted. Do you copy? Zit number two. Luc Hellscream out.'

He's wearing a *Star Trek* pin badge.

'Hi Alice, sorry about that,' he says after a few moments. 'My guild is in the middle of a raid, y'know. Come on up.'

I've genuinely no idea what he's talking about. I follow him through the kebab shop. His dad is busy decanting a large tub of mayonnaise into squirty bottles, a cigarette hanging from the side of his mouth.

I get an unwelcome flashback from last night

'Hello, Mr ... Bambino.' I smile, trying to be cheery.

He just shakes his head as we pass.

A door leads to the flat above. Shaun gestures me in and we climb a set of narrow stairs, passing grease-stained walls to make our way down a gloomy corridor to his bedroom. The air is filled with the aroma of meat fat. It's all very dark, which my hangover appreciates. The curtains are dragged closed, but at least he's made the bed. The rest of the room is like a space command centre. There are three computer screens, all displaying a game that looks like a knock-off *Lord of the Rings*.

There are two chairs at the bottom of the bed, one of them not unlike the sort of thing that I imagine pilots sit in, complete with cup holder and headrest. It takes up most of the floor space.

The other is a wooden kitchen chair. The walls are covered in *Minecraft* posters.

'This is nice,' I venture, glancing around.

'Thanks.' He sits on the wooden chair and gestures for me to take the good one. The warm leather hugs my bum cheeks. It's like sitting on a cloud, a warm, leather cloud. 'The modem produces seventy-two kilowatts of RAM.'

I make all the right noises, presuming that seventy-two kilowatts of RAM is something to be proud of.

'Will you live here next year?' I ask.

Shaun nods. 'I don't feel like living with young people.'

'I know what you mean. Did you hear in the student union, they were playing Radio 1?'

'There's no accounting for the tastes of today's youth.' Shaun smiles and I laugh. It's easy breezy, a laugh a minute until I realize that Shaun is five whole years closer to said youth than me.

'Anyway . . . I like your pin badge.'

'Thanks, you look nice too.'

So, this is going well.

'You still up for playing some *World of Warcraft*?'

'Absolutely.'

'What are you, then? Troll, human or dwarf? You can join our clan. We've a raid about to start in Ardenweald.' Shaun picks up a controller from the desk in front of us. Untangling it from a mass of wires that would put NASA HQ to shame.

Obviously, I've no idea what he's talking about.

'Um, what is *World of Warcraft* exactly?' Shaun hands me some white headphones. They're essentially long bits of wire compared to the contraption surrounding his own head.

'An MMPORG fantasy series.'

I'm still not exactly sure what we're dealing with here, but I just plump for human. 'Human please, I'd like to be human.'

He nods. 'Good choice.'

Then he taps away on one of his keyboards at lightning speed, and a woman wearing a sort of armoured bikini appears on the screen. I wonder if this is the manifestation of Shaun's ideal woman. She has significantly bigger boobs than me.

'You can come up with your own name.' He twists to look at me. 'Or there's a name generator we can use if you'd like.' He's tapping the whole time, setting up my profile.

'Definitely the generator.'

Shaun smiles and he has this ghost of a dimple on his right cheek. Interests and a dimple. Excellent.

The name generator which has appeared on one of his screens stops spinning.

'Undine Smethergell.' I lean over his shoulder to read my new fantasy name. Sounds significantly more badass than the real deal.

'Hellsman back,' Shaun announces to no one I can see. 'New clan member, Undine Smethergell.'

My character jumps into the world.

Right. I put my headphones in. I've read *The Hobbit* and I watched all of *Game of Thrones*. I can do this.

Two hours later and I'm gripped.

I'm told we're raiding. Shaun might as well be speaking a foreign language. He randomly shouts out phrases like 'retreat to Maldraxxus!' or 'blood elf to the left!' Freaky angels come down from the sky amidst lightning bolts. Giant trolls wielding axes stomp around. It's impossible to tell who is friend or foe. *The Hobbit,* it ain't.

Despite my confusion there is something primal about watching a man launch virtual warfare. Like the modern-day equivalent of a sexy Celt or a hot Viking raider. Shaun shouts random instructions into his headset while I duck and dive every time Undine and Hellsman look like they're about to run into trouble. Every now and then, he breaks off to take a swig from the cans of Mountain Dew he's brought out from a mini-fridge beneath his desk.

So, he's a young twenty-five. But he's good fun. He instructs me to push a button and Undine stomps all over a troll. I'm possessed by bloodlust and before I know it, stomping has become Undine's signature move. I stomp my way through two hours of foe, and we laugh maniacally every time one goes down under her thigh-high leather boot.

With a jolt, I realize that I need to leave to be in time for my shift at the Lotus Flower.

'Er, Shaun.' I tap him on the shoulder. He holds a finger up for me to give him a moment.

'Level forty-seven completed. Hellsman out,' he says into his mic, spinning round in his chair to face me.

'Wow! That was . . . wow.' I take my headphones off.

'It's a developed world,' he says. 'Next time you can be more involved in the raids and stuff. For a first-timer, Undine did great.'

As he speaks, Shaun sounds a touch breathless.

'Er, could I maybe have some water?' My mouth feels strangely furry after the Mountain Dew.

'Of course. Water's in the kitchen. Follow me.'

'I have to be at work in half an hour,' I say to his retreating back.

We walk through to a small galley kitchen. It takes a few moments for my eyes to adjust to the natural light.

'Where do you work?' He fills me a mug with water from the tap.

'The Lotus Flower. The Chinese? I don't love it but I'm hoping that I'll be able to work there while I'm at uni. Just for some extra cash.'

He nods. 'I'm thinking the same about the kebab shop. Dad's pretty gutted that I don't want to take it on long-term though.'

'I understand.' I have a drink. 'Today has been fun.'

Shaun gives another small smile.

'You know, my last girlfriend didn't want me to be friends with people who weren't gamers.'

'Didn't she? That doesn't really seem fair,' I tell him, feeling vaguely uncomfortable but not entirely sure why.

He nods. 'She thought they wouldn't understand the lifestyle.'

I don't think she's someone you should associate with, Alice, she's so vulgar.

I just know you're going to love my friends.

Why do you need your own friends when you have me?

'My ex was the same,' I tell Shaun. I push my fingers into the corner of my eyes to try and block out the tidal wave of memories. 'He wanted to control who I was friends with. But I don't think love should do that, do you?'

When I open my eyes again, Shaun is shaking his head from side to side slowly. Little dots dance across them. It's nice to be having another realisation that isn't accompanied by a panic attack. But it's still a little surreal to be having it in Shaun's galley kitchen.

'I'm sorry to hear that, Alice,' Shaun squints across at me.

Suddenly, I'm not entirely sure I am about to bypass that panic attack. I grip the kitchen counter tight.

'Sorry,' I tell him, 'I'm just realising some stuff.'

'That's no problem, Alice, would you like some more water?'

I nod, trying to concentrate on the breathing that I know will help.

I have to hold the cup with two hands.

'I'd really like to be friends. And I'm here if you ever want to talk through the stuff with your ex,' I say because it's true. Friends are something I didn't know I needed quite so much. I could always use another.

Shaun smiles; if he's a bit sad, he doesn't let on much. You can't go out with someone just because you feel sorry for them. Literally everyone deserves more than that. 'I'd like that too. Come on, I'll show you out,' he says.

I leave through the kebab shop, getting a grunted farewell from his dad. Or maybe it's just a grunt.

Outside, I take some deep breaths and stretch out my suddenly tight fingers, pleased that I'd just about managed to head off another panic attack.

Speed walking home to get my uniform, I WhatsApp Gabby.

> **Me:** I know I said this already, but I'm sorry that I let Charles stop us from being friends xx

It's close to 2 a.m. there, so I'm surprised that my phone buzzes with a reply immediately.

> **Gabby:** Who is this Charles you speak of?
> **Me:** Hahaha. I wish it was that easy xx
> **Gabby:** I highly recommend therapy. Been in it my whole life and look how normal I am

She sends a selfie of her cross-eyed and poking her tongue out.

> **Me:** How do you look so good with your eyes crossed? I'll think about it
> **Gabby:** It would do you the world of good, darling. Trust me on this one

Chapter Twenty-Five

'So, let me get this straight, you *watched* him play video games. All afternoon?' Joanie asks at the end of our shift.

'No, Undine got to do some stomping too.'

'Who the fuck is Undine?'

'Me, I'm Undine. It's part of the game.'

'What's it about, like?'

'No idea, to be honest. Fantasy or war, I guess. Lots of fighting. Lots of . . . ' I pause to take a drink of my Coke. We're gathered on the couches after work again.

'Stomping,' Joanie finishes for me.

'Thank you.' I lower my voice to a whisper. 'I decided in the end, though, we're better off as friends.'

'Look at you, friend-zoning people. You'd never have done that when you were all sad and desperate.'

I twirl some noodles round my fork. 'I've friend-zoned one person. Maybe love is rational and I'm just not ready to fall in love again.'

'But why though, it's not like you're still pining over Charles is it? You hardly even mention him anymore.' Joanie pauses for a second. 'Which, I'd like to add, is a massive relief for all of us.'

I roll my eyes.

'Maybe these are just the wrong men,' she says after a moment. 'I've said it before, and I'll say it again – I never knew what you saw in Andy.'

We've obviously abandoned our whisper enough for Andy to overhear us.

'Oi! I'm with someone new.' He heads to the toilet, *The Socialist Worker* tucked under his arm. 'Plenty of nudes.'

'That's, er, great, Andy. I'm glad things have worked out for you.' I turn back to Joanie.

'Seriously?' she says towards Andy's retreating figure.

'He's not that bad. A bit like pineapple on pizza. Not particularly welcome but it won't kill you.'

'Oh yes, well no wonder you two didn't work out then. Not exactly Romeo and Juliet, is it? "Thou dost remind me of a deep-dish Hawaiian".'

We're laughing then and shoehorning the words pineapple into all manner of sentences.

'Um, Alice,' Joanie says suddenly, wiping her eyes. 'I think you have a visitor.'

'What like a pineapple?' I roar.

'No, like an actual person.' She nods towards the doorway where Luke hovers, his gazed fixed on me. 'A really fit person.'

'It's Luke.'

'You didn't say how fit he was, Alice.'

'I . . . um . . . don't think I recognised it. At first.'

Blood rushes to my cheeks. And not just because of the pineapple thing.

Now my entire face is red.

'What do you think it means that he's here?' I ask, scrambling to put my coat on because – thankfully – it's time to go home anyway.

'You know,' Joanie looks over at Luke, 'we could just ask the man, save all this angst.'

'No.' I'm already moving away.

'Hey, Luke!' she shouts.

'Run, Luke, run!' I practically shove him out of the door.

We're stood by the giant flower-headed lions either side of the doorway, breathing hard. Or, at least, I'm breathing hard. Luke mainly looks confused.

'Luke . . . you're here?' I ask.

He clears his throat. 'I was passing and I'd thought I'd see if you needed someone to walk you home?'

The silence when he finishes speaking is thick like treacle, hanging there in the darkness.

'Okay, thanks.'

I don't think that is why Luke's here. But I can't call him out for being a liar. Not after seventy-one days of not seeing each other.

We set off, me stealing surreptitious glances at Luke. Oh Jesus, I really have missed him.

He catches me looking.

'Do you normally walk home alone?'

I have an image of Luke turning up at the end of every shift determined to walk me home. I don't completely hate that image. But it's probably best not to outright lie. 'I normally get a lift with Joanie and one of the chefs. Or I bring Dad's van when I can.'

Luke nods, appeased.

We walk in silence for so long that I wonder why Luke has turned up at all. It isn't for my sparkling conversation, clearly.

'How was the bingo?' he asks eventually. Apparently we're planning to ignore the fact that we haven't spoken in weeks. I can get on board with that plan to be honest, despite feeling . . . odd around Luke. Unsettled in a way that would have made me happy once, but now just makes me nervous.

'More complicated than it ought to have been.'

I remember my accidental text. Shame floods through me. Ah, yes. Last night . . .

'I got drunk. Very drunk.'

'I gathered.' He does the smallest of smiles. 'What?' He's looking at me.

I've stopped to stare. Because although stern Luke is handsome, smiling Luke is offensively attractive.

I can't tell him that I've stopped because I've missed seeing him smile. So instead, I say the next thing that leapfrogs into my brain. Which, highly unhelpfully is . . .

'So are you in love with Hannah?'

Luke frowns at me, the darkness making shadows across his face.

I just keep talking. Barely bothering to stop and breathe now. Honestly, a nice little bit of oxygen deprivation is exactly what my brain deserves. Take that, brain!

'I'm only asking because of the bet. Even though I know we called it off. Or you did I think. But from a philosophical standpoint, I'd like to know the outcome. That's it. It's purely, one hundred per cent about the bet,' I finish with a flourish.

Luke breathes out a sigh. I guess he must have excellent lung capacity as it seems to go on for quite some time.

'No, Alice. We aren't in love. We aren't even together.'

'You aren't? Right. Okay. But why the heck not? You were such a good match. Well, aside from the fact that she seemed really into astronomy.'

'Alice.'

'But then you know, Empedocles kind of said that opposites attract. Or like strife and love attract. I've been doing research for my uni interview. Did I tell you about that yet? Probably not since we stopped talking. I guess you'd be the strife.' I pause for a second to gasp in some air. 'But then Empedocles also said that you can bring people back from the dead with magic, so maybe . . .'

'Alice,' Luke says again. 'We were never together.'

No. This isn't true. I saw them. Weeks ago. I saw them outside the Welcome Centre.

'But I saw you together at the Welcome.' I can't even hide the sad lilt to my voice.

I'm sure Luke is frowning, thinking. But it's dark and I can't see properly.

'A bit of the ceiling had fallen in and I offered to help with the clean-up. But Hannah and I agreed after Dad's party that we're better off as friends.'

I nod, guilty that my fear of running into a loved-up Hannah has meant that I've got lax in my promise to help at the Welcome. I've been making Mum run the stolen food in there like a drugs mule.

But at Luke's words, my arms and legs are feeling like noodles. Of course, it's wrong to feel quite so euphoric in the face of the news that the Welcome Centre is literally crumbling to bits 'Great. I mean not great, just good. And only if you think it's good. Was it the horoscope thing?'

'No, Alice. It wasn't the horoscope thing.'

'Well, what a hopeless pair we are,' I say around a smile so bright you could probably spot it from space.

'But what about you?' Luke asks. 'You said the boxers text wasn't meant for me, but it must have been meant for someone.'

'Shaun,' I say. 'We're better off as friends too.' I'm still smiling.

'Okay, that's great. I mean, very good.' For the record, I'm living for awkward Luke. 'Anything else new with you?' he asks, recovering somewhat.

I shrug. 'Not loads. I've been prepping for my uni interview mostly. It's in two weeks. Or just less than two weeks. I went over Hume earlier.'

'That's fantastic, Alice. Really brilliant.' He pauses and then asks, 'What does Hume believe?'

I think back to today's flashcard.

'Hume believed that inductive reasoning and belief in causality cannot be justified rationally. He thinks that intuition comes from custom and habit basically.' I repeat verbatim what was on my card earlier.

'I've missed hearing you talk about philosophy.' Luke sounds just as surprised at his admission as I am. I'm blushing again. Thank God for the dark. 'And for the record,' he picks up quickly, 'it's actually right, what Hume is saying. Nonconscious emotional information does have a neurobiological explanation.'

I laugh. 'But hold your horses, are we actually agreeing here? Have we found a bridge between philosophy and biology?'

'Technically I think Hume did, but let's take the credit ourselves.'

'Okay, what you said.'

He nods but keeps talking. 'I've been doing some thinking recently, about other ways that biology and philosophy might have more . . . in common than we previously led ourselves to believe.'

This is music to my ears. 'Oh really? Do go on.'

'Well for instance, I presume you've heard about developments in epigenetics?' he asks.

I shrug. 'Maybe I heard it mentioned on some podcast once. I can't remember though. What's epigenetics?'

'Epigenetics is the study of how your behaviour and environment can cause changes that affect the way your genes work.'

Luke sounds like he's reading from his own flashcard.

'What does it have to do with philosophy though?'

'Essentially, it's about how our genes are affected by factors other than biology. Obviously there's more to it than that, but epigenetics demonstrate how our upbringing, our personalities, our personal . . . philosophies influence the expression of our DNA. It's an answer to the nature versus nurture debate.'

I don't know how Luke's students get through his lectures. Hearing him talk science is a lot.

'That's really interesting,' I tell him honestly. He hums his agreement while I wonder if getting older means realising that everything is just that bit more complicated than I'd thought it to be.

Luke turns to face me. For a second it looks like he's going to say something seminal. Or else kiss me. And while I absolutely should be thinking 'fucking finally', I feel a pinprick of panic instead.

It's completely and utterly unwelcome.

I don't know if Luke catches the unwelcome panic, or if he was never planning to kiss me in the first place. But we're so close that I feel his breath warm on my cheek when he says, 'Alice, would you like to go to the reunion together?'

I jolt back.

'You're going to that?'

He clears his throat.

'Didn't you get an invite on Facebook?'

'I got it but I don't exactly want to go. Why do you want to go? School was awful for you. Plus we left school fourteen years ago, who has a fourteen year high school reunion. That is not a thing.'

Luke shrugs, then dips his head to look at the floor. My seconds-ago flinch is forgotten.

'Luke Priestly, do you want to go to gloat about the fact that you're a fancy-pants doctor at a university now? Because I could totally get on board with that. We could go all Romy and Michelle on them.'

Luke laughs. 'I have literally no idea what you're talking about. I'm going because Gordon has asked me to and I owe him one for all the years where he was the only person who spoke to me.'

We set off walking again. 'Hey, I spoke to you. Remember, I said the award was shit.'

'Yes, I do remember that. But you only said that because I said that it was shit first.'

'My comeback was weak.'

He laughs. 'So will you come?'

On the one hand, from what I remember the reunion is two days before my interview. I should be using that time to cram my brain full of all manner of philosophers. Plus everyone knows that you go to reunions to gloat, and I am a person without gloat. But on the other hand, I do really want to go with Luke. I think I knew full well the way this was going as soon as he asked. Still, I aim for coy. Or coy-ish at least.

'I mean, I suppose I could go. Piggyback off your successes. I might even get myself a new frock.'

'Frock?'

I blink. 'Sorry, I'm spending too long with Mum. How're you planning on getting there? I really don't fancy taking the van.'

'I'll drive. I can pick you up.'

'Great, thanks.'

I look up and realize with a shock that we're outside my house already. I feel vaguely disappointed.

'You'll have to come for tea again soon.'

At this moment, I think it'd be almost impossible to deny Luke anything. Especially under the moonlight with his hair a bit windswept. 'Of course. I've missed Mick and Lilian.'

I glance behind me at my house, reluctant to leave and yet also nervous that Mum is spying on us again from behind the veil of the net curtains.

'I best get in then,' I say.

Luke nods slowly. Or maybe I'm just seeing it in slow motion. Noticing everything about him like I'm seeing him for the first time. 'Night,' I say. I sound like I've been drugged.

'Goodnight, Alice.'

Luke looks like he's going to say something else and I hold my breath.

But he doesn't. Instead, he stuffs his hands into his jeans pockets and I watch him walk off into the dark.

*

In the quiet of my bedroom, I unlock my phone. There are two missed calls from private numbers. This is really starting to get annoying. I don't have time to dwell on who might be persistently calling me, though, because I need to do this now, before I let myself back out. I type 'Women's Aid, Easington' in the search bar and watch as the poster from the Welcome Centre loads, alongside the Women's Aid website with a big 'Get Help' banner.

I exhale a shaky breath.

I can admit that my relationship with Charles wasn't healthy. Wasn't good. I've grasped it more and more with every panic attack.

But I want to want to kiss Luke. I want to move forward without the shadow of Charles. I cautiously look through the website, my head swimming at words like *gaslighting* and *financial abuse*. I read deep into the night, filling my brain with new knowledge.

It's a cliché, that saying knowledge is power. But it feels powerful to know this. Charles isn't special, he's not even particularly unique.

I think about what Gabby said about therapy, adding the details of the support group to my calendar in my phone. Because just knowing it's there for women like me, it makes me feel less alone.

Chapter Twenty-Six

Unknown number: Alice, it's Charles here. I've been trying to contact you. Could you please answer your phone? We can't find some files and it's pretty urgent. Between you and me, this new assistant is useless. It's not like when you were here. C x

I read the message and drop my phone. I fumble to pick it up, hitting delete as my hands shake.

I stamp down the urge to go and hurl my phone into the sea.

Rubbing one palm over my collarbone, I count my breathing, waiting until it's levelled out before I open my eyes.

I think about what I've learned these last two weeks.

How abuse isn't just stories of women fleeing in the dead of night. Of shelters for women with nowhere else to go. Of women trying desperately to get away. It is all those things and it's awful. But it's also coercive control. Financial control. I think of the seventeen missed calls I had yesterday – it's harassment.

I delete the message. Block the new number.

'What are you up to today, pet?' Mum asks through the bedroom door.

I jolt and shove my phone under my pillow. Looking guiltily at the door as if Mum can see right through it. 'I was going to go shopping.' Good, my voice is not stressy. Totally normal. 'It's that reunion thing tonight and I might buy a new dress.' I've thought about it and I can stretch to it. I've been saving half of my wages for months. The world isn't going to end if I buy a new dress.

I won't have to go back to Charles.

There's a pause.

'Are you sure you're okay in there?' Mum asks.

'Absolutely. All fine and dandy. Grand, you could say.'

Another worried pause.

'Maybe it'll do you good to get out. Are you going to Durham?'

Mum is clearly of the opinion that a shopping trip to Durham is the answer to all of life's grievances.

I make a sort of dithery noise.

'I could come with you?' she carries on through the door. 'It would be ever so exciting, like a mother-daughter day. We used to always have those.'

Mum is right. When I was little, we'd have Saturdays when we'd do something together. Just like baking, or going down to the beach. Sometimes Aunty Moira would come, depending on where she was at in the lifecycle of her current relationship. It had all started to seem a bit small when I was a teenager, so we stopped. Or I stopped, to be completely honest.

'All right, why not. Are you sure you have time?'

'Of course I do. I'd actually really love to buy you a dress for prom.'

'It's a reunion,' I call digging around for a pair of socks, 'And there's no need.'

'Still, I'd like to,' she insists, her voice getting further away as she retreats downstairs. Something warm and snuggly settles in my chest. Motherly love, the hot water bottle of all the loves. It dims thoughts of texts from exes and domestic abuse posters.

'Okay, then. Let's go shopping!' I say, basically to the walls of my room.

Mum calls from downstairs, 'Ready when you are, pet!'

*

There's something about Durham that makes it feel right. Being here. It just feels like an important place, as if serious things have been happening here for all of time. Which I suppose they have. I think about Luke's study, wondering if it'll be another thing to put Durham on the map. A study which proves whether love is inherently rational.

Whenever I think about it, it's all a lot more muddled in my head than when we first agreed to that bet. I was so certain then that true romantic love supersedes what is rational. Now, I'm not so sure. Now the thought of falling in love borderline terrifies me. Which isn't rational at all.

'I think your Aunty Moira bought them last time we were here.' Mum points to a mannequin wearing some nipple tassels in the Anne Summers window, planting an image in my head that I could honestly live without.

We're by the main shopping street. 'What should we try first do you think?' I ask.

'I always think Marks and Spencer is a good option,' Mum says. 'Their stuff is built to last.' Spoken like a true baby boomer.

M&S probably wouldn't be my first choice. But Mum is so enthusiastic about the new Per Una range that I can't resist.

Plus she's determined to pay. So onwards we head.

Mum's faith in the integrity of Markses is challenged when I find nothing in there. In fact, I find nothing in any of the shops, not for want of trying. I try on all sorts, including what I'm pretty sure is a wedding dress from Monsoon.

'I don't think it is for brides,' Mum says, her head round the curtain of the changing room. She's looking distinctly flustered and she's not the only one.

I pull at the tag. 'Apparently there's a matching veil.'

We regroup over tea. I know I'm breaking Mum's spirit with this trip because she doesn't even complain about spending £2.80 on a cup of tea. Instead, we huddle over Google Maps on my phone, plotting out a route that'll allow us to hit the maximum number of remaining shops in the quickest way possible.

And who doesn't love a mother–daughter day planned with military precision?

Fortified, once more into the breach we go. I've been missing from the shopping scene for so long that the return of the scrunchie has passed me by entirely, as has the unfortunate dawn of the crop top.

But nothing screams me. What *is* me these days?

'Perhaps if we had an idea of what you actually want? Maybe we need more tea!' Mum wafts her face as we emerge from a fruitless seven-dress foray in H&M. It's almost the last shop on our route.

'I don't know!' I wail, throwing my hands in the air as other shoppers dodge around me. 'Do you think I can pull off gold?' I grab the lapels of Mum's coat, 'Will I look like the Honey Monster?'

'You can wear anything you like, anything,' she says, in what sounds like increasing desperation.

'That's the problem, I think. I don't know what I like.'

I slump onto a bench by the river.

'Maybe we should just go home. I'm a lost cause.' Plus my feet are starting to hurt. I don't have the stamina for this.

Mum sets her shoulders and adopts the stance of a general in the final throes of battle. 'One last place. Come on, look!' She points towards Durham Vintage. 'We haven't been there yet.'

Chances are I am in no way cool enough to pull off a vintage outfit. But the looming prospect of not finding anything means that it's worth a shot. I will not be defeated. Not if I can help it.

If this were an action movie, it would be the bit where the hero gets up and keeps fighting after being shot like seven times.

I haul myself towards Durham Vintage with a determined focus.

It's warm inside, the air thick with dust and sticky in a way that seems old.

There's a hotchpotch of different things. Necklaces and bracelets hang from hooks on the walls, their big jewels catching and reflecting the light from the shop windows.

The smell is not old or musty, but worn, lived in. There's a philosopher, Marc Bloch, who says that history comes from humans and it's true. Every coat, jumper, earring has a story all of its own.

I run my hand down a rail of silk scarves, flighty under my fingertips.

'I like it here,' I tell Mum.

I've a feeling that my one last hurrah might take some time. The back wall is filled with vintage dresses. I'm drawn to them, with their bold patterns and thick fabrics. I dismiss a bottle-green taffeta number as too heavy, and a black and gold jacquard one because, to be honest, it looks like a curtain.

Then I spot a pale blue dress, tucked away at the end of the rack. It has a chiffon overlay that falls in layers over the skirt. There are short butterfly sleeves and a beaded red flower stitched at the waist. I run the tips of my fingers over the intricate beads, starting to think that maybe I've been going wrong believing that a man might be my soulmate. I don't need a man, I need this dress. This dress and I are meant to be. God, I hope it fits.

In the changing room, the zip slides up no problem. Nothing looks good in changing rooms, does it? Except this dress does. It's like I said, soulmates.

'What do you think?' I ask, stepping out from behind the dressing-room curtain.

Mum is either broken from our shopping expedition or feeling overly emotional because her eyes well up at the sight of me.

'Oh, Alice ... It's beautiful.'

I swish around and look at myself in the mirror.

It *is* beautiful.

My mind is quiet for once. Taking in the dress and me in it.

'It looks amazing!' A shop assistant with pixie hair bounces around just to the side of me. 'I've been waiting for someone to come in and pick this up. It looks perfect on you.'

I smile and flush a bit, like you're meant to when you get a compliment.

I look at the price tag. £48.

'It's a bit much,' I tell Mum. She's wiping under her eyes with a tissue.

'Nonsense. We'll take this, please,' she tells the assistant, whose already wide smile grows impossibly wider.

'Are you sure?' I ask Mum, really hoping that she is.

'Absolutely.'

'I know, I know! Hang on a sec.' The bouncy shop assistant disappears into what I guess is the storeroom, returning with a headband, the exact same red as the flower. Except it has little blue leaves embroidered onto it.

'It's lovely,' I say.

'I thought it would go so well. It's just come in.'

I duck down so that she can put it on and then she's fluffing my hair and flipping up the layers of the skirt, circling me and saying things like 'perfect, love it, YES!'

'She'll take that, too,' Mum pipes up as a particularly energetic fluff has me close to flashing my knickers at everyone in Durham Vintage.

'Honestly, Mum ... just the dress.' I already feel bad enough spending Mum's money. When did I stop being able to buy my own clothes? *Don't answer that*, my brain replies.

'Nonsense, see it as a decade worth of mother-daughter days.'

'But missing them was my fault, not yours.' I'm the person who never came home after university – not until this year, when my life fell apart.

'I could have played my hand better.' She gathers herself. 'Now, go get changed.'

I'm wise enough to recognize an olive branch when I see one, and accept it.

'Okay, thank you, Mum. I really appreciate it.'

She nods.

Pixie-girl has her hands clasped in front of her. 'That was the most beautiful thing I've ever seen,' she says and her eyes fill with tears.

Well, my life is nothing if not dramatic.

As a thank you, I offer to buy us tea from Nando's. I get a little zap of pleasure at the Durham Vintage bag at my feet. Whoever said that money doesn't buy happiness has clearly never found the perfect dress after traipsing round shops for five hours straight. Mum is busy telling me the story about how I got overly attached to a pair of pegs when I was little. I've heard it before, but it still makes me laugh.

'. . . and even though all the other pegs looked exactly the same, you always knew which ones were *your* pegs. You married them every day. Like a real Victorian urchin.'

'We'd been on a school trip to Beamish. They have that whole section on what it was like living in the Victorian era. I think that was where I got the idea from,' I say as the waiter brings our food. Mum shares Dad's aversion to flavour and had double, triple-checked that there would be absolutely no spice. She now eyes her butterfly chicken with great suspicion.

She shakes her head, patting the top of her food with a napkin. 'You know, I always felt guilty when you played with those pegs.'

'Don't worry, Mum.' I pick up my own burger, wondering if eating a meal like this will ever be something I don't have to do consciously. I know my food issues could be way worse; chances are I got away from Charles before they could really take hold. But it's still annoying. I keep talking to distract myself. 'Kids are random. Tyler is obsessed with herbivores. Last time I babysat he made me pretend to be a diplodocus for two hours straight. He kept feeding me lettuce from a bag.'

Mum laughs. 'No, I mean . . . I wished you didn't have to play on your own so much. All this looking for love . . . If we'd been able to give you a sibling . . .' Her voice trails off, but the message might as well be written on a banner and dragged through the sky by a plane. Mum takes a tentative bite of a chip.

I suddenly find that I'm having to work very hard to swallow. 'Honestly, Mum. Charles had nothing to do with you and Dad. Nothing at all. It was me. Please, don't worry.'

She nods slowly. 'We did want more children . . . it just wasn't meant to be.'

'I'm sorry if things were hard.' I give Mum's hand a squeeze.

She shrugs. 'We were happy with you. I just worry we put too much pressure on you.'

'Lots of people are only children, Mum. They don't all end up like me.' I'm not exactly sure which bit of the like me I'm referring to here. Likely the whole angsty package. I carry on, 'So much goes into making a person who they are. Luke was speaking to me about this thing called epigenetics. It's like your environment dictates how your genes work, but they're still your genes.'

Mum chews on a chip, looking thoughtful.

'Okay, if you're sure,' she says finally.

'I am. Absolutely sure.'

'Thank you, Alice. Things are on the up for you, now. A mum can always tell.'

Chapter Twenty-Seven

Luke: I'll set off just before seven to pick you up?
Me: Sounds good. See you soon

I feel like I have a kaleidoscope of butterflies in my stomach as I do my hair wavy and spend as much time as I have spare on my make-up. Charles would say that I've overdone it. But hand on heart, I can say that I don't care what his opinion would have been. Revelation.

I fix my headband, forever indebted to the excitable shop assistant. It and this dress are soulmates. When I go downstairs, Dad wolf-whistles and Mum tells me that I look very smart, but then blots at the corner of her eye with a hanky.

My phone pings.

Luke: Outside

I hurry to meet him.

It's early March and I haven't seen the sun in months, so going without a jacket might be a decision I live to regret, but I cannot, in good conscience, put my big coat over the dress. I clamber into Luke's (mercifully warm) car while Luke looks at me. He blinks several times. 'Alice. You look ... I mean you look very ...' he gives a small cough, '... beautiful.' Which makes me feel all warm and fuzzy.

'Thanks,' I reply. 'You look nice, too.' And he does. He's wearing a white shirt and some dark grey trousers. You'd have to be a troll to look bad in a white shirt like that.

We sort of just stare at each other for a moment.

I give a nervous laugh in an effort to break the tension that's tighter than my Spanx.

'Let's get going!' I say, breathlessly.

'Yes, really . . . let's get going.' Luke releases the handbrake, and he looks more than a little relieved to be setting off.

Maybe it's just the novelty of not having to risk life and limb in Dad's van, but I'm obsessed with watching Luke drive. He's just so unfailingly capable at everything. It's quite a turn-on. Who'd have known it?

After less than ten minutes, we pull into the school car park. Except it doesn't look like it used to when Luke and I came so many years ago. Gone are the peeling paint panels under row upon row of windows, and there isn't a Portakabin classroom in sight.

Instead, there's now a futuristic white-and-glass building with a sign which declares Easington Roman Catholic High School in silver letters. It's an acknowledged truth that almost everyone in Easington pretends to be Catholic to get their kids in here, because this is the higher-performing school and everyone is willing to put up with a few hymns and a couple of Hail Marys in exchange for a higher GCSE pass rate.

There's a sign over one of the doors that exclaims, 'Welcome Back, Class of 2010!'

'Looks like it's taking place in the gym,' Luke says, closing the door behind him. Is that a weird thing to find fit, a man closing a car door? Possibly.

Luke hasn't moved from where he's stood beside his car though, and I wonder if perhaps he's more nervous than he's letting on.

'Should we take a picture, maybe?' I ask. Just for something to say. Plus there's also a teeny tiny bit of me that thinks I'd like some photographic evidence of how good Luke looks tonight. For purely innocent reasons, of course.

I probably look better than I've looked at any point over the last five months and so I upload it to Instagram. Because any personal growth I've been doing lately does not extend to excellent selfies. You don't look a gift horse in the mouth and all that.

'Should we go in, do you think?' It sounds like a question because suddenly, I'm wondering why the hell we're bothering going to a reunion when we could just, I don't know, go back to Luke's flat or something. That sounds like a much better idea. Nice one, brain.

'We have to.' Luke, at least, looks pained at the prospect so it's good to know I'm not suffering alone. 'I told Gordon I'd meet him here.'

Bloody Gordon.

Luke smirks at me. I can't be completely sure that I didn't say that out loud.

We set off towards the double doors of the sports hall. I can feel my hands getting clammy, nervous at the prospect of attending a reunion with everyone who knew me at school but even more nervous at how I feel about Luke. It feels big. I don't remember feeling like this when I realized how much I liked Charles. All those philosophers are missing a trick. Love isn't all fancy words and high-concept feelings. It's pure terror. Plain and simple.

Not that I *love*, love Luke or anything, but you get the idea.

'After you . . .' Luke offers as we head through. The doors clunk behind us, and everyone turns to look.

Inside the gym, the lights are dim. There's an ageing DJ playing Destiny's Child, multicoloured lights beaming out of his kit. The floor is scattered with balloons. By one wall there's cling film-wrapped food set out on a row of school desks, along with several bottles of wine. It's your classic school disco, only we're all fourteen years older and alcohol doesn't need to be smuggled in.

People huddle at the edge of the dance floor and we scan the crowds, feeling like me and my dress have done well. We're maybe a touch more dressy than everyone else, but not by much.

I feel Luke's hand cover mine, grabbing on tighter than he likely needs to.

'Come on, let's get a drink,' he says. His shoulders are tense. 'Then I'll see if I can find Gordon.'

I nod, following behind him towards the row of glasses.

'What is Gordon up to these days?' I say over the music.

'He runs a tech start-up in Manchester,' Luke calls back to me.

'See,' I stop and gesture with my hands. 'Another point to my theory that *not* peaking at school is the key to long-term success.'

The song finishes right at the time I say 'success' and I end up shouting it, causing everyone stood around us to stop and gape. So much for incognito.

Luke smiles and his shoulders relax a touch.

We arrive at the drinks. I try to discreetly look for people I might recognize, but everyone is just generic adult.

Luke looks down at his phone and then says, 'Apparently Gordon's already here.'

I take a glass of wine and Luke has a Coke because he's driving. Then we do another scan of the perimeter of the dance floor.

'Over there, look,' I say, pointing to the far corner where Gordon Grahams is waving furiously at us.

We weave our way back to the other side of the gym.

'Gordon, hi.'

Gordon has not changed at all. His teeth are still rather large for his face. But his salmon suit is sharp. I take sharp to mean expensive when it comes to suits. Dad's one funeral suit is not sharp. So I'm pleased that Gordon seems to be doing well for himself.

'Luke, hi!'

Luke nods and waves a hand in my direction. 'You remember Alice King?'

I smile and give a little wave.

'Course I remember Alice. We sat next to each other in Year 8 geography.' Gordan turns to me, nudging Luke with his elbow. 'This one was incredibly jealous.'

'Oh, really?' I beam at him.

'Gordon,' Luke says in a voice that makes me break out in goosebumps.

Maybe this reunion will be better than I expect it to be ...

As the booze takes effect, people start to mingle.

I smile and nod at the news that Louise, my science lab partner, had twins last year and rents a place down in Peterlee. She has her version of Beyoncé's birth announcement shoot as her phone lock screen, and I admire her a great deal for that.

Andrew, my rugby-mad Year 10 boyfriend, now works as a prison officer I hadn't quite expected to hear the word 'shiv' quite so often tonight, but all in all, he looks happy.

Then there's Sasha, who took one for the team and became the teenage pregnancy statistic of our year. She went back to college and is a chiropractor now.

I enjoy talking to people that I went to school with, but I'm itching to get closer to Luke.

Glancing his way, I see that he's still surrounded by women. A small yet determined group who seem intent on getting his attention.

I shuffle a bit closer, hearing one of them declare that she's a pilates teacher and very flexible. Emphasis on the very. I'm sure it's Peggy; she used to be best buds with Sarah Smithins who snogged Luke on the down-low.

I clench my fists tight by my side.

To his credit, Luke seems surprised to be the centre of attention. I can't fight the urge to pull him away from all the people who made his life miserable in high school. But when I try to extricate myself and get to him I'm blocked by people. They pepper me with an onslaught of questions. I find myself mumbling vague statements, trying not to give too much away about my work-in-progress life, my earlier enthusiasm for the evening evaporating with each sympathetic look I accumulate.

'No, I'm not married.'

'Yes, still with my parents actually. I'm hoping to move out in September.'

'No, no children.'

'You want to get a move on. Nice dress, by the way.' Jade Bolton, mum of five, has me cornered.

'I don't think I need to be worried quite yet.' I throw out mental pleas into the universe. *Someone help! Please.*

The universe doesn't listen.

'I knew a woman who went through the menopause at thirty-three. All her eggs died off.'

Every question is leaving me more and more miserable. Or at least my answers are. At least Jade seems to like my dress.

I need to get away.

Luke is still being held hostage by his adoring fans. He's faring much better than he did at school.

I understand then it's not just me who thinks that Luke is a catch. There's likely a fair chunk of the human race who would agree.

Suddenly my efforts to get to rescue him seem just a little bit sad. He's fine. He's laughing right at this second. He absolutely doesn't need me.

I make my escape. I don't even make an excuse, just turn and walk away from Jade who is mid-sentence. Something about her friend's inhospitable womb being straight out of Gilead.

I head down brightly lit school corridors, trying the handles of classroom doors that all look the same and are all locked, until a science lab door finally opens and I go in and take a seat on one of those high stools they have.

I remember my own science lessons. Running my hand through the orange flame of a Bunsen burner. The thrill of setting magnesium on fire. Wondering why on earth iron was Fe on the periodic table.

So, new plan for the evening . . . hide here for an hour or so, claim a headache and then beg to go home. The dress can have another run-out somewhere less judgemental. I slump on the table, willing the time to pass.

Ten minutes later, I'm testing myself on the stages of the human digestive system out of an old, battered textbook. Nothing like finishing a highly dispiriting evening correctly identifying a rectum.

I jolt as the door creaks open and Luke's head appears around it. 'Luke!'

'You took a while to find.' He opens the door wider then, coming fully inside.

'It's only been ten minutes. You didn't have to come after me.'

I say this despite the fact that I'm very happy to see him. My face has broken out into a smile all of its own accord.

'I wanted to,' he says simply.

Luke leaves the door open, and the music reaches us, albeit faintly. 'Poker Face' by Lady Gaga is playing. Ironic. My smile is about ready to carve my face in two.

'What're you doing in here?' he asks.

'Thought I'd best brush up on my ileum from my anus.' I wave at the textbook. 'Seriously, when have we ever used any of this stuff again? Like, does anyone really need to know about the functions of the pancreas?'

He gives me a pointed look.

'Oh yes, biologist. Got it.'

Luke comes and sits next to me.

'You know,' I tell him. 'You shouldn't be in here babysitting me. Your people will miss you.'

He shrugs.

'Oh, come on. Aren't you even a little bit smug about the fact that they were all awful to you in school and now they're vying to win your hand?'

He pauses. 'I thought I might be a little bit smug,' he begins, 'but I don't actually want to make small talk with the girl who stabbed my hand with a compass in geography. More than once.'

'What? Who the fuck did that? Was it Peggy?' Suddenly I'm furious on his behalf.

'It doesn't matter, Alice.' He looks resigned.

'No, tell me who and I'll avenge you!'

'Alice . . .'

'I knew you got picked on a bit, but that's like next level, Luke.'

He shrugs. 'It doesn't matter . . . but, er, that's why I didn't want to shake your hand, that day of the awards. I'm not sure why I'm saying all of this now, but I just didn't want you to see the mess of my hand.'

I'm off my stool threatening to take down Peggy again while Luke is telling me again that it doesn't matter.

'It does matter,' I say with feeling, letting Luke position me gently back onto my stool.

'It doesn't. Their prefrontal cortex hadn't fully developed. It's why teenagers are awful.'

I think of Gordon, Luke's only friend at school.

'But not all teenagers are awful.'

Luke shrugs weakly.

'You weren't awful,' he says.

I feel like it might ruin whatever moment we're having here to say that his benchmark for awful was obviously really low if people were stabbing him in school.

'I can see you thinking hard,' Luke says, tucking some of my hair behind my ear in a move that makes my brain shut up a bit. 'And it doesn't matter anyway. I don't care what any of those people think.' I'm so relaxed listening to him I'm like a puddle on the floor.

'That's good, I suppose.' I sound drunk.

Luke gives a rare, genuine smile. Something clunks into place in my chest.

'Would you like to dance with me, Alice.'

It's unusual. Luke's voice with a nervous lilt.

'You, dance?' I ask, even as I slide off my stool, hardly sure that my legs will hold me up.

As if on cue the DJ starts up 'Love Story' by Taylor Swift as Luke takes my hand and we start to sway. He's so tall that even in heels I can lean my head against his chest. He twirls me out and then back into his chest. We're awkward and uncoordinated, but I do not care.

I nuzzle back against him again so that his heart beats into my ear. I can see his throat bob as he swallows. Feel the heat from his chest through our clothes.

We stay like that. Silently swaying. I half expect to have another episode. I steady my breathing, count it out like I used to. I try pressing my body tighter to his. I want to have made the most of this moment. I need to say something, to try and explain how we've ended up here. I look up at Luke.

'Alice, I really want to kiss you. Do you think I could? I don't want . . .'

I place a finger on his lips, my face tilted to meet his. 'I totally think you could.'

'You do?' His voice comes out deep and throaty.

Small smile.

Words might have failed me, but I can always manage some very enthusiastic nodding.

I close my eyes and the next thing I feel is Luke's lips.

It's tentative at first, a whisper of a kiss. As if he's worried I might break. I hope I don't break. I run my hands up the front of his shirt and loop them around his neck and press forward. At my invitation he deepens the kiss. His mouth is warm and soft I am not myself.

He has a hand in my hair now, kissing me with abandon and somehow – suddenly – in this empty chemistry lab, I feel free.

Chapter Twenty-Eight

I forget about time. I could emerge from this kiss like you might wake from a coma, only to discover that you've lost years of your life. It would be totally worth it.

The kiss turns impatient, demanding. At some point I have wrapped a leg around the back of Luke's, as if I'm considering scaling him. It's the sort of kiss you read about, the sort you see in films and think, *people don't kiss like that in real life.* I never want to let go. Never want it to end. I pour everything I have into it.

We come up for breath.

'You're beautiful.'

'I thought beauty was a trick of evolution?' I nudge him weakly in the ribs.

'It is. One of her better tricks.'

I kiss him again then. Standing on my tiptoes to reach. He pulls me against him so strongly that my feet leave the floor entirely.

It's perfect.

I lose myself as Luke rearranges his grip on me. Yes.

But then I feel it like a pebble dropping into my stomach.

The dread.

It ripples outwards.

No.

Not again.

I freeze. Stiff with terror. We're all going to die.

Luke stops immediately. Lets me go.

Charles, pulling me in close.

Charles telling me to stop being a baby and give him a kiss.

Being naked. Feeling naked.

Luke has taken a step back.

'No, no,' I wheeze. 'I'm so sorry.'

The edges of my eyes go dark.

'Hey,' Luke soothes. 'Just concentrate on taking some deep breaths, okay? I'm going to put my hand on your back to help. Is that all right, Alice?'

I huff out an assent, feeling Luke's warm hand rubbing small circles on my back.

We stay there, me hollowed out and stretched thin, Luke muttering words I can't hear until the stiffness begins to pass. My breathing regulates. I slump forward, my forehead landing in the crook of his shoulder.

'Shh, I've got you.'

I've no idea what to say. I'm so embarrassed I could weep.

I concentrate on my breathing, on the steady thrum of Luke's heart under my ear. I start to hear the music again in the distance. Slowly, the panic retreats, leaving me cold and shaken in its wake.

'That wasn't the first time, right?' he asks. I really shouldn't be surprised that Luke knows me so well.

I shake my head, still clinging to him.

'Right. They've happened every now and then. That day we first met. I'd just had one . . .' I sniff, not even realising that I've started to cry. 'I used to have them when I was a teenager.'

'Shit. I'm so fucking sorry, Alice.'

I clutch at Luke's biceps, hanging on for dear life.

'I had some myself, back in college.' His voice is calm, measured.

'You did?'

I feel, rather than see him nod.

'It took me ages to recognise what was going on at school. Although it's a panic attack, I don't feel panicked, not really. It's more like – God this sounds ridiculous – but it feels like the world is ending.'

'They're all different,' he says. I'm still not breathing right. 'They – they manifest in different ways.'

'Seem to.' I take some deep breaths. 'What helped you?'

I sense him hesitate before answering. 'Biology. Seeing them for the biological reactions they are.'

My heart still pounds. 'Tell me.'

'It's just the body's normal response to a threat. If, say, you saw a lion, your body would get flooded with adrenaline. It would give you energy to flee. That's why you breathe so hard too. You're stocking up on oxygen for your muscles. Getting ready to run.'

'I see.'

'But there's no lion. So you don't know why you feel like that.'

I don't like the thought that my body wanted to flee from Luke on a cellular level. Not when my heart was fully on board with all the kissing.

'Shall we get you home?'

I nod. 'I'm sorry for ruining your evening.'

'I thought we'd banned apologies?'

I give a weak laugh and follow him out. Luke's hand is over mine as the music grows louder. Together, we reach the double doors which open back into the sports hall. We pause. I rest my head against his shoulder as he looks down at me.

'I just need to go and tell Gordon we're leaving. Do you want to come or go straight to the car?' he asks.

'Car, definitely the car,' I say, because I still feel vaguely out of it, and also worried I'll do something I regret if Jade starts talking about the state of my ovaries again.

Luke passes me the key and I dart through the dim sports hall with my head low, careful not to look anyone in the eye. I hardly even notice the cold as I make my way to his Volvo. I let myself into the passenger side and then keep counting my breathing which I know will help.

With scant regard to the state of my mascara, I press the palms of my hands so deep in my eyes that when Luke appears and I pull them away, dots dance in front of my vision and I have to blink them away.

'Did Gordon mind you leaving?' I ask, my voice slightly hoarse.

Luke takes the key and starts the ignition. 'Not at all, he was in the middle of a mosh pit back there.'

I laugh at the thought of little Gordon Grahams in a mosh pit.

'I still can't believe that you drive a Volvo,' I say. Because I can't seem to find the words for what I really want to say. Need to.

'They can't be beaten on all the core components of car ownership.' Luke speaks while looking out of the rear-view mirror to reverse, and I get that he's just playing along. I appreciate it though. So much.

'Yeah, if you're a middle-aged man. Is coolness not one of the core components of car ownership?'

He moves to drive out of the car park and I can't help but notice that he's very . . . contained on his side of the car.

'What could be cooler than safety?' he says. 'You're involved in a pile-up on the motorway, say, you're surviving with all your limbs still attached to your body. Nothing sexier than literally walking away from a burning car.' He taps the steering wheel while I marvel at the inappropriateness of enjoying watching his mouth form the words 'pile-up'.

We set off towards my house, Luke's hands never deviating from their designated ten and two positions on the steering wheel.

At some point he must turn the radio on, as I realize that we're listening to indie rock on quiet.

'Is that okay?' he asks, noticing me looking at the music console.

'Yeah, course, fine.' I manage a smile.

I'm quickly learning that Luke doesn't mind silence. Silence with Charles invariably meant he wasn't speaking to me. But silence with Luke is different. Comfortable. Like he knows I sometimes need to be alone but not alone.

We pull up outside my house, except I don't want to get out of the car. I know we need to talk about what happened, I just don't know how to start it.

'Luke,' I go to say, at the same time that he says, 'Alice'.

'You go.' He nods towards me.

I feel tingly with nerves all over.

'I was just going to say sorry, for what happened back there,' I tell him. 'I really wouldn't want you to think I didn't enjoy the kiss, I really enjoyed the kiss. Like really, really.'

I think about adding another really, just for good measure, but Luke is . . . there's no other word for it, smirking at me. My cheeks flush with colour.

'I enjoyed it too,' he says and then after a pause, 'really.'

'Don't be a dick.' I laugh.

'But where does it leave us?' I ask then. 'I'd really like to do more of the kissing . . . obviously, but not if it, you know . . .' I trail off.

'Causes another panic attack?' Luke asks and I nod sadly.

He's twisted round in his seat to look at me and it's a crime against Hallmark movies everywhere that kissing Luke would make me feel like that.

'Plus I have my interview on Monday. That's literally three days away. I need to be in a good headspace for it.' I'm not sure why I'm talking so quickly.

'Hey, I get it, Alice. If this is all too much, we can be friends. Or enemies. Or whatever you want.'

'Is that what *you* want?' I ask. I remind myself that Luke is a self-proclaimed eternal bachelor. Doesn't believe in love and all that. And, oh God, I've fallen for the worst possible person.

'No.' The sureness of Luke's voice cuts through my spiralling panic. He holds his hands up. 'I'm not saying I know how to do ... this, or that I'll even be any good. But I ... miss you when you're not there. I don't know what's wrong with me, honestly.' He does a nervous laugh. 'So, I want to try, if you do.'

'I'm really scared,' I tell him honestly. 'But I want to try too.'

Luke thinks for a minute. 'How about this,' he suggests. 'Instead of jumping head first into something *more*, we just wait it out in the space between friends and whatever the next step is. Like a ... more than friends.'

I let Luke's words settle over me.

'A more than friends?' I ask and he nods. 'I like that.'

Luke breaths out and I get how nervous he's been this whole time.

'Do more than friends get to kiss?' I ask.

'No idea, I just made the whole thing up. I don't want to pressure you,' he says.

'I think it was when you touched ... er ... when you touched my bum. It brought back a bad memory. Of Charles.' I'm so hot that you could power half of London with the thermal energy I must be giving off.

Luke thinks he's business as usual when he says 'got that' but he's gone stock-still, gazing into the middle-distance with a distinctly murderous air.

'Luke.' I try to bring him back. His eyes meet mine.

'Have you ever ... considered talking to someone?' he asks. 'Someone who might be able to help.'

I nod.

I had thought about it when I'd spoken to Shaun. And when I texted Gabby too.

'There's a group, in the Welcome ...' I trail off. Wanting to explain more, but feeling like I just can't get the words out.

The twitch of the front room curtains catches my eye. Mum.

'I'd better get in,' I tell him, leaning forward just a touch.

He finds the certainty in my eyes and leaves the softest kiss against my lips. His hands are firmly in his lap, and I can't decide whether I want to be grateful or scream at the injustice at his lack of touch.

'I'll see you soon?' I say, my tone somewhere between a statement and a question.

'Course. You could come by the lab after your interview on Monday if you like?'

I really would like that. 'Perfect.'

Chapter Twenty-Nine

There's another awful comment under my photo with Luke. It just says 'whore', posted from an account with no followers. The internet is wild, isn't it? I still feel unsettled by it as I head downstairs on Saturday morning. I do have a nice good morning text from Luke though, so today is very much yin and yang so far.

The looks on everyone's faces tell me we're about to get heavy on the yang though. 'Who died?' I ask as I walk into the front room to find Mum, Dad and Aunty M all sat looking at each other forlornly. Then, realising that I have a very elderly Nana who might actually have died, I follow it up with, 'Shit, it's Nana, isn't it?'

Dad looks at me. The TV is off. I am very much braced for the worst. 'No, pet, your Nana is fine. But the Welcome Centre. The council can't raise the funds.'

I look at Aunty Moira. 'I thought you said they would? You said we had ages?' I ask, my head racing through all the things the Welcome Centre is good for. Dwaine's jazzy exercise class, the golden oldies mornings, the food bank, the Women's Aid support group that I've literally just decided to go to.

'It's these latest cuts,' she answers, unusually serious for once.

'There must be something we can do?' I look at Mum who shakes her head.

'Council wondered about having a fundraiser-type thing,' Aunty

M tells us. 'But what's the point? Folk round here don't have much money spare as it is.'

We're all silent while the news sinks in. I get what Aunty M is saying, I really do. No one in Easington has a lot. And I know what it's like to struggle for money, to worry about every pound you're spending. But I also know what it's like to just lie down and let things happen to you without fighting for what you want. I don't want that for the people of Easington. Surely we have to at least try?

'I think we should do the fundraiser, People here don't have much, but I know they'd give what they can. We can't go down without a fight,' I tell them as three pairs of eyes look my way. 'How long do we have exactly?' I ask.

'Till the first of May,' says Aunty Moira. 'After that, *Dave* can sell it. Apparently he has a buyer who wants to level the place. Put a Subway there or something. Why the heck would we need a sandwich shop when we have Star's? I've been speaking to the charities who use the place, to see if any of them could take it on. But the charity sector is struggling too.'

I ignore the sinking feeling. 'We've got two months then, to raise as much as we can.'

Mum nods. 'But . . . fifty grand?'

'Twenty-five,' Aunty M cuts in.

'I thought you said he was selling it for fifty?' I ask.

Dad's eyes ping-pong between us all like he's watching a Grand Slam tennis match.

'There's a scheme,' Aunty M tells us. 'If a community can raise a certain amount of money for places like this, the government will match it.'

'Well there you go!' I say with renewed vigour. 'We're already halfway there.'

'I don't think . . .'

'Not now, Mum. We don't need no Debbie Downers round here.

I'm going to meet Joanie now. I'll see if she can make some cakes to sell at the fundraiser or something. We can do this!' I say this with a big smile even though really, a bake sale is not going to make us twenty-five grand.

Aunty M, at least is roused by my very rousing speech in the front room. She smacks her thigh hard and declares, 'Course we bloody well can.'

I mean, we might not. Mum is right, twenty-five grand is a lot. But it's the principle of the matter. We're not just going to let this happen. If the Welcome Centre is going down, it's going down swinging.

'We can't just give up without a fight,' I say to Joanie, my head pounding as 'The Circle of Life' blasts through the Little Daisies sound system.

Joanie does not look good. She has her head on a table in the circus room. The circus room should not be entered into with a hangover. Joanie is eyeing a particularly exuberant ringmaster like she's about to strangle him with her bare hands.

'What. The. Fuck. Are. You. Talking. About?'

'The Welcome Centre, we need to do something to save it. What's the matter with you by the way?'

Joanie has massive bags under her eyes. A bit like a dead panda. 'Are you sick?' I ask.

A low-budget clown with cracked white face paint and a horrifying red smile leaps from behind the doorway and every child in the room screams and runs to their parents. Tyler burrows under Joanie's arm and onto her knee and she relaxes a bit, patting his hair.

'Flat across the hall were having a party all night. Hardly slept. Can someone get me some coffee?' Joanie shouts. Little Daisies isn't really the sort of place where you bark out orders. But the exuberant ringmaster, clearly fearing for his life, decides to break the rules and runs from the room towards the kitchens.

Joanie shakes her head. 'Right, sorry, I'm good. Tell me the plan again, this time slowly.'

I take a breath. 'So, Aunty Moira told me that there's a government scheme that'll match any funds the community raises to take over a building like this.'

I have the YouGov website open and I scroll down to show Joanie the relevant bit.

'It'd mean it would be owned by the community essentially. So all the stuff that it has now could still run. We might need a committee to oversee everything. But the important thing is that the building would be protected. So all we need to do is raise twenty-five grand.'

'Twenty-five grand!'

I ignore her outrage. 'Aunty M said the council were going to hold some sort of fundraising thing, to raise the money. But they abandoned the plan because it's too much.'

Joanie drums her fingers on the table. 'That *is* a lot of money, Alice.'

'I know, but we have to try surely? We can't go down without a fight.'

The parents of the birthday boy are having it out with the dodgy clown. It's quite distracting, but I gather my thoughts.

'Go play again?' Tyler asks. Joanie nods and giving the clown a rather wide berth, he runs back into the main play space.

'What are you thinking, to raise the money I mean?' Joanie asks.

'We could have different things, like, I don't know, a human auction for stuff that people might need anyway. That way they're only paying what they would have done.' I hesitate. 'I should probably speak to Hannah about it. She's so involved in the Welcome, she must be gutted that Dave's planning to sell it.'

Joanie looks up from where she's taking a long drink of what must be absolutely boiling coffee.

'Luke's Hannah?' she asks.

'I told you, they went on two dates. I was there for one of them.'

'Defensive much?' Joanie gives me what I think of as her Disney villain smile.

I lean forward to whisper. 'It's just that me and Luke kissed last night, at the reunion.'

Joanie smacks her hand on the table. 'Knew it! Tell him to pay up then.'

'I don't think I can. I had a panic attack after, and we did agree to be more than friends, but it's not exactly a declaration of love, is it?'

'A panic attack? Shit, Alice.'

'I've had them before. And Luke explained them to me, like biologically. They're still scary but I don't know, I kind of get why I'm having them now.'

Joanie blows a breath out.

'I think I need to park worrying about everything until after my interview on Monday. We still have time. But I wanted to run the Welcome idea past you. What do you think?'

Another hand slam, this time earning us a frown from a group of other mums sat sipping cappuccinos a table away.

'Fuck it, I'm in. Let's save the heap of shit.' She takes another drink of coffee. 'You want to go through some more interview questions?' she asks.

'Please, if you don't mind.' I pull out my now not insignificant stack of potential interview questions flashcards. They're held together with a hair bobble. I hand the pack to Joanie.

She pulls a card from the middle of the pack and clears her throat like she's reading the questions on *Mastermind*. 'Question one. Which philosopher said, "That which is not good for the beehive cannot be good for the bees"?' She flips the card over to check the answer.

'Marcus Aurelius,' I say, confident that it's correct.

'Good job, you're going to smash it.'

I really hope she's right.

Joanie continues quizzing me through our shift at the Lotus later. She has some flashcards stuffed into her waistcoat pocket and when we pass each other she mutters things like, 'What does consequentialism consist of?' and 'Whose philosophy was based on the principle of *Ren*?'

Trying to revise and waitress at the same time is harder than you might expect. Especially when all night I can't stop thinking about the Welcome Centre too. Of what'll happen if we can't raise the money.

When Paul comes over to the couches at the end of our shift, I brace myself for being publicly berated. Joanie is still rubbing her temples and groaning about the fact that she's been awake for two days straight. I don't feel too great myself and it takes me a few moments to tune into what Paul is saying.

'. . . we'll be knocking them on the head.'

'Knocking what on the head?' someone asks. Clearly I'm not the only person who zones out of Paul's speeches.

'The free food.'

Joanie snaps her head round with such vigour that I'm surprised she doesn't break her neck. She rounds on Paul, jabbing a finger at him. 'You can't take our meals. They make up part of our pay packet. Unless your next sentence is that you're about to give us a raise?'

Paul at least has the good sense to look uncomfortable.

'Look, my hands are tied.' He holds both his palms up, his hands seemingly the exact opposite of tied.

Oh my God, is this because we're stealing the out-of-date food?

'Bullshit. This place is full every night.'

'Stop being a troublemaker, Joanie,' Paul warns, his face flushing with anger.

'Don't troublemaker me, you bellend.' Joanie gets away with being meaner to Paul than the rest of us, because he relies on her to run the place.

'Right!' She address the other servers. 'We can't stand for this. Let's form a union.'

They all look at each other.

I want to help Joanie, but I'm also guilt-stricken that our food theft is causing the place to go under. 'What about a WhatsApp group, at least?' I suggest.

Everyone shifts about, but no one voices their support. No one does anything at all, aside from Andy who takes the whole thing as a sign that the revolution is about to begin and puts down his pint with a determined air. 'I'm with you,' he says.

Paul ignores him.

'That's settled then, and anyone who has a problem with it can leave,' Paul says, backing away from the couches. All the other wait staff look down, busy with what is, apparently going to be their last meal here.

'What if it's because of the food we've been taking?' I whisper to Joanie once he's far enough away not to overhear.

'We take it before it goes in the bin, Alice. The bin. Fuck. I hate being poor.' Joanie slumps back.

She's right. And I am done.

I make after Paul. 'You can't just stop giving benefits that make up part of our pay,' I tell his back. He turns to face me.

'Are we still talking about this? I told you, there's nothing I can do. If you want a job, you'll have to accept it.'

I wave a hand back to the couches, almost certain that everyone is watching me. It's bad enough that the staff here have to put up with an incompetent manager who turns a blind eye when the customers grope them, but having their wage packets reduced too? It's just completely not fair.

'Everyone here could all sue you for loss of wages. I have a bit of experience in admin. I'd help them.'

'I think you're forgetting something'' He jabs a finger at me.

'What's that then?' I ask, outraged.

'You're on probation, you haven't passed it. I'm letting you go. You've never been any good anyway.'

I'm too stunned to speak. To think I felt guilty minutes ago. Now I'm gutted that I won't be able to steal any more food from under Paul's nose.

Joanie comes up from behind me, anger radiating off her like cosmic rays from the sun.

'Don't,' I tell her, shaking my head. 'You need the job for now. For Tyler.'

I can see the war of emotions on her face.

'I don't want to work here anyway,' I tell basically the whole entire staff. 'If you ever want to drive this numpty out of town,' I hook a thumb over my shoulder towards Paul, 'give me a call.'

Andy starts up a slow clap.

'What will you do?' Joanie asks as I get my coat.

'It'll work out,' I tell her, with more confidence than I feel. I actually feel the unwelcome return of gnawing panic. I won't have a wage, however meagre it might have been. I won't have security. Again. But I can't let on to Joanie; she can't quit too. 'We'll get you out of here next.'

'God, I hope so. It'll be even worse now that you're not here.'

'I think that's the nicest thing you've ever said to me. I feel like we should hug. Do you think we should hug?'

'Fuck no.'

All righty then.

Chapter Thirty

I'm sat in a long corridor waiting for my interview, trying to block out everything that has happened since Friday night and hoping that I don't have a panic attack. It's not exactly the Zen-like state I was hoping for.

If this were a movie it'd be one of those scenes where a line of hopefuls who all look essentially the same sit patiently with crossed ankles, portfolios clasped to their chests, waiting to be called in by some director extraordinaire.

However, this is not a movie. So it's just me in a corridor on my own, five hundred flashcards clutched in a death grip. My foot is tapping so much that I'm sure it's trying to communicate with my brain via Morse code. Something along the lines of, *You have no business being here.*

'Just a few minutes, Ms King.'

A middle-aged man shows a young woman out of a door at the end of the corridor.

The other candidate looks ten years younger than me, and is in denim overalls with rainbow hair and a nose ring. She seems exactly the sort of person who'd be accepted to study philosophy. I can see her now, sipping soya chai lattes and musing on whether nature is inherently ordered. The image does nothing for my raging imposter syndrome.

She nods at me, acknowledgement that we're civil people who

happen to be vying for the same thing today. My foot resumes its tap in earnest. *SOS. SOS*, it beats out.

'We're ready for you now, Ms King,' the middle-aged man calls to me and I head towards him, hoping that I don't look as shaky as I feel. Potentially drunk is not the first impression anyone wants to give in an interview.

'Alice! Welcome. Please take a seat, I'm Dr Kamaria.' A woman in a bright pink dashiki greets me from the corner of a huge wood-panelled office. She's by a wall of books where two chairs sit opposite one. I take the one.

'This is Mr Clark, who leads on the moral theory course.'

Mr Clark looks to be the sort of man who plays badminton and listens to Classic FM.

'Nice to meet you,' I squeak.

'And you, Ms King.' He takes the final seat. I'm so nervous, there's a good chance this is going to start with me puking on them. I clasp my hands together and plaster on a fake smile.

'So, how we like to do these interviews is to keep things fairly informal. It's not a philosophy test or anything like that, we'd just like to get to know you as a person a little. See what makes you tick,' Dr Kamaria says. 'Does that sound okay?'

I think of my hundreds and hundreds of flashcards. 'Yes.' Possibly only the bats can hear me.

'And do you have any questions at this stage?'

'No.' I curse myself. I should have had an intelligent question ready to go.

'We'll each be taking some notes, if that's okay?'

'No problem.'

Dr Kamaria smiles at me and I relax a tiny fraction.

'Then let's begin.'

The first part of the interview is straightforward enough. They assure me that my A level grades are impressive and ask me why I'm applying now, of all times. I expected this question and so rattle off the answer I've already thought of.

I tell them how maybe I wasn't ready to go to university when I was eighteen, how I hated the idea of doing badly at something and so quit instead of sticking it out.

'I'm much more resilient now,' I tell them with some certainty. 'And I've never lost my love of philosophy. If anything, being back in Easington, it's grown. When I started my degree in London, it was full of people who *knew* they belonged there. Like, they just knew it. They had this confidence that I didn't. But people from Easington deserve to feel like they belong in places too.'

'Hear, hear!' Dr Kamaria says, and I feel my confidence growing. It's got to be a good sign if the person in charge of the whole thing is agreeing with you, hasn't it?

'It sounds like the philosophy of power is something you might like to pursue study in?' Dr Clarke says. I wonder if he's quite as wowed by my outburst.

'Absolutely.' I nod. 'And love, I've always been interested in the philosophy of love. That's what my A level coursework was on.'

I might be imagining it, but Dr Kamaria sits up a little straighter.

'Do go on, Alice,' Dr Clarke says.

'I agreed with Bertrand Russell. That a life without love isn't worth living.'

'Russell is generally popular amongst applicants, let me tell you that,' Dr Kamaira laughs.

'I bet. It's tempting, the philosophy that love conquers all. Except it doesn't, not really.' I think of Joanie, stuck in a job she hates for Tyler's sake. 'It doesn't conquer poverty, or hunger.' I think of Charles. 'And sometimes truly awful behaviours are carried out in the name of love. Love is a choice. It's an action that you can take or not take and then keep on taking. And it doesn't just have to be romantic love either. You choose to love in all relationships.'

'So you are suggesting that love is more complicated than Russell claimed?' Dr Clarke asks.

I suddenly realize that I have absolute confidence in what I'm saying. 'When it comes to love . . . I think that anyone who believes that they've arrived at the answer hasn't thought deeply enough about the question.'

And that's me, isn't it? All this time I've been waiting for a man to fall in love with me when really, it's a million times more complicated than that. It's not about getting someone to love you, it's about loving people and being loved for who you are.

Both Dr Clarke and Dr Kamaria are nodding.

'Thank you, Ms King. Is there anything else you'd like to add?'

I'm still a bit out of it from the revelation I've just had. But I manage to shake my head.

'You'll be able to check your offer via the UCAS portal,' Dr Clarke says.

I get to my feet and offer a clammy hand out for a shake, which no one seems to mind. Or maybe they're just being polite.

'Take a seat.' Luke gestures towards a run-down office with a few worn chairs and a small expanse of kitchen worktop piled high with mugs. As promised, I've come to meet him after my interview but now that I'm here, I'm struck unresponsive by the sight of him in a lab coat.

'I'll just go put this away.' He holds the lapels of the lab coat and I give an effusive 'Thank God'. Which earns me a small smile.

Once he's back, in a navy shirt which is only marginally less distracting than the whole lab coat set-up, and he's fished through all the mugs in the hunt for a reasonably clean one and made me a coffee, we sit opposite each other.

I blow on the tar-like substance, looking around the messy office.

'Has anyone ever told you that scientists are slobs?'

'I think we have to be so methodical in our work, we give in with the rest.'

'By that rationale, I should be the sort of person who has all their coat hangers facing the same way. Except I'm not.'

'That's actually an indicator that someone's a sociopath. Serial killer territory.'

'Shit, really?'

He laughs. 'No. Come on then, how did it go?'

'It was actually amazing. It didn't feel like an interview at all, just like a talk about philosophy. I really hope they let me in. I feel like I've done what I can.'

I'm doing my best to keep my expectations in check. By that I mean wrestling them back from the dark blue yonder of outer space.

'Fantastic, Alice. Well done. I'm sure they'll offer you a place.'

'Can't you put in a good word for me?' I ask him, sipping at coffee so potent I probably won't sleep for a week.

'That would be unethical,' he says, raising an eyebrow.

I make a note to poke Luke into being mock stern again at a later date.

'I know, and anyway, it'd be easy to let you save me, but I'd rather save myself thank you very much.'

'Glad to hear it. When did they say they'd let you know?'

'I find out through the application portal. I never even heard back from the other two, so there's like a ton riding on this. In the meantime, I'd better look for a job.' While I'm talking, I stand up and move to sit next to Luke on the little two-person couch he's on. It's one of those cheap ones with scratchy material and no arms, and it's about as sexy as my unemployment chat.

I look towards the office door; the place seems quiet enough.

'Hello,' he says, turning slightly to towards me. I look at where his leg is next to mine. He wears suit trousers well. There's an inch of space between us. I'm not overly fond of the inch of space, but we've agreed to take things slowly.

'Hello,' I say back. 'I just thought that maybe I should get some sort of a reward for doing so well in my interview.'

Luke twists fully round to look at me properly. 'I see, and what did you have in mind?'

'A kiss, at least?'

'I'm sure that can be arranged.'

The actual kiss is short. Because we're in public and we're both worried that I'll panic. Luke's hands stay firmly against his side and the whole thing only lasts a couple of seconds. But still, it lights me up like a set of Christmas lights. And I know for certain that I want more.

I'm floating on a cloud of good feeling by the time I arrive back in Easington. I'm almost certain that the interview went well and the fact that it doubled up as a sort of therapy session for me, one where I realized that I'd been going about this whole love thing completely wrong, well, that was just the icing on the cake.

Even if I have always put romantic love on a pedestal, it's not that I didn't know that there were other types of love out there. Philosophers almost universally agree on the fact. These past few months, I think I've been inadvertently dousing myself in the love of my family and friends. And learning to at least *like* yourself is a pretty big deal too. It feels good to have these realisations properly nailed down.

I'm so pleased at the direction that my musings have taken that I don't notice the Mercedes parked outside Mum and Dad's house. Or the car door slamming as I turn my key in the lock.

I'm halfway through the door and someone is saying my name. 'Alice.' I freeze.

'Alice.' He says it again and goosebumps break out all down my spine.

I turn slowly to face him.

'Alice,' he says a third time, opening his arms wide like he might want me to fall into them. Except I don't, of course I don't. He must grasp this, because he puts his arms back down by his side then. 'Well, silly, aren't you going to invite me in?' Charles asks, shoving past me.

They're not home. All I can do is follow Charles into the empty house.

PART FIVE

CHARLES
(again)

'Love shouldn't hurt'

Chapter Thirty-One

Charles looks exactly the same as he always has done. His blonde hair is slicked back and he's smiling a perfect white smile. By the time I follow him into the front room, he's already on the couch. Manspreading to the max.

'It's freezing in here,' he says, rubbing his hands together. 'Did your parents ever get that smart meter I suggested? They really can't be beaten on energy efficiency.'

I've mostly been hovering dumbstruck in the doorway. I can feel the panic rising, threatening to crest inside me, but I concentrate on my breathing. Think of Luke telling me that it's just a biological response and when I do talk, my voice is surprisingly steady.

'What are you doing here?' I ask him.

His smile grows even wider. 'I've come to take you home, silly. Don't pretend that those Instagram posts weren't for my benefit? That you wanted me to see how well you were doing?'

I move to stand by Dad's chair, keeping a wary eye on Charles.

'I've no idea what you're talking about. You finished with me. You have another girlfriend?'

His smile drops, just for a fraction of a second.

'Who?' he asks, 'Ophelia? That's been over for ages.'

This is news to me. It doesn't make me happy, not like it would have done in the past. It makes me nervous. Each breath is getting harder and harder, like I'm being squeezed.

'You need to leave,' I tell him.

'Alice, be reasonable. We were always so good together, and like I said, your Instagram ... you've proved a point. You'd become incredibly needy before, but now I can see that you don't *need* me. That's very attractive.'

Wow, he talks some rubbish. But amid the garbage, I do notice one thing he said.

'Was it you? Who kept sending me awful messages and commenting on my posts?'

Charles's eyebrows lift, just the tiniest amount, and I know I'm right. Suddenly, I'm not sure how safe I feel.

This time when he talks, his voice doesn't have the same sickly-sweet tone. It's more purposeful, demanding. 'Why would I do that? Not everything is about you, Alice. Now, do you have anything you want to bring with you when we head back?'

'Head back?' My voice sounds hoarse.

'Home.' He gestures towards the window and his car.

'This is my home.'

His glance bounces between the patterned carpet, the net curtains and Mum's collection of porcelain figurines. 'No one would want to stay here,' he scoffs – and then I lose it entirely.

'I want to stay here, Charles. No wait, I *am* staying here. You aren't a good person and you *cheated* on me. I'm done, I've moved on.' I think of Luke and the inch of space he leaves and the fact that I only ever feel unfailingly safe with him. I point towards the door. 'Now get out.'

Charles tenses, like a cat that's about to pounce. But I'm not a mouse, not anymore.

'Go,' I tell him.

His cheeks have red patches as he pushes himself up off the couch. But instead of going towards the door, he's coming towards me. 'If I'm going home, you're coming with me.'

'I'm not going anywhere.' I stand my ground, though I'm suddenly very aware of the fact that Charles is a lot bigger than me. My breaths start coming in short sharp bursts.

He grabs my arm. I stare down at his grip on me in horror. 'What are you doing? You're hurting me!' He looks down too. Lets go.

'You need someone to make these decisions for you, Alice. Just come on now, stop this nonsense.' Charles puts his hands on his hips.

I've no idea what's going to happen next. All I do know is that I'm not getting into that car with him.

'Come on, Alice.' He holds out his palm like he expects me to link my hand with his and suddenly I'm furious that he'd think I would ever go back to him after everything that's happened.

I grab the first thing I can. It's the picture of me winning my arts award. Luckily the corner is sharp.

I jab it at Charles.

'You need to go now.'

Charles's eyes go wide in alarm at the fact that I've armed myself. Albeit with a plastic picture frame.

The front door opens.

'Go on then, I'll have a quick cuppa,' Aunty M says, just as she and Mum come into the front room to the freeze-frame of me holding out the pointy corner of the picture towards Charles.

For a second, neither of them moves. But then my arm drops a touch and a sob escapes me and in a flash Mum has her arm round me and Aunty M is marching towards Charles then manhandling him by the shoulders towards the door.

'What the fuck is wrong with you people?' Charles's face has turned a shade of purple that cannot be healthy. His hair is becoming dishevelled. I glance down. A shoelace is undone. Anarchy.

'Go, now,' I tell him as Aunty M is shoving him through the doorway.

'You heard the woman,' she tells him cheerfully.

'You are never, ever welcome in my house,' Mum calls behind him, mustering a level of venom beyond anything I've ever heard her say.

Charles mutters something that sounds suspiciously like 'lunatics', and I think I hear Aunty M whack him as she leads him towards the front door.

I collapse onto the floor, just crumple, still holding the picture of me and Luke together.

'Well.' Aunty M comes back into the front room wringing her hands as if she's just taken out the bin bags, 'I don't know about that cup of tea, Cheryl, I think we all deserve something a bit stronger.'

'I think you're right, Mo.'

Mum disappears into the kitchen as Aunty M sits on the floor next to me, crosses her legs and gives my knee a squeeze.

I feel oddly numb. There was a time when Charles coming back for me was everything I wanted but now I just feel . . . relief that I'll never have to see him again. I'm going to call the police. Look into a restraining order.

Mum joins us on the carpet, handing round mugs filled with no small amount of a brown spirit.

'Cheers!' Aunty M says. 'For being rid of the posh twat once and for all.' We all clink mugs and take a drink. Whatever it is, it burns like hell.

'He really was the poshest of posh twats,' Mum says, potentially drunk from one single swig. I don't think, in my whole entire life, that I've ever heard Mum swear. It sounds so wrong that I start to laugh. And once I start, I can't stop. Maybe I too am pissed after a single toast.

'The way I was going to stab him with the photo frame.' I can hardly breathe for laughing.

'It's only plastic.' Tears are rolling down Mum's face as she and Aunty M join in with the laughter.

'I only came in to talk to you about a job, Alice. Didn't expect to see you ready to commit murder.' Aunty M gives a massive belly laugh. I'm almost certain that she and Mum would have helped me bury the body.

'A job?' I ask, sobering up, just for a second.

'Tomorrow, pet, we'll talk tomorrow.' Aunty M pats my knee again. 'Enjoy your moment for now.'

Later that evening, the crash comes. I'm lying on my bed in the crook of Luke's arm as he smooths my hair down my back. Of course he came straight over once he heard what had happened. I'm somewhere between awake and asleep, wrapped up in his warmth. My limbs feel like they're made of lead. I'm not sure I could move if I wanted to.

'Is there a biological reason why some men are like him and some women are like me?' I ask him, not turning up to look at him but staring straight ahead at my wall.

'What do you mean?'

'Like is there something faulty with him? That he goes on like that.'

'No, I don't think so, Alice.'

'But there must be. You said about teenagers, how some of them can't help it. Maybe it's the same.'

'I think I used the teenage thing to make myself feel better. But men like Charles, there are so many things at play, so much that goes into making them what they are. More than anything, though, some people are just knobs.'

I laugh and then just listen to Luke breathe, steady and sure. It's the last thing I feel, the rise and fall of his chest as my eyes finally close.

It's a mild evening when I finally push through the doors of the Welcome Centre a week later. It feels unnaturally bright inside, like I'm under a spotlight or something.

But they're there, most of them smiling. Milling around by the hatch to the kitchens, pouring drinks from the big teapot.

Women of all shapes and sizes, all ages, who've been through something and come out the other side of it. They're all looking at me.

I give an awkward wave.

'Hi, I'm Alice,' I tell the room.

I'm not here to make some grand announcement. Or to tell everyone my story right away.

I'm here because that poster is absolutely, completely right.

Love should never hurt.

PART SIX

ALICE

(or Alice and Luke, depending on how
much of a romantic you are).

*'Sometimes, love is a bubble
pod in your parents' yard.'*

Chapter Thirty-Two

Me: Hi Hannah, it's Alice. You know, from the BBQ. I heard about the Welcome Centre and I just wondered if we could meet to discuss an idea I've had, for keeping it open

I wait on my bed for a reply to come through. Hopefully, the fact that I had to mention the barbecue doesn't work against me.

It takes ten minutes before my phone pings,

Hannah: Hello Alice, that's a nice idea. But I thought the council couldn't afford to take it on?

Me: I have an idea, please just meet me to chat about it? If you think it's daft, we can leave it

There's another five-minute pause.

Hannah: Okay, when?

Me: Star's at 3?

Hannah: I'll see you there

I blow out a huff of relief and then move on to my next, equally awkward message.

Group Chat: Exes

I add Dwaine, Andy and Shaun, getting to work on a message before I can talk myself out of what is potentially a terrible idea.

> **Me:** Hi everyone, hope you're all well. You're probably all wondering why I'm getting in touch, but basically I need your help with something important. If that's okay, message back and maybe we could meet? Thanks, Alice

My phone pings immediately.

> **Shaun:** Shaun here — I would be happy to meet, Alice

Dwaine's reply comes after an hour or so.

> **Dwaine:** Sorry, in the middle of leg day. I don't see why not …

Andy's is the last to roll in.

> **Andy:** What day is it? Aye, lass, we can meet. So long as you're not trying to steal me away from my new missus ☺

I assure Andy that I'm not and the four of us agree to meet at Star's later that afternoon. I should have time to get Hannah on board with my plan before they all arrive.

I check the time, 10.10 a.m.. My phone call is already ten minutes late. This is what Aunty M said though, that it's chaos over there. It's taken them two weeks to even sort out a phone interview. Apparently the charity sector has suffered from the same cuts that plague the council.

Finally, after five more minutes, my phone rings.

'Hello, Alice King here.' I answer in my best 'I am mature person and I really want to come work for you' phone voice.

'Hello, Alice, sorry I was running a little behind. I'm Janet, I run the Durham branch of Women's Aid. I'm sure your Aunty Moira told you that I'm in desperate need of an admin assistant, I just can't keep on top of the work at all. Sadly we're getting more and more calls.'

'That is so sad,' I jump in, confused between being sad about all of the women who need help, or a little bit happy that for the first time in Easington's history, connections are getting us where we want to be. 'I would absolutely love to come and work for you, if you'll have me. I have ten years' experience as an admin assistant at Beck Health Cafés, I really think I could do a good job, but more than anything, I want to come and help with the work that you do. And I have experience in applying for restraining orders and also of going to one of your groups.' There's conviction in my voice, and not even the fake type you normally adopt only for interviews. I really do mean what I say.

'Look,' Janet starts, 'I'll level with you. The pay is awful, and we can only offer part-time hours at that. But your aunty said you'd do a great job and that you have a plan to help keep the community centre open, which would save me an enormous headache.'

I'm nodding along, even though Janet can't actually see me.

'I'm going to do my very best. I have some meetings about it this afternoon, actually.'

'Brilliant. Keep me posted and we'll see about a start date.'

I do a silent 'yes, yes, yes!' and then attempt to will my voice back to professionalism as I say, 'Thanks so much, Janet. I should say, though, that I'm waiting to hear back from Durham, I've applied to study philosophy in September. If it all works out, I'd love to do both though.'

'That's fine. Moira mentioned as much. We can adjust your

hours. Hopefully by then things will be a bit more ordered around here anyway.'

Tears are rolling down my cheeks at the thought that I'll be able to go and help with the work they do at Women's Aid. If I get into uni too, it'll be perfect.

As I sit nursing what is likely to be my first of many cups of tea in Star's, waiting for Hannah, I wonder just how long my good fortune is likely to last.

I mean, is it ever a good idea to meet four-fifths of your exes on a random Thursday afternoon. It seemed like a solid plan this morning, but now I'm 95 per cent nerves.

'Hannah!' I practically throw myself out of my seat when I see her coming towards my table at the back of the café.

She isn't smiling when she spots me, but then my smile is possibly bright enough for the both of us as she sits down.

'Order whatever you like,' I tell her, 'it's on me.'

Apparently guilty, semi-unemployed me is very magnanimous. Stupidly so. But like I said, bag of nerves over here.

Hannah orders a cup of coffee and then folds her hands. Her jumper is neatly ironed and her hair is in a ponytail. Even before Stephanie the butcher gave me choppy layers, my hair never all stayed in the same bobble.

'I don't have ages,' she says. 'I left Dad watching TV, but he can't be on his own for too long.'

'Course, how is Mr Hall?'

She shrugs. 'Okay, mostly.'

Hannah's coffee comes and I know that it's now or never for my pitch.

'Right,' I start. 'I know you probably don't like me that much, and I get it, I do. I told you that there was nothing going on with me and Luke, which wasn't true. But I didn't know how I felt at the time and I'd been through some shit and you got caught in the middle of it all and I'm sorry.'

Hannah sips delicately at her coffee, looking at me over the top of her cup. I take it as a sign to go on.

'But the people of Easington deserve to save their Welcome Centre. If we can raise half the money that Dave wants, the government will match it and the community will become the owners.'

Hannah has leaned forward in her seat, just a little bit.

'The community?' she asks.

'Yeah, we'd have to have a committee or something like that. I thought you'd maybe want to be in charge of that. My aunty works at the council and she said they'd help manage it.'

'But how do you suggest we raise the money?' She's not laughing me out of the place, that's good.

'A fundraiser. The council thought about it, but then abandoned the idea. But if we all give a bit of what we can, maybe it'll be enough. I'd love your input.'

She taps her fingers on the table.

'And you and Luke?' she asks.

'Sort of together,' I admit. 'I really am sorry.'

She does a deep breath out. 'Glad to hear it, I'm never wrong about these things.'

'Wait, you're not mad?' I ask. In my head, we've been embroiled in a love triangle.

'Why would I be mad? We went on two dates. And one of those was awful. He's a nice guy, not for me though.'

'Right. Riiggghhhttt. Well, that's fantastic!' I'm so enthusiastic I actually propel myself upwards a tiny bit. I'm literally taking off with enthusiasm.

I talk Hannah through my plans so far. I'm thinking some sort of event down at The Buccaneer, since it's big enough to host a lot of people and the Welcome itself is out.

She offers a few ideas of her own (like asking the bar to give us a cut of sales) and after half an hour, I'm feeling much more relaxed and also vaguely optimistic about the future of the Welcome.

'I'd better get back to Dad.' Hannah stands up and pulls on her coat.

'Course, I'll add you to the WhatsApp group.'

She has the last bit of her coffee.

'Why are you so bothered about the Welcome Centre?'

I try to compose myself and try not to let my mind go back to two weeks ago, with Charles.

'It's just, you know, the important stuff that goes on there. The food bank and ... plus, there's the fact that Women's Aid run that support group. I don't want that to close,' I reply honestly.

Hannah looks at me then.

'Okay, let's make sure it doesn't.'

I feel, on the whole, that this afternoon is going as well as it can by the time Hannah leaves. However, as I see Dwaine arrive, I am once again struck by the thought that this is, at best, a dodgy idea. Clearly Dwaine has jogged here; his shirt has essentially moulded itself to his body.

I manage a tentative little wave as he comes to sit at the table.

'Do you want a drink?' the teenage waitress asks.

I watch as Dwaine attempts to ascertain whether Star Bucks sells anything which wouldn't throw out his daily macros. In the end, he opts for water with a slice of lemon. I order another cup of tea.

'Alice.' He finally turns to me. 'How've you been?'

I remember the last time that I saw Dwaine. Panting and shaking. I rub a hand over my collarbone. 'Good,' I say. 'Better, at least.' Movement in our direction draws my attention.

'Look, there's Shaun. Hi, Shaun!' My wave this time has a little more oomph behind it. Shaun is, after all, the only man I didn't have a breakdown in front of.

We have a bit of a palaver wrestling chairs from the tables nearest us to join our own. At least Star's is mercifully quiet.

'You're right on time,' I tell Shaun as he orders a can of Dr Pepper.

'Of course.' He shows us his arm and the massive watch that's on it. 'This is an atomic watch. It's radio calibrated to be incredibly accurate.'

We manage a good effort at a bit of small talk. Shaun is almost all set for September, seeing as he got offered a place without needing to interview. I keep checking the UCAS portal, but there's no news yet.

No, now is not the time to panic about that.

I'm saved from my spiral by the late arrival of Andy, who stumbles through the door covered in paint.

'Sorry, lass. Our Cindy surprised me at work.'

Cindy, I realize, is Andy's new girlfriend.

'No problem, thanks for coming.'

Andy orders a coffee and asks the waitress to tell Bob in the kitchen to put a splash of something in it. We all pretend not to hear.

'We're old pals,' Andy informs us. 'Always buys a paper from us.'

'Right.' I clap my hands to gather the meeting. 'Now that you're all here – and thanks for coming by the way – I just wondered, that is I, er . . .' I peter out as they all stare at me.

'Spit it out, lass. We don't bite. Well, not unless you want us to,' Andy winks. His heavy-on-the-Irish coffee has arrived remarkably quickly. He takes a long sip.

I rub a flattened palm over my collarbone again.

'Right, it's just that I wasn't in a good place when we dated.' I clear my throat. 'What you should know is that I'd been in an abusive relationship.' They all turn quiet. 'And I hadn't worked through any of it.'

'I'm sorry about that, Alice,' Shaun says.

'Me too.' Dwain.

Andy pulls me into a cross-table hug that leaves me covered in paint. 'I never understand why folk do that. I love women me.'

'Thank you.' I rush on knowing that If I stop now I'll never start again. 'You couldn't have known and I'm not sure you'd have been able to help if you did. But I wondered if you could help now? Not help *me* but other women.'

The three of them go silent, looking at each other before all nodding.

'Absolutely,' Andy says. 'To women!' He forces Dwaine and Shaun to high-five.

'To women!' I join in to yet more high-fiving.

'Great, guys,' I sniff, emotional all of a sudden.

'What do you want us to do, Alice?' Shaun asks.

'Well, you know the Welcome Centre is up for sale?' Cue some muttering. 'We want to buy it, as a community. We're running a fundraiser, likely at The Buccaneer, to get us started. Where you all come into it is that I was hoping you'd be willing to volunteer your . . . talents to raise some cash.' I turn to Dwaine. 'Like, Dwaine, you said you had a black belt or something?'

He nods his head slowly. 'Karate, judo, jujitsu, American wrestling.'

Jesus. 'Brill, well I wondered if you might do some self-defence classes, for anyone who wants to come? Or maybe some personal training, just a little, and donate the money you make. I thought about it, and you could advertise your other classes at the same time.'

Dwaine smiles. 'I'll help. It's a right pain trying to find some-where else to host my disco dance class as it is.'

'Fantastic, thank you!' Next I turn to Shaun. 'When my ex and I broke up, he found out what I was doing pretty easily and left awful comments all the time. I wondered if you could help people set tighter security on their social media. If that's something you know how to do? People could just pay as they feel, so no one is excluded.'

He blinks at me. 'That's a good idea, Alice.'

'So would you be willing to help?'

'I would. I could speak to Dad about doing a special kebab or something too? One where profits go straight to the fundraiser.'

'That would be amazing! Great idea.'

Shaun beams.

'Actually,' I ask, 'would you be able to check the security settings on my phone now? I think I changed them all, but I'd prefer a professional eye over them?'

Shaun takes my phone and we all watch for a second as his thumbs fly around at lightning speed.

'Here.' He hands it back a few minutes later. 'Anonymous himself wouldn't get in now.' I'm not 100 per cent sure who or what Anonymous is. But I guess that's the point.

I smile at him. 'Wow, thanks so much, Shaun!'

'Don't tell me, don't tell me,' Andy says, pulling his shoulders back. 'You want me to sing at this thing, really draw in the crowds.'

This isn't actually why I'd invited Andy. I was hoping that he'd help out with painting and decorating the Welcome Centre. But he looks so happy at the prospect of being asked to sing that I can't bring myself to tell him no.

'Thanks, Andy. I'm sure more people will come if they know you're singing.' Truly, I feel like the opposite is true. And Joanie is going to kill me. Still, I'm not about to dampen the good feeling that hangs around our table like mosquitoes by a swamp.

'I really appreciate all your help. I'll be in touch with the details of the event.'

Shaun stands up first. 'I have a raid starting in fourteen minutes,' he explains, looking at his watch.

'No problem.'

'And I'm due back at the gym.' Dwaine follows suit.

'Thanks again.'

'Guess I'd better get ready for tonight, it's a pity I won't see you at work, Alice. We've really got over our bad break-up, haven't we?' I wonder how potent his Irish coffee could have been; he seems to have forgotten the circumstances of our parting ways. I take it that he's probably been doing a fair bit of day drinking too.

'We sure have, Andy,' I tell him, like he's an ageing great-uncle who's forgotten that we're not still in the rationing era. 'But I'll still see you around.'

The four of us head to the till to pay.

'Thank you all,' I tell them once we're outside. 'I'll be in touch.'

For a moment after they leave I stand on the pavement and look up at the sky. For once, it's actually a clear blue — rare in this part of the country. My home. Hope bursts through my chest instead of panic. I'm getting there. Or at least I think I might be.

Chapter Thirty-Three

Save the Welcome Centre — a call to action! As many of you know, the Welcome Centre is up for sale. We, as a village, have two options. We can either accept this and have no more coffee mornings, no more exercise classes, no more food banks . . . or we can fight it.

We say we should fight it. And if you agree, come along to The Buccaneer on Saturday 30th March and help Easington save our Welcome Centre. Tombola, auction, entertainment, drinks and more! Food provided by Easington's answer to Paul Hollywood — the Cake Fairy. Doors open at 3 p.m.. Come along and see what's available!

The Facebook notification pings through, followed almost immediately by alerts on the WhatsApp group I now have with Hannah and Joanie.

> **Joanie:** Hannah, did you compare me to Paul Hollywood?
>
> **Hannah:** I did indeed, you're welcome 😊
>
> **Joanie:** Couldn't I be Mary Berry?
>
> **Me:** Come on, there's only one Mary
>
> **Me:** What if no one comes?
>
> **Hannah:** They will. There's already a comment on the post

I check the comments section. Sure enough, Andy has written, 'Count me in! Women have been even more oppressed than men, we can stand for it no longer, comrades!'

That he's then gone to the quite considerable effort of creating a pair of punctuation boobs, with brackets and full stop nipples, undermines his sentiment somewhat.

> **Joanie:** I still can't believe you got the sack from the Lotus and then found the perfect job right after
>
> **Me:** I wish you could quit already
>
> **Joanie:** Mate, me too
>
> **Hannah:** I knew there was something I needed to tell you, Joanie. My star sign said I'd be extra forgetful this week!
>
> **Joanie:** Come again?
>
> **Hannah:** Jasper has got another job. You know the chef? He wanted someplace with an oven that works every time
>
> **Joanie:** No way?
>
> **Me:** OMG Joanie, you can get a job at the Welcome when we save it!
>
> **Joanie:** Still seems a lot of ifs and buts to me

Maybe I'm being a bit greedy asking the universe to grant all my wishes – there's no magic lamp buried in the Arabian desert after all – but I really do hope that Joanie will get that job.

> **Me:** Hang in there just a bit longer. Things are going our way now

Offer Status: Unconditional Offer

I refresh the page. It's still there. Refresh again. Still there.

I got in.

To Durham. Philosophy. I got in. My brain is clearly so over-whelmed that it's only working in short sharp bursts.

I got in.

'I got in!' I yell, this time thumping downstairs to tell Mum and Dad.

'What's going on?' Mum comes in from the kitchen.

I'm out of breath with excitement. And a bit of nerves, but mainly excitement.

'I got a place at Durham,' I tell her, holding out my phone so that she can see the . . . yep, the offer is still there.

'Oh, that's wonderful, Alice! Gary, isn't that wonderful?' She claps her hands together.

You can tell how monumental an occasion it is by the fact that Dad has muted the TV.

'Let's see it then,' he says and I show him my phone too.

'I bet they don't go handing out unconditional offers to just anyone,' he says, puffing his chest up a bit. I think it's likely the fact that my A levels are over a decade old and therefore definitively in the bag, but I'm not about to dampen the glow of parental pride that I'm currently basking in. Not when we've had years of it being as sparse as oxygen at altitude.

Mum agrees wholeheartedly with Dad.

'Have you told Luke?' she asks. To say that Mum is Team Luke would be the understatement of the century. The second she heard he was a doctor she'd put him on a pedestal somewhere close to Alan Titchmarsh. Every time he (Luke, not Alan Titchmarsh) comes round, she rolls out the Hobnobs. The chocolate ones.

'Not yet, I just found out. I'm going to his in a minute anyway, if I'm still okay to borrow the van, Dad?'

'Aye, I'm done for the night. You go enjoy yourself.'

I do a very effusive goodbye and then I'm not so much as

whipping down the B1283 towards Luke's flat as I am shuddering and hoping the clutch makes the full journey.

Luke and I are still in the more than friends category, the parameters of which we've had to suss out for ourselves, seeing as it's not a real category of relationship. So far, we've agreed that more than friends means we *aren't* more than friends with anyone else. There's also a fair bit of kissing in the more than friends zone. Luke, always excellent at anything he does, is an excellent kisser.

Happily, all kissing so far has been panic attack-free, though much like when he's driving the Volvo, Luke's hands rarely stray where they shouldn't.

I'm not sure whether to be incredibly grateful for his restraint or disappointed at the lack of ravishing.

Buzz. Buzz. Buzz.

'Hello?'

'Luke, it's me.'

'I know. I heard the van.' I think I hear a smile in his voice, but I can't be sure.

'Can I come up, then?'

'Course. Sorry, one sec.'

There's a clunk as the door lock releases and I push through. I take the stairs to Luke's floor two at a time.

Rounding the corner, I see he's there in the corridor, a tea towel over his shoulder. It seems ridiculous now that in those early weeks I never appreciated just how handsome Luke is.

He's Jupiter and I'm a tiny hopeless asteroid careering towards it. The gravitational pull kicks in big time.

I planned on playing it a bit cool, the fact that I got accepted into Durham.

'Guess who got into uni?' I rush out, not giving him chance to reply. 'Me, it's me!' Maybe I've never had an iota of cool when it comes to Luke.

'That's fantastic, Alice. I knew you could do it.' Luke picks me up and spins me round right there in the corridor. I take the opportunity to breathe in the scent of the side of his neck.

'Hi,' he says as he puts me down, his cheeks tinged a bit pink.

'Hi.' I smile back.

'We should go inside,' he says, looking back to his flat.

'Let's.' The air between us feels charged tonight.

To distract from the fact that I'm potentially gazing at Luke like I want to jump the poor guy, I look around his flat. The remnants of an old mill gutted and turned into flats, it's all exposed brick and glass. It's not the first time I've been, but it is the first time Luke has cooked for me here. On an evening. You know, the time of day when sexy times are most likely to happen.

Note to self, must never say the words 'sexy times' out loud.

The whole flat is pretty small – the kitchen is just off the living room and there's a mezzanine level which I presume is where he sleeps.

Don't think about his bed. Don't think about his bed!

Not. Now. Brain.

'Sorry about the mess, I ran over in the lab today,' he says.

'Uh huh. Such a shame you don't keep the lab coat here. You didn't bring it home as a one-off today, did you?' I look around, hoping to see it but just noticing the fact that it is all a bit messy. Just like the office was. There's a hastily squared pile of letters on the coffee table and the leather couch has a mismatch of cushions, a jumper slung over the back.

'It *is* a mess, isn't it? I know what you said about scientists and chaos but for some reason I just can't get over the fact that you don't live in a hermetically sealed vacuum and just hook yourself up to an oxygen cylinder.'

'You did bring your own tank, didn't you? There's only enough air in here for ten minutes.'

'A joke, this early in the evening!' I declare. 'Are you high?'

'No. And like I said, I don't like things too tidy. It unsettles me.'

'I'm basically your perfect woman then.' I clap a hand over my mouth as soon as I say it.

Luke rolls his eyes but doesn't deny it. And look at that, I'm floating in a haze of happiness somewhere off into the stratosphere.

This man is full of surprises.

'Do you want wine?' he asks.

'Why not, just a bit, since we're celebrating.'

He comes to sit next to me on the couch, clinking his wine glass with mine.

I take Luke in. He's obviously showered; his hair is still wet at the ends, making it a little bit curly. He smells damp and delicious. I go red at my own thought process.

'I hope sea bass is okay?'

'Course, that's great. I'm starving. Thank you for cooking after you've been at work.'

'No problem.' He gets off the couch but gestures for me to stay. It's tan leather and so big that I feel like a child sat on a giant's sofa.

He moves to the kitchen, returning a few minutes later with a plate of real food. I join him at the little breakfast bar he has along a stretch of kitchen worktop, mentally adding 'man carrying plate' to the list of things I find sexy about Luke. He's just really . . . carrying those plates. The food I'm presented with looks like it's come straight out of *Good Food* magazine. There's little squares of potatoes to go with the fish, and some roast vegetables. Having wrestled with a potato peeler quite a lot myself these last few months, I recognise that Luke has gone to an awful lot of trouble with this meal. The whole thing is so very . . . Luke. Careful, considered, thoughtful. I feel a rush of something that feels suspiciously like love. We haven't talked about the bet for weeks, months even. And I can't imagine that Luke is the sort of person who would refuse to say something he felt if it meant losing a bet, but still . . .

'You're thinking awfully loud over there,' Luke says from where he's sat next to me on his tool.

'And here I thought you were some great biologist extraordinaire. You can't *hear* thoughts.'

He raises a single eyebrow at me.

'It's just this food, it's so good.' I continue to talk after swallowing a mouthful of sea bass. Luke does a sort of smirk but it is good. My brain is mercifully quieter when it comes to food these days. I wouldn't say I'm entirely worry-free. But that's one of the things that going to group on Mondays has taught me. Recovery from all things is rarely linear.

Luke smiles.

'Second small smile,' I say without thinking.

'Pardon.'

'Er, I just meant that you did your small smile.'

He looks at me and I keep talking.

'It's like you have three states of being. Serious, small smile and big smile. I love big smile, but I'll take small smile when I can get it.'

He runs his hands over his jaw.

They're good hands.

Manly.

Fearing it'll give the game away, I resist the urge to start fanning myself.

Small smile again. This one is decidedly sexy. As if he knows my thoughts have taken a seriously non-PG turn.

Luke clears away the plates, refusing my offer of help. He returns with chocolate shortbread, *in a biscuit tin.*

'Oh well, I couldn't possibly eat it!' I declare, taking a big bite.

Our stools, which have a decided swivel to them, have sort of turned inward so that our knees are touching. I wonder if Luke is as affected by the knee touch as me. He seemed pretty affected when we had our first kiss in the science lab.

Now is not the right time to be thinking about that kiss.

Except now that it's there, the kiss that I shouldn't be thinking about is impossible to dislodge from my brain. And despite my best efforts to focus on something else – war, famine, incurable diseases – the only thing I do think about is the sensation of Luke's lips on mine.

I lean forward imperceptibly.

So does Luke.

My hand is on his knee.

His don't move.

'It's okay, you can touch me.'

'We should go slow,' he says.

'Glaciers have moved faster than us, Luke. Now touch me.'

He waits another beat. But this time there's no panic when he winds his hands into my hair. The feel of his fingers against my scalp makes my skin prickle. Other than that time on my bed, when I'd practically glued myself to his side after Charles had shown up, Luke and I haven't done much touching. It's an oversight I intend to rectify immediately.

'This hair.' He spreads his fingers so that the strands fall through them. Luke continues to talk more to my hair than to me. 'You know at school I used to try and sit behind you. I loved looking at your hair.' He pauses and visibly cringes. 'Wow, that sounds creepy.'

'At school?' My voice is unnaturally high.

Small smile.

'At school,' he agrees. 'But you never even noticed me. No matter how much eyeliner I wore.'

I laugh and lean forward more as Luke keeps playing with my hair. 'I did notice you. I thought, "Wow, his nail varnish is so shiny". So there, your efforts weren't completely in vain.'

I find the thought of Luke liking me, liking me even just a tiny bit at school, thrilling. Like little jolts of lightning, this knowledge I now have bursts through me, rockets under my skin.

It makes me brave.

'And anyway, I notice you now.'

Big smile.

'Uh huh.'

'Can I kiss you?' he asks.

'Yes. Please.'

Before I know it, his lips are on mine. Finally, we're getting somewhere.

Except as soon as the thought manifests, it's over. Too quickly. Not at all the kissing marathon I was hoping for. Luke's hands are back by his sides. How disappointing.

'Was that okay?' he asks.

'Yes. Absolutely. Let's do it again. Put your hands on me.'

Horny Alice is mouthy.

'I want to touch you. But I don't want to hurt you.'

'You won't.'

This time I take matters into my own hands.

I stand up on shaky legs.

Don't make a tit of yourself.

Brain, you are not welcome here.

Luke hasn't moved.

'Please tell me you're coming? This is starting to get embarrassing.'

In a flash, he's standing. Pressed up against me. I love it.

My brain starts to short-circuit and my skin is hotter than the surface of Mercury.

'Will you tell me what you like?' He pulls my hair to one side and plants a chaste kiss behind my ear.

I'm genuinely at risk of spontaneously combusting as we move through the flat and climb the steps up to Luke's bedroom.

Luke pauses. We're at the foot of his bed. I look down.

There's some sort of . . . I think it's a rug on the floor. It's made up of knots of fabric. It's the ugliest thing I've ever seen.

'Your bedroom rug is hideous,' I say. Luke looks too. And then we're laughing. I'm clutching my stomach, we're laughing so much.

'I hate that rug. Mum bought it for me.'

'So many colours.'

'Too many.'

I wipe a tear from the corner of my eye. I look back up at Luke, suddenly serious. 'I'm not sure I know what I like.' I answer his question from minutes ago.

'Let's slow down.'

'No.' Even I'm surprised at how firm I am. 'I just meant that I don't normally . . . er . . . you know.' It turns out that it's very difficult to gesticulate the word 'orgasm' and by the time I'm done trying, you could toast marshmallows on my forehead. 'So don't worry about putting any extra effort in.'

'I'll be putting extra effort in.'

I reach round and unzip my dress.

'You're so beautiful, Alice.' I step out of my dress as Luke stares at me and I supress the urge to squirm. 'We'll figure everything out together.' He brushes his lips against mine. 'We won't do anything until you're ready.'

'Okay. Now take your shirt off.' He stares at me, wide-eyed. 'Focus, Luke. Your shirt.'

His hands tremble on the buttons before he shrugs it off.

I'm distracted. Not distracted enough to notice that Luke is fit. Like, really fit.

'Whoa. How do you look like that?'

Luke shrugs but his gaze is glassy. 'It's simply a case of upping your—'

'Actually, I don't care.'

I trail my fingers down his chest.

'You don't want to talk nutrition?'

I quiet him by unclipping my bra.

Luke remains as serious Luke. Serious Luke has never been my favourite Luke. I think perhaps I've underestimated his appeal before now.

We're kissing properly then. Finally. And it's everything I remember.

My hand slides up across warm skin. I can feel his heart beating hard.

His hands have still barely moved.

'Luke.' I bite the join of his neck and shoulder. 'Touch me.'

'Tell me what feels good.'

His hand goes up my back as he kisses my neck.

'That, I like that.'

We tumble sideways onto the bed, shoulders and legs and elbows everywhere. The kisses get lower, and I look up to the ceiling and mutter a silent prayer.

'And that.'

He kisses my collarbone.

'And that.'

And I do. I really do.

Finished, we lie looking at each other. Luke is playing with the ends of my hair and I'm so very close to saying the three words I thought earlier. They bash against my lips, fighting to get out. But for now I force them down and cuddle up to Luke.

Chapter Thirty-Three

'So, it was good then?' Joanie asks.

We're in my bedroom, getting ready for a night at the bingo. Which means we're taking it in turns to stand on the tiny amount of floor space to shimmy into our clothes.

Joanie has a rare night of freedom and, in a spur of the moment decision, I invited Hannah too. Something I'm now living to regret as I cast a nervous glance her way. She's only just met Joanie and I think we need to ease her in gently. 'Joanie, please, we're not talking about my S-E-X life!'

Gabby is on video call, my phone propped on my pillow so she can see what's going on. Between her and Joanie, it's quite the friendship onslaught.

'Alice gets giddy when she's had good s-e-x,' Gabby supplies and I let out a nervy giggle.

'Plus you've been smiling like you've won the s-e-x lottery all afternoon. It tells me everything I need to know.'

They're not wrong, my jaw has a persistent ache. Not that being with Luke has miraculously cured all my issues. It hasn't. It's just that it's nice to have someone else to work through things with. I particularly liked it when we worked through them on the couch. And in the shower.

'How's your dad?' I ask Hannah, keen to move the conversation away from my sex life.

Hannah is brushing her auburn hair on the bed. 'He's doing okay, thanks,' she says. 'Mrs Finney from across the road is sitting with him tonight. She'll call if anything goes wrong.'

'He's so lucky to have you,' I say.

'Thanks. I always wanted to be a counsellor. One day I might get round to it.'

'That would be so cool.'

'Pass me my fishnets will you?' Joanie is sat on the edge of the bed. I pull them out from where they've wormed their way under my pillow and pass them over just as my phone pings.

'Looking good ladies,' Gabby wolf-whistles. 'I wish I could be there for the event Alice, you'll let me know how it goes?'

I promise to and we all say our goodbyes before the call ends. A message comes through from Luke.

Luke: Have a nice evening. Mum and Dad say hi xx

'Oh my God, you're going to be unbearable as a girlfriend, aren't you?' Joanie is smiling though.

I look up from my reply. 'I . . . don't know if that's exactly what we are yet,' I answer carefully.

'You know what I say? If it looks like a duck, quacks like a duck, it's a duck.'

'Who's a duck?' Hannah asks.

'No one's a duck and I've literally never heard you say that phrase.' Still, I make a satisfied noise. Luke and I really do need a proper talk soon.

'Are you girls ready up there?' Mum calls.

'One sec, Cheryl!' Joanie replies, adding her tenth, and final, layer of eyeshadow. Her outfit is mostly netting.

Mum and Aunty M are waiting for us at the bottom of the stars.

'Come on then, lasses!' Aunty M calls impatiently. 'The minibus is waiting.'

Laughing for no good reason, we run down the stairs, out of the house and scramble into the minibus, calling bye to Dad as we go.

At the Mecca we take our usual table and I introduce Joanie and Hannah to Mum's work friends.

Everyone orders a drink-drink, other than Hannah, who settles on Coke.

'You're not drinking?'

She shakes her head.

'Dad, you know?'

I nod.

I take a sip of my warm wine, thinking that if there was ever anything fair with the world, Joanie would win tonight.

Several hours later, I start to wonder if Joanie is perhaps the anomaly to Luke's theories about luck. Because she does seem to have basically none.

'How can you have no numbers?' I half yell at her.

'It's really very simple, Alice. They didn't call any on my card.'

'Jager, jager, jager,' Aunty Moira chants, arriving back from the bar with a tray of shots that only Mum and Hannah decline. I wince as the alcohol burns off a layer of my oesophagus.

'We've done like ten games and you've never had more than three numbers a go!'

'You know, I'm sat right next to you, you don't need to shout. Can't you just sit quietly like Hannah?' I look over at Hannah who is gently humming. We're moments from cartoon birds coming to land on her shoulder.

'No. Look we have one more game. You'd better win this time,' I tell Joanie in what is perhaps an overly aggressive manner.

'Right. I'll try harder to control the balls coming out of that tub on stage shall I?'

'That's all I ask.'

Our last game starts. I squint as my own numbers blur into one.

Once. Twice. Out of the corner of my eye, I notice Joanie blotting out numbers on her card. It's not enough, though. I've twice as many crossed off as her. And we're getting too far into the game now. They always last a certain amount of time before someone shouts,

'BINGO!'

For God's sake.

Whoever has won is getting some serious cheers, unnecessarily loud. They don't need to be so over the top about it. Rubbing it in like that. It's making my ears ring.

Joanie smacks me on the back. 'Alice, tell your mum congratulations!'

'Mum?'

'She won, Alice! Ten grand!'

The rooms spins.

I look at Mum. She's in total shock.

'Mum!' I launch myself over the table, remembering too late that it's full of half-drunk drinks.

'I can't believe you won!'

'Thank you, Alice. It's quite a shock. I don't think I ever ...' She's preternaturally calm. 'Would you mind coming over to that desk with me? That's where you're meant to go when you win.' She points to a booth along the back wall.

'Course!' I agree like a woman who still thinks she can walk in a straight line.

We stumble past the other tables, Mum doing the odd cele-bratory wave.

'Congratulations!' someone in a bright blue and orange uniform tells her. 'There's just a few forms to fill out. You can do it now, if you have time?'

'Of course.' Mum takes the BIC pen and starts to fill out her details.

'I can't believe you won!' I tell her, talking really fast and only slurring the occasional word. 'What're you going to spend it on? You could go on a cruise! Or get a new kitchen. I know, you could retire properly.'

'That's what I wanted to talk to you about, Alice,' she says.

'It is?'

'Yes.' She doesn't look up from her forms. 'I was thinking of giving the money towards the repairs to the Welcome Centre, if that would be okay with you?'

I'm so shocked that it takes me a minute to dredge up a sentence.

'But you've literally just won. Why are you thinking of giving it all away?'

'Why would I need ten thousand pounds?' she asks matter-of-factly.

'But Dad—'

'Your dad will feel the same.'

'But he ... cruise ... your kitchen.'

'My kitchen is just fine. In fact, I have everything I need. Isn't that what that philosopher man says? About being contented with what you have? You have his quote on your cork board.'

I realize that Mum is talking about Socrates, who did say something like that. I wonder how he'd feel about Mum describing him as 'that philosopher man'.

I crush her in a side hug.

'You're amazing. Yes, please give it to the Welcome Centre. We can make them put a plaque up for you.'

'I don't need a plaque.'

'You're getting a plaque.'

'Why are you crying, Alice?'

'Because I'm really drunk. And also, it's a lovely thing you're doing. Did I mention the drunk thing?'

'There, all done.' She slides the forms back to the worker.

'The money will be in your account in seven to ten days,' he replies.

As we walk back to the table, ready to give Joanie and Hannah the good news, I text Luke.

> **Me:** Can't believe it. Mum just won a ton of money and she's giving it to the Welcome Centre! And also I STILL want to get in your boxers
>
> **Luke:** On my way …

Chapter Thirty-Five

'Testing, testing!

The mic screeches. Joanie has carved a small semi-circle of space on the floor at The Buccaneer. We'd agreed that she should do the auction, seeing as she's more of a familiar face round here. But I'm due to say a few words beforehand. Mum, Dad, Dwaine, Andy and Shaun, along with an assortment of tradespeople, are lined up looking nervous off to the side. Dad apparently called in a few favours and Easington's barter economy has really come through for us. Meaning that we have an electrician, a clairvoyant and a funeral director all willing to offer their services.

Joanie passes me the mic and I clutch it tight, willing the shake of my hands not to show. But then I think of all the people at my group who've had to be braver than me, and actually, making a mini speech doesn't seem like such a big deal anymore.

'First of all, thanks for coming everyone.' I'm wearing the dress I bought in Durham Vintage. There's a good chance that The Buccaneer has never seen such finery, but it's giving me a much-needed confidence boost right about now. My gaze meets Luke's and he gives me a small nod.

'As you hopefully know by now, today we're raising money for the Welcome Centre.' I look to where my new boss, Janet, is stood off to the side, next to Nana. Nana is busy smuggling Tyler pink wafers when she thinks no one is watching. 'Everyone here probably has their own reasons for wanting the Welcome to stay open. For me it's the fact that Women's Aid run a weekly session there. Women's Aid is a charity that helps women who face domestic abuse.' I cough. 'I think everyone knows that domestic abuse happens.' My glance carries around the room. 'But we assume that it isn't happening to people we know. Because domestic abuse happens in the shadows, and it doesn't always look like we might expect. Or it happens to women who already struggle to find a voice.' Another cough. 'It means so much that you're all here. That as a community we're trying to save the Welcome Centre. Remember, love shouldn't hurt. Thank you!'

Andy is clapping louder than I've maybe ever heard anyone clap ever. Each smack of his hands like a mini sonic boom. But then the rest of the crowd is joining in and I get a fair few smacks on my back as I move to stand next to Luke again.

'You're incredible,' he whispers beneath the applause. I shiver at having his mouth so close to my ear and wish that I wasn't in a room full of people, half a foot away from my immediate family.

Joanie has the mic now. 'Thank you, Alice. And if any of you fuckers don't donate, you'll have me to deal with.' She casts an accusatory glare around the room.' Everyone squirms. 'Right, let's get this show on the road.'

The meat raffle is called. Dad, who seems to have purchased half a book of tickets, wins a tray of pig parts. He whoops and cheers like a man whose diet is not already predominantly bacon.

Next comes the auction. 'The rules are simple,' Joanie says. 'I'll tell you what these good people are offering, and you bid for them. Highest bidder wins. No kinky stuff though, I know what you lot are like.'

Mum goes a couple of shades paler at the laugh Joanie gets.

'First up then, step this way Gary!' Dad shuffles to stand awkwardly next to Joanie. 'You might recognize Gazza as your local friendly plumber. Rated the third-best plumber in the village according to ratemytrade.com, though we all know that the Tap People's people delete dodgy reviews.' She gives an exaggerated wink. 'Gary's Golden Showers and Other Plumbing Services is offering a day's plumbing work. So if you have some knobbly pipes or you're having to take the occasional cold shower, then Gary is your man.' She claps him on the back.

Mum and Dad had been effusive in their agreement to be part of the auction. I wonder now if they might have some regrets.

The bidding is more frenzied than I expected it to be. Possibly because some people are well on their way to drunk. It's quite challenging to tell the difference between hand movements and genuine bids. I end up back on the stage, trying to help Joanie figure out who is bidding what. It turns out that plumbing problems are endemic in Easington. In the end, Dad's services sell for £150.

The auction carries on. A clairvoyant sells her skills for over £200. Bought by a glassy-eyed ex-miner who apparently fancies a chat with his dead brother.

Dwaine gives a little spiel about the new self-defence class he's running. And even though it's completely free, people start to bid for it. In the end, Aunty Moira pays £500, hollering about Dwaine's jawline and asking whether clothes are optional at the session.

I start to think that I should have included something about the objectification of men in my speech.

By the time Joanie has sold her services as the Cake Fairy and instructed everyone on how to pay by cash or PayPal I reckon we've made a fair amount of money, but not the fifteen grand we still need.

'We've had an online donation come through,' Hannah announces from where she's sat on a little table by the stage, laptop plugged into a socket there. 'Oh wow, it's for five grand!'

There's a collective 'ooh'. 'It's from Gabby!' Hannah says her name and immediately my eyes fill with tears.

'Is that the woman that sent you the card with the,' Mum drops her voice, '. . . boobs on it?' Trust Mum to still hold that against Gabby, despite the fact that she's just gone some way to saving the Welcome Centre.

And even though I know that £5,000 isn't to Gabby what it is to the people here, there's no law which says that rich people have to use their money for good, is there? I send her a WhatsApp.

Me: I can't ever thank you enough x

Gabby: Don't even think about it. Enjoy your event.

Talk soon x

I send back a line of hearts.

'This is what we're talking about, people!' Joanie has got very shouty into her mic. I'm thinking that she might put it down, now that the auction has finished, but instead she says, 'And now folks, we have one more very special donation.'

We all look around, wondering who the mystery donor might be. As per, my eyes are drawn to Luke, who is standing at the edge of the stage. He is exuding stress. His shoulders are raised and he's balled his hands into fists. I wonder what the hell is going on as Joanie walks towards him.

'Over to you, Luke.' She passes him the mic.

'Do I really need this?' he asks, looking down at it in his hand. But then he must decide that he does, because he lifts it to his mouth and I have no idea what's happening.

'Quiet, you lot,' Joanie barks at the crowd who go immediately silent – because she's bloody terrifying.

'I'd like . . .' He stops and then starts again. 'I'd like to donate five hundred pounds, please.' He's looking right at me. 'Payment for a lost bet.' His voice gets clearer at the end though the tips of his ears are pink.

There's another communal gasp. No one can say that our event
didn't bring the drama.

I seem to be walking towards Luke, and maybe I've always been
walking towards Luke. I come to a stop in front of him, my heart
so full it can't possibly be contained in my chest.

I feel everyone moving around us. But Luke and I are still stood
in our places, gazing at each other.

'The bouncy castle is open folks!' Joanie has taken the mic from
Luke again. 'Anyone wishing to avoid Andy singing, I suggest you
head there now!' So many people rush the doors, they get jammed.

'Hey,' Andy protests before snatching the mic from Joanie.

'Luke, I—'

'Can I go first?' he asks.

'Course.'

He takes a deep breath. 'I just wanted to say that I don't
expect anything. You don't need to say it back. The donation, it
comes without expectation. I ... I'm not good at this.' He does a
nervy laugh.

'I don't know. You're better than you think.'

He laughs properly this time and I smile up at him.

'I thought that to win the bet, the other person had to fall in
love too?'

He shrugs his shoulders. 'I changed the premise.'

Behind us, I hear Andy start up his set. And him belting out
'Staying Alive' isn't quite the romantic backdrop to this type of
conversation I might have hoped for.

'You, the great Luke Priestly, have changed the premise of a bet?'

He grins at me, relaxed now. 'The great Luke Priestly, I like that.'

'I'll bet you do.'

'Going to get it embroidered onto a cushion.'

I laugh and then say, 'You were right, I won the bet.'

'You did?' Luke asks.

I lean up to kiss him, just a quick one that's absolutely not enough, 'I really did.'

Looking around the room, all our friends and family are here. Hannah and Mr Hall are chatting by her laptop table and Shaun is in the corner working on the teenager from Star Bucks' phone. Dwaine is in the centre of a group of women from the defence class. Aunty Moira stands a few metres away from Andy as he starts up a rousing rendition of 'Love Changes Everything', lighter raised aloft as if she's front row at a concert. Mum and Dad are across the room, laughing with some friends.

For some reason, Andy doesn't sound quite as bad as usual tonight.

'Good job, guys.' Joanie pushes between us. Tyler is next to her and looks at Luke as if he's a new species of herbivore. Luke, in turn, offers his hand to introduce himself in a move that makes me all warm and fuzzy.

'Do you think we made enough money?' I ask her.

'We're still short,' she says. 'But there's the money from the bar to tot up and whatever we get from Bambino's kebab special. They're running it all month.'

'There's hope then.' I'm completely at risk of crying again.

'Course there's hope, Alice,' Joanie huffs. 'There's always hope.'

Chapter Thirty-Six

Joanie: Fuck yeah we did it!!!!!

For the second time in my life, I've made the front page of the *Easington Gazette*. This time, for raising enough money to save the Welcome Centre.

I can only presume that Mum is throwing me yet another surprise party in honour of that fact, because I've been banished to my bedroom for most of the afternoon. A few hours alone doesn't feel like the punishment it once did.

'Alice, you can come down now,' Mum calls from the bottom of the stairs.

I fold the newspaper back up and head downstairs, knowing the score by now. 'I'm on my way,' I yell. Honestly, I don't feel like I have another party in me, but I'll suck it up, for Mum's sake.

Except ... there's no one here. Or no one who isn't Mum and Dad anyway. And the front room looks just like normal. Aside from the extra frame above the mantelpiece.

'What's going on?' I look between Mum and Dad stood together in the front room. 'Why are you smiling? And why are you holding hands?'

They *never* hold hands. I've kind of gathered over the last few months that Mum's love language revolves around making food, and Dad's around eating it.

'You need to go into the garden, Alice.' Mum is grinning so wide that I'm surprised her face doesn't split in two.

'What? Why? We don't have a garden.'

'The yard, then.' She rolls her eyes. I try to peer out through the back window, but someone has pulled the curtains shut.

'Tell me right now what's happening.'

They both shake their heads and then they shepherd me through the kitchen towards the back door.

'Have fun.'

Dad pulls open the door and Mum shoves me through it.

And I stop dead.

My heart is in my mouth.

Because there, in the yard, is a blow-up see-through dome, filled with fairy lights. And in front of it is Luke.

'You got me a bubble pod?' I ask him, amazed because it is inconceivable that Luke has rammed a bubble pod into Mum and Dad's yard. It cannot be the case that it is full of fairy lights. And I'm just not willing to accept that he has somehow got a table inside and covered it with flowers.

Luke does a small cough.

I'm pretty sure my mouth is just hanging open.

'You talked about it once.'

He looks sheepish.

'Pardon?'

'That time in Star's, when you were talking about exercising on the beach with Dwaine, you said "it's no bubble pod".'

I laugh once. Then I realize that Luke is deadly serious. I'm not hallucinating. There's a bubble pod in the yard.

'Will you come inside with me?' Luke glances up and I notice that all my neighbours are hanging out of their bedroom windows, trying to get a good look. Some are taking pictures. There's not a hope in hell that we'll avoid the village Facebook gossip site.

I nod, taking his hand.

We have to squeeze past the coal shed to get into the entrance.

'I can't believe you got me a bubble pod.'

Inside it's like ... it's like being in a beautiful, well, bubble. The ceiling is full of fairy lights and it's eerily quiet. I glance at the table covered in flowers.

'You organized all this?'

'I did.'

I turn slowly on the spot.

'You know. For someone who claims never to have had a proper girlfriend, you are acing this.'

He shrugs. 'Of course I'm acing it.'

'Wow, I really must love you, I even love you when you're being arrogant.'

'Arrogance can be very attractive in a mate. And I love you too.' Not sure I'll ever get tired of hearing that.

I laugh then. Take in the pod some more.

'How?'

'I hired it from a man with a van in Newcastle.'

Luke pulls a chair out for me, and I slope into it.

'I've been thinking,' he begins, sitting in the chair opposite me and pouring me some a cup of tea from a little teapot that Mum must have helped him fill, 'about our bet.'

I take my delicate cup.

'You have?'

'I have.'

'And what have you been thinking? Because if you're about to launch into another "I don't believe in love" speech, you've picked a very poor setting for it.' I wave around at the sparkly pod. 'And also, you've already admitted defeat.'

'I have and I'm not planning on ruining your victory. I've just been thinking that perhaps the premise of our agreement was never sound to begin with.'

I have a sip of tea.

'What if, essentially, we believe the exact same thing?' Luke asks, piquing my interest. 'Go on,' I say.

'I was doing some research in the library yesterday. It was some dusty old journal, but it started with a reminder about who the father of science was. Do you know who it suggested?'

I hazard a guess. 'Newton ... Einstein ... those are the only dead scientists I know.'

Luke shakes his head. 'Aristotle,' he says.

'No way!' I'm smiling.

'Yes,' he says.

'Well, anything good enough for Aristotle is good enough for us.'

'Exactly.'

I'd always assumed that happiness was loud as an emotion. That it announced itself with a clash of cymbals. Fireworks. A finishing line that declares, 'Welcome to happiness, you made it!' But it's not like that at all. Contentment is quiet. Peaceful.

Probably, things like happiness and love look different to us all. I'm still not claiming to know what love is, even if being with Charles taught me a lot about what it isn't. But right now, love for me is in a bubble pod in my parents' yard. Loving Luke makes me immeasurably happy because he loves me back the right way.

'Thank you, for all this,' I tell him, waving a hand around the bubble pod, but meaning so much more.

Chapter Thirty-Seven

FOUR MONTHS LATER

'And you're sure, absolutely sure that you don't want to, I don't know, write a letter of resignation like a normal person?' I ask from next to the half beast, half flower statues that frame the entrance of the Lotus Flower restaurant.

'Are you kidding me?' Joanie does a maniacal laugh. She's been looking forward to today an unnatural amount. She's even arranged to have Luke watch Tyler for half an hour because she wants to commit every second of what's to come to memory without the distraction of her small child.

Now that we're here, Joanie narrows her eyes at the door. 'You've already talked me out of egging the place. At least let me stick it to Paul to his face. You can't take that away from me, Alice.'

I set my shoulders.

'All right, all right. Come on then.'

I push open the doors to the Lotus Flower, doing an exaggerated waft of my hand to Joanie.

Paul rounds the bar as soon as we're both inside. 'What're you doing here?' He looks past Joanie towards me. 'Come to beg for your job back?'

I scoff as Joanie says, 'You really are a conceited arse, Paul.'

'Yeah, yeah, whatever. Jo, your shift doesn't start for half an hour yet. Come bother me then.'

Joanie pulls herself up to her full height. Which is still, admittedly, pretty small and says, 'Fuck you, Paul. I quit.'

'She sooo quits,' I add ineffectively. We both have our hands on our hips. I've never felt more badass.

Paul laughs, but he's started to sweat more than normal, so I think he might really be more than a little nervous at the prospect of losing Joanie. 'You can't quit. Where else are you going to get a job?'

'Funny you should ask that, but you're actually looking at the Welcome Centre's new part-time, school-hour chef.'

The council ran interviews for the new chef as part of their promise to help manage the Welcome Centre. They were impressed with Joanie's 'community spirit' and 'caring nature'. Plus Aunty M had done a fair bit of coaching before the interview.

Paul is still stuttering about indignantly, but Joanie just talks over him.

'And every single person I make a prawn sandwich for, I'm going to tell them how badly you treat your staff here. And then maybe with a bit of luck, you'll get the sack!' she says cheerfully.

Paul has turned an angry red. Like a giant spot almost. But Joanie isn't done. 'And for the record, these things are hideous.' I had talked Joanie out of egging the joint, but I'd been right on board with her plan to hack up her waistcoat. She now produces the bits of pink silk that she has painstakingly butchered and scatters them onto the floor, looking Paul dead in the eye. For a final flurry, she grabs a handful of change from the tip box. 'Just taking what I'm owed,' she sing-songs. People mostly leave a few coins in tips, so I'd be amazed if Joanie has so much as 50p, but the effect is very dramatic. And Paul looks too terrified to speak. Joanie casts him one more scathing look before turning to me. 'Shall we get off then?' She smiles like Ursula did when she stole all those souls.

'Absolutely, bye Paul.' I do a cheerful wave that causes him to turn puce.

'You know,' Joanie says as we leave, 'I'm going to forever regret not getting to pelt him with rotten eggs.'

'That's all right,' I tell her as we head away from the restaurant, back towards Mum and Dad's house. 'We all have to learn to live with regret.'

There's a small posse of people on the pavement outside Mum and Dad's terrace by the time we get there. From what I can tell, Luke is pretending to race Tyler halfway down the street. Each time he takes an early lead but then hops about on one foot shouting, 'The alligator got me again' and letting Tyler win the race, even if he is doubled over laughing. Sometimes, I wonder how my heart still fits in my chest. (I make a mental note to relay this thought to Luke later, because I'll forever love annoying him.)

Mum, Dad and Aunty M are all busy loading up my worldly goods into the back of Luke's car. He was right, the Volvo boot is deceptively spacious.

'You're really going then?' Joanie asks as Tyler runs over to her. Luke lifts his hand up in a wave, a bit red from all the running, and then disappears inside.

I nod. Nervous, but sure I'm making the right decision. 'It's too far, with work. And I start uni properly in a couple of weeks.'

Tyler has attached himself with the stick of a limpet to Joanie's side so she walks with him glued to her leg. 'I guess it's good that they agreed to be flexible with your hours.' Joanie is saying nice things, but she sounds like a petulant toddler.

I stop to look at her. 'You know I'll come back, like, all the time right? And I still want to babysit Tyler as often as you need. Plus I'm still going to the sessions on Monday nights. I'm not giving that up. You'll basically see me as much as you do now.'

Her shoulders drop, just a touch. 'I'll miss you, that's all.'

I bump my arm into hers as we near the house. 'I'll miss you too. But it's only Durham. It's not far. There's a great bus route.'

'Fine,' she huffs, but she's smiling. 'Come on Tyler, let's go see if Aunty Cheryl has any of the good biscuits.'

'The Hobnobs are in the second cupboard,' Mum calls to Joanie as she and Tyler disappear inside.

'Thanks for watching Tyler,' I say, sliding up to Luke where he's stood on the pavement holding a box of miscellaneous items from my room. It looks to be mostly wires.

'It's fine. I like him more than most adults,' he says as I laugh, giving him an appreciative once-over. It never ceases to amaze me, the weird things that I find sexy about Luke. I add 'man holding cardboard box' to the list that lives for free in my head. It's the sunglasses too, they're doing things to me.

I'm sure Luke knows that my thoughts have veered decidedly in the direction of the gutter, because when he looks down at where I've pressed myself into his side, his cheeks have a faint flush.

It was a big decision, the one to move in with Luke. Even though I *know* that Luke wouldn't do what Charles did, I still find it hard to trust my own judgement sometimes. Luke waited, patient as ever, and in the end we agreed to get somewhere new, together. So that it doesn't feel like I'm living in his space.

It just doesn't make sense to live apart in the same city. Not when we're going to be so busy, what with me working and going to uni and Luke still involved in the study. Apparently, so far the findings support the premise that love is irrationally rational. People fall in love with who they're meant to, but no one can quite explain how or why. So I guess we were both right. And figuring it out is going to keep Luke busy for years yet.

'I think that's the last of it,' Dad declares, placing a lone shoe on the pile of junk that I've filled the back of Luke's car with. 'Just in time for *Bargain Hunt*.'

Mum is stood in the doorway, her eyes looking decidedly watery. Aunty M has an arm around her.

'I'm going to be back in two days!' I tell them, welling up myself.

'I know, I know,' Mum sniffs, 'I'm just really proud of you.'

'We all are, pet,' Aunty M smiles, before looking at Luke. 'Don't give us a reason to come after you.'

'Wouldn't dream of it,' he says smoothly.

'Nah, you're all right,' Aunty M agrees. 'Come on Cheryl, let's go get the tea on.'

After extracting one last promise that I'll be back in two days and that yes, I'll stay for tea and pork chops would be lovely, they all leave to go inside.

Then it's just me and Luke, alone on the pavement.

He holds out his hand and I interlace our fingers.

'Ready?' he asks, smiling.

I look up at him, smiling back. In the beginning, love didn't come easy for me and Luke. We've had to figure a lot out – about each other, but mainly about ourselves. Falling in love with Luke didn't feel like chance or fate. It wasn't Cupid and a heart-tipped arrow. Loving Luke elevates everything, but it feels like a choice.

And maybe when it comes down to it, those are the loves that really matter. The ones you choose and the ones you keep on choosing every single day. And I choose Luke.

'Ready,' I tell him. And I totally, absolutely, am.

Acknowledgements

Firstly, I'd like to say a huge thank you to anyone who has read this or *My (extra) Ordinary Life*. More than once, messages from readers have made me sob. I appreciate you all so much.

Thank you to the whole team at Simon and Schuster. In particular, my editor Molly. I feel ridiculously grateful to have the great fortune of having you as my editor. You don't even get how brilliant you are. Thank you also to Harriett, my publicist extraordinaire, Sarah, India (who designed this gorgeous cover) and Sara-Jade for being such a champion of romance fiction. I really do believe that you're all the best in the business.

To my agents new and old! Hannah you were one of the first people to have read this and I think maybe talked me down off a ledge with it. I'm starting to forgive you for leaving, though only just. And Mads, for being an incredible support and all-round fantastic agent. I feel so lucky that I get to work with you. Thank you!

Writing can be a slow and solitary process, so I'm endlessly grateful to my writing friends who keep me vaguely sane through the whole thing. Even though I'd likely get more writing done if I didn't spend so much time messaging the pair of you, thank you to Mira and Emma especially.

Thank you to Gemma Moon for checking the philosophy in this for me! Any mistakes are obviously my own but your message that, 'Luke would definitely be a hard determinist' made me laugh. And to all of my friends who read early drafts and then continue to buy multiple copies of my books, I'm so grateful.

To Mum and Dad, as always, I'd be a total mess without you – I'm often that anyway, but I'd be even more so! I said to a great friend once that I didn't know if I was fully qualified to write a book about love. Her reply was that I have three kids so of course I am. It's really stuck with me (Vicky, you are very wise). And Elodie, Hugo and Kit, she's right – I love you a ridiculous amount.

Lastly, I want to acknowledge that whilst Easington Colliery is a real place, I've taken some rather extreme liberties with almost everything about it. I grew up in Hartlepool and what I hope is accurate is the sense of community and pride which, in my opinion, defines this area of the country. More than one character here has been inspired by my childhood. I hope in time that we have more writers from places like Easington and Hartlepool. The people there, like anywhere, have stories that deserve to be told.